PRAISE FOR CAROLYN BROWN

The Family Journal

"Brown takes a snapshot of the heart at its most vulnerable and then puts it in our hands for safekeeping. *The Family Journal* dares to expose every emotion we're too afraid to face but determined to conquer anyway."

—Amazon review

"Reading a Carolyn Brown book is like coming home again."

—*Harlequin Junkie* (top pick)

The Empty Nesters

"A delightful journey of hope and healing."

—*Woman's World*

"The story is full of emotion . . . and the joy of friendship and family. Carolyn Brown is known for her strong, loving characters, and this book is full of them."

—*Harlequin Junkie*

"Carolyn Brown takes us back to small-town Texas with a story about women, friendships, love, loss, and hope for the future."

—*Storeybook Reviews*

"Ms. Brown has fast become one of my favorite

nce Junkies

"A road trip full of laughs, tears, and deep friendships that proves that heart is truly what makes a family."

—*Em and M Books*

"Carolyn Brown delivers another heaping dose of comfort reading with her latest book . . . all about supportive friendships and overcoming grief and loss. Girl power for the win!"

—*Rainy Day Ramblings*

"Sometimes if you are lucky, you pick up a book at just the right time in your life that every emotion written by the author resonates and you cannot put it down. *The Empty Nesters* by Carolyn Brown is that book for me."

—Goodreads review

The Perfect Dress

"Fans of Brown will swoon for this sweet contemporary, which skillfully pairs a shy small-town bridal shop owner and a soft-hearted car dealership owner . . . The expected but welcomed happily ever after for all involved will make readers of all ages sigh with satisfaction."

—*Publishers Weekly*

"Carolyn Brown writes the best comfort-for-the-soul, heartwarming stories, and she never disappoints . . . You won't go wrong with *The Perfect Dress!*"

—*Harlequin Junkie*

The Magnolia Inn

"The author does a first-rate job of depicting the devastating stages of grief, provides a simple but appealing plot with a sympathetic hero and heroine and a cast of lovable supporting characters, and wraps it all up with a happily ever after to cheer for."

—*Publishers Weekly*

"*The Magnolia Inn* by Carolyn Brown is a feel-good story about friendship, fighting your demons, and finding love, and maybe, just a little bit of magic."

—*Harlequin Junkie*

"Chock-full of Carolyn Brown's signature country charm, *The Magnolia Inn* is a sweet and heartwarming story of two people trying to make the most of their lives, even when they have no idea what exactly is at stake."

—*Fresh Fiction*

Small Town Rumors

"Carolyn Brown is a master at writing warm, complex characters who find their way into your heart."

—*Harlequin Junkie*

"Carolyn Brown's *Small Town Rumors* takes that hotbed and with it, spins a delightful tale of starting over, coming into your own, and living your life, out loud and unafraid."

—*Words We Love By*

"*Small Town Rumors* by Carolyn Brown is a contemporary romance perfect for a summer read in the shade of a big old tree with a glass of lemonade or sweet tea. It is a sweet romance with wonderful characters and a small-town setting."

—Avonna Loves Genres

The Sometimes Sisters

"Carolyn Brown continues her streak of winning, heartfelt novels with *The Sometimes Sisters*, a story of estranged sisters and frustrated romance."

—*All About Romance*

"This is an amazing feel-good story that will make you wish you were a part of this amazing family."

—*Harlequin Junkie* (top pick)

"*The Sometimes Sisters* is a delightful and touching story that explores the bonds of family. I loved the characters, the story lines, and the focus on the importance of familial bonds, whether they be blood relations or those you choose with your heart."

—*Rainy Day Ramblings*

The Strawberry Hearts Diner

"Sweet and satisfying romance from the queen of Texas romance."

—*Fresh Fiction*

"A heartwarming cast of characters brings laughter and tears to the mix, and readers will find themselves rooting for more than one romance on the menu. From the first page to the last, Brown perfectly captures the mood as well as the atmosphere and creates a charming story that appeals to a wide range of readers."

—*RT Book Reviews*

"A sweet romance surrounded by wonderful, caring characters."

—*TBQ's Book Palace*

"Deeply satisfying contemporary small-town western story . . ."

—*Delighted Reader*

The Barefoot Summer

"Prolific romance author Brown shows she can also write women's fiction in this charming story, which uses humor and vivid characters to show the value of building an unconventional chosen family."

—*PW Weekly*

"This story takes you and carries you along for a wonderful ride full of laughter, tears, and three amazing HEAs. I feel like these characters are not just people in a book, but they are truly family, and I feel so invested in their journey. Another amazing HIT for Carolyn Brown."

—*Harlequin Junkie* (top pick)

The Lullaby Sky

"I really loved and enjoyed this story. Definitely a good comfort read, when you're in a reading funk or just don't know what to read. The secondary characters bring much love and laughter into this book—your cheeks will definitely hurt from smiling so hard while reading. Carolyn is one of my most favorite authors. I know without a doubt that no matter what book of hers I read, I can just get lost in it and know it will be a good story. Better than the last. Can't wait to read more from her."

—The Bookworm's Obsession

The Lilac Bouquet

"Brown pulls readers along for an enjoyable ride. It's impossible not to be touched by Brown's protagonists, particularly Seth, and a cast of strong supporting characters underpins the charming tale."

—Publishers Weekly

"If a reader is looking for a book more geared toward family and long-held secrets, this would be a good fit."

—RT Book Reviews

"Carolyn Brown absolutely blew me away with this epically beautiful story. I cried, I giggled, I sobbed, and I guffawed; this book had it all. I've come to expect great things from this author, and she more than lived up to anything I could have hoped for. Emmy Jo Massey and her great-granny Tandy are absolute masterpieces not because they are perfect but because they are perfectly painted. They are so alive, so full of flaws and spunk and determination. I cannot recommend this book highly enough."

—Night Owl Reviews (5 stars and top pick)

The Wedding Pearls

"*The Wedding Pearls* by Carolyn Brown is an amazing story about family, life, love, and finding out who you are and where you came from. This book is a lot like *The Golden Girls* meets *Thelma and Louise*."

—*Harlequin Junkie*

"*The Wedding Pearls* is an absolute must read. I cannot recommend this one enough. Grab a copy for yourself, and one for a best friend or even your mother or both. This is a book that you need to read. It will make you laugh and cry. It is so sweet and wonderful and packed full of humor. I hope that when I grow up, I can be just like Ivy and Frankie."

—*Rainy Day Ramblings*

The Yellow Rose Beauty Shop

"*The Yellow Rose Beauty Shop* was hilarious, and so much fun to read. But sweet romances, strong female friendships, and family bonds make this more than just a humorous read."

—*The Readers Den*

"If you like books about small towns and how the people's lives intertwine, you will love this book. I think it's probably my favorite book this year. The relationships of the three main characters, girls who have grown up together, will make you feel like you just pulled up a chair in their beauty shop with a bunch of old friends. As you meet the other people in the town, you'll wish you could move there. There are some genuine laugh-out-loud moments and then more that will just make you smile. These are real people, not the oh-so-thin-and-so-very-rich that are often the main characters in novels. This book will warm your heart and you'll remember it after you finish the last page. That's the highest praise I can give a book."

—Reader quote

Long, Hot Texas Summer

"This is one of those lighthearted, feel-good, make-me-happy kind of stories. But, at the same time, the essence of this story is family and love with a big ole dose of laughter and country living thrown in the mix. This is the first installment in what promises to be another fascinating series from Brown. Find a comfortable chair, sit back, and relax because once you start reading *Long, Hot Texas Summer*, you won't be able to put it down. This is a super-fun and sassy romance."

—Thoughts in Progress

Daisies in the Canyon

"I just loved the symbolism in *Daisies in the Canyon*. As I mentioned before, Carolyn Brown has a way with character development, with few if any contemporaries. I am sure there are more stories to tell in this series. Brown just touched the surface first with *Long, Hot Texas Summer* and is now continuing on with *Daisies in the Canyon*."

—Fresh Fiction

Miss Janie's Girls

ALSO BY CAROLYN BROWN

CONTEMPORARY ROMANCES

The Banty House
The Family Journal
The Empty Nesters
The Perfect Dress
The Magnolia Inn
Small Town Rumors
The Sometimes Sisters
The Strawberry Hearts Diner
The Lilac Bouquet
The Barefoot Summer
The Lullaby Sky
The Wedding Pearls
The Yellow Rose Beauty Shop
The Ladies' Room
Hidden Secrets
Long, Hot Texas Summer
Daisies in the Canyon
Trouble in Paradise

CONTEMPORARY SERIES

THE BROKEN ROAD SERIES

To Trust
To Commit
To Believe
To Dream
To Hope

THREE MAGIC WORDS TRILOGY

A Forever Thing
In Shining Whatever
Life After Wife

HISTORICAL ROMANCE

THE BLACK SWAN TRILOGY

Pushin' Up Daisies
From Thin Air
Come High Water

THE DRIFTERS & DREAMERS TRILOGY

Morning Glory
Sweet Tilly
Evening Star

THE LOVE'S VALLEY SERIES

Choices
Absolution
Chances
Redemption
Promises

Miss Janie's Girls

CAROLYN BROWN

 Montlake

Published by Montlake, Seattle

www.apub.com

Amazon, the Amazon logo, and Montlake are trademarks of Amazon.com, Inc., or its affiliates.

ISBN-13: 9781542023047
ISBN-10: 1542023041

Cover design by Laura Klynstra

Printed in the United States of America

This one is to my own two girls,
Amy Brown Morgan and Ginny Brown Rucker.
To list all the reasons would take a book, not a page!

Prologue

Christmas, 1961

S arah Jane Jackson, Janie to her friends, looked around at the
stark room and set her suitcase on the floor. This was it—home
for the next few months. Her father, the Reverend Arnold Jackson,
stood off to one side twisting his fedora in his hands as if he didn't know
what to say. If it had been her mother standing by the door, she would
have been preaching a sermon.

A smile tickled the corners of Janie's mouth at the thought of her
mother standing behind the lectern at the church. Her father was the
preacher at a church in Whitesboro, Texas, and her mother was sup-
posedly the dutiful wife who submitted to his every whim. Yeah, right!
When they got home from church, it was her mother, Ethel, who ran
the show, and nobody crossed Mama. Janie was pretty close to convinced that the devil himself was afraid of Mama.

If Mama said that Janie had disgraced the family, then by damn,
she expected the girl to bow her head in total shame and hide under the
bed for the rest of her life. Too bad Janie didn't feel the same way about
that, or about thinking a cussword. There was no changing the fact,
though, that if Mama said Janie was going to a maternity home until

the baby was born and then giving up her bastard child, then Daddy would bring her without an argument.

A door at the end of the room opened, and a girl with long red hair, blue eyes, and a belly swollen out even more than Janie's said, "Guess you're my new roommate. I'm Greta. What's your name?"

"Janie." She tugged her shirt down over her pleated skirt, which would no longer button.

"Okay, then." Janie's father settled his hat on his head and glanced at the door as if he couldn't wait to get out of the room. "You get this over with, and we'll discuss where you'll go after it's done. Your mother thinks you might do well at Aunt Ruthie's place."

Her mother had harped on what would happen to her if the family's good name was ruined and that they needed to get *this* over with and never mention it again. *This* always brought a sneer to her face, and never once did she call it a baby. The world would come to a complete end for sure if anyone should learn that the preacher's daughter was "with child." Not even her mama said the word *pregnant* except in whispers, and heaven forbid that any God-fearing Christian would tell a girl that there were ways and means to have sex and keep from having a baby.

There'd been so much tension in the house that Janie had considered running away. If she just disappeared, then Ethel could claim that someone had kidnapped her daughter, and everyone in town would bring over tuna casseroles and homemade desserts and commiserate with her. Janie was so deep in her own thoughts that she forgot about her father and the new girl, and suddenly everything seemed very awkward.

"Why Aunt Ruthie's place?" Janie asked. "Why not just sell me into slavery in some faraway country?"

"Don't get sassy with me, girl. Your rebellion is what got you in this mess." He glared at her. "There's worse places than Birthright, Texas."

Janie inhaled deeply and let it out slowly, counted to ten, and bit her tongue. So her father thought that was a bad place, did he? Well, she wasn't about to tell him that she'd rather live with Aunt Ruthie than her mother.

"You'll be taken care of." Arnold Jackson seemed to be trying to fill the heavy silence in the room more than comfort her. "And the child will have good Christian parents to give it a good home."

Janie heard the emphasis he put on the word *Christian*, as if she were nothing more than a heathen for getting herself in *trouble*.

He took a deep breath and went on. "It won't ever be branded a bastard that way."

Those were the exact words her mother had used as they were leaving the house two hours ago. No hugs. No tears. Just those words. Her baby might grow up thinking it had married parents, but the truth would come out someday. It always did.

She ignored her father and scanned the room. There were two twin beds covered with pink chenille spreads, two small desks with wooden chairs pushed up under them, and one window covered with plain white curtains.

"All right then, this is goodbye." He still didn't offer his daughter a hug. Maybe if he showed her any affection, God would strike him dead for consorting with the enemy.

Janie looked him right in the eye. "Will I ever be going back to Whitesboro?"

"Probably not," her father answered as he stepped out into the hallway. "But we'll figure all that out in good time. We'll have to talk to Aunt Ruthie before we decide where you'll be living after you leave here."

"Yes, sir." She followed him to the door and watched him hurry down the hallway and turn the corner. It wasn't until he was out of sight that she let one tear escape.

Greta crossed the room and handed Janie a tissue. "Not exactly the way you thought you'd be spending Christmas Day, is it? Who was that man?"

"That was my father, the Reverend Arnold Jackson." Janie dried her eyes and blew her nose. Then she threw the tissue in the trash can beside the empty desk and made a vow that she wouldn't shed another tear for the way her parents had treated her. "It's not the way I wanted to spend Christmas, but then, according to Mama, I don't deserve to worship the baby Jesus. God, this room looks like a prison."

"What did you expect?" Greta asked. "A five-star hotel with pictures of pretty roses in gilded frames hanging on the walls? There won't be mints on your pillow every night, either, and you don't get room service. You got the speech before you came up here, didn't you? No outside contact with anyone, especially the miserable son of a bitch that got you pregnant. No personal anything. Just have your baby, give it to loving parents to raise, and leave so the next pregnant girl can have your spot. Chop, chop! There's a couple that can't conceive waiting, and you're here to make them happy."

Janie sat down on the edge of the bed that looked less used. "That's not exactly what they said."

"Pretty damn close, though, isn't it?" Greta eased down on the other twin bed. "Might as well unpack. Tomorrow we start back to school. I'm a junior, and my baby is due in six weeks. My roommate just left yesterday. She had a baby boy. She got to hold him for an hour before they took him away. When's your baby due?"

"The doctor said toward the end of April." Janie threw her suitcase on the bed and opened it. "Where are you from?"

"Little town south of Richmond, Virginia, but we're not supposed to talk much about where we came from or exchange personal information." Greta winked. "You're breaking the rules."

"If we hadn't broken the rules already, we wouldn't be here." Janie picked up seven pairs of white cotton underpants and looked around.

4

Greta pointed toward a set of double doors built into the wall with drawers below them. "Bottom two are yours. When I move out, you can put your things in the top two. Biggest belly gets the upper ones, so it doesn't have to bend as far."

Janie opened the third drawer and put her panties to one side. "So basically, we are supposed to have *this*"—she laid a hand on her stomach—"that's what Mama always called it, anyway. It was never a baby or her grandchild. Once we have it, we're supposed to hand it over like it's a hamburger at a café and never think about it again."

"Yep," Greta answered. "Who's Aunt Ruthie?"

"Mama's great-aunt," Janie said. "My folks think they're punishing me, but I'd rather live with her in a town that doesn't even have a grocery store than go home to them. Where are your folks sending you?"

"I'm going back home, but there'll probably be a set of rules engraved in stone and set up in my bedroom. God only knows that I sure won't ever again be allowed to roam free and wild or go to the horse stables without a chaperone. You'd think getting pregnant out of wedlock was a sin that would cast a person straight into hell, wouldn't you?"

"According to my mother, that's where I'm headed. When this is over, I'm supposed to spend hours and hours on my knees begging God for forgiveness for my sin." Janie took her toiletries to the bathroom and began to pace the floor. "Someday in the next hundred years, it won't even be a big deal, and women won't be looked down on for doing what men have been doing for years. I hope I live to see that day. My brother, Luther, got his wife pregnant before they married, and Mama and Daddy adore her."

"I bet they told everyone that the baby was *premature*." Greta put air quotes around the last word. "That's what happens when the baby comes before nine months after a couple gets married. Boys don't get sent away to homes, because they can't get pregnant. The sin is always on us girls. Folks don't worry about them, because what boys do isn't obvious to the world like a swollen belly is. Short story is that boys will be boys, and they can't ruin the family reputation." She laid a hand on her stomach. "I hate these smocks they make us wear."

She's right, the pesky voice in Janie's head said. *Boys live by different rules than girls, and you know it, but someday things are going to change. Wait and see.*

"My folks are telling people that I'm on a mission trip with Aunt Ruthie for this semester." She tucked a strand of dark-brown hair back up into her ponytail.

"I'm away on a tour of Europe." Greta shrugged. "That's what my folks told everyone anyway. A private tutor went with me and my grandmother, who really is away on a long tour, and I'll be joining her as soon as the baby is born. The tutor will really be teaching me while we're traveling, so that when I go back for my senior year, no one will ask questions."

Since the day the doctor had told Janie that she was pregnant, no one in her family had spoken about it. She and her mother had sat on the front pew at church just like always, and her father had aimed his sermon right at her for the next four Sundays. It seemed that just by doing the very thing that her mother and father had done to bring her into the world, she'd turned herself into a modern-day Jezebel, someone who was totally unfit for polite society.

The lady in the office on the first floor had suggested that things would be better if she didn't make close friends here in the maternity home, and she'd signed a paper saying that she wouldn't try to contact her roommates after they had given birth and left, or anytime in the future. She was to finish out her time until the baby was born, and then she was supposed to never think about the experience again. That would make her whole and fit when it was over, and ready to find a good husband.

Janie felt a weight lift from her heart and soul at just being able to talk with Greta about her situation. Maybe they would be friends.

Maybe not, but having someone to talk to eased the pain in her heart of being given away like a puppy.

She opened the curtains and looked down at the parking lot below. Snow flurries flew around, and her father held his hat down with one hand as he hurried over to his shiny black car. He had a folder under his arm—probably all the papers she'd signed.

He got into his car and didn't even look up to see if maybe she was in the window. Cold and indifferent, she thought, like the day he had taken her into his study and told her that he and her mother had arranged for her to go away to a maternity home in Dallas. They would leave on Christmas morning, and the folks in his congregation would think that they were simply going to spend the day with Aunt Ruthie in Birthright, like they always did. According to her mother, the Good Book said that the elder of a church should take care of the elderly, and since Aunt Ruthie was old, they shouldn't leave her alone on the holiday. Everything had been carefully planned so that no one would ever know about the disgrace Sarah Jane had brought on the Jackson family.

Her mother had come into the study while Janie was still reeling from that news of her banishment and had reminded her wayward daughter that her ancestors had helped in the founding of Whitesboro. Now that daughter had put a huge blot on the family name. Janie had heard about the family's involvement in the history of Whitesboro so often that she could have recited it back to her mother, but she had kept her mouth shut. Ethel Adams Jackson had a mean right hand, and she didn't spare the force when she got mad. Janie had sported a red handprint on her face lots of times after she had smarted off to her mother. Evidently, that was another sin, somewhere down below pregnant before marriage but still on the list.

Janie had looked up the history of Whitesboro in the school encyclopedia to make sure it was true, not merely some lore her mother had made up and told her from the time she was big enough to listen. That's when she found out that after the Civil War, the women in

Whitesboro were prohibited from going out on Saturday nights because shootings were so common. Like the men from the Adams family were not involved in a single one of those shootings—truth probably was that they just didn't get caught. What Janie thought didn't matter one little, tiny bit. Her mother's precious family tree wasn't so pure and spotless, and it was all Janie's fault.

"How old are you?" Greta broke the silence between them.

"Fifteen, but I'll be sixteen on March fifteenth," Janie answered.

"Beware the Ides of March," Greta said.

"Mama brought that up a lot, especially this last month, when she found out that I'd brought shame upon the almighty family tree. You would have thought that there was a book in the Bible called the Gospel According to Shakespeare, and the first verse had to do with the Ides of March. The rest would have been about wayward daughters who ruin the family name," Janie said as she watched her father drive away.

"Amen!" Greta raised a hand toward heaven. "I bet every girl in here has heard all about that. Who's the father of your baby?"

Janie whipped around and glared at the girl. "Kind of nosy, aren't you?"

"All we've got is each other for the next six weeks. We'll be escorted to classes like we're prisoners," Greta informed her. "Actually, I guess we are. We're being punished for messin' around before we were married all legal-like. Our sentence is the time we have left in the months it takes to produce a baby and give it away. We don't have much choice in whether we want to keep it or not. Our parents put us here because we're underage, and the law says they have authority over us. I know because my dad's a lawyer, and, believe me, he read me chapter and verse from the law books about his rights and mine. My mama raises Thoroughbred horses. And yes, I'm nosy. If we talk to each other, maybe it'll help us both keep from losing our minds in this place." She swung a hand around to take in the whole room.

"A boy who worked on my grandpa's farm last summer. He told me he loved me and that I couldn't get . . ." Janie struggled with the word, even though she was mad enough to spew cusswords.

"Pregnant," Greta filled in. "We can say the word in here. The devil won't come up and pull us down to hell for saying it out loud."

Janie took a deep breath and continued. "Pregnant, except on two days each month. He said that it was the rhythm method." Evidently, Greta hadn't been raised in the same atmosphere Janie had. "I guess he was wrong about those two days, because here I am."

"Guys will tell a girl anything when they want sex," Greta said. "Crazy, ain't it? The guys brag about it, and we're not supposed to say the word above a whisper. They must enjoy sex, the way they chase after it, and no one tells us jack squat about how to keep from getting pregnant. I found out too late that there are ways and means. Of course, since girls like me and you aren't married, we can't have that new pill they've come up with. It's not fair, but it's the way it is. I hope I live to see the day when we can brag about having sex if we want to and we don't have to be ashamed that we're pregnant and not married."

Janie smiled for the first time. Greta had rocks for brains if she thought that her lifetime was going to be long enough to change the world that much. "I hope that someday unmarried women can get the pill. My mama fusses about the world going to hell in a handbasket because women are demanding their rights. She says that women should be content to do what God intended them to do, and that's having babies and keeping house."

"Me too. When I get old enough, I'm going to march with those women who want the right to keep their babies and use birth control." Greta sighed.

"Did you like it?" Janie changed the subject.

"Are we talking about sex?" Greta asked. "Not so much the first time. But later, with another boy, I did. A lot. He kind of knew what to do. The first one wasn't very good at it."

"Two boys?" Janie gasped. Ethel Jackson would have dropped down on her knees at the front of the church and prayed for Janie until she starved to death if she found out that her daughter had been with two boys.

"Yep," Greta said. "The second one is the father of this." She pointed at her belly. "But he joined the army when I told him I was pregnant. Not that he would have had to do that, because my daddy would have never let me marry him. He might have killed him or had him killed, but Daddy wouldn't ever let me marry beneath the family name."

"Did you want to?" Janie asked. "Marry him, that is?"

"Not so much," Greta said.

Janie had never talked so openly with anyone in her entire life about anything. She'd always been the preacher's daughter, and folks didn't discuss that kind of thing in her world. Girls like Greta were considered wild—sleeping with two different boys and then *admitting it*. Didn't matter how rich they were; good girls like Janie didn't associate with them.

"What was your baby's father like?" Greta asked.

"He had dark hair and brown eyes, and he came up from Mexico with his dad to work for my grandpa." Janie sat back down on the bed.

"Holy crap on a cracker," Greta gasped. "Did you tell your folks about him?"

Janie shrugged. "Mama would've killed me graveyard-dead if I didn't tell her. If it had been a white boy, I might not be here. Daddy would have made him marry me. I'm glad he wasn't a white boy from a decent family. I don't want to be married." That was the first time she'd admitted she didn't want to be a wife. Having a man tell her what to do, when to do it, and how to do it didn't sit well with Janie. Even though her mother ruled the house, in public she put on a submissive face and deferred to her husband. That had confused Janie ever since childhood.

Two men, though, before Greta was married—she could almost hear her mother gasping for air. But it was downright liberating to say that she wanted more out of life than to have to submit to a man's every whim.

"When you first came in here, I thought you were going to be all shy and backward," Greta said. "I couldn't get my last roommate to talk much. She didn't want to give her baby away, but . . ." She shrugged again. "You're in the tenth grade?"

"Yes, I am." Janie had decided in that short time that she liked Greta. "And you're in the eleventh? Daddy said I'll have school here."

"That's right—we'll be in the same room together," Greta said. "We go from breakfast to the classroom and then to lunch. After that we come back here to do our homework. From three to five we can go to the game room if we want, and then there's supper. Saturday, we do laundry. Sunday is chapel and boredom."

Just like prison, Janie thought.

But at least you've got someone to talk to, and that makes things so much better, the voice in her head said.

Amen, Janie thought.

Greta went into labor on Valentine's Day. Janie never saw her again. The very next day, a new roommate showed up—a short blonde-haired girl who was hard as nails and would be staying in the maternity home for six months. She took her things out of paper grocery bags and tossed them into the bottom two drawers with no respect for organization. She flopped down on the bed and laced her fingers over her stomach.

"I'm Elizabeth. I'm seventeen, and this is my second trip to this place. How long have you been here?"

Janie pulled out the chair to her desk and eased down into it. "I'm Janie, and I've been here since Christmas. You've really been here before?"

"Two years ago," Elizabeth said. "When are you due? You look like you're having a baby elephant."

Janie raised her eyebrows. "I feel like I'm havin' one, too. I'm due at the end of April."

"You won't go that long." Elizabeth sat up on the edge of the bed and eyed her. "You'll deliver early. You're too big already. Are you keeping it?"

Janie shook her head. "I didn't know that was an option."

"Not if we're under eighteen," Elizabeth said. "But at least we get three squares and a bed until the kid is born. My stepdad threw me out when he found out he had gotten me pregnant."

"What did your mama say?" A few months ago, the idea that a man would do that to his stepchild would have shocked Janie, but not since hearing a few of the girls' stories in this place.

"Mama is an alcoholic and does whatever he says, and she never believes me, but she did call the folks here and got me into the home, again, so I guess she ain't all bad," Elizabeth said. "I'll be eighteen the week after this one is born, so I'm not going back home ever. How old are you?"

"Sixteen in another month," Janie answered.

"I was your age when the first one was born. He belonged to my boyfriend." Elizabeth pushed a strand of blonde hair behind her ear. "I wish this one did, or that I could tell the nice people who will get the baby that the father is a bastard who takes advantage of his stepdaughter."

"What happened to your boyfriend?" Janie asked.

"He died in a car wreck two weeks before I found out I was pregnant," Elizabeth told her. "If the baby boy that couple took home looks and acts like him, they've got a good child. Danny was a good man—maybe I should say boy, since he was only sixteen at the time."

Elizabeth was right in her prediction about Janie not carrying the baby full term. On the afternoon of April 15, Janie was doing her algebra homework when her water broke. Elizabeth hurried out of the room to the only phone on the third floor—a wall-hung black one that could only call the nurse's station. In ten minutes, a lady in white appeared with a wheelchair and motioned for Janie to sit down.

Elizabeth waved and yelled, "Good luck."

"Thanks," Janie managed to say before the lady took her out of the room.

Janie delivered a five-pound baby girl at one minute until midnight. At three minutes after midnight, she delivered another baby girl only three ounces bigger. She got to hold her twin daughters, with their jet-black hair and tiny little fingers and toes, for one hour before the nurse took them away. Watching that woman walk out of the room with her beautiful babies was the hardest thing Janie had ever had to endure, and she swore she'd never go through it again.

Four days later Aunt Ruthie showed up at the hospital to take her to Birthright, Texas. Janie's milk had come in that morning, and her breasts felt as if they were made of concrete. They throbbed, and the front of her blouse sagged with the moisture. For the first time since she had been taken away from her home, Janie wished that she could talk to her mother. She'd know what to do about the pain and the embarrassment of having big, sticky circles on her shirt. But her mother and father had been called to run a mission in Mexico and were packing to leave.

As Janie took one last look at the room and waved at Elizabeth, she made a vow that she would march with Greta for women's rights when she got old enough. She shouldn't have to leave her babies behind, and she should be able to buy birth control pills if she wanted to have them.

60 years later

Chapter One

Birthright, Texas, population forty, was the only place Noah Jackson had ever truly felt at home, so why was he dreading going back there? He kept time to the country music on his truck's radio as he fought the Houston traffic. Once he was through town, the drive north would be a piece of cake. In five hours he'd be sitting in his great-aunt's driveway. By suppertime he should be unpacked and moved into the big two-story house on the east end of the town.

"Town," he chuckled. "Birthright can barely be called a community these days."

The bumper-to-bumper vehicles finally broke up, and he could drive the speed limit. He'd promised Miss Janie, his great-aunt, two years ago that when she needed him to come stay with her and manage her affairs, he would be there. She was his last living relative, and he owed her that much and more for always having a stable place for him and his parents to land between army bases.

A week ago, Miss Janie had called him. "It's time," she had said. "The doctor told me today that I've got cancer in addition to this forgetting disease"—she refused to call it Alzheimer's—"and it's not treatable. The cancer is going to cause the other problem to speed up, so I need you to come home, Noah. Please don't let me die alone in a nursing home."

"I've just finished a case," he had told her. "I'll get things in order here and be there the first of the week. Can you manage until then?"

"Sam comes by every day," she answered. "But he won't let me drive anymore. I forget how to get home even from church. I hate that I have to disrupt your life, darlin', but I want you here with me"—she paused and took a deep breath—"and I want you to find Teresa and Kayla. You're a private investigator, so you can do it. I need them here with me."

His head had swirled around in circles that day as he'd promised to do his best to find the two girls Miss Janie had fostered more than a decade ago. He had no idea where they might be, since neither had kept in touch with Miss Janie very well. She had mentioned getting a few Christmas cards and a couple of letters from one of them. On her birthday last March, she'd cried because neither of them had come home to see her ever. Noah had wanted to strangle the both of them.

A loud horn from the vehicle behind him snapped him back to the present. The light had turned green, and he was first in line. He took his foot off the brake, but his mind kept going back to Miss Janie as he drove.

Two years ago, she'd called him when she was first diagnosed with Alzheimer's. He'd driven up to see her that weekend, and she had insisted that he start the proceedings to put her affairs in order. Now he had power of attorney and was the executor of her will. For the past year, he'd paid her bills because she couldn't remember if or when she had taken care of them.

That was the day she'd told him about the babies she had given birth to back when she was sixteen. He had wanted to do more than strangle his great-grandparents for the way they had treated his sweet great-aunt. Once he'd done some research, though, he found out that it was not an isolated case. Women who were under eighteen had to abide by their parents' decisions concerning their rights to keep a baby, or babies, as had been the case for Miss Janie. Her parents, Arnold and Ethel, had made her give the babies up for adoption and had then parked her in Birthright, Texas, with an old-maid aunt.

"I wanted to keep them so badly." Miss Janie had wept into a lace-edged hanky when she told him about them. "Aunt Ruthie told me later that she even offered to help me raise them, but Mama said I'd shamed the family name. We weren't supposed to ever talk about it, but Aunt Ruthie and I did, and we celebrated their birthday every year."

Just thinking about how distraught she'd been even after so many years put a tear in Noah's eye. If his father, General Adam Jackson, had been alive, he would have told him for the hundredth time that he was soft—that he should have joined the army so they could make a man out of him.

Even though Noah had finished law school, landed a job in a big Houston firm, and had been very successful for the next two years, "the General," as Noah called him, had died a disappointed man. His only child had not followed in his footsteps, or his grandfather Luther's for that matter.

The General would have been even more disappointed if he'd been alive when Noah gave up his position in the law firm and went to work with his friend Daniel as a private investigator. The old man probably would've turned over in his grave if he'd known that Noah was having doubts about staying with that job and was glad to have a few months in Birthright to decide what to do with his life.

"You can shoulder part of the blame for this," Noah whispered as he passed the sign welcoming him to Fairfield, Texas, population 2,951. "You were rooted in the army, but the only roots you gave me was Miss Janie's place. In my mind, that was going home. I've had wings but no roots, Dad. At thirty-one, I'm ready to stop chasing my passion and settle down to it."

You will join the army when you finish college. His father's last words when he and Noah's mother left him at the university came back to haunt him. Maybe if he had done what the General wanted him to do, he would have put down roots in the army and this feeling of dread wouldn't be getting heavier with every mile.

He pretended he was in court and had to defend the feeling in his heart. The dread was not because he was going back to Birthright, but it had to do with the fact he would be watching the only living relative he had left die by degrees. She might not even know him by the time she'd drawn her last breath. That was the sorry culprit taking away his happiness over going home.

You always were too soft for your own good. The General's words popped into his head again. *I've been gone too much to make a man out of you, but the army will take care of that, and then I can be proud of you.*

"The only person ever proud of me was Miss Janie," he muttered. "She came to my college graduation, encouraged me to get my law degree, stood by me through bad times as well as the good ones. She's told me more than once to follow my dreams, even if they changed by the week."

The chains holding back his happiness began to loosen as he got closer to Birthright, and by the time he'd pulled into the driveway, he was whistling. Miss Janie was sitting on the porch swing, and she got up, shuffled over to the top of the stairs, and held out her arms for a hug.

Noah was home.

He walked into her arms, and peace filled his whole being when she hugged him. No matter what happened in the next few months, he could face it, because this was where he belonged.

"I'm so glad you are home. I can rest easy now," she said. "Your first job is to find Teresa and Kayla. I need to see them before I die."

"I'll do my best," Noah promised, but he sure didn't look forward to bringing Miss Janie's two foster daughters back into the house after the way they had left and never even returned for a short visit.

"I have faith in you." She rolled up on her toes and kissed him on the cheek.

❖ ❖ ❖

Yawning as she left a patient's room, Teresa Mendoza started down the hall to make sure Opal Cunningham hadn't kicked her covers off. The poor old dear's feet got cold in the night, so Teresa always looked in on her right before she clocked out.

She would be off from the nursing home for two whole days, stuck in her boring, tiny one-bedroom apartment unless they called her to work overtime—better to take any shift they offered her.

She had reached the end of the hallway and was in the lobby when she heard someone knocking on the glass entry door. When she turned around to see who in the world wanted to come visit patients at almost eleven o'clock at night, she froze. Exhaustion had her seeing things. That could *not* be Noah Jackson.

Evidently, he knew she was staring at him because he kept pointing at the door. She blinked several times and then rubbed her eyes, but he didn't disappear. He had grown from a lanky boy into a tall, broad-shouldered man with the same piercing blue eyes and jet-black hair. She felt like she was in one of those dreams that move in slow motion as she crossed the floor and punched in the code so he could come in out of the hot Texas air.

"Teresa, I found you." He grinned.

"What are you doing here?" Her voice sounded flat even to her own ears. "Why were you looking for me?"

"I need you to come back to Birthright and work for me," he answered.

"Doing what? Working at the huge hospital or the fancy nursing home?" she smarted off.

Birthright had been nothing more than a rural community when she'd lived there with Miss Janie Jackson. The town couldn't have grown enough that there was a place for her to work there.

"Miss Janie is dying," he said. "I need someone to live with us and help me take care of her."

Her heart went out to her foster mother but going back would mean returning to the pain of being an outcast who seemed to have no place in any world. Being a foster kid set her apart from the rich kids for sure. Coming from the background that she had before Miss Janie took her in, she wasn't accepted by the middle-class kids, either. Although she loved Miss Janie and appreciated her for taking her in and giving her a decent home, that couldn't make up for the feelings of rejection she associated with that area of Texas.

"I have a job. Hire someone else."

His big blue eyes bored into her brown ones without blinking. He wore his hair shaggier these days and kept a little scruff on his face. Apparently, he had not gone into the military like his dad had expected him to do.

"I don't want anyone else," he said. "Miss Janie wants her girls to come home, to be with her these last days. I've spent a lot of money and resources tracking you down. You could have at least put a return address on those damn Christmas cards."

"Why would I do that?" she asked. "The government stopped paying her when I had my eighteenth birthday. And I'm not responsible for what money you've spent. That's on you, not me. Tell Miss Janie hello for me." That she didn't want Miss Janie to be disappointed in her decisions wasn't any of his business.

"You can take care of strangers but not the woman who gave you a fit place to live?" he asked.

There it was. He'd finally played the you-owe-her foster card. She clamped her jaw shut so tightly that it ached, but at least she wasn't spewing out a line of swear words so hot that they would set the lobby on fire.

"And what happens when she's gone? I might not be able to get this job back," she said through clenched teeth. "Did you think of that?"

"Why are you so angry?" Noah asked.

"Have you forgotten about the screened porch at Miss Janie's house?" she threw back at him.

"I'm sorry about that, Teresa. I really did like you, and"—he stumbled over the words—"it was only a few stolen kisses, but if my mama or my father had found out, they would have killed me. You know my parents . . . the General . . . they would have thought making out with you at Miss Janie's house was disrespectful of her hospitality."

He blinked and looked down at his hands. "I need help, and Miss Janie wants you girls to come home. She cries for you and Kayla and asks me every single day if I've found you. I'll pay you twice as much as you make here, plus you'll have room and board and only have to take care of one patient."

For any other person she might have jumped on the offer, but this was Noah, the boy she'd fallen in love with at fourteen and had never really gotten over.

"How long has she been sick?" she asked.

"A couple of years ago she was diagnosed with Alzheimer's. The disease has been taking over pretty fast, but until last June she was able to manage with a little help from her neighbor Sam. She said she was fine, but then Sam called to say she was forgetting how to get home from the grocery store and even church. I talked to her doctor and decided it was time for me to come take care of her." Noah's voice cracked toward the end of the explanation.

"Did she really ask for me?" Teresa asked.

"She keeps begging for her girls to come home," Noah answered. "When I found out you were a nurse's aide, I figured that it would take care of two things. She would be pleased that one of her girls came home, and she knows you so she wouldn't mind you helping her."

"Why didn't you ask Kayla?" Teresa asked.

Kayla was a year younger than Teresa. Kayla had been a wild card from the beginning, and when Teresa left, Kayla still had a year to go before the government tossed her out into the harsh world.

"I can't find her, and chances are that she doesn't have the training you do," Noah answered. "I've got to get back. Sam is staying with Miss Janie, and I told him I'd be back by daybreak. Here's my card—the house phone number is written on the back in case you've forgotten it. Just think about it. If you don't show up by the end of the week, I'll start looking for full-time help somewhere else." He started for the door.

"Six, seven, eight, nine," she called out.

He stopped and glanced over his shoulder. "What does that mean?"

"That's the code to open the door."

He chuckled.

"What's so funny?" she asked.

"That would be the first thing most folks would punch in." He hit the right buttons and disappeared out into the night.

Teresa turned and started toward the office and tossed the card in the trash can on the way. She punched out, picked up her tote bag full of empty supper containers, and headed back across the lobby on her way out to her truck. Stopping in her tracks, she stared at the trash can for several seconds. Her heart told her to at least pick up the card and take it with her, but she had vowed she would never let her heart make decisions for her again. Besides, she hadn't been back to see Miss Janie since she'd left all those years ago. Miss Janie would know that she'd failed—both when she quit college and when she had married Luis. When she reached the door, she punched in the code and made it all the way to her vehicle, tossed her tote bag on the threadbare passenger's seat, and drove home.

She stripped out of her scrubs, took a long, hot shower, and put on a faded nightshirt. Normally, she went right to sleep when she crawled into bed, but this wasn't an ordinary night. For the first time in over sixteen years, she'd seen Noah Jackson again. She'd thought when she'd

24

married Luis that she was over that little teenage crush, but evidently not, because merely being in his presence had created the same heat that those few forbidden kisses had caused.

Maybe she shouldn't have been so hasty in throwing away the card. He had offered her a lot of money to come back to Birthright, and if she was honest with herself, she owed Miss Janie more than a few months of care. If guilt had a color, it would be black, and if it could be weighed, it would be heavier than a full-grown elephant. The feeling bore down on her so hard that she could barely breathe.

Miss Janie had been there when she'd needed someone, and now the sweet old lady needed help. That Noah would be in the same house didn't matter. Those few stolen kisses had happened years ago, and it was time she stopped thinking about them.

"Dammit!" She sat up and pounded the lumps from her pillow, throwing herself backward once done. Dark clouds floating back and forth over the quarter moon created shifting patterns on the ceiling and the walls of her tiny bedroom. That alone seemed like an omen, telling her that even though she'd been through a divorce a year before, there was light in the darkness.

"But is going back to Birthright the clouds or the light?" she whispered.

Never know until you try, the pesky voice in her head told her.

At three thirty, she slung her legs over the side of the bed and stood up. She found a pair of pajama pants in the clean laundry basket and put them on. Then she went out into the darkness, padded down the steps of her garage apartment in her bare feet, and got back into her truck.

Thank goodness no one was in the home's lobby, and the code wouldn't be changed until the seven o'clock shift came to work. She pushed the right buttons, found the card in the trash can, and tucked it into the pocket of her nightshirt.

When she got back home, she laid the card beside her cell phone and went back to bed. She closed her eyes and crashed almost at once. She awoke at noon and reached for her phone to see if she had been offered an extra shift, but there were no messages. She would have rather worked a double shift that day to give her something to occupy her mind, but oh, no, the fickle finger of fate had to point right at the card on her nightstand.

There will be no peace until you do this. That voice in her head was back.

She turned the card over and called the number. When Noah answered, she said, "I'll be there Saturday afternoon," and then hung up before he could say anything. She didn't need his thanks, or even twice what she was making. She just needed a lot less guilt about not making a bigger effort to visit or call Miss Janie and a lot more peace in her heart, and once her decision was made and she'd given her word, she had both.

The day started off well, and there didn't seem to be many good days anymore. At least not since Noah had moved into the big old rambling two-story house with Miss Janie. Ever since the doctor discovered that she had a rare form of bone cancer a few months ago, the dementia seemed to be on a fast track.

Thank God Teresa had said she'd come back to Birthright and help. At least he hoped that her terse phone call had been serious and that she really was going to show up that day. Once he had her number, he'd tried to call her back a couple of times, but she hadn't answered.

"I love this screened porch and the smell of roses." Miss Janie took a long breath. "I was scared when Mama said I had to come here to live, but I'm glad she did. Aunt Ruthie was a wonderful person. Did I ever tell you about my girls?" she asked.

"Yes, ma'am, and I believe they might be coming home soon." Noah knew he was her only living relative, which was why he'd come home to Birthright, Texas, to stay with her.

"They had beautiful black hair," Miss Janie sighed.

There was a moment of silence, and then she went on. "And even though folks say that a baby's eyes change from when they're born, I know they stayed brown like their father's. He was a very handsome boy. I want to see my girls before I die, and I don't care how much money you spend to find them."

"They'll be home soon. It's a lovely day, isn't it?" Noah tried to steer the conversation away from the girls. When she mentioned the two girls she had fostered, she got weepy. To see his sweet great-aunt cry broke his heart.

She crossed her arms and glared at him. "Why are you still here anyway? I hired you to find my girls, not make my breakfast."

"I'm your great-nephew, Noah. I used to come see you fairly often," he said gently.

She narrowed her eyes and stared at him for several more seconds. "You're Luther's grandson, right?"

"Yes, ma'am. Luther was your brother, and his son was Adam. I'm Adam's son, Noah," he explained like he did at least twice a day.

"Adam and Noah, just like in the Bible. Daddy used to preach about those two men, and David and Daniel. Were they twins like my girls?" she asked. "I have trouble remembering what Daddy said about them."

"No, they lived in different times," he told her.

"I wanted to keep my girls." She teared up. "In those days we didn't get an option about keeping our babies."

Two years ago, when she'd been diagnosed with Alzheimer's, she'd told him about the twin girls she'd given away at birth and had insisted that he find them for her. He'd had to jump through a few hoops, but he finally located them—in El Paso, Texas—and found out that they'd died together in a car wreck when they were twenty-five years old. One had been married two years without any children; the other one had still been single.

When he'd told her about her daughters, Miss Janie had wept for a week, and then one morning she'd come out of her bedroom and asked him if he'd found her girls. He was hoping that when Teresa came back to Birthright, if she did, Miss Janie would forget all about the babies that she'd birthed and concentrate on at least one of the girls she had fostered when they were teenagers.

Janie's gray eyebrows knit together, and she tilted her head to the side. From the few pictures that Noah had seen of her, she'd once had brown hair. Now her thin hair had grayed, and her blue eyes had faded, as if so many of the memories of her life had washed out from her mind. "What month is it?"

"Today is the first day of August and it's Saturday," Noah replied. "It'll be fall pretty soon, and then winter will come on fast after that. Then it will be too chilly to sit out on the porch for breakfast. Why don't you eat your breakfast before it gets cold?"

Fine screen wire covered three sides of the wide porch, letting the breezes flow through but keeping the mosquitoes out. When Noah was a boy, he'd begged his mama and daddy to let him sleep out there, but they never did.

She pushed her plate back. "I don't want eggs. I want chocolate doughnuts and milk."

The doctors had said she'd probably be gone by Christmas, so Noah figured it didn't matter what she ate. *Let me eat what I want and die when I'm supposed to*—that's what she always said, even now. He took the plate back to the kitchen and brought out a box of chocolate doughnuts from the pantry. He poured a tall glass of milk, put both on a tray, and carried it out to the porch.

"Look at that sunrise." Miss Janie smiled. "Aunt Ruthie and I watched a sunrise like that the morning she brought me here to live. Where is Aunt Ruthie? Has she gone to the store?"

"No. She died the day I was born," Noah gently reminded her. "Remember when you told me that there are only so many souls in heaven and they have to be reused, so I got Aunt Ruthie's when she died? And it would help me to grow up independent and able to make up my own mind about things?"

Miss Janie giggled like a schoolgirl. "Aunt Ruthie could make the devil sit on the front row in church and get saved, sanctified, and even dehorned. She was a tough old bird." She lowered her voice to a whisper. "I was kind of afraid of her when I was a little girl, but when I came to live here, I learned really quick to love her. I never told her that. I should have."

"Was she mean?" Noah asked.

"No," Miss Janie replied. "And she wasn't exactly strict—she was set in her ways. Did I tell you that she got me a job at the school? She took care of the cafeteria, and when I graduated, she talked the superintendent into giving me a job working with her. The next year the secretary job came open, and I applied and went to work for the high school principal. I saw dozens of principals come and go before I retired."

"You did tell me that." Noah was glad to hear her talking about something other than her girls.

"When does school start back this year?" Miss Janie asked. "I have to go two weeks early to get things set up for the kids."

"Not for a while yet." Noah watched her eat several doughnuts and drink the whole glass of milk.

"Is Luther coming this summer?" she asked. "I always look forward to his visits."

"Grandpa died a while back," Noah reminded her.

"Luther died?" Miss Janie's eyes misted over. "So now I'm all alone in the world? When is the funeral?"

"You're not alone. I'm here with you. I moved in last June, and we set up an office for my investigative work in one of the upstairs bedrooms." Noah laid his hand on hers.

She dried her eyes and blinked several times. "Of course you did. Did you find my girls?"

"I'm still searching for them," he answered.

Teresa packed everything she owned in three boxes and the now-ragged suitcase that Miss Janie had given her when she graduated from high school. Since she hadn't given a thirty-day notice, she lost the deposit on her garage apartment, and she'd used nearly all of her meager savings to put a new alternator in the truck so it would get her from Hope, Arkansas, to Birthright. She had thought she would use the money to replace at least two of the bald tires on the vehicle, but tires weren't worth much if the damn truck wouldn't even run. Maybe the bald tires and prayers together would get her there.

The sun peeked over the eastern horizon by the time she tossed the boxes and the suitcase into the back of the truck. She locked the door to her tiny apartment and turned the key over to the manager of the place. Noah said that she'd have a place to live until Christmas, and she sure hoped he stuck to that.

Her cell phone service died at noon that Saturday because she used a pay-as-you-go plan and hadn't bought a refill card. She was still fifty miles from her destination, so she really was traveling on a prayer from that point. She tossed the phone over on the passenger seat and figured if she had a blowout, maybe some kind soul would call Miss Janie's house and Noah could come help her. He had said he would pay her, and God only knew how bad she needed the money, but a fresh wave of guilt washed over her when she thought about charging him to help with Miss Janie.

The truck might be running on fumes, but the radio still worked, so to keep her mind off the thoughts of blown-out tires or no fuel in the tank, she turned the dial.

"And here's 'Storms Never Last' by Miranda Lambert. She sang this recently at the Grand Ole Opry, and I was privileged to be right there on the front row," the DJ said.

"I hope you're tellin' me the truth, Miss Miranda," Teresa said as the words flowed by, talking about bad times passing with the wind.

An hour later, hungry and hoping that there were some leftovers from dinner, she parked in front of the big two-story house that intimidated her every bit as much now as it had the day she'd moved a box of clothing into it just before eighth grade. Black clouds rolled in from the southwest, and a loud clap of thunder followed a jagged streak of lightning. Teresa didn't have time to sit there and think.

She could see the sheets of rain coming toward her, and if she didn't get her things from the bed of the truck and onto the porch, they'd be soaked in a few minutes. She rolled up the window, jumped out, and grabbed the suitcase and one box and jogged across the yard. Her jet-black ponytail flipped back and forth as she ran to the truck for the other boxes. A hard wind blew the first raindrops across her face as she hurried up onto the porch with the last box. Out of breath, she knocked on the door.

After a week of giving herself lectures concerning Noah, she thought that she had things under control, but when he was right there on the other side of the door, her knees turned to jelly.

"Come right in." He stood to one side. "Can I help you with—"

"Yes . . . ," she butted in. "Three boxes. I can get the suitcase."

They'd gotten all her things inside when another crack of thunder brought a deluge with it. Miss Janie came out of the living room and stared at Teresa for the longest time, as if she wasn't sure who she was; then her frail hands went to her cheeks and her eyes widened. "You found one of my daughters. You did it. You found one of my babies. Come here to Mama, darlin' girl, and give me a hug. Have you seen your sister? Is she coming?" She opened her arms.

Teresa didn't mind being called Miss Janie's daughter. Noah had said that she had developed Alzheimer's, so that was understandable, but Teresa damn sure didn't want to be recognized as Kayla's sister. That girl had been a handful the whole time they had lived together in this house, and all they'd done was argue and bicker.

Miss Janie wrapped Teresa up in her arms and wet her shoulder with tears. "I'm so sorry I gave you away. I thought about you girls every single day and prayed that your adoptive parents were good to you. What did they name you, child?"

"My name is Teresa Mendoza, and I haven't seen Kayla." Poor Miss Janie hardly looked like the same strong woman who'd cried as she'd stood on the porch and waved goodbye as Teresa went away to college. That little secondhand car Miss Janie had bought for her had served her well. She almost wished she were driving it back here.

"Oh, no!" Miss Janie took a step back and put her hand over her mouth. "They split you up and put you in different homes. I wanted them to keep you together."

"Miss Janie, Mendoza is my married name, but I'm divorced now." Teresa shot a look at Noah.

"That's good." Miss Janie dried her eyes. "I'm glad we can be a family again. Maybe your sister will come later. How long has it been since you sisters have seen each other?"

"A long time," Teresa muttered.

"Are you hungry?" Miss Janie asked.

"Starving," Teresa admitted. "I drove straight here and didn't stop for breakfast." She didn't say that she was afraid if she killed the engine of her old truck, she might not get it started again.

"Well, let's get you fed, and then Noah can help you get things up to your room. I want to know everything about the people who raised you," Miss Janie said as she shuffled back down the wide hallway to the kitchen. "What do you want? Noah is right good at making breakfast."

"Whose plate is that?" Teresa pointed to a plate of scrambled eggs, bacon, toast, and hash browns.

"That would be what Miss Janie didn't want this morning," Noah explained.

"I'll heat it up in the microwave and have that," Teresa said. "No use in wasting food."

Miss Janie sat down at the table and frowned. "Young man, who are you? Are you the one I hired to bring Teresa to me, or are you her husband?"

"I'm Noah, your nephew," he said. "Luther's grandson."

"That's right." Miss Janie touched her forehead with her fingertip. "Teresa, darlin' girl, you will have to overlook my forgetfulness. Sometimes I can't remember too well, but I remember the day you two were born very well."

"You'll have to tell me all about that day." Teresa bit back tears. She worked with Alzheimer's patients in the nursing home, but seeing Miss Janie like this was tougher than she'd expected it to be. Poor soul thought that she'd birthed Teresa and Kayla, and on the same day, which would make them twins. Teresa remembered the day when Social Services came to the trailer to take her out of her school in Sulphur Springs to a group home up near Paris, Texas. When Miss Janie had heard what happened, she had stepped in and applied right then for an emergency foster care license and had taken Teresa out of the group home and to Birthright with her that very night.

"I will," Miss Janie agreed. "Leaving my sweet babies in that home was the saddest day of my life."

The microwave dinged, and Miss Janie started to stand up. "It's time for me and Greta to go to class now. The bell has rung, and our teachers get upset if we're late."

Noah laid a hand on her arm. "Today is Saturday. You don't go to class today."

"That's right." Miss Janie settled back down as Teresa retrieved her food from the microwave and started eating.

"Tell us more about that day you gave the babies away." Noah took a seat at the other end of the table.

"What day?" Miss Janie's gray brows drew down into a heavy line. "Noah, who is this woman? I told you not to hire someone to take care of me. I've been doing all right on my own since I was sixteen and Mama and Daddy put me here."

"This is Teresa. She's one of your girls that you wanted me to bring home," he said.

"My girls aren't grown women," she argued. "You were going to find both of them. Where's the other one?" She frowned.

"That was sixty years ago, Miss Janie. You took in Teresa and Kayla when you retired. You became a foster parent to help Teresa and then Kayla," Noah said. "Your babies would be sixty now, not twenty-eight and twenty-nine."

She shook her head. "Don't you try to fool me. I gave birth a few days ago. I still hurt from it. Where's Aunt Ruthie? She'll tell you that I'm right."

The poor old girl really was confused. She had never married nor had children. "I'm so sorry that you hurt. What can I do to help you? I can ask about pain pills, or we can go sit somewhere where the chairs are softer."

"You've had a lot of excitement yesterday and today," Noah said. "Maybe you just need to rest a bit. It is past time for your little afternoon nap."

"I am very tired," she agreed. "And I'm still sore from the birth, but at least the milk has dried up. That was so painful, and so embarrassing the way it kept making my shirts all wet. Aunt Ruthie says it'll get better in a couple of weeks. I wish I could hold my babies one more time. They were so little, and I wanted to keep them so bad."

As she got up out of the chair, she held the bottom of her stomach and walked slightly bent over, like a woman who'd recently had a baby. Teresa laid her fork down and hurried to her side. "Let me help you."

"Thank you." Miss Janie smiled shyly. "I never realized how much having a baby would hurt, but I'd do it all over again to be able to hold them for another hour. You're a good nurse. What's your name?"

"I'm Teresa, and you are Miss Janie, right?" she answered.

"I'm Sarah Jane Jackson. I'm sixteen. The father of my babies is in Mexico now. He's a sweet boy, but I didn't love him. I'm glad I didn't marry him," Miss Janie whispered. "I don't want to get married—not ever. I don't want a man to run my life for me. I want to do that for myself."

"I understand," Teresa said, but she didn't really. Miss Janie had expressed Teresa's thoughts exactly about not wanting a man to run her life, but what was all this about giving birth? When Miss Janie sat down on the edge of the bed, Teresa knelt in front of her and removed her bedroom slippers. "Are you cold? Do you want me to cover you with that nice fluffy throw?"

"No. I want Aunt Ruthie's quilt." Miss Janie pointed to a patchwork quilt draped over a rocking chair.

Teresa shook out the folds and covered Miss Janie with it. "There now. You rest, Sarah Jane, and I'll be back to check on you a little later."

"Thank you," Miss Janie said. "You're one of the good nurses. The one I had last night was really hateful."

"I do my best." Teresa tiptoed out of the bedroom and eased the door shut. When she got back to the kitchen, her food was cold, so she reheated it again in the microwave.

"Okay, Noah, you need to explain to me what's happening here," she said. "You didn't mention anything about babies or tell me how bad she is when you offered me this job."

Noah's tired blue eyes met hers. He raked his fingertips through his dark-brown hair and squared his shoulders. "I'm so glad you're here

35

to help me. Seems like she gets worse every hour, and there are some things I can't do for her like you can. She's got bone cancer that's spread through her whole body and Alzheimer's on top of that. The doctor has given her anywhere from four weeks to three months, but probably the end will come closer to the six-week mark. But there's the possibility she might still be here at Christmas."

"I know that." Teresa brought her plate back to the table. "But what's all this about babies?"

"When they first diagnosed her with Alzheimer's, she called me." Noah's deep voice still made chills chase up and down her spine like it had when she'd met him for the first time. "She wanted to get everything out in the open, so she told me that she'd had twin daughters when she was sixteen. I thought she was already advanced in the dementia and only *thinking* that she'd given birth, but I followed the thread of what she told me and did some research. She was remembering that part right. She really did give birth to twin daughters when she was sixteen."

"Why didn't she keep them?" Teresa asked between bites.

"I did some research on that, too, and back then she wasn't given a choice. Because she was a minor, her parents got to decide what happened. Her parents sent her to a home for unwed mothers in Dallas. She gave birth, and then they sent her here to live with her great-aunt Ruthie. From what little she's told me through the years, she and Aunt Ruthie got along well, but down deep I don't think Miss Janie ever got over giving those babies away. She begged me to find them for her, and I did. Unfortunately, they were both killed in a car wreck when they were twenty-five. She took the news hard, and then she started telling me to bring y'all home to her. Somehow she transferred all the feelings she had for those two little dark-haired daughters over to you and Kayla."

Teresa finished off her breakfast. "She thought I was a nurse when I helped her into bed."

"When she wakes up after her nap, she's usually a little better," Noah told her. "When she gets stimulated, she gets really angry at me.

She'll do the same with you. Don't take it personally. It's the disease. I've got a list of what to not mention when she's not herself. We try not to say 'remember,' but instead ask her to tell us about when she was a certain age. So just don't disagree with her, but try to steer her into another conversation."

Teresa bit her tongue to keep from snapping at him. She didn't need a crash course on how to deal with dementia. "I don't need you to tell me how to do my job. I worked with patients like her in the nursing home," Teresa said. "I know how to handle them."

"Good," he said.

"And while we're at it, we should get my duties defined a little better than you did when you hired me," she said. "Am I to do cleaning or cooking?"

"We have a housekeeper who comes in every other week. I've been doing the cooking, but if you want to do that, I won't fight with you. However, your main job is to help me with Miss Janie. She's so wobbly, I'm afraid that she'll fall in the shower, and she'd be mortified if I saw her naked," he answered.

"So would you," she told him.

"What's that supposed to mean?" His eyes narrowed into slits.

"Think about it." She took her plate to the sink, rinsed it, and put it in the dishwasher. Then she poured herself a cup of coffee.

"I still don't know what you're talking about," he said.

"Think how you'd feel if you had to give Miss Janie a bath. You'd be worse than mortified, and things would be awkward between y'all," she told him. "I'm going up to my room to unpack. I can carry my own boxes. I don't need your help."

"All right then, do it on your own, but you don't have to be afraid I'll kiss you again," he smarted off.

"If you did, you'd be pushing up daisies. I'm not that same little backwoods girls with no confidence. Oh, and unless I'm really busy, I'll do the cooking. If what you make is like this coffee, it won't be worth eating," she said.

"I made the breakfast you just ate," he reminded her.

Yes, you did, and if you'd been dying, Luis wouldn't have made a meal, she thought, but Noah didn't need to know that.

"I can do better," she threw over her shoulder as she left the room.

Chapter Two

Teresa carried two of the boxes up the stairs, set them in the hallway, and went back for the last of her things. When she had left to go to college eleven years ago, she'd thought she was ready to set the world on fire. She was going to prove that a foster kid could do great things, and then she had met and married Luis Mendoza. He had promised to love, honor, and be true to her right there in front of the judge at the courthouse the week before Christmas—and she'd believed him. That was the first of many mistakes she'd made where Luis was concerned.

She was shocked when she opened the door to her old bedroom and saw that it hadn't been touched since the day she left. The doll Miss Janie had given her their first Christmas together stared up at her from the miniature cradle that sat next to the rocking chair in the corner. She'd been too old to play with dolls when she got it, but now she kind of understood why Miss Janie had given it to her. With their darker skin, she and Kayla must've reminded her even back then of the two little baby girls she'd given away, and she'd never been able to give her own daughters a doll.

Teresa sank down in the rocking chair and took in the room bit by bit. Pink rose wallpaper, lace curtains, pink bedspread, and crocheted doilies under the silver comb and brush set on the oak dresser. It was like stepping through a fog into a different time. Tears rolled down her cheeks when she remembered how vibrant Miss Janie had been the day she'd shown Teresa the room for the first time. Now that sweet, kind lady was gone and only a shell remained. The first time she'd seen the room, awe and disbelief had washed over her—this was her very own bedroom. She had waited until Miss Janie had left her alone in the room that day before crying then, too. She wiped her eyes on the tail of her T-shirt and pushed up out of the rocking chair. She couldn't sit there blubbering all day. She had work to do, especially since she'd made those smart-ass remarks about cooking.

Miss Janie must've either cleaned the bedroom once a week or had someone do it for her, because she didn't even see a speck of dust on the closet shelf when she put one of her boxes up there. Then she unzipped her suitcase and unpacked it. She hung up her jeans and shirts and set a pair of boots and one of sandals on the floor. She remembered Miss Janie inspecting her room on Saturday back when she was in middle school. More tears flowed, and this time she sank down onto the floor and admitted to herself that the reason she hadn't come back to Birthright was that she didn't want Miss Janie to know that she'd failed. She had stopped going to classes and had gotten married before the first semester had even ended.

"So much for staying in school and getting my nursing degree like Miss Janie wanted me to," she muttered.

The sound of uncontrollable weeping floated up the stairs, and she stepped out into the hallway. Noah's deep tones in a muffled conversation and Miss Janie's sobbing sent her down the stairs in a hurry.

She met Noah in the downstairs hallway. "This time I don't know what to do with her. Can you go in there, please? Maybe seeing you will calm her down. Right now she's sixteen, and today she arrived here to live with Aunt Ruthie. I swear she feels like she gave birth a couple of days ago and can hardly move. I'm going to call the doctor."

Teresa left him standing in the hallway, rushed into the bedroom, sat down on the edge of the bed, and took Miss Janie's hand in hers.

"What's the matter, darlin'? What can I do to help?" she asked.

"I want to hold my babies again. I don't want to give them away. Aunt Ruthie told me that she offered to help me raise them, but my parents won't hear of it. I've shamed them, and they won't let me keep my babies," she said between bouts of sobbing. "Help me, please."

Teresa remembered a patient in the nursing home who'd had dementia and had evidently lost a child when she was a young woman. Someone had finally had the foresight to give her a baby doll, and she had taken care of it like it was real until she'd died a few weeks later.

"If you won't tell the head nurse on me, I will bring the babies," Teresa whispered.

"For real?" Miss Janie's eyes lit up. "You can do that?"

"Yes, I can, but you have to promise me that you won't cry like that anymore. You break my heart when you do," Teresa answered. "All you have to do is tell them to get me when you want to see the babies. I'll sneak them out of the nursery and bring them right to you."

Noah met her at the doorway and whispered, "Are you bat-crap crazy, woman? The only way we're going to get two babies is to steal them from the hospital in Sulphur Springs, and I'm not going to jail for kidnapping."

"I'm not crazy, and I know what I'm doin'." Teresa brushed past him.

"I doubt that," Noah called after her. "If there are babies upstairs, I'll eat my socks."

"You better take your shoes off and get out the mustard. I hear socks are a bit hard to get down without some mustard and a little pepper," she shot back at him.

Hoping that Kayla hadn't taken everything out of her room when she left, she went there first. Other than the fact that the walls in Kayla's room were pale green and Teresa's were light yellow, the rooms were exactly alike—her baby doll still slept in its little cradle. Teresa picked it up, made sure the blanket was wrapped neatly around it, and then retrieved the one from her room. When she reached the bottom of the stairs, she cradled one in the crook of each of her arms and headed toward Miss Janie's room.

Noah met her in the hallway again and held up a finger. "The doctor says the pain in her pelvic bones is probably what is causing that feeling that she had after giving birth. What are you doing with those dolls?"

"These are not dolls today. They are real babies, and don't you say anything to contradict that. My heart breaks when she sobs for the babies that she can't have, so we're making substitutions," Teresa answered. "Can she have more medicine for the pain?"

Noah shook his head. "She's on the maximum dose that she can have without going to the hospital. She made me promise not to let her die anywhere but right here. The doctor says that she'll probably spend more and more time in bed from now on. She's going to know those are not living, breathing babies."

"Watch and learn," Teresa told him.

Miss Janie's eyes widened, and a smile covered her face as she held out her arms for the dolls. "Put a pillow in my lap so they can lie side by side."

Noah did what she asked, and Teresa gently laid each doll down. "They're beautiful babies. Do you think their eyes will stay brown or turn blue like yours?"

"They'll stay brown like their daddy's eyes. Thank you for bringing them to me. You done good, gettin' them past the head nurse." Miss Janie reached out to touch each of their little faces. "They're sleeping. How long do I get to keep them?"

"As long as you want," Noah said from the doorway.

"I don't want to give them away," she said.

"Then you don't have to," Teresa told her. "We'll arrange it so that you can have them right here with you. We'll even help you with them until you can get on your feet. You had a lot of stitches, and they take a long time to heal."

"This is wonderful." Miss Janie couldn't take her eyes off the two dolls. "You"—she pointed at the one on her left—"you are Mary Jane. And you"—she moved her bony finger to the other one—"you are Madeline Ruth, and I will call you Maddy." She began to hum a lullaby and sway back and forth. "You can go now. I'm good as long as I don't have to give them back."

"We'll need to put them in the nursery at night so you can rest, but we'll take good care of them when they're away from you," Teresa told her.

Miss Janie's chin quivered. "But I can keep them until bedtime, right?"

"Of course," Teresa said past the grapefruit-size lump in her throat. "Or until it's feeding time. We'll take care of that in the nursery, too, and if you get tired and want to rest, you let us know."

Miss Janie started to hum again and waved Teresa and Noah away.

"That was genius," Noah whispered. "Where'd those dolls come from anyway?"

"Miss Janie gave me one for Christmas the first year I was here, and then the next Christmas she gave one like it to Kayla. We were too old to play with them, but I'm damn sure glad she gave them to us," Teresa told him. "Someone in the nursing home did this for a dementia patient. I'm glad it worked for Miss Janie."

"Well, I sure hope it continues to work. Thank you," he said. "Thank you, and I'm so glad you've dealt with this kind of thing before now. The doctor said that, between the cancer pain and the Alzheimer's, she might get hung up in whatever age she had the most trauma or happiness—either one. She could think she's sixteen until the day she passes away," Noah told her. "Or she might still go back and forth. We should be prepared for either or both on an hourly basis, but if she stays in bed more and more, we'll have to get a bed with rails."

"I've dealt with folks like her in the nursing home," Teresa said. "If she breaks a hip or an arm, she'd be in even worse pain. I'm going back upstairs to unpack the rest of my things, and I'll get something going for lunch. Is there anything Miss Janie isn't supposed to eat?"

"She doesn't have much of an appetite, so I let her have whatever she wants. Sometimes she eats chocolate doughnuts three times a day," Noah answered. "You're taking all this better than I thought you would."

"Do you mean with Miss Janie or with you?" She raised a dark eyebrow.

"Both," he answered.

"Miss Janie needs me, and I owe her more than I can ever repay. And you, well, we're both adults and not lovestruck teenagers." She shrugged. "We've grown up and we're not even the same people we were back then. So you let her have whatever she wants to eat? Do you offer her wholesome food first?"

"Eat what I want . . ." Noah grinned.

"And die when I'm supposed to," Teresa finished the sentence for him. "I remember hearing her and Sam's wife say that lots of times. At this point, she *should* get whatever she wants." Teresa had no desire to stand in the hallway and make small talk with Noah. She was there to do a job, pay back her debt to Miss Janie for taking her in, and save enough money to live on until she could go back to her old job and have enough saved up that she could rent a better apartment and not have to work double shifts to survive.

If it's all that simple, then why am I so damned emotional? she asked herself as she wiped away another tear making a streak down her cheek as she headed back to her room.

When she got there, she sat down on the floor and opened the last two of the three boxes. The third one held her keepsakes from the past eleven years, and it was already on the closet shelf. When she left to go to college, she'd emptied four dresser drawers. Now she only needed one, for her underwear and nightshirts, which had been packed in the second box. The last box held a coat, a hoodie, and a couple of pairs of sweatpants that wouldn't fit into her suitcase. Other than two pairs of jeans, a couple of secondhand-store dresses, and a few T-shirts already hanging in her closet, that was it. She'd lived in scrubs for the most part since she started working at the nursing home right after she and Luis married.

Her unpacking done, she kicked off her shoes and stretched out on the bed. The ceiling became a screen for memories that played out in slow motion. There was one of her mother coming out of the only bedroom in the trailer and stumbling into the kitchen. She flipped the cap off a bottle of beer onto the floor and told Teresa to get up off her lazy ass and pick it up. The next vision was of the police and the Social Services lady who took her from the house. Her mother stood in the door with a bottle of whiskey in one hand, and she didn't even wave with the other one. She learned later that one of her teachers had seen bruises on her and called the police.

Teresa remembered keeping her eyes straight ahead and not even looking back at the ratty trailer. Living in the group home the lady was telling her about as they rode into town couldn't be any worse than living there, where her mother couldn't even make a decent taco or tamale without burning the meat.

Another vision made its way to the ceiling. This time it was Noah at fourteen. He'd come to visit Miss Janie that summer, along with his parents, and he'd kissed her. They were sitting on the porch swing when it happened, and he'd told her that she was pretty. She'd never forgotten that kiss and the way it made her feel—all gushy inside and flushed on the outside. Maybe that was just a typical first kiss, but she'd never captured that kind of excitement or feeling again, not even with Luis.

In the same sense, she'd never felt as dirty as when he told her afterward that she shouldn't tell anyone about the kisses. When she'd asked him why, he'd said, "You know why." But she hadn't known—not until he had explained it to her when he came to the nursing home. She had jumped to conclusions and look where it got her. Her mother hadn't given a damn about her. To have one that would think it disrespectful to kiss a girl on the porch was still a little foreign to Teresa.

Chapter Three

Teresa had finished putting a pot of black beans in a slow cooker to go with the enchiladas she planned to make for supper when she heard voices outside on the porch. Even though the thermometer said it was already past ninety degrees, Miss Janie had insisted on sitting on the porch swing that afternoon.

Teresa strained her ears until they hurt, then finally went to see who Miss Janie was talking to. She found eighty-year-old Sam, Miss Janie's neighbor, sitting on the porch step and fanning himself with his sweaty old cowboy hat.

"Well, hello, Mr. Sam. How are you doin' today?" she asked. "Can I get you something to drink?"

"Well, hello to you, too, Teresa. I'd love a beer," he said, "but if you ain't got one, tea would be fine. And, honey, it's just Sam, not Mr. Sam. That makes me feel like I'm older than I am. Us old guys don't have no business out in the afternoon heat. As the crow flies, it's less than a quarter of a mile from my place to here, but that's across two barbed-wire fences and a pasture. Driving means maybe half a mile all total. My old bones don't jump barbed-wire fences, and with hunnerd-degree temperatures, I damn sure wasn't walking anywhere." Sam was a short fellow who lived in bibbed overalls and boots, and Teresa could vouch that his hat was at least fifteen years old.

"We've got beer. Can or bottle?" Teresa asked.

"Ain't nothing like a bottle." Sam grinned.

"Miss Janie, can I bring you something?" she added.

"Cookies and milk, and bring enough for Sam," Miss Janie answered.

Teresa went straight to the kitchen and put the old folks' orders on a tray. Sam and his wife, Delia, had always been kind to both Teresa and Kayla as next-door neighbors. Teresa had always loved those two old folks for being so open and accepting when it came to them—Teresa was at least half-Mexican and Kayla was half-black. As she headed down the hallway to take a tray out to the porch, she smiled at the memories of them coming to Miss Janie's to play dominoes or canasta on Sunday afternoons.

"Is part of that for me?" Noah asked as he stepped out of the living room and held the door for her.

"Nope," she answered. "It's for Mr. Sam and Miss Janie. She seems to be doing good today. She knows Sam."

Teresa went straight over to the porch swing and stooped down far enough that Sam could take his beer and a couple of cookies. "How's Miz Delia doin'?"

"Lost her to cancer last year." Sam's voice cracked.

"I'm so sorry," she said as she sat down beside Miss Janie and held the tray in her lap. "I didn't know."

Dammit! Every time she turned around, something emotional happened to put tears in her eyes. She reached up and wiped them away with the back of her hand.

What did you expect? the voice in her head chided. *You've been gone eleven years. Babies that were born the year you left are almost teenagers, and folks have died. If you'd been coming home regularly, or even called Miss Janie once a month, you'd know these things.*

"Well, honey, I reckon you didn't get much news from home what with the way things are. When did you get back?" Sam turned up the bottle and gulped several times.

"Couple of days ago," Teresa said.

"You should've been here the past two years," he scolded.

"I realize that now," Teresa said.

"Where's Kayla?" Sam asked.

Miss Janie's chin began to quiver. "I want my other child to come home to me. I can't die until she's here. I need to tell her how much I love her. You'll have to go inside and see the babies before you leave, Sam. They're beautiful." She lowered her voice. "I think Aunt Ruthie talked to someone, because I got to keep them."

"Ruthie can be a handful when she wants to be." Sam chuckled. "My Delia and Ruthie pretty much ran this part of Texas when . . ." He stopped and bit off a chunk of cookie.

". . . Still chokes me up to talk about them women," he said when he'd swallowed. "They was both so happy when Janie came to live here. Neither of them had kids, so they kind of treated Janie like their own. Delia would've been lost without Janie when Ruthie passed on so young."

"Hi, Sam." Noah brought a beer out and joined them. "Think we'll get a snow tomorrow?" he teased.

"Sure we will, soon as pigs sprout wings and fly," Sam said. "We are goin' to have a hard winter, though. Y'all can depend on that."

"Kayla needs to get home before it starts snowin' and winter sets in, Noah," Miss Janie said. "You found Teresa, so you can find her. And I want to see Greta again, too." Miss Janie picked up another cookie with one hand and the glass of milk with the other. She dipped the cookie into the milk and said, "I wonder if Maddy Ruth and Mary Jane will like to dip their cookies."

"I'm sure they will," Teresa said. "When they get old enough, they'll do all kinds of things."

"Like build a snowman," Sam said. "How big was that one you and Delia built the winter that you came to live here?"

"Taller'n you," Miss Janie giggled.

"That ain't sayin' much." Sam laughed with her. "I should be gettin' on down the road. I've got to pick up a few things at the feedstore for them worthless sheep I keep around the place. Y'all need anything?"

"Nope," Noah answered.

"Why don't you come over about five and have supper with us?" Teresa asked. "I'm making enchiladas, black beans, and Mexican rice. There's plenty for all of us."

"I'm so glad you dropped by to see Teresa," Miss Janie said. "Noah is going to find Kayla real soon. My babies are all grown up now and coming home to stay with me, and Greta will come visit if she can. I'm so happy."

Poor old darlin'. It has to be exhausting for her to live with a mind like that, Teresa thought. *One minute she is sixteen and the next she's either jumped forward or backward to another time or place.* Even though dementia wasn't anything new to Teresa, it was tougher seeing it afflicting a family member like Miss Janie. There were those blasted tears damming up behind her eyelashes again.

"They grew up, didn't they?" Miss Janie said. "I didn't think I'd ever get to see them again when they took them away from me at the home, but Noah found Teresa. Now he'll find Kayla, and we'll be the family we should've always been. They were raised up out around El Paso. Just think"—she paused long enough to get a third cookie—"they were that close all this time and I didn't even know it. But in those days they wouldn't tell us who adopted our baby. We had them, got to hold them for a few minutes, and then they were gone."

Times had sure changed since Miss Janie had had her babies. Teresa couldn't imagine being told that she couldn't keep a child if she wanted to, no matter how young she was when she gave birth.

"I'll be back for supper around five," Sam said. "I love good enchiladas. Did your mama teach you to cook?"

"Nope," Teresa answered. "Mama didn't like the kitchen so well. She used to say that my grandmother did, but I never got to know her or any of my other relatives. Miss Janie taught me to love cooking."

Miss Janie waved goodbye to Sam and then smiled up at Teresa. "Did I tell you that I named them Maddy Ruth and Mary Jane? But the folks who got them changed their names, I'm sure," Miss Janie said. "I'm sleepy. Nurse, would you help me back in bed? I'm really sore, and I need to rest."

"Yes, ma'am." Teresa stood up. "I sure will. You can get a little nap before Sam comes back for supper."

By the time Teresa got her settled, Sam had gone and Noah was back in the living room looking over what appeared to be legal documents.

"Need something?" He looked up.

"Are you even searching for Kayla, or have you given up?" she asked.

"The way you two fought and bickered, I'd think you'd want me to give up," he challenged.

"There's not an ounce of love lost between us, but if Miss Janie wants to see this Greta or her before she dies, then I'll tolerate Kayla." Teresa bit her tongue to keep from adding, "Like I tolerate you."

"Greta's not coming. She was her roommate in the home where Miss Janie had the twins. She had me search for her a couple of years ago, and we found out that Greta had died from a heart attack when she was seventy. She'd gotten married when she was thirty and had two boys, who are still living and running the horse ranch in Virginia. From what Miss Janie told me, Greta was pretty sassy. She said that you reminded her of Greta, but I always thought that Kayla could beat you for sass any day of the week. You might have some spunk, but that girl was hard as nails."

"Don't underestimate me"—Teresa sat down on the sofa—"or you might wind up in trouble."

"Right back at you," he told her. "I'm still looking for Kayla. I traced her to San Antonio, but her trail has gone cold. She's off the grid. No credit cards. No job that pays social security. Nothing."

"Did you check the morgues?" Teresa asked.

"Yes, I did," he answered. "And the hospitals. I even had a fellow PI put a man out on the streets to see if she is a working girl."

"She's a survivor and don't you forget it. Most of the time she's meaner than a constipated cougar, but I don't think she'd stoop that low." *Where did that defense of Kayla come from?*

"Like you said, she's a survivor. I met her one time, and she had a lot of anger in her, even after living here with Miss Janie those years," Noah said.

Teresa frowned at Noah. "When were you back here?"

"Right after you left for college. My folks and I had finished a four-year stint in Germany, and they were on their way to Japan. We stopped by to see Miss Janie, and then they dropped me off in San Antonio for college and they left," he answered. "Kayla was starting her senior year, and she was wound tighter than a two-dollar watch, as Miss Janie used to say."

"You got that right, but don't waste any more of your time and money looking for her on the streets. She used to be an excellent shoplifter, so she'd turn to stealing first." Teresa stood to her feet and took a couple of steps toward the hallway. "Try looking at housekeepers. She might do that, and lots of folks pay housekeepers in cash, so that might be the reason you're having trouble finding her."

"I never thought of that. I didn't know that she liked to do that kind of work. Thanks for the tip," Noah muttered.

Teresa stopped in her tracks and whipped around to face him. "You are welcome. I want Miss Janie to leave this world in peace. The only time I ever knew Kayla to knock the chip off her shoulder was when she was around elderly people. She adored Delia and Sam. I bet you find her doing a job that pays cash and maybe living in a homeless shelter."

"Miss Janie said she left a note and ran away with some kid named Denver. I did think for a while that maybe she had four or five kids by now and is a stay-at-home mom," Noah said. "But with what you just told me, I'll tell my PI to look in the other direction."

"Kayla swore she'd never have kids," Teresa said. "She practically raised her younger siblings, and she said she'd never trust a man to be a good father."

"She must've had a tougher life than I even imagined," Noah said.

"You don't know anything about how either of us lived before Miss Janie took us in."

Teresa left the room, checked on Miss Janie, and then went upstairs. Teresa remembered Denver from high school. He'd come from a good family, but he had always been worthless. He was one of those tall, dark, and handsome boys who could sweet-talk a girl into the back seat of his car with no problem. Teresa wasn't a bit surprised that Kayla had run away with him right after she graduated.

Given her foster sister's temper, she would be surprised if they were still together. Denver didn't take orders well, not even in high school. He was constantly in detention for being late, swearing at teachers, and fighting. His parents went to bat for him every single time he got in trouble—nothing was ever his fault. He wouldn't be able to hold down a job.

Kayla might've supported him for a while, but she'd begin to see through him before long, and she wouldn't be able to hold her temper, either. The reason that Noah couldn't find her might be that she'd found another man who'd treat her right and had taken his name.

That wouldn't change her social security number, the voice in her head said.

Before she could argue that point, she heard Miss Janie crying and hurried back down the stairs to see what she could do to help. "What's the matter, darlin'?"

"I want Kayla to come see me. I'm dying, and I've got things to say to her," she sobbed. "She was such a tormented little soul. I need to talk to her."

"Noah is doing his best," Teresa said.

Miss Janie sat up and slowly slung her legs off the side of the bed. "Noah is building an ark. He doesn't have time to look for Kayla. You need to do that for me."

"Yes, ma'am." Teresa extended a hand to steady Miss Janie when she stood up. "I'll do that as soon as I make supper. You want to go to the kitchen and help me?"

"I want to go to the front porch. I need to be sitting there in case Kayla comes home. She might forget which house to go to, but if I'm right there, she'll see me." Miss Janie groaned when she took the first step. "My legs ain't what they used to be."

Teresa looped Miss Janie's arm in hers like she'd been taught in the nursing home. "Use me to lean on, and your cane for support on the other side."

"You're a good nurse," Miss Janie told her. "I wonder what Kayla turned out to be."

"Probably someone who can boss everyone around," Teresa said.

Miss Janie frowned. "Don't judge her, honey. That's the way she copes. She had a hard life."

Like I said to Noah, we both did, Teresa thought as she helped Miss Janie out to the porch swing and got her settled.

"Could I get you something to drink or a little snack?" Teresa asked.

"Don't need a thing right now except to see my other baby girl," she answered. "Were y'all identical twins, or could they tell you apart?"

"We were different. Her hair is curlier than mine, and she has green eyes," Teresa answered. *But those weren't the only differences between us,* Teresa thought as she sat down beside Miss Janie. Kayla had already built a hard shell around herself when she arrived at Miss Janie's house. The only time that Teresa ever saw her soften was when she talked to

Miss Janie, Sam, or Delia. In the years that they were foster sisters, Teresa had never been able to chip a bit of the hard shell away, so after a while she'd given up trying. The day that Teresa left for college, Kayla didn't even come down to the porch to wave goodbye.

"I can't wait to see her." Miss Janie sighed. "Every car or truck that goes by, I keep prayin' it will turn into our driveway."

For her foster mother's sake, Teresa hoped the same, but for her own sake, Teresa dreaded the day.

Chapter Four

Teresa awoke on Thursday morning in a cold sweat. She had dreamed that Luis showed up in Birthright with a sad story about how his second wife had left him, and he wanted another chance with Teresa. When she told him that wouldn't happen until the devil sold snow cones in hell, he shot her right between the eyes. Everything went dark, and she felt as if she were falling into a black abyss. When she came to herself, she was sitting up in bed with a death grip on the pillow.

She pushed back the cover and shivered as the cold breeze from the vent above her bed rushed over her sweaty skin. Her legs were still shaky from the dream, but she made her way to the bathroom at the end of the hall. She drew the curtain around the tub, adjusted the water, and took a warm shower.

The evil look in Luis's eye when he pulled the trigger kept coming back to her as she fixed breakfast that morning. Like most days, she kept the food warm on the top of the stove, and everyone ate when they were ready. That morning was different, though. For the first time, Miss Janie used a walker instead of a cane, and she arrived just as Teresa was flipping the last pancake out of the cast-iron skillet.

"Look at you with new wheels." Teresa tried to keep her tone light and encouraging, but her heart sank. From cane to walker, then to a wheelchair, and last, bedfast. She'd seen the progression in her line of work too many times to think that this new thing was just for a day.

Miss Janie inhaled deeply as she sat down in the chair that Teresa pulled out for her. "I love the smell of coffee and bacon all mixed up together when I wake up in the morning. I'm glad you still like to cook. I loved it when you spent time in the kitchen with me."

Noah came inside from the screened back porch and went straight for the coffeepot. "Did you have a good night's rest?"

"Yes, I did, but it's getting harder for me to get in and out of my bed. Seems like the floor is ten feet away from my feet," she said, then lowered her voice to a whisper. "Who is that woman cookin' breakfast?"

"That's your daughter Teresa," Noah told her.

"My daughters are Maddy Ruth and Mary Jane. I would never name one of them Teresa," she said.

"Why not?" Noah asked.

"Because Teresa was a girl in our church that was mean to me," Miss Janie answered.

Why did you even take me in? Teresa wondered as she put a pancake and two strips of bacon on a plate.

"How old are you today?" Noah asked.

"I'm seventeen." Miss Janie tipped her chin up defiantly. "I'm not old enough to keep my babies, but I can have coffee." She picked up her cup and took a sip. "Mama and Daddy don't let me have coffee, but Aunt Ruthie says anyone who can give birth to babies is old enough to drink it. I wanted to add cream and sugar to it the first time I had a cup, but Aunt Ruthie said life didn't come all sweetened up, and neither did her coffee."

Truer words have never been spoken. Teresa's nightmare came back, and her hands shook so badly that she almost dropped the fork she was using to turn the bacon. Teresa's life hadn't simply been black coffee—it had been bitter, burnt espresso. She took down plates from the cabinet and got silverware from the drawer.

Miss Janie frowned. "Why are we having bacon for supper?"

In the blink of an eye, Miss Janie had jumped into the time machine.

"This is morning," Teresa gently reminded her, "and we're about to have breakfast."

"I get confused. Of course it's morning. The sun is coming up in that window." She pointed. "And it goes down in my bedroom window. Have you found Kayla? I need both you girls to be home with me. I need to die, but I can't until y'all are here with me like I was with Aunt Ruthie and with Delia."

"I'm doing my best," Noah said.

"Well, do better," Miss Janie said sternly. "I want to see what she's done since she left me. Before Mama and Daddy sent me away, I dreamed about being a nurse, but I went to work at the school with Aunt Ruthie and never did do that. I'm glad one of my girls grew up to be a nurse, and I need to see what Kayla has made of herself."

A nurse's aide was a long way from what Miss Janie had said, but if she wanted to think like that, Teresa wasn't going to correct her.

"Hello!" Sam's gruff old voice rang out as he came in through the back door. "I'm letting myself in. Is breakfast ready?"

"You bet it is," Teresa answered. "Come on in and help yourself."

"I hate to cook, and you said I was welcome over here anytime, so I decided to take you up on it." Sam went to the stove and filled a plate, then took a seat next to Miss Janie. "How you doin' this mornin'?"

"I'm pouting because I hired those two to find my other baby, and they ain't doin' their job." She crossed her arms over her chest and pushed her plate back.

"Well, maybe she'll feel that you're lookin' for her and will come home on her own." Sam dove into a stack of four pancakes.

"You think so?" Miss Janie's eyes lit up.

"I believe that if we pray hard enough and long enough with our whole heart, anything is possible," Sam answered between bites.

"God didn't hear my prayers to heal Aunt Ruthie and Delia, so why should I trust Him now?" Miss Janie asked.

"We can't blame God for our old bodies wearin' out," Sam told her. "That's the way of things, but He might lay it upon Kayla's heart to come home if you really want to see her. Never hurts to try. I read in the newspaper that the Sulphur Springs High School is havin' their ten-year class reunion the weekend of the homecoming football game." Sam glanced over at Teresa. "You goin' to attend?"

"No." Teresa shook her head. "I've been out eleven years, and they only have reunions every five. This would be Kayla's ten-year class get-together. If she was here, I doubt that she'd go."

"Why not?" Sam asked.

"We were nobodies at school," Teresa said.

"My girls weren't nobodies," Miss Janie argued. "They were beautiful and popular, and they were both cheerleaders. Maddy Ruth was the president of the student council. I was proud of them."

Teresa almost choked on a bite of bacon. Neither she nor Kayla had been anything other than a couple of outcasts. They certainly didn't hang out with the popular girls. Miss Janie's mind wasn't only having trouble sticking around in a single time frame—now she was flat-out rewriting history books.

Sam caught Teresa's eye and winked. "I bet when Kayla comes home she'll want to go to the reunion for sure. The kids will miss you not being there this year, Miss Janie. They always looked forward to you making the rounds and telling them all hello."

"They always have cake at every reunion." Miss Janie smiled. "Do we have cake, Teresa? I could sure use a piece and some good cold milk to go with it."

"No, but I'll make one today, and we'll have it for dinner," Teresa answered.

"Chocolate?" Sam and Miss Janie asked at the same time.

"If that's what y'all want, it'll be ready by noon, but you've got to promise to eat your fried chicken first," Teresa replied.

"We will," they chorused together the second time.

Noah was glad that Teresa was there. She had been able to get Miss Janie to eat healthy food better than he could, and she'd stepped into the caregiving position like she was made for it. Every time he looked at her, he remembered those stolen kisses and the way they had made his pulse race. She'd been a pretty teenager, but she'd grown up to be a beautiful woman. They were adults now, not teenagers, but he still felt like the latter when she was around him.

And she's made it clear that she doesn't feel the same, the pesky voice in his head reminded him. When he passed her on the way to take his empty plate to the sink, his elbow brushed against her shoulder. The embers of an old fire he thought had been put out stirred inside his heart. She seemed to still have a chip on her shoulder about those teenage kisses, and he—well, his chip wasn't on his shoulder but in his pocket, in the form of a five-year sobriety coin. Yes, she might have a past, but so did he, and after the way her mother had drowned herself in booze, Teresa would never be interested in a recovering alcoholic.

Besides all that, Noah had control of her and Kayla's inheritance from Miss Janie—she thought he'd be better at talking to them about it. Maybe she had known about those kisses . . .

He was supposed to decide how to give it to them once he found them. Should he hand it over to them in a lump sum or give it to them in monthly checks? This position complicated everything. He had tried to talk Miss Janie into putting another lawyer in charge even before he knew Teresa was coming home, but she'd have none of that. No sir. Her only living relative was a good attorney, and he would handle her affairs the way she wanted him to.

Sam nudged him with his shoulder. "You look like you're trying to solve the problems of the world."

"I was thinking about a case." Even if it wasn't the truth, it wasn't a lie, either. How he handled his great-aunt's property was a case.

"Shouldn't a PI be off investigating stuff?" Teresa asked.

"I have been working on finding you," he answered. "Now that you're here to help with things, and as soon as we locate Kayla, I'll take a few cases."

"But first you find Kayla," Miss Janie said. "I don't care how much money you spend. I want my daughter to come home."

"Why did you foster me and Kayla? You were almost ready to retire when you brought me home, and you brought Kayla in right after your last year at the school."

"I had one more year when the social workers came to the school to inform us that they were taking you from your mother's home." Miss Janie smiled. "I was dreading living alone in this big old place, and I'd been watching you girls out on the playground for years. If I had to make a trip over to the elementary school, I'd wait until lunch recess so I could see you—you both looked like how I imagined my girls growing up."

She narrowed her eyes and lowered her voice. "And . . . I hated y'all's mothers for not taking care of you right. I even wondered if my girls were being treated like that, and then finally one day, the social worker came to the school to talk to me and some of the teachers. That's when I knew I had to take you home with me. I needed someone and you needed a home. I got approved to be your foster mother, and you came to live with me."

She paused again and then went on. "Folks had invited me up to the senior citizens place in Sulphur Springs, but who wants to drive that far every day to have lunch and play dominoes? You had dark skin like my babies, so I could pretend you was mine. Where are my babies again? Did they have a good home?"

"I'm sure they did," Sam answered. "Me and Delia used to talk about how nice it would be if Birthright had a senior citizens place of our own. We might be a small community, but I bet we'd draw people from the outlying communities as well, especially since it's hard to get around much as we get older. But the town never did anything with the idea." He paused. "I should be goin'. Them four sheep of mine are going to be carryin' on if I don't get some feed out to them."

Noah poured himself another cup of coffee and headed toward the stairs. "Why do you keep sheep, Sam?"

"Delia liked to watch a baby lamb romp around in the springtime. When it got up big enough, we gave it to one of the farm kids to show at the county livestock show, and she got a big kick out of seeing if her baby won a prize," Sam explained as he carried his plate to the sink. "Feedin' lambs reminds me of her smile, so it's worth keepin' more around."

"Please come again, Sam," Teresa said. "There's always plenty, and we love the company."

Sam removed his cowboy hat from the hook beside the back door and settled it on his head. "Thanks again for that, but if I'm goin' to be eatin' here, I'll have to contribute a little. I bought some beef from Jimbo Turner down the road from me last week. I'll bring over some steaks when I come back."

"That would be great," Noah said, "but you sure don't have to bring anything. Teresa always makes plenty, and if you'll eat with us, I don't have to live on leftovers."

"Boy, ain't you learned that leftovers is the best part?" Sam laughed as he disappeared out the back door.

What Sam said stayed with Noah all the way to his bedroom-office combination on the second floor. Leftovers were the best part. Did that pertain to life as well as food? After the main course was served, did the part that was left behind become better? If so, then what remained of his heart and life when he got sober would be the good years, right? Would Teresa or any other woman ever see it that way?

He sat down at his desk and pulled up the file that had Teresa's and Kayla's inheritance documents in it. Deciding how and what to do with all that money gave him a headache. He knew exactly what he would do with what Miss Janie had left him. He planned to live in Birthright and do his PI work out of the house right there.

Man was not made to live out his days on earth alone. His grandfather's booming preacher's voice rattled around in his head. Luther Jackson, brother to Miss Janie, had joined the service to get away from his religious family. Miss Janie said that after several years, her brother got tired of running from God, and although he made a career of the military, he became a chaplain.

"Maybe man was made to have a wife," Noah muttered, "but there's not many available women in Birthright, Texas."

Chapter Five

*K*ayla Green awoke to the sound of gardeners working on the flowers that hot summer morning. She shielded her eyes against the sun coming through her bedroom window. When that didn't work, she reached for the spare pillow and slammed it down over her face. Gardeners weren't supposed to be there on Sunday, not even if it was hot as hell and the roses and lantana needed tending to. The sprinkler system should take care of that on the one day that Kayla could sleep late.

She finally tossed back the covers, grumbled the whole time she got out of bed, and put on a pot of coffee. Since she was already up, she thought about going to church, but that would require getting dressed, and she liked to lounge around in her pajamas on Sunday until noon. Then she would do what grocery shopping needed to be done and catch up on laundry.

Thinking of church reminded her of going to services with Miss Janie. She'd been glad to get dressed up in a nice, clean outfit those days, and even more glad that the snooty girls she went to high school with went to the bigger churches over in Sulphur Springs. She liked all the elderly people in the little Birthright church so much better than those hateful bitches.

But the other thing that it reminded her of was the smell of the church bus when it came around to their neighborhood on Sunday morning. Kids who had parents to take them to services didn't ride the bus—just the ones whose parents had partied hard the night before. Kayla was one of those children who never had matching clothes or hair that was combed. She was one who hadn't had a bath the night before or brushed her teeth that morning and had contributed to the smell in the bus. Her mother didn't make her younger siblings go to church, but then they belonged to Kayla's stepdad, so they were white—not half-black like Kayla.

She'd gone to church all of three times. After that, she would hide behind the house, then sneak off to the woods for two hours until she heard the vehicle delivering the kids back to the neighborhood. Then she would go back into the house, get out the hot dogs or maybe open a can of soup, feed the other three kids, and try to clean up the mess from the night before. They usually ate in front of the television or on the porch, because her stepdad got really mad if they woke him and her mother before they were ready to get out of bed.

The memories of Billy Joe Green's thick belt coming down on her back and butt made her shiver even after fifteen years. She shook her head, trying to erase the picture of his eyebrows drawn down and his mouth set in a tight line as he jerked his belt from the loops in his jeans, but it was burned into her brain.

She'd found a little peace when she went to church after she'd left Denver, but not enough to give up her morning that day. "The apple doesn't fall far from the tree," she whispered as she poured a cup of coffee and carried it to her recliner.

In spite of Miss Janie's help and raising, Kayla had taken up with a man who was just like her worthless stepfather. Billy Joe Green and Denver both always had an excuse for quitting their jobs, and they attacked every problem with violence. Like mother, like daughter. That's what she'd heard whispered by her schoolteachers, and even her classmates, and she'd proven them right up to a point. Eighteen months ago, Denver had lashed out at her for the last time, blaming her for him losing his job. She'd walked out that evening with nothing but the clothes on her back and the hundred dollars she'd saved from her tips working as a waitress.

"Kayla! Come down here!" Mrs. Witherspoon yelled from the bottom of the stairs leading up to Kayla's one-room apartment. The woman wasn't easy to work for, but Kayla's job as housekeeper came with a free garage apartment, which beat living in a box under a bridge, and the old girl was happy to pay in cash.

Kayla pulled a pair of shorts on and let her nightshirt hang free. "Yes, ma'am," she called out as she started down the stairs, only to find Mrs. Witherspoon and a policeman waiting.

Mrs. Witherspoon shook her finger at Kayla. "What have you done? If you've been in trouble with the law, then I'll fire you on the spot."

Kayla rubbed her sweaty hands on the back of her shorts, but she couldn't stop her heart from racing. Denver had found her; she was sure of it. He had told her that he'd kill her before he would see her with another man.

"She's not in trouble," the policeman said. "I just need to talk to her for a minute or two."

"Well? Get on with it." Mrs. Witherspoon crossed her arms over her chest. "I've got to get to church, and if Kayla is in trouble, I need to know before I leave. She might steal me blind."

"She's not in trouble," the policeman stated again. "A private investigator came to my office yesterday. He said there's some family looking for you over in northeast Texas, down south of Paris. He left this letter for me to deliver to you. I wouldn't have known where to bring it, but I'm friends with this lady's"—he pointed at Mrs. Witherspoon—"this lady's grandson, and he spoke about you cleaning her house. I recognized the name." He handed her the letter. "Hope it's not bad news."

"Well, if that's all it is, I'm going to church. I'll see you in the morning, Kayla, bright and early. You need to polish the silver coffee service.

I have my club meeting tomorrow evening, and I expect things to be ready." Mrs. Witherspoon turned and marched back toward the house.

"Thank you," Kayla told the policeman, but it took all her willpower not to tell Mrs. Witherspoon to kiss her naturally born half-black ass.

She carried the letter back up to her tiny one-room apartment, which had come furnished with a twin-size bed, a table and one chair, a recliner, and a combination cabinet, stove, and refrigerator over in one corner. Her hands shook as she fell back into the worn recliner, and she noticed the return address. The letter was from Miss Janie, not her mother, thank God. Had it been from her mother, she would have burned the damned thing without even looking at it.

A wave of guilt bigger than a tsunami washed over her. Within a week of running away with Denver, she'd known it was a big mistake, but she couldn't go back and admit it to Miss Janie. Besides, the government had stopped paying for her upkeep when she turned eighteen, and Miss Janie had been kind enough to let her stay until she graduated. She'd even offered to pay for Kayla's college, like she had Teresa's.

"Not even the wonderful Teresa stayed in school, though. She dropped out to get married." Kayla remembered the first Christmas card that came to the house after Teresa left.

She turned the letter over several times in her hands. Miss Janie was dead. Kayla could feel it in her bones.

Finally, she slipped a thumb under the edge of the flap and opened it. Three one-hundred-dollar bills fell out into her lap. Tears flowed down Kayla's cheeks. Miss Janie had left her an undeserved gift, and she'd never know how much Kayla appreciated every dollar, or how much she needed the money.

She dried off her cheeks with the back of her hand and unfolded the letter, expecting to find something handwritten in Miss Janie's perfect handwriting, but it was a typewritten letter on letterhead from Noah Jackson, Attorney at Law and Private Investigative Services. She remembered Noah very well even though he came to the house only once. His father was in the military—she couldn't remember which branch—and his mother was kind of high class in Kayla's estimation. They had stayed only a few days because Noah was due to start college and his folks were moving to Japan.

Noah wrote that Miss Janie was dying of cancer and had Alzheimer's. Kayla heaved a sigh of relief—Alzheimer's and cancer were bad, very bad, but at least Miss Janie wasn't dead, and she wanted Kayla to come home. The money was to get her there by whatever means she wanted, and she read that she would have free room and board if she would help take care of Miss Janie.

Kayla eyed the letter as if it were a poisonous snake. Did she really want to open up that can of worms again? Go back to where she'd had even less self-confidence than she had right then? Where people followed her around in the stores because she might shoplift like her mother had been known to do, or just because she had dark skin?

"The apple and all that," she muttered.

What if Teresa had been summoned to Birthright, too? Could she stand to live in the same house with her again? All they did was argue and bitch at each other—they fought about everything from who used the last of the shower soap to who hated the other one the most. The only time they were civil was when Miss Janie was in the room, and even then, it was a chore.

Kayla closed her eyes and flashed on a picture of her bedroom at Miss Janie's house. She couldn't expect it to be the same as when she left it, but it was twice as big as her tiny room above Mrs. Witherspoon's garage. If she went back, she could make peace with all the regrets she'd piled up inside her heart, and the letter said that Noah would pay her a salary to help take care of Miss Janie. She couldn't take money for that job, though—not when her foster mother had dragged her out of the pit where she'd been living and treated her like a daughter.

Determination flashed through her as she opened her eyes—she was going back to Birthright. She picked up her phone and found the bus station—a bus left going east to Dallas that afternoon at one o'clock. Kayla packed her suitcase and wound duct tape around the outside to keep it from falling apart. Even though Denver had never hit her, he did have tantrums and throw things. The nice luggage that Miss Janie gave her for graduation had been the object of his last fit.

She wrote a note to Mrs. Witherspoon and put it in the mailbox. She'd been paid on Friday, so she would forfeit only one day's work by leaving without giving notice. Then, at noon, she hitched a ride into town with one of the gardeners. She paid for a ticket on the next bus leaving for Dallas and never felt so free as she did when Abilene disappeared behind her.

After half an hour, she began to worry. Denver had family in Sulphur Springs. What if he'd gone back there after she'd left him? That was exactly what she got for not thinking things through. She started making plans as she watched the flat countryside going by at seventy-five miles an hour. If he was there, she would go to the courthouse and get a restraining order against him. Of course, he wouldn't think twice about walking right through it, like the Dixie Chicks sang about in "Goodbye Earl." Maybe if Denver did do something stupid, she would take care of him the same way the girls did in their song. After all the places where she'd put her head at night in the last year and a half, jail didn't look scary at all.

After a two-hour layover in Dallas, Kayla climbed aboard the bus to Sulphur Springs. During the hour-long ride, she mentally counted the money she had left several times. The ticket had cost ninety dollars, and she'd spent five on a chicken sandwich and a glass of sweet tea in Dallas. That meant she had two hundred left of Noah's money, and she'd barely managed to save about that much during the past six months while working for Mrs. Witherspoon. The old lady had counted the slices of bread and grains of salt to be sure "her girl" didn't rob her.

Once Kayla made up her mind to do something, she seldom looked back at her decision, but it was full-steam ahead. Yet when the bus came to a stop at the Pilot gas station in Sulphur Springs, the steam ran out and she questioned if she was doing the right thing. She still had enough money to purchase another ticket. She could go to Tulsa and get a room in a cheap hotel for a couple of days while she looked for work.

You are so stupid. Denver's voice popped into her head. *You can't use Mrs. Witherspoon for a reference after quitting your job.*

She sat still until everyone else had gotten off the bus before she finally stood up, stepped out into the hot air, and picked up her taped suitcase from the ground. She was on her way inside the station when she heard someone call her name. She whipped around to see Sam Franks, Miss Janie's neighbor, not ten feet away.

"Mr. Sam?" she asked, to be sure she wasn't hallucinating. She hadn't told a soul that she was going to Sulphur Springs, so why was he there?

He poked a thumb at his chest. "It's me in the flesh. You going through, or do you need a ride to Birthright?"

"What are you doing here?" she asked.

"Nellie Thompson is coming home from Houston after visitin' her daughter for a week. She asked me to pick her up and take her home. There's room in my old truck for one more passenger if you need a ride." He gave her a quick hug.

She'd always loved Mr. Sam and Miz Delia. They'd treated her like she was kinfolk that they liked.

"I'd love one and thank you." She couldn't believe her luck. Kayla waved to the older woman, whom she'd met at church, as she got in.

A minute later, Sam spotted Miss Nellie and then helped her into the truck. Teresa slid over to the middle of the bench seat and sat between Nellie and Sam on the ten-minute trip to Birthright, and Nellie talked the whole time about everything from her grandkids to how much she missed her cats. Listening to her tell stories about her kids and cats brought back memories of ten years earlier, when Nellie would come sit on the porch with Miss Janie. They'd been friends—not best friends, like Miss Janie and Delia were—but they were in the same Sunday school adult class, and Nellie had always known the latest gossip.

When Sam finally stopped in front of her house on the west end of Birthright, she patted him on the shoulder and said, "Thanks so much for coming to get me, and for taking care of my precious Bonnie and Clyde while I was gone."

"Didn't mind a bit," Sam said.

Kayla slid across the bench seat and grabbed Nellie's luggage from the truck's bed. "I'll take this in for you."

"Thank you, darlin'," Nellie said. "Tell Miss Janie I'll be down to see her once I get settled in. This travelin' is tough on a ninety-year-old woman. I'm glad you've come home. Last time I went to see her, she was cryin' because her girls were so far away."

"I will sure tell her." Kayla had never known anyone to cry about her—not even her own mother. "And I'm glad to be back for a while."

Nellie laid a wiry hand on Kayla's arm. "Don't you leave until she's gone. Her heart was broken when you girls didn't come see her, and now her mind is all jumbled up. I think it's like havin' four jigsaw puzzles all mixed up together."

"Yes, ma'am." Kayla patted Nellie's hand and then slipped free of it and jogged back to the truck.

Birthright was so small that Kayla often wondered why they didn't use one welcome sign and paint the goodbye on the other side. In what seemed like the blink of an eye, Sam was parking his rusty old truck in front of Miss Janie's house.

She'd thought she'd have a few moments to catch her breath from the truck to the porch, but Miss Janie was sitting on the porch swing, and be damned if that wasn't Teresa right beside her.

Sam hopped out of the car and yelled, "Look who I found at the bus station when I went to get Nellie!"

"She's here." Miss Janie squealed like a little girl and held up her arms. Teresa helped her to her feet, and she shuffled across the porch. "My other baby has come home. Sam, you prayed, didn't you?"

How in the world had that strong woman she'd left behind gotten so feeble? Ten years before, Miss Janie had still had a bit of brown hair left in the gray. Her bright-blue eyes had been full of laughter and witty sayings. Now she had wispy gray hair and she'd aged forty years instead of ten. If a strong wind whipped through Birthright, she'd need rocks in her pockets to keep it from blowing her away. And to top it all off, she was talking like Teresa and Kayla were her real daughters, not just foster children.

"I sure did." Sam stood to the side and grinned. "And God answered my prayers."

"Hello, Kayla," Teresa said.

Kayla wasn't sure how she'd be received after ten years, but Miss Janie opened her arms wide, and Kayla walked right into them.

"I might believe that God is good now that you're home," Miss Janie said. "Come and tell me about the people who adopted you. Were they good to you?"

Kayla glanced over at Teresa.

"Miss Janie, how old were you when you had to give us away?" Teresa asked.

"Sixteen, but that was a few years ago." Miss Janie sighed. "Now we're all together again."

Kayla left her suitcase sitting on the porch and supported Miss Janie back to the swing. She looked over Miss Janie's head and mouthed toward Teresa, "What's going on?"

"Play along with whatever she says," Sam whispered from behind her.

From Noah's letter, she knew that Miss Janie had Alzheimer's and also cancer, but Kayla didn't expect to find her looking like she did.

When Kayla ran away with Denver, Miss Janie was still helping out with funeral dinners, taking food to new mothers, and was a force to be reckoned with in Birthright.

"I knew Noah would find my girls." Miss Janie's eyes sparkled. "I felt it in my heart. You grew up to be beautiful. What's your name? You would've been Maddy Ruth if I'd gotten to keep you. Tell me about the people who adopted you."

"I'm Kayla Green. Don't you remember me, Miss Janie?"

"Now, now!" Miss Janie patted her on the back. "We don't have to keep secrets any longer. Times have changed. You can call me Mama now. Is that your suitcase? Have you had supper? Teresa made tortilla soup for supper and there's plenty left over."

"Yes, that's my suitcase, and I could eat. Thank you, ma'am." A vision of a spotless kitchen where three meals a day had been prepared flashed through Kayla's mind.

"We have a lot to talk about. I want to know everything. Did you go to church? Were you a cheerleader like Teresa was?" Miss Janie pushed up out of the swing.

Sweet angels in heaven. What had she agreed to? Miss Janie had had a mind like a steel trap, and now she thought Kayla was her real daughter and that she'd been popular in high school. Noah hadn't mentioned anything like that in his note when he'd sent the police to find her.

Miss Janie stopped inside the door and frowned. "Sam, thank you for finding my baby. These other two wasn't havin' any luck with it. I knew you could do it, though. You should come on in and have a bowl of soup, too."

"I happened to be at the bus stop when she came in." Sam followed them inside. "Noah must've been the one who really found her, right, Kayla?"

"Yes." Kayla picked up her suitcase and carried it inside. "He sent a letter by the police this morning. I caught the first bus out of Abilene."

Kayla took a deep breath as she took the first step inside the house. She'd always loved the smell—a faint aroma of roses and food mixed with something lemony that Miss Janie brewed up for cleaning. Kayla associated the combination with safety.

She was standing in a long hallway that ran from the front porch to a door leading out to the back porch. Miss Janie had told her that the house was built that way so the breezes could flow into the place. A hall tree stood against the wall to Kayla's right. Hats hung on the four hooks, and boots were lined up on each side of the antique piece of furniture. She recognized a pair of the boots as her own. Not one thing had changed in the past decade. The living room was to her left and stairs leading up to the second floor, to her right. She headed toward the next door to the left, into the kitchen. The one right across the wide hallway went into Miss Janie's bedroom. She peeked inside before she entered the kitchen. The same cute little lamps were on each end of the dresser. The four-poster bed bore the same quilt, and the rocking chair, its pink-and-white-checked cushions.

Miss Janie was already sitting in a kitchen chair when Kayla stepped through the door. A confused look passed over her face. "Where's Aunt Ruthie? She always sits right here." She pointed at a chair beside her. "I wanted her to meet you. We used to talk about my girls so much. I know she'd love to finally see you for herself."

"Well, hello, again. Look who finally made it home." Noah came into the kitchen from the back porch. "I got a phone call this morning from the private investigator I had workin' on findin' you. He said the police had delivered my letter, but I didn't know if it paid off."

"I'm here." Kayla waited for someone to tell her to help herself to the soup or to tell her to sit down.

Miss Janie pounded on the table with her fist. "I asked y'all about Aunt Ruthie. Someone needs to tell her to come in here and meet Maddy Ruth. She should see the little baby I named after her."

"Aunt Ruthie has been gone for thirty years," Noah told her.

"Why didn't someone tell me?" Miss Janie began to weep.

Kayla rushed to her side before Teresa could and bent to hug her. "I'm so sorry that we didn't tell you, but we didn't want to upset you."

Miss Janie blinked several times before her expression changed. "I remember now. We had her funeral at the church. I get things all jumbled up. But now that my girls are home, I'll get all better. We can be a family at last."

"That's right," Teresa agreed. "Soup's on the stove. Jalapeño corn bread is under the cake dome. Chocolate cake is over on the bar. Y'all help yourselves."

"You aren't goin' to play the perfect hostess and serve me?" Kayla raised a dark eyebrow at Teresa.

"You're a big girl." Teresa's tone dripped icicles. "Help yourself or starve."

"Well, I ain't about to go hungry," Sam said as he walked in from the porch. He opened a cabinet door and got down a bowl. "I love soup and corn bread."

Kayla ignored Teresa like she'd tried to do when they lived in the house together those four years. She followed Sam's lead and ladled up a bowlful of soup, plopped a square of corn bread into it, and sat down at the table. Not gobbling it down like a hungry hound dog took a lot of self-control, but she managed to use her manners—like Miss Janie had taught her when she had come to live at the Jackson house. She'd been scared out of her mind that day, maybe even a little more than today, but by damn Teresa wouldn't ever know it.

"Who adopted you?" Miss Janie asked. "I wanted to meet them, but things weren't done that way back then."

"The Green family were wonderful parents," Noah answered very quickly.

"Yes, they were." Kayla played along even though it was a big, fat lie. Her mother and stepfather had abandoned her when she was fourteen years old.

"I'm so glad you had a good family, but now you are back with me where you belonged all this time. I thought you and Mary Jane were identical twins, but I can see now that I was wrong." Miss Janie stared at Kayla like she was a celebrity.

Holy hell! Teresa would never be mistaken for Kayla's sister, much less her twin. Kayla had gotten her kinky hair from her black father and the freckles across her nose and her green eyes from her white mother. Teresa was part Mexican, with good hair and flawless skin without a single freckle.

"Maybe after I eat, I could have a long, hot bath and wash my hair," Kayla said, trying to buy some time to figure out what she'd walked into. On one side, Miss Janie was as warm as sunshine. On the other, the chill from Teresa frosted her to the bone. There had never been any love lost between them, and like when she'd come to live there, Kayla had the feeling she was trespassing on Teresa's territory.

"Of course, darlin'." Miss Janie yawned. "This is your home now. We're all three finally together. I'm going to take a little nap now, and we'll talk more when I wake up." She stood up and kissed Kayla on the forehead as she shuffled off toward her bedroom. "I never thought I'd see my babies again. I'm so glad to get a second chance to show you that I've always loved you."

The minute Kayla heard the bedroom door close, she locked eyes with Noah. "Babies? What's going on?"

Noah explained about Miss Janie giving birth to twin girls out of wedlock when she was sixteen, and now that her mind was scrambled, she thought Kayla and Teresa were those two babies. "The doctor says she'll most likely be gone by Christmas, so if you could stay until then and let her die in peace, thinkin' that she finally reconnected with her babies, it would be great."

"I ain't got nowhere else to be, so I might as well stick around until the end." Kayla carried her empty bowl to the sink, rinsed it, and put it into the dishwasher.

"Thanks," Noah said. "I've got work to do in my office, so like Miss Janie said, make yourself at home."

"Why don't you call her Aunt Janie?" Kayla asked. "I always wondered about that when you came here to visit that time."

"I have no idea why," he answered. "Everyone else, including my dad, called her Miss Janie instead of Aunt Janie, so I did, too."

Sam finished off his soup and went for another bowlful. "Y'all girls realize she's very serious about you calling her Mama, don't you? And I can feel the chill between the two of you. You've got to at least pretend to get along to make her happy. You owe her that."

"For a place to stay until Christmas, I'll try," Kayla told him, and then locked eyes with her foster sister. "How about you? Stayin' until the end?"

"Yes, I am," Teresa answered. "I'm not so sure we're that good at pretending, Sam."

"Then learn." Sam shook his finger at both of them. "Miss Janie deserves to die in peace."

Chapter Six

*E*vidently, she was supposed to act like she was at home rather than a guest, so Kayla dumped her dirty clothing out onto the floor. She sorted it by color and fabric, like Miss Janie had taught her when she was fourteen. To do laundry without plugging money into the machine to start it seemed strange. Kayla hadn't had that privilege since she ran away with Denver. What she couldn't wash out in the kitchen sink by hand had to be taken to a Laundromat.

She put several pairs of underwear, half a dozen T-shirts, and a couple of pairs of khaki shorts that she'd gotten at a church clothes closet into the washer and started it. While that ran, she headed upstairs to take a long bath. When the claw-foot bathtub was nearly full, she sank down into the warm water and sighed. To have a bath in a deep tub was something she'd never take for granted again. In her tiny room above the garage, she'd had a shower stall so small that she could barely turn around in it. When she'd moved in, she'd thought she'd died and gone to heaven. Living on the street for six months, she'd been lucky to get washed up in a service station bathroom. She ducked her mass of curly black hair under the water and then worked sweet-smelling shampoo that Miss Janie had always bought special for her type of hair into it. This was nothing short of pure heaven.

Dusk was settling when she finished her bath, found the hair product that Miss Janie kept for her in the cabinet, and worked it into her hair. The Mimosa Hair Honey shine pomade was ten years old, but it still did wonders. She checked her reflection in the mirror and then got dressed in clean jeans and a T-shirt and went back downstairs, where Teresa sat in the kitchen having a slice of pecan pie with ice cream.

"Do I really have to act like you're my sister? Anything else I need to lie about?" Kayla asked.

"You lie all the time, so it shouldn't be a problem," Teresa answered.

"I see you haven't changed any." Kayla passed by her on her way to put her clothing into the dryer and start another load. "You're still as big a smart-ass as ever. Got any more of that pie?"

"Nope." Teresa shoved the last bite into her mouth and answered around it. "But there's chocolate cake over there." She pointed toward a domed cake plate.

"Did you make it?" Kayla glanced over at the cabinet.

"Yep, I did, but I promise I didn't poison your part of the food," Teresa answered.

"I wouldn't put it past you, but since Sam ate some and he didn't fall over on the floor with froth coming out of his mouth, I'll take a chance," Kayla told her.

"I wouldn't poison you." Teresa poured herself a glass of lemonade but didn't offer Kayla any. "It would be a waste of good food."

Noah came into the kitchen and cut himself a slice of cake and got the milk jug from the refrigerator. When he reached for a glass, he turned toward Kayla. "Should I pour some for you?"

"Yes, please, and thank you." Kayla smiled.

"Hey, don't look at me like that," Teresa said. "You lived here as many years as I did. You know where things are, and you can wait on yourself."

"I already figured that out." Kayla could hear the coldness of her own voice. "But you don't have to be such a"—she stopped and grinned—"such an old witch about it."

"You almost made a mistake there," Teresa said.

"What'd she do?" Noah asked.

"I called her a bitch one time, and she tried to shake my teeth out of my head." Kayla cut herself a piece of cake. "She's mean as a rattlesnake, and that word sets her off, so be careful not to call her that. I also remember that *you* didn't finish college, so what did you become?"

"I married a man who said we needed two incomes. I worked at a nursing home and got my nursing aide's certificate by going to night school. Never had the money to get the nursing degree I wanted. How about you?" Teresa answered.

"Why, I was the personal aide to the president's wife in the White House," Kayla smarted off. "What do you think I did? I lived in a travel trailer most of the time with Denver. He was as worthless as the last sheet of toilet paper on the roll. I supported us by doing waitress work. I'm not perfect like you." Kayla's tone was pure sarcasm.

"One twin is always the good one. Least I went back to school," Teresa smarted off right back at her.

Kayla ducked her chin and glared at Teresa. "Don't you know? I'm the twin that gets to have all the fun."

"Were y'all this hateful to each other when you were here?" Noah asked.

"We lived together in this house, and I can count the times we were friends on one hand. I was the poor little half-black girl with the kinky hair like my father and green eyes and freckles like my white mother. Teresa was the pretty Mexican girl with good hair and the cute figure," Kayla said.

"Oh, get over yourself," Teresa scolded.

"Well, evidently y'all haven't kept in touch since you left. Didn't you ever wonder about each other?" Noah asked.

"I didn't have anything to say to her," Kayla answered. "And maybe we did act like sisters. Haven't you ever heard of sibling rivalry?"

"Yes, I have, and I've seen it before," Noah replied, "but I believe I'm seeing it in Technicolor right now."

"Well, I sent Miss Janie a Christmas card every year, and I usually wrote her a letter on her birthday in March," Teresa said, and then turned to face Kayla. "Did you remember to do that?"

"Nope," Kayla said. "Don't judge me. I barely made enough money to pay the bills. I didn't have money for things like cards, and I hate to write letters."

"What did Denver do?" Noah asked.

"He couldn't hold down a job for more than a few weeks at a time, and whatever money he made went to buy pot for him and his buddies. Go ahead and tell me you're not surprised." Kayla shot another dirty look toward her foster sister.

"I married at nineteen and divorced last year," Teresa said. "I can't judge you. My husband couldn't keep his pants zipped around other women. I stuck with him until he left me for a woman that had two kids by him already, so it's only a matter of which one of us has been the biggest fool," she said. "I'm going to get Miss Janie ready for bed before I go upstairs."

"If you're taking care of her, then what's my job?" Kayla asked.

"As Miss Janie gets more and more feeble, it'll take both of you to care for her," Noah answered. "I'm going to leave it up to you to work out a schedule about the cooking and care."

"What about housecleaning?" Kayla asked.

"We have a lady to come in and do that." Noah cut himself another slice of chocolate cake.

"I can take over that part," Kayla offered. "I've been working for a bitchy old girl the past six months, taking care of her fancy house. I'll be glad to keep this one clean."

"All right then." Noah started out of the room. "I'll call the cleaning service from Sulphur Springs and tell them we won't need them anymore. I write paychecks on Friday. Do you need an advance until then?"

"No, I'm good. Is Teresa gettin' paid?" Kayla asked.

"Yes, I am," Teresa answered.

"Don't you feel guilty taking money from someone who did so much for both of us?" Kayla asked.

"She's left y'all a bit of an inheritance," Noah said. "Consider your payment for this work as part of that."

Kayla was shocked to even think that Miss Janie would leave her something after the way she had treated her foster mother—leaving in the middle of the night with nothing but a few lines written on a piece of notebook paper and put under the sugar bowl on the table.

Teresa checked on Miss Janie one more time on her way upstairs that evening. She was sound asleep and looked more peaceful than she had since Teresa had arrived, but then she had her babies at home with her. Now she could skip over the line separating the living from those who were already in eternity.

Teresa's shoes felt as if they were weighted with lead as she climbed the stairs. She hadn't wanted to be paid to take care of Miss Janie, but Noah had insisted when he'd written her paycheck. Teresa's heaviness of body and soul had nothing to do with losing her job but with knowing that she didn't deserve any kind of inheritance from Miss Janie.

She hadn't opened her box of memories in a while, but that evening something kept nagging at her to get it down from the closet shelf. Maybe it was Kayla's return. She took down the box, set it on the bed, and removed the contents one by one. First was the only picture she had of her with her mother. Angelina, or Angel, as she insisted that Teresa call her. Angel had a cigarette in one hand and a bottle of beer in the other and had struck a sexy pose. Teresa was sitting on the other side of the porch steps leading into the trailer. In the background, one of the many guys who came and went was standing in the doorway bare-bellied. He held up his middle finger to whoever was taking the picture. The man looked a helluva lot like Luis, Teresa's ex-husband, but the picture had been taken twenty years ago. Maybe the stance or the crude gesture was what reminded her of him, and not so much the facial features.

She laid the picture aside and brought out a faded pink satin ribbon. Angel had tied that around Teresa's hair when she enrolled her in kindergarten. That was the last day Teresa had ever felt pretty.

"What's that all about?" Kayla asked from the doorway.

Kayla's voice startled Teresa so badly that she felt an adrenaline rush. "Don't sneak up on me like that."

"I didn't," Kayla said. "I came up the stairs, went to the bathroom, and saw you standing near the bed like a statue. Where did you get all that stuff anyway?"

"It's personal stuff that I've kept." She put the ribbon and the picture back in the box.

"I didn't ever have much worth keeping, but I did keep a notebook that Miss Janie gave me to write down my thoughts." Kayla shrugged. "But then you—"

Teresa put up a palm. "Don't start that crap about me havin' a better life than you. We all had our burdens to carry, and mine wasn't a bit lighter than yours."

"You don't know everything about my life." Kayla took a step into the bedroom.

"And you don't know much of anything about mine," Teresa told her. "But we need to get along as best we can for Miss Janie's sake now."

"As long as you don't try to lord it over me, I'll give it a try," Kayla said.

"If you don't knock that chip off your shoulder soon, I'm going to really do it for you," Teresa threatened.

Kayla gave her foster sister the evil eye. "Bring it on, big girl."

Teresa sat down in the rocking chair. "Girl, you ain't had it a bit worse than I have. Luis refused to let me continue in college. He said that it took two people to make a living, and I could hustle my butt out there and find a job. When I came home and told him I'd gotten a job cleaning at the nursing home but I had to work the three-to-eleven shifts, he didn't even care about that. But then why should he? That gave him time to come home from his day job, clean up, and go out with his buddies to drink beer and chase other women. So don't go pouting thinkin' you had it so rough."

"At least Luis worked." Kayla sat down on the edge of the bed.

"Denver was a spoiled brat," Teresa said. "I never could see why you were attracted to him."

"He told me I was pretty," Kayla whispered. "And we had sex when I was fifteen. After that, he was kind of nice to me at school. It's not easy to never fit in anywhere. Denver gave me a place, even if I was only on the fringes."

"Miss Janie didn't let us date until we were sixteen," Teresa said. "And what do you mean by kind of nice?"

"As long as I was his booty call, he let me hang out with him and our friends, and he was so mean that no one dared bully me after that." Kayla kept her eyes on the memory box and didn't look at Teresa. "His folks kicked him out about that time, and he lived with some of his worthless friends until we graduated. The rest is history. We were going to set the world on fire. He had a car, and I had a few dollars saved from my allowance."

"Then you found out that it took more than that to blaze a trail in the world, right?" Teresa agreed. "Luis and I were going to live in a mansion by the time we were married ten years. We were going to have a family, and everything was going to be perfect."

"You got it." Kayla almost smiled. "But guess what? Perfect ain't anything but a pipe dream. Why didn't y'all have kids?"

"I'd gotten on the pill when I went to college, and after his first affair, I didn't miss a single one. I even set an alarm on my phone to remind me that it was time to take it," Teresa replied. "How about you?"

"He said if I got pregnant, then I could figure out how to pay for an abortion. He didn't want snotty-nosed kids—his words, not mine—running around his feet. I didn't have a phone, but I took that pill faithfully at eight o'clock every evening when I got home from work. Thank God the health clinic provided them free." Kayla shivered.

"Real bastards that we got, weren't they?" Teresa said.

"Apples don't fall far from the tree, and we kind of proved it, didn't we?" Kayla stood up.

"I was thinkin' more that the guys we took up with did that." Teresa could hardly believe that they were talking civil to each other after the way they'd slung words around earlier.

"Think about it. We're damaged goods. Our folks didn't want us. Most foster homes wouldn't have taken us in as old as we were. Miss Janie was kind enough to realize we needed a stable home, but we were way past what those counselors call our formative years," Kayla told her. "My folks moved off and left me. You got taken out of your home because your stepdad was beating on you and your mama."

"Our judgment ain't too good, is it?" Teresa followed Kayla out into the hallway. "But we've both got a fresh chance right now. Let's make the most of it."

"We'll see," Kayla said. "We are who we are for the most part. As for me, I don't intend to ever trust another man."

"Me, either," Teresa said.

Kayla started toward the stairs and turned around. "Good talk, but don't go thinkin' you're my real sister or that you can tell me what to do."

"Right back at you." Teresa closed the door to her room, sat down on the floor, drew up her knees, and rested her chin on them. She'd said that she could never trust another man, but there was something still unresolved between her and Noah. She could tell by his expressions that he could feel it, too. She might put her faith in him, but she had so much baggage in her past that even if they did admit the attraction, she'd probably end up like Kayla—just a booty call.

No, it was far better that she simply resisted all those emotions she felt when he was around. Shove them into the dark corners of her heart and never let them see the light of day. Banter with him like she'd been doing and then get on with life after Miss Janie was gone. Until then, she had her work cut out for her.

A sharp knock on her door startled her for the second time that day. Expecting it to be Kayla, she yelled, "Come on in."

Noah slung the door open, and from her angle on the floor, his silhouette filled the doorway and blocked out the light. His broad chest looked like it was at least an acre wide and narrowed down perfectly to his hips. He wore cowboy boots and snug jeans, and his hair was shoved up under a black felt cowboy hat. She'd never seen him dressed like that, but the look was downright sexy. He took a step inside and flashed a brilliant smile.

"Do you think you and Kayla could hold down the fort for a few days?" he asked. "I've got a case over around Texarkana. I'll leave some money for y'all for anything you might need while I'm gone and my cell number in case you need me."

"We'll manage," Teresa said. "I'm settled in pretty good right now, and it looks like Kayla is here for the long haul, so go on. When are you leaving?"

"First thing tomorrow morning. I should be gone Monday through Wednesday if everything goes well," he answered.

"Well, you sure look like you'll do just fine," she told him.

The three of them were adjusting better than she thought they might. She was enjoying doing the cooking and spending time with Miss Janie. Kayla had offered to help with the cleaning duties and with Miss Janie when Teresa needed her. And now Noah trusted them enough to go away for a few days on a job.

"Thanks for doing this. I've had to turn down some work since I got here because of this situation, and it's tough on the reputation. I get a lot of my work by word of mouth," he said.

"No problem," she assured him. "So, you'll be back Wednesday?"

"Hopefully, but Thursday at the latest," he said as he started down the stairs.

"Safe travels," she called out.

"Thank you." Noah waved back.

"Out of sight, out of mind," she muttered, but she didn't believe a single word.

Chapter Seven

Noah propped a pillow against the headboard of the bed in a cheap hotel on the outskirts of Texarkana. Ever since he moved from Houston to Birthright, he'd had second thoughts about what he wanted to do with the rest of his life. He'd gotten scholarships to go to college, but he'd still had a lot of money tied up in student loans. He had found out right fast that eighty-hour weeks and all that stress weren't what he imagined his job would be, but he was stuck with the only real skill he had until his good friend Daniel Freeman, who had gone to law school with him, had quit and joined his father's private investigator firm. That sounded like a fantastic idea to Noah, so when Daniel offered him a position, he jumped on it. He put in the hours and passed the test to be a PI, and after a year of working with the Freeman Firm, he'd left the company to start his own practice.

He picked up the mystery book he'd brought along and began to read. The story was about a PI who was always bumbling things up. So far, he'd never made any of the mistakes the character in the book had made, but after a year of this business, he was doubting it was for him after all. Sitting in a motel, waiting for dark so he could hit a couple of bars, when he'd rather be in Birthright—well, he had a lot of decisions to make by Christmas.

He hit the first bar at ten o'clock, sat on a stool at the far end of the counter, and sipped on a nonalcoholic beer until the right man came inside. The guy slid into a booth in a dark corner and ordered two beers. By the time the waitress delivered them, a woman had joined him on the same side of the booth. Noah positioned his phone so he could get several pictures of them kissing.

That woman looks younger than his daughter, Noah thought as he pulled up the family picture the man's wife had given him.

It's not your job to judge, that pesky voice inside his head reminded him. *You are here to verify that he's having an affair, deliver the evidence, and be on your way.*

"But I don't like being a part of breaking up homes," he muttered.

"What was that?" the bartender, a cute little blonde who couldn't be a day over twenty-one, asked.

"Sorry, I was talkin' to myself." Noah laid out a bill on the counter and carried his beer to the booth right behind the couple.

He turned on the recorder on his phone and decided they were, beyond a doubt, the stupidest couple he had ever surveilled. Even in the noise of the bar, he could hear them loud and clear.

"You'll tell her tonight when you go home," she said.

"If she's asleep, I'll do it in the morning before I go to work. By this time tomorrow night, we won't have to hide things any longer. I love you, Chrissy."

"Oh, Marcus, I love you, too."

More kissing and then Marcus said, "Let's leave these beers behind and go celebrate in our room."

Noah knew the make and model of Cheating Husband's truck, so he waited a couple of minutes before he followed them out. He got a few more shots of them all hugged up and making out next to a small compact car as he walked to his vehicle. Then they separated and each drove, as luck would have it, to the very hotel where he was staying. By the time they got into their room, he'd shot a dozen more pictures.

Figuring that his job was done, he went into his room, loaded all the pictures and the audiotape into his laptop, and sent them straight to the man's wife. She responded by saying she would send a check for the rest of the money she owed him.

"Well, that was easy enough," Noah said aloud.

His phone rang and the ringtone let him know it was Daniel. "You still in Texarkana?" Daniel asked as he picked up.

"Yep, got finished with a case, and I'll be headed home tomorrow morning," he answered.

"Got time to do a favor for an old friend?"

"Sure," Noah said. "What do you need?"

"I've got a job that involves insurance fraud," Daniel replied. "The feller lives in Fulton, Arkansas. That's not far from Texarkana. Name is Quinn McKay, fifty-nine years old. I need pictures of him lifting or doing anything strenuous. I can be there Thursday to spell you if you haven't gotten something by then. It pays the going rate."

"Text me the address, and I'll take care of it for you," Noah told him.

"Will do." Daniel ended the call, and the text came through in seconds—name, address, and a picture of the guy.

Noah fell backward onto the bed and stared at the ceiling. He was anxious to be home, but he couldn't very well refuse to give Daniel a hand, not after all the help he and his dad had given him.

This will give you a while to think about what you want to do with your life going forward. The voice in his head sounded an awful lot like his granddad Luther Jackson.

Knowing what Noah did now about Miss Janie's past, he suspected that his grandfather did know about his sister's pregnancy. Were there more skeletons in the closet?

"We all have skeletons," he whispered. "I know a little about Teresa's past, and the investigator in me would like to dig deep into her life, but that's her privacy and her story to tell me if and when she trusts me enough with it."

Yeah, right. You want to know everything about her, he thought. *You want her to trust you, and you're just dying to trust her enough to tell her your story.*

"Maybe so, but it probably won't ever happen," he muttered.

"Why are you doing this today?" Teresa asked Kayla when she got the cleaning supplies out. "Haven't you ever seen all those embroidered tea towels in fancy stores? Monday is cleaning day."

"I don't go by what fancy towels say. I don't care if it says Monday is cleaning day. This week it's going to be on Tuesday," Kayla answered. "In the house where I grew up, every day after school was cleaning day. That way I could get rid of all Billy Joe's empty liquor bottles from the night before, and I could wash the sheets from my bed," Kayla said. "You got a problem with me cleaning the place today?"

"Not a single one," Teresa said, "but stay out of my room. I'll keep it clean."

"Afraid I'll steal something?" Kayla asked.

"Do I have reason to be?" Teresa asked.

"Not anymore, and when I did shoplift, it was only food because I was hungry. I haven't had to do that in years." Kayla took her bucket and marched up the stairs without a backward glance.

"Nurse! Nurse!" Miss Janie's weak voice called out. "I'm ready for the babies now. Can you bring them to me?"

"Of course, I can." Teresa hurried up the stairs to get the dolls. She'd worried about what living with Kayla as an adult would be like, but so far it was pretty much like living with her as a teenager. She still had a chip the size of a cruise ship on her shoulder and blew up at anything Teresa mentioned.

Kayla's door was open, so she dashed inside and grabbed the doll from the cradle. She was coming back out when Kayla blocked her way.

She popped her hands on her hips and cocked her head to one side. "You're like the pot calling the kettle black, aren't you? Why are you stealing my doll?"

"Miss Janie wants the babies. Here—carry one of them." Teresa handed Kayla's doll to her.

"What in the hell are you talkin' about?" Kayla asked, but she followed her down the stairs.

When they reached the bottom, Teresa looked back and shook her head. "Don't hold it like that. Pretend it's a real newborn baby. She thinks these dolls are her babies. Today she's sixteen."

"How long will she be that age?" Kayla asked.

"Two minutes, two days." Teresa cradled her doll in her arms like a real baby. "Or maybe two seconds. We play along with whatever age she is."

"We don't call her Mama at this age, then?" Kayla asked.

"Nope, that's only when she's about forty or fifty," Teresa answered.

"Is she ever in her seventies?" Kayla whispered as they entered the room.

"Seldom. We cherish those times." Teresa smiled at Miss Janie. "Here you go. They've had their baths and been fed. They were such good babies all night long—you should be so proud."

Miss Janie smiled shyly. "Aunt Ruthie was right. We can raise them ourselves. Who is that?" She pointed at Kayla.

"She's a new nurse that Noah hired. Her name is Kayla. She's very good with babies, and she's had lots of experience." Teresa wasn't lying about that. Kayla had practically raised several younger siblings before she got put into foster care.

"You'll tell me if she's mean to them, won't you?" Miss Janie asked.

"I'll fire her if she's ugly to the babies," Teresa promised as she laid one of the dolls on the pillow in Miss Janie's lap, then motioned for

Kayla to do the same. She was more than a little surprised that Kayla didn't have something to say, or maybe even kick her in the shins for the comment.

"I trust you." Miss Janie began to hum as she gently touched the dolls' faces.

"You call me when you're ready for us to take them back to the nursery." Teresa tiptoed out of the room with Kayla right behind her.

"You don't have the authority to fire me," Kayla said.

"No, I don't, but if it makes Miss Janie feel better, then we will pretend that I do." Teresa went to the kitchen, sat down in a chair, and put her head in her hands to catch her tears. "My heart breaks for her every time she wants the babies."

Kayla pulled out a chair and sat down beside her. "I had no idea that she'd be like this, but why did you ever let her think those dolls were real babies to start with?"

"She mourned for the little girls she gave away. I had a patient like that in the nursing home, and when the nurses gave her a doll, it soothed her." Teresa took a paper napkin from the holder in the middle of the table and dried her face. "I keep thinking about the turmoil she lived with all these years."

"Nurse! Nurse!" Miss Janie yelled.

Teresa hopped up and hurried across the hall.

"I've got a hangnail"—she held up her index finger—"and I'm afraid I'll scratch one of the babies with it."

"Why don't we take the babies back to the nursery, and I'll give you a manicure this morning," Teresa said. "You can even pick your nail polish. There's pink and red both on your dresser." She motioned for Kayla to come get the dolls. "Can you carry both of them?"

"Sure, I can," Kayla said. "Then I'll get back to cleaning."

"You still got a driver's license?" Teresa whispered.

"Yes, I do, even though I haven't owned a car in months," she replied.

"I needed to go grocery shopping today, but I'm afraid to leave her with you until she gets to know you better at the age she is right now. Would you mind doing that and cleaning later?" Teresa gently laid a doll in each crook of Kayla's arms.

"You're going to trust me with your vehicle?" Kayla asked.

"No." Teresa laid the pillow from Miss Janie's lap to the side and helped her sit up. "You can take Miss Janie's car. Keys are hanging by the back door, and the credit card that Noah left is on the credenza in the hallway. The list is on the front of the refrigerator."

"Why can't I drive your car?" Kayla asked.

"Because it's that old truck out there in the driveway. The tires are about to blow, and you'd be runnin' on fumes to get to a gas station," Teresa replied, and then focused on Miss Janie. "There, now, darlin', you lean on me, and we'll do your nails in the kitchen. And I forgot to put tampons on the list, and we're out of shampoo."

"Any particular brand?" Kayla asked.

"I usually get whatever is on sale." She led Miss Janie across the hallway and into the kitchen. "Have you decided on a color?"

Miss Janie giggled. "Mama says red is for hussies and that good girls don't wear red. Greta did when we were in the unwed mothers' home. She did my nails one time and I felt really rebellious."

"Then shall we do them red again?" Teresa asked. "I won't tell on you if we do."

"Yes." Miss Janie clapped her hands. "Mama shouldn't have made me go there. If Aunt Ruthie hadn't talked to them, I wouldn't have my babies today. How long until I stop hurting from giving birth?"

"It'll go away soon," Teresa told her as she started out of the kitchen to get the little zippered manicure set that had always been on Miss Janie's dresser, and the bottle of polish.

"Why did she ask that?" Kayla whispered as she followed her.

"Because the cancer is in her bones and the pain must remind her of the way she felt after she gave birth," Teresa explained. "Oh, and we need more detergent while you're at the store."

"I understand. See you in a couple of hours. Think it would be all right if I got a pizza for dinner on the credit card?" Kayla asked.

"I don't see why not," Teresa replied. "That sure sounds good."

"Oh. My. Goodness." Miss Janie had gotten up and was standing in the kitchen door. "Do I hear my girls being nice to each other?"

Teresa headed on into the living room. "Don't worry. It won't last long, Miss Janie."

Miss Janie raised her chin a notch and looked down her nose at Teresa. "I told you to call me Mama. We don't have to pretend anymore. I'm claiming you and Kayla as my daughters. I've been sitting here thinking about whether you would have been Mary Jane or Maddy. I think maybe Mary Jane fits you better."

Teresa took her bony, spider-veined hand in her own and led her back to the kitchen table. "Tell me about my daddy. Was he a good man, or did he run off and leave you without even looking back?"

"Jesus was a good boy, but he was only a kid like me. He was sixteen that summer and I was fifteen." Miss Janie smiled. "I thought it was funny that his name was spelled like the Jesus in the Bible but pronounced different. I shouldn't have laughed about it, but when I wrote it in my diary, it looked like Jesus had gotten me pregnant."

"Did you tell your parents who your babies' father was?" Teresa asked.

"Yes I did, and Daddy was mad at me." Miss Janie's smile faded at the memory. "But Mama was even worse. You'd have thought that Jesus was the devil. If it had been a nice white boy, things might have been different."

"What did they do?" Teresa asked.

"He'd already gone back to Mexico when I found out I was pregnant. Daddy would never have let me marry Jesus, and besides, I didn't want to marry him." She lowered her voice. "Daddy was a little bit prejudiced, and Mama was a whole lot. They were mad enough at me when they thought it was a boy from my school, but they wouldn't even look at me when they found out who he was."

"Did you want to have sex with Jesus, or did he force you?" Teresa thought about the times she'd hidden under the porch or in the backyard to keep from having to fight off her mother's boyfriends.

"Jesus would have never forced me to do anything. He was too sweet for that. I think you got that from him. Kayla got my strong will," Miss Janie said, and then in the blink of an eye, her expression changed. "I'd like to go take a nap now. I'll get my nails done later."

"You can hold on to my arm so you don't fall." Teresa led her back to the bedroom. Lately, she'd been sleeping more and more. Noah said the doctor told him to expect that, but Teresa loved the precious moments when Miss Janie was lucid enough to recognize her as Teresa, the child she'd saved from a group home.

Miss Janie looped her arm into Teresa's and sighed. "How long does it take for the stitches in my bottom to heal up?"

"Quite a while, but I'll check and see if you can have some more pain medicine for that," Teresa answered.

"You better let me make a bathroom stop on the way," Miss Janie said.

Teresa helped her with that, and when she'd taken off her slippers and covered her feet with a throw, Miss Janie latched on to her arm.

"I'm glad you girls came back to help me," she whispered. "I didn't want to go to a nursing home. I hate that I'm a burden, but when I'm gone, I fixed things for all of you."

"All of us?" Teresa asked.

"You and Kayla and Noah, the loves of my life." Miss Janie's eyes fluttered shut and she began to snore.

The last five words that she'd said played through Teresa's mind as if they were on a loop. *The loves of my life.* Teresa wondered who or what were the loves of *her* life.

She'd thought that Luis was and had endured his cheating because she had loved him. She'd learned that indifference was the opposite of love, not hate. When the time came for her to sign the divorce papers, she flat-out didn't care anymore. She even felt sorry for the woman he was already living with. That poor soul had children with him, so they would be connected forever.

Getting back her self-esteem had been a long and rugged road, and from where she stood, that light at the end of the tunnel or road, or whatever it was called, was still just a dot out there on the horizon.

Kayla felt like a kid with a five-dollar bill in a candy shop when she pushed a cart into the grocery store that morning. She didn't have to keep a running total of what she spent in her head so that she wouldn't spend too much. Too many times, she'd had to decide what to put back, but not today.

She was reaching up for a bag of flour when a strong male voice behind her said, "Let me get that for you, miss."

"Thank you." She turned around only to end up face-to-face with Will Barton, the shyest kid and the biggest geek in high school.

"Is that you, Kayla?" he asked.

"Yep, it's me," she answered. "What happened to your thick glasses?"

"Traded 'em in for contacts right after high school." He smiled. "You and Denver moved back to this area?"

"No, only me. I'm at Birthright with Miss Janie," she told him.

"I heard she had Alzheimer's and cancer. Sorry to get that news. She was a lively old girl, even after she retired. She used to come in for groceries every week and tell me how proud she was of me," he said.

"You work here?" she asked.

"Yep. I manage this store and do the buying for the other three in the chain," he answered. "Is Denver joining you later?"

"I hope not," she spit out so fast that it shocked her.

Will chuckled. "Never did see what a pretty girl like you saw in that loser anyway. Well, I got to get back to the office. Good to see you again—tell Miss Janie I said hello. Hey, are you going to the ten-year class reunion?"

"I didn't even realize we'd been out of school that long."

Will flashed another grin. "I'm sure they'll miss us both terribly if we don't show up."

"Yeah, right." Kayla smiled back at him. "They'll all mourn our absence."

He was still chuckling when he headed back down the aisle and turned the corner. Kayla wished she'd taken a picture of him. No way was Teresa going to believe that the biggest nerd in high school had turned out like that.

She had a cart full of groceries and almost fainted when the cashier rang up the total. Never in her entire life had she spent nearly two hundred dollars on food that only had to last a week. The back seat was completely full and two small bags rested in the trunk of Miss Janie's old 1976 Ford Maverick when she pulled out of the parking lot. The old baby-blue vehicle might be close to antique status, but it still drove like a charm.

Will's clear blue eyes still teased her mind as she drove home, and she liked the fact that he had a sense of humor. Why hadn't she noticed either of those things when she was in classes with him? Most likely, it was because back in high school he always sat on the front row. Even with his glasses, he had trouble seeing the board.

And you had your mind so set on Denver that you couldn't see anyone else, the voice in her head reminded her in a blunt tone.

"Guilty as charged," she said out loud as she drove through Birthright.

Miss Janie had told her that at one time the town had been known as Lone Star and that it had a school. Her aunt Ruthie had been one of the students in the last graduating class in 1948. Kayla didn't know why she remembered that bit of trivia. Now the town had a population of forty—well, maybe forty-three since Kayla, Teresa, and Noah were living there again.

"Population explosion," Kayla whispered as she parked as close to the back door of the house as she could get.

Teresa met her in the kitchen with a worried look on her face. "Thank God you're home. I need help."

"What happened?" Kayla asked.

"Miss Janie is sitting on the floor beside her bed. She says her legs don't work anymore, and I can't lift a deadweight," Teresa answered.

Kayla followed her across the kitchen and the hallway and right into Miss Janie's room.

"Who are you and what are you doing here?" Miss Janie frowned.

"I'm here to help Teresa get you into bed. What happened?" Kayla sat down on the floor beside her.

"My legs don't work no more." Tears flowed down Miss Janie's face. "Please don't take me to one of them homes."

Teresa eased down on the other side of her and wiped the tears away with a tissue. "We'll never do that, Mama. Your girls came home to take care of you. We'll be right here always."

Kayla slipped an arm around her shoulders. "That's right, Mama. If your legs don't work, we'll get a wheelchair so you can still have breakfast on the back porch some of the time."

"You are good daughters. Promise me"—she looked from one to the other—"that you will let me die right here in my house when the time comes."

"We promise," Teresa and Kayla said at the same time.

"Call the nurse to come get me up and back into bed," she said.

"How about you let us do that?" Teresa said. "The nurses are all busy right now."

"I raised two good girls. Where are the babies?" Miss Janie asked.

Lifting a deadweight, even if Miss Janie wasn't the woman she used to be, wasn't easy, but they managed to get her into the bed. She wanted the babies brought to her as soon as she was settled.

Kayla retrieved the dolls from their bedrooms and carried them into Miss Janie's bedroom gently, as if they were real babies. She wondered how much different her life would have been if she'd gotten pregnant the first time she and Denver had sex. She would have a teenage son or daughter herself right about now. The idea of trying to raise a child almost gave her hives, especially if it was a boy who turned out to be like Denver.

"Here they are," Kayla said as she came into the room.

"Why are you bringing your dolls in here, Kayla? They belong upstairs in the little cradles I had made for them," Miss Janie scolded. "Did I break a hip? My legs feel funny."

"No, you didn't break a hip," Kayla answered. "I thought you'd like to see that we've kept the dolls nice all these years."

Miss Janie rubbed her shoulder. "Did I fall?"

"No, you slid down into a sitting position, but I can call the doctor if you think I should," Teresa answered.

"Why would you do that? You're a nurse," Miss Janie said.

"That's right, but to be on the safe side, I'll give him a quick call." Teresa took the dolls from Kayla and whispered, "Stay with her until I get back, and then I'll help you unload all those groceries."

Kayla sat down on the edge of the bed and said, "Miss Janie, how old are you?"

"It's not polite to ask a woman her age." She pouted. "But I'll be seventeen on my next birthday."

"And you came to live here when you were sixteen?" Kayla asked.

"Yes, I did. I was terrified at first, but Aunt Ruthie was so nice to me. She didn't put me down for what I'd done. Where is she? Did she go to town and leave me with you?" Miss Janie asked.

Lord have mercy! Kayla hoped that when her own time came, she died in her right mind. Poor Miss Janie. This had to be a miserable existence.

Teresa motioned for Kayla to join her in the hallway.

Before she left, Kayla patted Miss Janie on the shoulder. "I've got to get the groceries into the house before our ice cream melts. I'll be right back, though."

Teresa led the way back to the kitchen and turned around at the cabinet. "The doctor says he's been expecting this and that she won't be able to walk anymore. She's ready for a wheelchair now." She bit back a sob.

"We'll do what we can. We promised that we'd let her die at home, but the Miss Janie we knew when we were kids is gone already. It's only a matter of her heart figuring out that it's time to stop beating," Kayla said.

"I've got so many regrets." Teresa wiped away a tear and hugged Kayla for the first time ever.

Chapter Eight

This morning is turning into Freaky Friday, Teresa thought. Miss Janie was the child and she had become the parent. In Miss Janie's jumbled mind, Tuesday was Sunday, and she'd demanded that she get out of bed and go to church.

"I promise it's Tuesday, and church services are not held on Tuesdays," Teresa assured her.

Miss Janie crossed her arms over her chest and said, "If I can't go worship, then I'll just starve and go see Jesus in heaven."

"Which Jesus?" Kayla entered the room. "Our Lord and Savior, or my father?"

Miss Janie picked up one of the dolls beside her and threw it at Kayla. "Don't you claim to be fathered by Jesus. And why do I have your dolls in my bed, anyway? Good God, I'm not a child. I'm a grown woman, and I want to go to church like I've done every Sunday since I came here to live with Aunt Ruthie."

"Your legs aren't working right now," Teresa told her. "Maybe next week the medicine the doctor is giving you will help you walk again. Until that happens or we buy a wheelchair, you can't go to church."

"Then one of you go and record the service so I can hear it." Her eyes finally settled on Kayla. "You need it worse, so you go."

"How am I supposed to record the services when I don't have a cell phone?" Kayla asked.

"Find one." Miss Janie tossed the second doll out of the bed and onto the floor. "And put those back where they belong."

"Miss Janie, how old are you?" Teresa asked.

"I was thirty on my last birthday." She raised her voice and glared at Teresa. "Don't ask stupid questions."

"Why is it so important that you go to church this morning?" Kayla asked.

Miss Janie's face softened. "They already had Aunt Ruthie's funeral, didn't they? Did I miss it? I promised her on her deathbed I would never miss church, even if I was still mad at God for taking my babies away from me. I never go back on my word. I've been in the church here in Birthright every Sunday except when I was sick since I came to live with Aunt Ruthie. When did they bury Aunt Ruthie?"

"You told me that you went to Aunt Ruthie's funeral. She's been gone for years," Kayla said.

"Are you still mad at God?" Teresa asked to distract Miss Janie from the time shift.

"No. I made my peace with Him when Noah found you girls and y'all came home to me. I'm hungry. When are we having breakfast?" Miss Janie asked.

"How about a chocolate cupcake and a glass of milk?" Kayla asked.

Miss Janie giggled. "Don't you try that on me. You think if you can talk me into eating a cupcake, then you'll get to do the same. Eat your bacon and eggs first, and then you can have dessert."

Kayla went to the kitchen to heat up the plate of food. Teresa picked up the two dolls and laid them on the other bed. Kayla's lips trembled, probably with tears, when she returned to Miss Janie's still-angry expression. "Why did you blame God for taking your babies?"

"Daddy was a preacher, and Mama was a dutiful Christian wife. At least she was that in public. She was the boss at home," Miss Janie

answered. "If Daddy had been a farmer or maybe even a bartender"—
she giggled—"then he and Mama might have given me a choice in what
I wanted to do with my babies."

"That made it God's fault?" Teresa asked.

"Of course. Didn't you hear me? Daddy was a preacher. God ruled
our lives." Miss Janie frowned like Teresa was having trouble following
the conversation.

Kayla laid a hand on Miss Janie's arm. "I understand."

"So do I, now." Teresa sat down on the edge of Miss Janie's bed.
"Would you like for us to get a bed that you can lower and raise, and
maybe a wheelchair so we can go out on the porch every day?"

"That would be nice." Miss Janie yawned. "I'm sleepy now, so y'all
can go. I'll call you when I need you. I think I'm going to like this new
nurse."

"That's good." Teresa covered Miss Janie's feet with a crocheted
throw.

Teresa poured them each a glass of lemonade when they reached the
kitchen. "Have you been to church since you left Birthright?"

"Not one time. Have you? And are you losing your mind, too?"

"Why would you ask a stupid question like that?" Teresa asked.

"You poured lemonade for me. You never did that before." Kayla
grinned.

"You never deserved it before," Teresa smarted off. "And to answer
your question, I have not been to church. Not even when Luis and I
got married. He was a practicing Catholic. The only place of worship
I'd ever been to was the one here in town with Miss Janie. He told me
that the Catholic Church wouldn't recognize our marriage."

"That made it easy for him," Kayla said. "Did you blame God for
the parents you got?"

"Yep," Teresa answered.

"Do you remember when you realized that you'd gotten lousy parents?" Kayla toyed with her glass.

"Second day of kindergarten." The pain that came with the way she felt when she got to school that day was as fresh as it had been back then. "The other little girls had bows in their hair and cute little outfits. My hair was a tangled mess. I had dressed myself that morning in wrinkled jeans that were a size too big and a shirt that was a size too small. How about you?"

"Oh, I remember, all right, and Christmas always brings the memories to the surface, even though I don't want to think about that time," Kayla replied. "God could have sent a good man to marry my mama before I was born instead of my stepdad. He never let me forget that he'd done me and my mama a big favor by marrying her despite her having an ugly kid. I was supposed to be grateful that he provided a home for me and put food in my mouth. The first time he slapped me across the face was when I asked if I could have a new dress for the Christmas program at school. I was in the first grade, and the other girls were talking about what they were going to wear. He told me that I wasn't better than his kids, and they dressed out of the free church clothes closet. Mama jumped into the battle and told me I should appreciate my daddy because he worked hard for his family."

Teresa took a sip of her lemonade. "Mama lived with several men, and I heard the same stories. Daddy worked hard and paid the lot rent on the trailer for us that month. 'Daddy' was simply whoever she was sleeping with at the time. I was in maybe the third grade when I figured out that I'd had so many daddies that I couldn't count them all on one hand. A guy came around that summer handing out invitations to Vacation Bible School and told Mama that they'd take me and bring me home in a church bus. That was my first time to go, and that's when I decided if God really could do anything, then He must hate me a lot."

"Ever decide that it wasn't God's fault?" Kayla asked.

"Workin' on it," Teresa answered.

"Me too, but sometimes the goin' gets slow." Kayla kept her eyes on what lemonade was left in her cup. "Look at us, acting like we're in group therapy. Ever go to any of that kind of thing?"

Teresa drank down several gulps of lemonade. Did she really want to share any more? She took a deep breath, let it out slowly, and said, "Yes, I did. There was a group therapy in the basement of a church that dealt with cheating and/or abusive spouses. I went a few times."

"Did it help?" Kayla asked.

"I learned that until I got ready to admit I was an enabler for letting Luis treat me like he did, there weren't enough sessions in the world that would help me," Teresa answered.

"You wanted help in dealing with him, not you, right?" Kayla asked.

"Sounds like you went to a few sessions, too," Teresa said.

Kayla shook her head. "Not me, but one of the girls I worked with did, and she told me about it. She thought if she went to therapy, she could figure out a way to change him. I kept telling her that it wouldn't work."

"What happened?" Teresa asked.

"He left her for another woman. Maybe he was kin to Luis," Kayla replied. "And then she took up with another man as bad or worse than that guy. We are who we are, Teresa, and we have to want to change that a whole lot to ever get through it or around it."

"How bad do you want to change?" Teresa asked.

"I'll ask you the same question," Kayla shot back at her.

"That's complicated."

"Damn straight it is." Kayla did a head wiggle. "Maybe what we need to change is our choices and our circumstances. Think God will be kinder to us if we do that?"

"Well, we've got a chance to do both if we stick around here," Teresa agreed. "Maybe that old saying about God helping folks who help themselves will apply."

Kayla finished off her lemonade and pushed her chair back. "I'm willin' to test that theory. I guess there ain't nowhere to go but up from here."

"Yep." Teresa did the same and carried both their glasses to the dishwasher. "Thanks for the therapy session."

"Thank Miss Janie." Kayla headed out of the room and then turned around. "She's the one who brought up the subject and got me to thinking about being mad at God."

Noah's truck smelled like coffee, cheese-flavored chips, candy bars, and pastrami sandwiches by Wednesday morning. Quinn McKay hadn't made so much as a step outside the door of his house. His wife even brought out the trash and took in the paper. Maybe the insurance company had been wrong to think that Quinn was trying to defraud them.

He was on his third bag of chips when Quinn came out of the house on crutches. According to the files that Daniel had sent over, the man had been hit by a car while crossing a street, suffering a fracture to his leg and some kind of pinched nerve in his neck. Noah could see the neck brace from here. Two years ago, Quinn had been stepping off a curb and someone had run over his foot. A year before that, he'd been rear-ended by another vehicle and had suffered severe neck problems. Either he was the unluckiest man alive, or else he'd cried wolf too many times and this last accident was unfortunately legit. Given his history, his problem now was that no one believed him.

For some reason, Noah had thought that the man would be a big fellow, and it turned out he was right. This guy probably made the bathroom scales groan, and he was every bit as tall as Noah, which would put him over six feet. Noah took pictures of him using the crutches to get into his truck. When he drove away, Noah followed him to a convenience store, where he got out without the crutches and filled the gas tank. Then he drove west toward Texarkana.

"Where are you going, Quinn?" Noah asked himself out loud.

He tailed him all the way to the east edge of Texarkana, where the man got out of his truck with no neck brace, slung a bag of golf clubs over his shoulder, and swaggered off to the links. Noah shot pictures of him through the whole process. Then he got out of his own truck and followed the guy onto the course. Quinn met up with a couple of other guys for some good old boy backslaps, and then Quinn McKay, the man who'd been *terribly* injured by a car, teed off.

Noah sent dozens of photos to Daniel and then called him. He answered on the second ring and said, "You have made an insurance company very happy, and this is enough to give them cause to go after whatever doctor this guy is working with. Job well done."

"Thanks. You know . . . this might be my last case," Noah said. "I've had a lot of time to really think about what makes me happy. This isn't it."

"I'm sorry to hear that, but what's this next step gonna be?" Daniel asked.

"I'm thinking about hanging out my shingle in Birthright," Noah said out loud for the first time.

"You want to practice law in a town of forty people? Are you crazy?" Daniel asked.

"Maybe so, but I can take the cases no one else wants. Word of mouth will get around the area, and I'll stay as busy as I want to be. With my inheritance, I don't need the money, so I could do pro bono work for folks," Noah answered. "I can have my practice in Birthright, and I bet clients will come to me from all the neighboring towns, including Sulphur Springs."

"How many lawyers are already in Sulphur Springs?" Daniel asked.

"Nineteen last time I counted," Noah chuckled. "But hey, none of them will work for pennies like I will."

"You're crazy," Daniel said.

"You could be right, but I've had a lot of time to think about things these past two days," Noah said.

"Well, good luck, and when you're starving, holler at me. We've always got a place for you in our firm," Daniel told him.

"That's good to know, and thanks. Keep in touch. Bye now." Noah ended the call.

Fulton, Arkansas, wasn't much bigger than Birthright. There sure wasn't a hotel in the place, and Noah had needed to be on twenty-four-hour surveillance. He had taken short catnaps and eaten in his car, and only took fast bathroom breaks to the nearest convenience store, located down the block from where Quinn McKay lived.

Noah got into his truck, made a couple of turns, and was soon back on Highway 30 headed west. His mind kept running in circles and coming back to that word *defraud*. Since they'd arrived at Miss Janie's house, Teresa and Kayla had been good about helping, and they both had a lot of patience with his great-aunt. But he had to wonder if they were sticking around to see how much of an inheritance Miss Janie would be leaving them.

Miss Janie herself had said many times that the apple didn't fall far from the tree, and he'd proven that day that people aren't always what they seem to be. He was never sure who she meant when she said that, but when he thought of Kayla, he wondered what the tree she fell from might have been like. The social worker had told Miss Janie about her mother abandoning her.

And Teresa? Miss Janie had told him back when she was still lucid that Teresa had been taken from her mother because the woman was unfit. She hadn't even tried to get Teresa back. About a year after Miss Janie had kept her from going to a group home, the mother left town, and no one had ever heard from or about her again. Noah had thought that maybe he'd find Teresa living with her when he'd started his search, but her mother was living in Bell Gardens, California, and was working as a bartender.

Bringing Teresa and Kayla into her home might have made Miss Janie feel like she was redeeming herself for giving away her own little babies. She'd said that at that moment she knew she had absolution for her sins.

Each of them had brought their own collection of baggage with them to Birthright. If Miss Janie was in her right mind, she might be able to help them figure things out.

A smile tickled the corners of his mouth as he thought about everything that had happened in the past few days. "You sly old gal," he laughed. "Somewhere in that tangled mind of yours, you've brought us all back to the house so we can sort out our problems, haven't you?"

It is what it is. The whispered answer in his head sounded like Miss Janie's voice.

Chapter Nine

noah was five miles outside of Tyler, Texas, that Wednesday afternoon when he got a phone call from Teresa.

"Hey, are you still coming home tomorrow?" she asked.

"No. I'm on my way home right now. I got finished early," he answered. Her voice warmed his heart and made him wish he were already there, but he had at least another hour of driving. "What's going on?"

"Everything is pretty normal for this place, but Miss Janie can't walk now. She slid down on the floor and couldn't get up. Since then, we're having to lift her. We need a wheelchair. A hospital bed and a bedside potty chair would be nice, too, and maybe a shower chair. Thank goodness she had a walk-in shower installed in the past ten years," Teresa answered.

He could have listened to her soft southern voice read the dictionary, but then, he'd been sitting in a car with no one to talk to for two days. "I'm actually about to reach the Tyler exit, so I'll pick up what you need there and have it to the house in the next couple of hours. The job I was doing, plus another one, ended quicker than I thought they would."

"That's great," she said. "We'll be looking for you."

"Got sweet tea made up?" he asked.

"Always," she answered.

Her voice changed slightly, and he could imagine her smiling.

"Sweet tea is about the only normalcy left here," she continued.

"Then by all means, let's keep some made up. We need something normal around there," he said. "I see a medical supply place up ahead of me. See you soon."

Blake Shelton was singing "Goodbye Time" when he ended the call. He sat in his truck and listened to the whole song. The lyrics of the song told the story of someone losing the love of his life and having to tell her goodbye. Noah wondered if the song wasn't an omen—with Miss Janie's new development, it wouldn't be long until he'd be saying goodbye to her. According to his father, men did not cry, but as Noah wiped tears from his cheeks, he disagreed.

"Goodbye time is tough," he whispered, and tried to think of something he could look forward to saying farewell to. The thought of his PI work ending put a smile on his face instead of bringing tears to his eyes. He could choose his clients and his hours and be doing something for the people of his community at the same time. That would make Miss Janie happy.

He was able to purchase all three items Teresa had asked for at the store, and the salesclerk even helped load the boxes into the back of his truck. For the next hour, he listened to the same country music station, and every single song seemed to have a message for him. Luke Combs was now singing "Beer Never Broke My Heart."

He could sure enough agree with every word except for the thing about beer. Whiskey and his own stupidity had been the two things that had caused him to hit rock bottom and get his heart broken in the process. On the day after Thanksgiving he'd have been sober for six years. He'd found a meeting in Sulphur Springs and tried to get in one a couple of times a month. So far that had been enough, but still the day might come when he would want to fall off the wagon, and if that happened, he knew where to go.

Jason Aldean was singing "Rearview Town" when he turned off the interstate north toward Birthright. "Another omen," Noah whispered. "Only it should say *life* in the rearview rather than *town*."

The crunch of gravel in the driveway sent Teresa's pulse up a notch or two as she sat on the porch with Kayla and Miss Janie. Noah was home.

That last word played over and over in her head. Was Birthright really her home? True enough, it had been the most stable place she'd ever lived. She'd seen a sign years ago at a craft fair that said "Home is where the heart is." If that was the truth, then no place was home. Since she was a little girl, her heart had been floating around like one of those fancy satellites in space.

As Noah got out of the truck, she could see the tiredness in his face. Dark circles ringed his eyes, and his smile had dimmed. Whatever job he'd been on had robbed him of good sleep. She recognized the signs from the times when she had spent sleepless nights in the trailer worrying about whether one of her mother's boyfriends might either knock her around or get all handsy with her.

"Luther!" Miss Janie squealed and clapped her hands. "You made it home."

"I sure did. How are you, Miss Janie?" He crossed the yard.

"Why are you callin' me that?" She stuck her lower lip out in a pout. "You always call me Sarah Jane."

"Sorry," Noah apologized. "You look so cute with your friends, I thought you looked like a Miss Janie today."

She giggled. "I kind of like it, so I forgive you. Come and tell me about the war. You know I always crave news about where you've been. You don't write nearly often enough." She held up her arms for a hug. "Mama says it's because that woman you're keeping company with takes up all your time."

Noah hugged her and then sat down on the top step of the porch. "Let's talk about you instead, and you can tell Mama that I'm not dating that girl anymore. I'm getting serious about a nurse I met. What have you been doing since I was home?"

A shot of jealousy chased through Teresa's heart. Was Noah talking about himself, or was he pretending to be Luther? Had there been a recent serious relationship in his life?

"I broke my legs," she answered. "My nurses told me that you'd bring me a wheelchair to use until they get well. Did you remember?"

"Yes, ma'am, I did." He pointed toward the truck. "It's right out there, and look what else I got you." He brought a chocolate bar out of his shirt pocket.

"You always remember how much I love candy." Her old eyes sparkled as she reached for it.

"Be careful," Teresa warned. She could feel a blush creeping up the back of her neck, but she couldn't get rid of the picture in her head of him with another woman, and she flat-out did not like it. "You might fall off the swing." Kayla took the candy from him, tore the wrapper free, and handed it off to Miss Janie. "Noah is sweet to remember to bring you something."

"Why are you talking about Noah?" Miss Janie asked. "This is Luther, silly girl. Noah couldn't buy candy. He only had whatever they took on the ark, and he lived a long time before I was born." Miss Janie took a bite. "This is so good. I haven't had one of these since you came home last time. Mama says that it'll ruin my teeth and make me fat. Don't tell her you brought it, okay?"

Noah put a finger over his lips. "It'll be our secret. What else does Mama tell you when I'm gone?"

"That I must be a good girl and sit up like a lady and to stop rolling my eyes at her. Sittin' up ain't too hard, but sometimes I turn my back and roll my eyes," Miss Janie said between bites.

"Why do you turn your back?" Kayla asked.

"Because if she sees me, she slaps my face real hard, and it hurts." Miss Janie put a hand on her cheek as if she could feel the pain by talking about it.

"Does Daddy say anything when she hits you?" Noah asked.

Miss Janie shivered. "Her slaps don't hurt as bad as his belt. He didn't have to whip you because you were a good boy, but he says girls got to learn their place so they'll be good wives. Let's go inside and get some milk. If you ask for it first, Mama won't say no."

Teresa blinked back tears. Who would ever have thought, as kind and sweet as Miss Janie had been to her two foster daughters, that she'd been an abused child? She'd made the comment that she didn't ever want to get married. No wonder, if she thought those whippings went along with being a wife.

"How about I get your new wheelchair out of the truck, and we give you a ride in it?" Noah asked. "No racing through the house, though. You might break something, and that would make Mama mad for sure."

Miss Janie clapped her hands and squealed like a little girl. "I promise I'll be careful." She lowered her voice. "But I might race down the hallway if Mama isn't looking."

"I'll help you bring it and whatever else is out there," Teresa offered, and stood up.

Kayla moved closer to Miss Janie. "If y'all need me, just yell. I'll stay right here with Miss Janie, in case she needs help eating all that delicious chocolate."

"Thank you," Miss Janie giggled and took another bite.

When they'd crossed the yard and were almost to the truck, Teresa remembered to say, "Welcome home. Miss Janie missed you."

"Thanks." He grinned. "Is she the only one who missed me?"

Granted it had been a while, but Teresa knew flirting when she saw it, and Noah was definitely flirting with her. She air slapped him on the arm. "Of course not. We all did."

"Well, it's good to be back." His smile got even bigger. "I missed being home."

He didn't say he missed her in particular, but the twinkle in his eyes gave her hope. Then the smile faded, and he pulled the box with the wheelchair out of the back of the truck.

"This sure happened fast," he said.

"I expected a gradual thing, too, but one minute she's shuffling along with a walker and the next she's flat on the floor and her legs won't work." Teresa followed him across the yard.

"The doctor said we could expect anything, and the decline could be slow or come along in the blink of an eye," Noah said.

"What were you doin'? Or is it classified?" she asked.

"Surveillance for an old friend," he told her. "I got all the information he needed, so now he doesn't even have to go. I owed him because he's the guy who helped find you and Kayla for Miss Janie."

Well, thank God for that guy, whoever he is, she thought.

"Looks to me like you could use about twenty hours of sleep," she said as she watched him use his pocketknife to open the box.

"Is that the voice of experience I'm hearing?" He pulled the chair out, popped it open, and attached the footrests.

"Yes, it is. Anytime I could work a double shift, I did it," she answered.

"You're working triple shifts every day here," he reminded her as he picked up the chair and started toward the porch with it.

"But here I only have one patient, not a whole wing," she told him.

"How do I get into that thing when my legs don't work?" Miss Janie frowned at the two of them. "The doctor says my hip isn't broken, so I don't know why they won't work."

"Maybe they'll get well if you stay off them," Kayla said. "And we'll carry you to the chair like we did when we brought you out to the porch."

"Good thing I didn't eat two candy bars." Miss Janie giggled. "I'd be so fat you couldn't pick me up."

Teresa had to fight more tears. The poor old girl had lived with abuse like she and Kayla had, and she'd never talked about it.

"Did Aunt Ruthie ever punish you with a belt?" Teresa asked as she and Noah put Miss Janie into the wheelchair.

"Aunt Ruthie loved me." She lowered her chin and looked up at Teresa. "She said she never married because she wasn't going to have a man tell her what to do, and if she ever had a child, she'd never whip it with a belt."

Noah and Teresa locked eyes over the top of Miss Janie's head. Without saying a word, they both understood a little more of Miss Janie's struggles and how those had made her the woman she'd come to be.

They managed to get the chair through the front door, and Teresa wheeled her into her bedroom. The other two followed behind her. This was sure easier than trying to carry an elderly woman from the bed to the porch or to the living room several times a day.

When Teresa parked the chair beside the bed, Miss Janie held up her arms for Noah to lift her up and lay her down. "How'd you like that ride?" he asked.

"It don't go fast enough," she said. "Now, y'all get on out of here and let me go to sleep. The babies will wake up in a little while and need me."

"Time travel," Teresa whispered to Noah and Kayla.

"And some folks deny the possibility of such a thing." He laid a hand on Teresa's shoulder. "If y'all got this under control, I'm going to clean out my truck, then get a shower and do a load of laundry."

"We got it." Teresa was surprised that her voice went an octave higher than normal, but that her pulse raced from his touch—not so much. That happened every time Noah was even close to her. For several minutes after he'd gone, she could still feel the warmth of his hand on her shoulder. She hoped Kayla couldn't see her discomfiture.

Once Miss Janie was settled in and had closed her eyes, the women tiptoed out of the room and eased the door shut. Kayla led the way to the kitchen and poured two glasses of sweet tea and then set a platter of cookies on the table.

"How'd you feel about what Miss Janie told us about her dad's belt?" Kayla asked. "You ever experience that kind of thing?"

Teresa took a big gulp of her tea and then set it down. "Of course. Did you?"

"My stepdad loved to beat on me. I was the cause of everything that went wrong at our house, no matter what. Stuff that happened when I wasn't even there was my fault," Kayla admitted. "But I got to thinkin' while she was sayin' those things, if she could become the sweet lady who took us into her home after the treatment she got from her parents, then maybe there's a chance for me to be less bitter."

Teresa nodded at the thought. "My mother was draggin' men into the trailer all the time. Sometimes for a weekend, sometimes a month or two. They liked to knock me around like they were my daddy, or else try to feel me up like I was their girlfriend. I learned to sleep with one eye open." She stopped and took a long drink of her tea. "I've been thinkin' more about things this past week than I have in years. Old hurts and memories of the divorce that I thought I'd destroyed have surfaced. I guess it's coming back here that's brought them out again. I'm not sure there's enough time left in my life for me to ever be a sweet old lady."

Kayla narrowed her green eyes at Teresa but didn't say a word.

"Don't glare at me, woman," Teresa said. "I didn't say I couldn't change somewhat. I said I might never be a sweet old woman."

"That's better." Kayla pushed her chair back, rounded the table, and got out a quart of ice cream. "We never know what the future might hold. Ever see that really old movie called *Overboard*? Goldie Hawn found her family and wound up with a bunch of little boys before the end of it."

Teresa nodded. "What's that got to do with anything?"

"There are single men out there with families who might be the very person waiting to fall in love with you," Kayla answered as she opened the silverware drawer and took out two spoons.

Teresa was wondering if there really were any good men left in the world, and if there were, did she even want to be with one of them, when Noah walked into the room. He wore a pair of gray sweatpants, a snow-white T-shirt, and no shoes. He went to the coffeepot, and in minutes, the aroma filled the whole kitchen. While the coffee perked, he took the lasagna that was left over from supper the night before, cut off a slab, and stuck it in the microwave.

Watching him right then, living in the same house with him these past weeks—Noah was one of the few good men left in the world. Any man who would put his life on hold to come to a place like Birthright to take care of his ailing great-aunt had to be a good person. What would it be like to be in a serious relationship with him? Was he the single man Kayla just mentioned?

"Y'all can have that ice cream and cookies," he said. "I've lived on sandwiches and junk food since I left. I'm so glad to find some leftovers in the fridge."

"Good thing you got here when you did," Teresa said. "Anything Italian doesn't last long around here."

"Or Mexican," Kayla said. "Teresa made enchiladas yesterday. You should've been here then. I ate the last of it this morning for breakfast."

"Y'all are killin' me," he groaned. "Will you make more next week?"

"Yep, but you have to be here to get any of it," Teresa answered. "If you're off on one of your trips, then you'll lose out, again."

"Believe me, honey, I'll be here." The microwave dinged, and he took the lasagna to the table and sat down. "I'll have some of those cookies for dessert. As Miss Janie used to say, 'It don't get no better than this.' Y'all know something—I believe being around Miss Janie has healing powers."

Noah definitely seemed more relaxed and less tense than he had been before he left. What exactly had happened on that trip?

"That's what we were just talking about," Teresa said. There was that squeak in her voice again, but then, Noah's knee was right next to hers under the table.

"I've been wondering . . ." Kayla dipped deep into the ice cream. "Y'all don't laugh at me, but something I overheard Sam and Miss Janie talking about a couple of days ago has stuck in my mind. What would it take to start up a place here in Birthright for the senior citizens? You know, like they have in the big cities, only smaller—where old folks can gather up and play dominoes and have lunch together."

"To start with, you'd have to have a place," Noah answered.

"And money to get things going," Teresa added. "And I'm not laughing at you. If we had the money and a place, I'd do that in a heartbeat. I love working with old folks, and together we could do the cooking."

"I can't imagine you two working together every day," Noah said.

Kayla shook her spoon at him. "Miracles do happen."

Teresa slid a sideways glance over toward Noah and hoped that Kayla was right.

Chapter Ten

noah thought he could sleep for at least twenty-four hours when he went to bed at nine o'clock on Friday night. Things had been going so well, he'd been sleeping like a baby, but not last night. He awoke at five thirty the next morning. No matter how hard he tried, he couldn't force himself to get back to that dream he had been having. He and Teresa had been sitting at the kitchen table looking over a legal document that had to do with a business. At one time she'd leaned over and kissed him on the cheek. No matter how tightly he shut his eyes, he couldn't figure out what was on that piece of paper. He didn't care as much about that as he did going back into the dream to kiss her again.

Finally, he got out of bed, went downstairs, and put on the first pot of coffee for the day. As soon as it dripped, he poured a mugful and carried it to the back porch to watch the sunrise. Later, he would go into the small office he'd set up in his upstairs bedroom and begin to take care of all the legalese of starting a new business, but that could wait.

Teresa padded barefoot out to the porch with a cup of coffee in her hands. "Good mornin'. What are you doin' up so early? I figured you'd sleep until noon."

Her black hair looked like a messy haystack piled on top of her head. Her pajama pants and faded red T-shirt hung on her body.

To Noah, she'd never looked sexier.

His breath caught in his throat, making his voice come out a little hoarse when he said, "Guess my body got enough rest." He motioned toward the chair right beside him. "Have a seat and watch the sunrise with me."

When she sat down, he caught a whiff of coconut and vanilla mixed together and realized that her hair was still damp. A vision of her in the shower popped into his mind. He could imagine her light-brown skin, all slick with soap, and her head thrown back to show her long, graceful neck as she rinsed the shampoo from her hair. He blinked several times before the picture in his head disappeared.

"Do you always get up this early?" she asked.

"Usually not before daylight, but I am an early riser. Since I've been in Birthright, things have been a little crazy," he replied.

"I sure enough understand that," Teresa said. "Kayla and I have decided to take turns sleeping in the same room with Miss Janie. She tries to get up by herself at night to go to the bathroom. When she could walk, it wasn't a big deal, but now someone has to help her. That new bed we set up in there has been great, though. I stayed with her last night. Kayla is with her now. I never thought I'd say this or feel this way, but I'm glad Kayla is home."

"Don't know how I'd survive without y'all. No way would Miss Janie let me do personal things for her, and strangers terrify her nowadays." Noah would rather be talking about anything other than his great-aunt's privacy.

"We owe her that much and more. We made some very bad choices in life. That's on us, but she gave us a good home and did her best to steer us right," Teresa said.

"Are you talking about your marriage?" he asked.

"That and staying with him when I knew he wasn't faithful. Looking back now, I realize I figured all men were like him since that's what I'd grown up with." She shrugged. "Some of the men that *visited*"—she put the last word in air quotes—"our trailer were married. I even saw them dropping their kids off at school the morning after they'd stayed the night with my mama. When I finally realized that wasn't the way things should be"—she paused long enough to take a sip of her coffee— "I told Luis to go live with his latest fling."

"What brought you to that conclusion?" he asked.

"There was this old couple in the nursing home who'd been married more than sixty years. They had so much love and respect for each other that I asked them to tell me their story. They even had a king-sized bed in their room instead of two twins because neither of them could sleep without the other. They'd had struggles in their life, but they'd always had enough love for one another to get them through the tough times. I'm talking raising three kids and living on a shoestring part of the time—without any cheating or abuse. That's when I decided if I couldn't have what they'd had, I'd do without," she answered.

Noah hadn't seen that kind of love in his grandparents or his parents. Sure, they'd stuck together until "death parted them" like they'd promised in their marriage vows, but it hadn't always been with love and respect. Knowing Miss Janie like he did now, he could understand her whole family so much better. It had all stemmed from her father and mother being so religious that their son rebelled and joined the army. Then his son followed in his footsteps, which meant that Noah was supposed to do the same. In his own way, he had rebelled by not serving his country. Maybe that's why, even with his law degree and PI license, he couldn't find his place in the world. He put all that on a back burner to think about later and returned his attention to Teresa.

"So how did Luis react when it was over? Did both of you cry, or were you angry?"

"He was relieved and told me if he could stay in the house we were renting and keep the furniture, he would give me a couple thousand bucks to find a new place. I was glad to let him have the place. I rented an apartment, and for the past year, I haven't had to come home to clean up full ashtrays and empty beer bottles."

"Did your mama drink a lot?" he asked. "You don't have to answer that. I don't mean to pry."

"Yes, she drank a lot. Cheap men bought her cheap wine or whiskey or tequila. Those with more money bought her better wine, good whiskey, and top-shelf tequila. She seldom bought it for herself because she didn't have the money to do so, unless she caught me doing something, punished me, and made me pay her whatever I was earning at the time to show me the 'responsibilities' of life."

"How about you?" Noah asked. "Did you drink?"

"Nope"—she shook her head—"never even been drunk. I had the occasional beer at Luis's family reunion, or a margarita on New Year's, but I've always been determined not to be like my mama. How about you?"

Teresa waited several minutes for him to answer. Maybe he was tired of all this heavy talk and she should steer the conversation toward the beautiful sunrise coming up over to their left. Trees that had been nothing but dark blobs had begun to have details like limbs and leaves. The sky turned shades of pink, orange, and lavender against a backdrop of blue sky with big fluffy white clouds drifting back and forth as the wind carried them.

She wished she could take the question back when his expression went blank. He'd gone into a dark place, and she had caused it. "I'm sorry. That was me prying. Let's talk about something else."

Finally, he cleared his throat and said, "I'm a recovering alcoholic."

That shocked her speechless for a full minute.

"How long have you been sober?" she asked.

"More than six years," he answered without looking at her.

She had vowed to never, ever get involved with a drinking man again, but more than five years sober was a good testimony.

"As you pointed out—we've all brought baggage back to Birthright with us." She shrugged.

He jerked his head around, and their eyes locked. "You aren't going to pry like I did?"

"Nope," she answered. "If you want to talk, you will. If you don't, then it's not my place to force it out of you. Since I got back here, I've talked to Kayla, and it's helped me a lot to know I wasn't the only one with a horrible past."

"Have you told her everything?" he asked.

"Some things are so painful that it's hard to talk about them." She finished off her coffee and set the mug on the wide arm of the chair. "Maybe someday she and I will trust each other to tell it all, but not yet."

"Do you know the difference between an alcoholic and a plain old drunk?" He reached across the narrow distance and laid a hand on hers.

"Yes, I do." She smiled. "Mama said it often enough that it's burned into my brain."

"Drunks don't have to go to those damned old meetings," they said in unison.

He removed his hand and took a sip of his coffee. "I take it that your mother never went to the meetings?"

"Not while I was living with her." Teresa wished that he hadn't taken his hand away. She liked the way it made her feel all warm and fuzzy inside. "I hope that wherever she is now, she's realized she has lots of problems and has done something about them. That is, if she's still alive. With her lifestyle, she could be dead."

That word—*dead*—sounded harsh in Teresa's ears, and yet it was the truth. Suddenly, she felt guilty because she'd never tried to contact her mother after she'd disappeared from Sulphur Springs. If as an adult, she'd found her, was it possible that Teresa could have helped her turn her life around?

"Your mother was in California working in a bar a few months ago. I don't know where she is now, but . . . ," he said. "But I did find her if you ever want to reach out."

"Thank you, but I don't think I'm ready to open up that can of worms. I do think it's ironic that Kayla's mother and stepdad went there, too." Teresa grinned. "Makes me wonder how many deadbeat parents head west. We were talking about you, though."

"I have a sponsor in Houston that I still check in with every week, and there's a meeting in Sulphur Springs I attend a couple of times a month," he said.

"Why haven't you gone to your meetings more often?" she asked.

"Couldn't leave Miss Janie," he answered. "Sam came over every week and sat with her for a couple of hours for me to go to the grocery store, but I couldn't ask him to do more than that. I might start going to one a week since y'all are here."

They watched the sun rise over the horizon. Then it became a round orange ball sitting on the top of the tall trees. For the first time since she could remember, contentment twined its way into Teresa's heart and soul—she was home right here in this tiny little Texas town with a population of forty.

"You know, Miss Janie's daddy, Arnold Jackson, was also a preacher," Noah said. "One of them hellfire and brimstone kind that preached against liquor of any kind, women working outside the home, and for the man being the absolute boss. As often is the case, my grandpa, Miss Janie's brother, Luther, rebelled. He joined the army right out of high school, wound up getting his girlfriend pregnant, and married her. She was a career woman who never missed a day of work except for the few weeks she took off to have my father. Grandpa loved his whiskey. He told me once that Great-Gramps Arnold threatened to disown him, like he'd disowned Miss Janie, if he didn't stop drinking."

So, Noah's grandmother had been a nurse? That was interesting, Teresa thought.

"So, her brother knew about the babies?" Teresa asked.

"No one talked about it, but he had to have known since they banished her to Birthright and seldom even came to see her," Noah answered.

"What happened to Luther?" Teresa asked.

"Grandpa died of cirrhosis of the liver," Noah said. "He always had liquor in the house. According to what my dad told me, he grew up thinking that everyone had a few drinks before dinner each night. My dad followed in Grandpa's footsteps and joined the military. The same disease that got Gramps killed him, and Granny died soon after from a heart attack. I grew up an army brat and Daddy used to bring me here when we had time between moves to visit Miss Janie since she was the only relative we had left."

"Bet that was tough since Miss Janie didn't drink," Teresa said.

Noah chuckled. "An alcoholic is challenged but never defeated. Daddy brought it inside a second suitcase. I snuck my first drink of bourbon when I was thirteen. By the time I went to college, I was drinking every day."

She could have gone to parties and drank every day in college, too, but she'd wanted to study hard and make something of herself.

Don't get too self-righteous, the voice in her head scolded. *After you met Luis, your grades fell and you didn't even finish the first semester.*

"How did you ever pass your classes?"

"Drinking was a big part of me—I don't know." He raised both shoulders in a shrug. "But I had good grades, got into law school, and passed the bar exam. My dad wasn't real happy with me, since I was supposed to be a third-generation soldier, but at least I wasn't a preacher. I like to think that brought him a little comfort."

"What changed all that?" She leaned in closer to him.

"I hit bottom," he answered.

Kayla stuck her head out the door. "Good mornin'. Miss Janie had a good night and is still sleeping, so I had a great night. I went ahead and made breakfast. Waffles and sausage will be ready in ten minutes."

Teresa jerked upright with a surge of the fight-or-flight adrenaline rush. She'd been so engrossed in what Noah was telling her that Kayla scared the bejesus out of her. When she caught her breath, she asked, "Need some help with breakfast?"

"I never turn down help. You can fry the sausage," Kayla answered.

"To be continued?" Noah asked.

"Our hour of therapy is up, but we can always book another time," she teased, and wished that they really had more time.

"Sunrise tomorrow?" he asked.

"Depends on whether Miss Janie has a good night or a bad one." She headed into the house.

"What was that all about?" Kayla whispered. "Seemed pretty intense out there, and you were talking therapy? Do you and Noah have something going?"

"We were just teasing." Teresa wasn't ready to share. "He got up early and made coffee. I couldn't sleep, so we were watching the sunrise."

"Nothing as romantic as watchin' a sunrise together, is there?" Kayla's green eyes twinkled.

"Nope," Teresa answered honestly. There wasn't a thing romantic about alcoholism. She could preach sermons about the effect it had on the children of drunk parents.

"So . . . changing the subject, since you evidently don't want to tell me what y'all were talkin' about," Kayla said, "have you thought about the idea of a senior citizens place?"

"That's the reason I couldn't go back to sleep this morning," Teresa answered. "I doubt that Miss Janie is going to leave us enough to start up something like that, but it would sure be a dream come true. I've loved working with elderly folks, and Sam was right when he said this community could use a place like that. It's hard to be housebound in Texas."

Something had been going on out there on the porch. Kayla would bet every freckle on it. The air was almost too heavy to even get a breath when she'd stuck her head out the door. Both Noah and Teresa had looked like they'd gotten news that someone had died. Teresa might be telling her the truth about it not being romantic that time, but Kayla had seen and felt the sparks between them in other situations. Still, she wondered what they'd been talking about. If Teresa needed time to think about whatever they were discussing, she would give her the room to do just that—and then she'd get the whole story out of her.

They put breakfast on the table without any more conversation, right up until Miss Janie yelled out for the nurse. Teresa started in that direction, with Kayla right behind her. Then she heard the back door close, and Noah joined them in the bedroom.

"I need to go to the bathroom, and I'm hungry," Miss Janie said. "Are you the doctor, young man?"

"I'm Noah," he said.

"Well, I don't care if you built the ark or not," Miss Janie said. "You need to get out of here so I can go to the bathroom."

"Yes, ma'am," he chuckled, and left the room.

Kayla was better at getting her out of bed, and in a few seconds she had her turned around and sitting on the potty. While she did that, Teresa straightened the sheets, folded the throw that Miss Janie was partial to, and got everything squared away.

"When I'm done, I want to go to the kitchen in my new chair. Eating in bed don't seem right. Mama never allowed such things, not even when I was sick. She said the table was made for meals." Miss Janie was careful to keep her gown pulled down to cover her knees.

"Your mama's not here, so we can do whatever we want," Kayla told her.

"I'm all done." Miss Janie reached for the toilet paper on a nearby table.

"How old are you today?" Teresa asked as she handed her a wet washcloth for her face and hands when she'd finished.

She drew her eyes down as if she was trying to remember, and then she smiled. "I was seventy-five on my last birthday. I'm glad you girls came home to help Noah with me. I've got cancer, you know, and he can't take care of me proper-like—not like you girls can. How long can you stay? Do you have jobs that you need to get back to? Lordy, Lordy, it's been years since I laid eyes on y'all."

Kayla could hardly believe her ears. Miss Janie was lucid! "We're glad to be here. You took care of us when we needed it, and we want to be here with you."

Hearing Miss Janie say "Lordy, Lordy" brought back good memories.

"We can stay as long as you need us." Teresa brushed Miss Janie's wispy hair and added a little hair spray.

Kayla helped move her over to the wheelchair and tucked a throw around her legs. "And I'm here for as long as you need me."

Miss Janie sighed and smiled. "We can catch up on everything at breakfast. Teresa, you can push me into the kitchen. Do I smell sausage? I love waffles and sausage."

"That's exactly what I made this morning," Kayla said. "And Teresa is making beans and ham and fried potatoes for dinner. She's going to fry up some okra, slice some tomatoes, and make some corn bread, too. I remember that's one of your favorite meals."

"I had a horrible time getting you to eat when you came to live with me. You wouldn't try anything new, and you hated it when it was Teresa's turn to choose what we had for supper."

"I hadn't had much variety until I came here," Kayla said, "but I've learned to eat more in these past years. How about a cup of coffee while I make your waffles?"

"Great." Miss Janie smiled again, lighting up her eyes. "Well, good mornin', Noah," she said when she saw him sitting at the table. "Were you glad to see the girls come home?"

"Yes, ma'am." Pure shock registered in his expression. "Did you get a good night's sleep?"

"Yes, I did. I guess the cancer is keeping me from walking, right?" she asked.

Teresa pushed her up to the table and sat down to her left. "That's what the doctor says."

"At least I didn't drink myself to death like Luther did. Do any of y'all say grace?" she asked.

"We did when we lived with you." Kayla was still amazed that Miss Janie was in her right mind.

"That's right." Miss Janie nodded. "I thought it would be good training for you. Noah, you can say it this morning."

They all bowed their heads and Noah said a simple prayer. Kayla was afraid that in that length of time, Miss Janie's mind would slip back to another time in her life. When he said, "Amen," she looked across the table to see that Miss Janie had snatched a piece of sausage from the platter and was biting into it.

"Mama would have slapped me for this, but I'm dying, so I can do what I want," she told them. "A good daughter never ate with her fingers, and they did not sneak anything until the husband was served. I'm so glad I never got me one of those husband critters. No offense, Noah."

"None taken," he said. "Did you and Luther get along?"

"I idolized him," she answered as she poured syrup on her waffles. "I didn't even fault him too much for having a drink or two. Daddy was so against drinking, but then he was the head of the almighty household. That's kind of funny, really. He put out that myth with his long Sunday-morning sermons, but it was Mama who really ran things. She's the one that made the decision to send me away and who wouldn't even let me come back home. Aunt Ruthie told me that Daddy wanted to send me right here to Birthright to stay with her and let me make up my own mind about the babies. But Mama said no, and that was that."

Everyone at the table waited for her to go on. No way would any of the three of them break this magic moment. "She hated Aunt Ruthie, so she thought it would punish me for my great sin to send me to live with her. When I was a little girl, Aunt Ruthie kind of scared me. She looked like one of those spider monkeys from the zoo—a skinny woman with a thin face and beady little eyes that could look right into a person's soul and read their thoughts. She came and got me at the home for unwed mothers. She talked to me all the way back, and by the time we got here, I found out I'd misjudged Aunt Ruthie. She was old, maybe fifty." She laughed out loud. "That's old to a sixteen-year-old girl who's scared out of her wits. Aunt Ruthie was Daddy's aunt, but she was the oldest and Daddy was the youngest of ten kids."

She stopped long enough to eat a few bites, and Kayla thought that any moment now, they'd lose her, but then she went on. "Aunt Ruthie was one of those free-thinking women. She inherited this place from her mama when she died, because she'd stayed around and taken care of her. My mother wanted this place sold and divided among all the children instead of Aunt Ruthie inheriting everything, but she had taken care of her mama, so, in my opinion, it should've been hers. I guess they'll all work that out in heaven—if they get there." She giggled.

"What's so funny?" Kayla asked.

"I'm not so sure about Aunt Ruthie getting to heaven. She told me some stories on her deathbed that made even me blush, and I thought I was pretty worldly by then," Miss Janie said.

"Were you mad at Luther when he drank himself to death?" Noah asked.

"Yes, I was," she said.

Kayla noticed that the light was leaving her eyes, so she hurriedly asked, "Why did you decide to be a foster mother to me and Teresa?"

"You needed a home. I had a big house. I was lonely"—she hesitated—"and you both had brown skin like the babies I gave away. I was looking for redemption."

"Did you find it?" Kayla asked.

"Yes, darlin', I did. I love you both, and I think I found a measure of peace in getting to raise y'all for a few years." Miss Janie smiled.

"Did you never fall in love?" Teresa asked.

Miss Janie shook her head slowly. "There was a teacher"—she paused—"and we . . ." The light was fading fast. "I'd like some cookies and milk now."

Kayla wanted to know more about the teacher. Had they had a relationship? Was he her age? Why didn't they commit to each other?

"How old are you?" Teresa asked.

"I'm seventeen, and I'll be a senior next year at the Sulphur Springs High School. Are you friends of Aunt Ruthie's?" She pursed her lips.

Kayla realized more in that brief moment than ever before how miserable it must be to constantly move from time to time. Two minutes ago, she'd been seventy-five, and now she was seventeen.

"What are you studying?" Noah asked.

"Home economics is my favorite class. I'm hoping that when I graduate, I'll get a job with Aunt Ruthie in the lunchroom at the school," she said with pride.

"Would you like to go to college?" Noah asked.

"Of course I would, but that costs a lot of money, and Daddy says that girls don't need to go to college. He says that they don't need an education to rock a cradle or cook a fine supper." She leaned forward and lowered her voice. "Don't tell Aunt Ruthie, but I'd like to design clothes for rich people, but folks from Birthright don't do those kinds of things."

"I liked home economics because I love to cook." Kayla hoped that by mentioning that she liked the class, maybe Miss Janie would remember back when Kayla took it at school.

"That's nice," Miss Janie said. "Would you get me some cookies and milk and push me out to the back porch? I'd like a little fresh air now. Tell Aunt Ruthie to come join me."

"Yes, ma'am." Kayla got up and pushed the wheelchair outside. "Is this spot all right?" she asked.

"No. I like it over there by that little table, so I have a place to put my milk," Miss Janie answered.

Kayla rolled her to the right spot and sat down beside her. "It's going to be a pretty day. Do you remember the first day you were here?"

"Of course," Miss Janie said. "Aunt Ruthie made a pot roast and hot yeast rolls. She thought Daddy and Mama might come to see me after all, but they didn't. They were packing to move to Mexico and be missionaries for five years." She picked up her milk and drank all of it.

"Think you'll ever see them again?" Kayla asked.

"Right now I don't care if I do or don't. I feel like I've been abandoned," she whispered. "Aunt Ruthie says that she's glad they didn't come to dinner and that she's really mad at her niece for the way she's treated me. You should go on inside and help Aunt Ruthie with the dishes now."

"I sure will. You holler when you want to come back in, and one of us will come out and get you," Kayla said.

"I can roll myself." Miss Janie almost snorted. "I'm not a baby."

"I bet you can," Kayla agreed.

When she got back to the kitchen, the table had been cleared and she was alone. She leaned against the sink and thanked God that Miss Janie had seen something in her to warrant taking her in when not even her own mother wanted her.

Chapter Eleven

*T*eresa took a deep breath and let it out slowly when she found her pink diary still hidden away in her desk drawer. The little book had never left the desk except for one time when she was a freshman in high school. She had taken it to school because after Miss Janie had given it to her, Teresa had vowed that she would write in it every single night, and she'd forgotten to put anything down the night before. She'd had some free time after the English test that morning, so she had taken out the diary and written that she wanted to be a nurse after she finished high school. She had sat beside Prissy Wilson in that class, and the girl had jerked it out of her hands and read what she had written.

"Are you crazy?" Prissy had said, loud enough for everyone around her to hear. "Someone like you could never be a nurse. That takes college, and you're a foster kid." She had flipped her long blonde hair over her shoulder, and her clique of popular girls had added their own little snickers.

Thinking about the humiliation of that day, Teresa wished now she'd asked her to explain that comment. Did *someone like her* never have a chance at an education like Prissy Wilson had?

She tucked the diary back into the drawer, went down to check on Miss Janie, and found Sam and Kayla sitting beside Miss Janie's bed.

"Good mornin'," Sam said. "I stopped by and Kayla treated me to leftover breakfast. I'm goin' to weigh two hunnerd pounds if you girls don't stop feedin' me. If I wasn't so damned old and if I hadn't promised Delia there'd never be another woman in my life, I'd ask Kayla to marry me."

"Why Kayla and not me?" Teresa asked.

"I got my reasons, but they don't matter none, since y'all are both too young for this old rooster. Kayla, are you goin' to your class reunion?" Sam asked.

"I always go to the alumni dinner," Miss Janie said. "But since my hip is hurting, I guess I won't go this year."

Teresa patted her arm. "Maybe next year you'll be all healed and you can go then. This year we'll send Kayla to it, and she can tell everyone that you said hello."

Kayla shook her finger at both of them. "No, thank you. I didn't fit in with that bunch of kids when I was in school, and I'm not going to go and let them put me down again."

Miss Janie's chin began to quiver. "You have to go or else no one will be there to tell them hello for me."

Kayla cut her eyes toward Teresa. "Look what you caused."

"I always go to the reunion, and the kids miss me if I don't." Tears welled up in Miss Janie's eyes. "I'm glad I broke my legs in the summer, so I don't miss the first day of school."

Teresa wondered how many of the thousands who'd passed through the high school would remember the school secretary or even come to the funeral when she passed away.

"It'll be good for you to go to the reunion," Sam said. "Ten years changes a lot of people. Going might make you feel better about them, and about yourself. Besides, you need to bring home stories to tell Miss Janie."

"All right then, I'll go," Kayla agreed.

"You will come back, won't you? You promised you'd stay with me." Miss Janie's expression had gone from happy to weepy to frantic in a matter of minutes. No wonder she needed so many naps—that had to be exhausting.

"I'm not going anywhere today. We were talking about my class reunion. I'll go, but I'll only be gone for an hour or two." Kayla reached through the hospital rails and held Miss Janie's hand.

Teresa could loan Kayla a dress. She had a cute little sundress that she'd gotten at a thrift shop before the divorce last year, but she'd never had a chance to wear it herself. She grimaced at the idea of her foster sister getting to wear one of her few pretty things before she did.

Do it for Miss Janie's sake, the voice in her head said loud and clear.

But I never got to wear it, Teresa argued. *And she's only been nice a few times in her life, so why should I let her have my best summer dress?*

"We could go shopping for a dress. There's a couple of thrift shops in Sulphur Springs." Teresa was willing to compromise that much.

Kayla shook her head. "Hell no! What if I bought something that had belonged to one of the girls I graduated with? That would only give them more ammunition to throw at me."

"I'll loan you a pair of my overalls," Sam chuckled. "You can fancy them up with fake diamonds on the pockets. Girl, you need to get comfortable in your skin and not give a damn what folks think. Prove 'em wrong by showin' 'em who you are at heart."

"Where's Noah?" Miss Janie asked.

"Right here." Noah came into the room and stood behind Sam's chair.

"I want you to take Kayla shopping for a new dress for the reunion," Miss Janie said. "I will pay for whatever she needs."

"Yes, ma'am," Noah said.

Everyone's willingness to help—especially Sam's words—pierced Teresa's heart like a sharp dart. "I have a dress she can have. It will look better on her than it does on me, anyway."

"Why's that?" Noah asked.

"Why is what?" Teresa answered with a question.

"Why would it look better on her?" Noah asked.

"Because it's green. I was always a little jealous of her eyes. Mine are plain old dull brown." Admitting that she liked anything about her foster sister, even now that they were grown women, wasn't easy.

"You were jealous of me?" Kayla's eyes popped open as round as pancakes. "I was always envious of you for your good hair and gorgeous complexion. I always felt like a misfit with freckles."

"You fit here." Miss Janie turned away from the television. "Both of my babies grew up to be lovely women. You got your daddy's skin and my freckles. Your eyes are the same color as Aunt Ruthie's, and she had curly hair. I wish I could have kept you and watched you grow up."

Kayla squeezed her hand. "You used to tell us that everything happens for a reason."

"I did?" Miss Janie frowned. "I don't remember too well some days. What were we talking about? Have the babies been good?"

"Yes, they've been really good all day, and they slept through the night," Teresa answered.

"I'm so glad." Miss Janie smiled. "We were talking about dresses, weren't we?"

"Yes, we were," Kayla answered. "Thank you, Teresa, for the offer of your dress. I would definitely like to try it on."

"Bet that hurt." Teresa grinned.

"Why would you say that?" Sam asked.

"She's never thanked me for anything in her life," Teresa answered.

"Never needed to." Kayla let go of Miss Janie's hand and stood up. "But if I borrow your dress, I can always back out of going. If money was spent on one, I'd feel obligated to go. One question, though? Are you going to be mad at me if I get blood on it?"

"Why would you get blood on it?" Noah asked.

"The juniors and seniors had art class together, and Prissy Wilson was downright mean to me," Kayla explained. "I'm not takin' bull crap off her. If she says an ugly word to me, I intend to use her blonde hair to mop up the floor."

"That's my girl." Miss Janie clapped her hands. "Prissy always was a bitch."

"Miss Janie, I can't believe you said that," Teresa gasped.

Miss Janie crossed her arms over her chest. "Truth is truth. Prissy was a smart-ass little girl, and she grew into a first-rate bitch who controlled her friends. I never did like that kid. If her mama left *her* in a ditch, I wouldn't have taken her in. Bullying other kids made her the queen of Sulphur Springs. Well, mark my words: her comeuppance will arrive one of these days, and it ain't goin' to be pretty."

Teresa hadn't realized that Prissy had been mean to Kayla. She had thought she was the only one that Prissy and her posse picked on. She had thought of dozens of questions she'd written down that she wanted to put to Miss Janie if and when she was lucid, but she was so shocked she couldn't think of a single one after what Miss Janie had said.

"I read in the newspaper that she's the president of the alumni association," Sam said. "I sure wish I was a fly on the wall to see Kayla put her in her place."

Kayla started toward the door and then turned back. "Noah, do you want to be my plus-one?"

"Nope, but if you need someone to bail you out of jail, just call me." He grinned.

Teresa didn't even realize she was holding her breath until Noah turned down the invitation. Lord, what a mess it could turn out to be if Kayla liked Noah. Teresa had just begun to get along with her foster sister, and they were dreaming about starting a little business together. Both of them liking the same guy could be catastrophic.

Noah turned his attention to Miss Janie. "I thought you might like to go sit on the porch and get some fresh air this morning. The girls will get you in your wheelchair. We can have a cup of coffee and have a visit."

"I'd love that. Teresa, you can get me up. Sam, you and Noah go wait on the porch," she said.

"Yes, ma'am." Sam pushed up out of the chair with a groan. "These old bones are about worn out."

"Mine, too, but they were good to us for a lot of years," Miss Janie agreed.

Teresa had no problem getting her into the wheelchair, but when she started to push her down the hall toward the porch, Miss Janie held up a hand.

"Stop right here for a minute," she said. "Feel that breeze? They don't build houses like this no more."

"No, they don't." Teresa didn't have the heart to tell Miss Janie that cool air from the air-conditioning vent right above her was causing the breeze. There was no way any kind of wind could find its way through two glass storm doors.

"When I'm gone, I want y'all to promise me that you'll convince Kayla to stay here awhile. She's not as grounded as you are," Miss Janie whispered. "She needs family."

"Of course we will," Teresa agreed. If Miss Janie asked her to gather up the stars into a big basket, Teresa would give it her best shot.

"You three were like my own children. Noah, because this was the only stable place he knew, what with his family being transferred from here to Kalamazoo every couple of years. And you girls, y'all were my redemption. Kayla just hasn't gotten roots yet like y'all have. Now, let's go to the back porch," Miss Janie said.

Teresa wasn't sure just how deep her roots went, but she would do what she could, especially for one of Miss Janie's lucid moments. Besides, neither of them would ever realize their dream of a senior citizens place if the other one left Birthright. "I promise, but you aren't leaving us anytime soon."

"I ask for forgiveness for all my sins every time I close my eyes, just in case." Miss Janie smiled. "We hear in church that God is merciful, so maybe He will let me into heaven. I hope so, because I sure want to see Aunt Ruthie again."

"Who else do you want to see in heaven?" Teresa asked.

"If I get there, I want to see my girls," she answered, "and ask them to forgive me for giving them away. But I hope they put my mama and daddy in a different section than me."

Teresa had not given much thought to eternity or who might be in heaven, but she understood Miss Janie's statement very well. If her mother, Angel, made it to heaven, Teresa wouldn't want to be in the same area as she was, either.

When they reached the porch, Miss Janie took one look at Sam and began to cry. "Oh, Sam, I miss Delia so much. Her funeral today was beautiful. We did good picking out that pink casket for her. She always loved pink so much."

Sam patted her hand. "Yes, she did. We'll both miss her."

Teresa noticed that Sam's Adam's apple bobbed several times after he answered Miss Janie. She hadn't thought about how hard it must be on Sam to see his dear old friend like this, or to have such memories of Delia brought up so often. When Miss Janie said something like that about the casket, it had to cause him pain.

Kayla brought out a tray with cups and the full coffeepot on it, poured for all four of them, and then sat down on the swing beside Miss Janie. "I stirred the beans while I was in the kitchen."

"Appreciate that." Teresa nodded.

A lovely breeze stirred the leaves of the pecan tree beside the house and brought the aroma of roses and honeysuckle with it across the porch.

"This was always my favorite place the five years I was here. I'd bring a book and a blanket out here in the winter and read for hours." Teresa inhaled deeply. "Every time I caught a whiff of roses after I left, it reminded me of this spot right here." She didn't say that she often remembered stolen kisses when she smelled the roses and honeysuckle.

"Honeysuckle does the same for me," Noah said. "When I was a little boy, I begged my parents to let me sleep out here, but they never would. A couple of times since I've been back, I have, though."

"Was it as much fun as you thought it would be?" she asked.

"Nope," he chuckled. "Even with a blow-up mattress and my own pillow, I figured out that I like central air-conditioning too much for this."

"Guess we outgrow our childhood fantasies, don't we?" She took a sip of her coffee.

"Yep, we sure do," Kayla agreed.

Miss Janie took two sips of her coffee and nodded off. Yet when a buzzard screeched overhead, she jerked her head up. "I'm ready to go take a nap now. Mama says that sleeping in the day is bad, but me and Aunt Ruthie like our little naps."

Teresa rolled her back through the kitchen and into her bedroom. Before she helped her out of the wheelchair, she fluffed up her pillow and made sure the sheets were smoothed, falling into the regular rhythm of the nursing home. She wondered how her former patients were doing and if any of them had passed on since she left.

"You're a good nurse," Miss Janie bragged on her.

"Thank you, ma'am." Teresa would far rather have been told that she was a good daughter than a good nurse, but that wouldn't be the truth.

When she went back through the kitchen, she checked on the pot of beans and ham cooking on the top of the stove and the enchilada casserole that was ready for the oven. The clock said it was still two hours until noon, so she put half a dozen cookies on a plate and carried them out to the porch.

"Thought y'all might want a little something to go with your coffee. Where's Sam? He was here a few minutes ago."

"He went home, but said he'd be back after a while for some of those beans," Noah answered as he picked up a cookie from the plate and dipped the edge in his coffee. "We were talking about the future. What do you plan to do after . . . ?" He stammered over the words. "After Miss Janie isn't with us anymore? Do you and Kayla really think you might put in a place for the old folks to go have lunch and play games?"

"That's just a pipe dream. We'd need money for something like that. I haven't made any plans," she said.

"I'll try to find some houses to clean. I bet I can make a living just working for the folks from here to Sulphur Springs. To give the community a place is a pipe dream, like Teresa said, but maybe if we work hard and save our money, we can do that sometime in the future," Kayla added.

"Would it make a difference to either of you if you started drawing a monthly check from the trust fund that Miss Janie set up for both of you?" he asked. "Maybe later this week, we'll ask Sam to come over for a little while, and we'll all three go to the bank and get y'all set up. What we need in this area is someone to do elderly babysitting, or like Kayla said, clean houses, or maybe even start a little business if there was a building available. In the big cities you can find folks who can do that, but—"

"Trust fund?" Teresa butted in.

"When Miss Janie's folks died, the money they had went to her and my granddad. Aunt Ruthie owned the oil rights to most of the county, so she had a healthy income from that. From what I can see, Miss Janie never touched that money and lived on what she made working at the school. Long story short is that the three of us—you, me, and Kayla—are inheriting a lot, but in trust. We'll get a certain amount each month, but we won't be able to touch the principal. She wanted to be certain that we wouldn't get old and have nothing—Miss Janie's words, not mine," he explained. "You don't have to get a job. You can pretty much do whatever you want. Go back to school to get your degree or even take a year or two to decide." He paused. "Or start that business y'all have been talking about. Give it all some serious thought, though. Don't jump into something and then decide you don't want to do it. That would break Sam's and all the rest of the folks' hearts."

"Are you serious?" Kayla gasped. "I thought the inheritance was getting to be here with her a few months or weeks."

"I'm very serious. Of course, until she's gone, you will earn a pay-check each week like I promised," he told them.

Teresa could hardly take in what he'd said. Part of her was happy; the other was angry. "We don't deserve this, Noah."

"Doesn't matter if any of us deserves it. It's what she wants done, and truth be told, I think she'd like for you to work together and give back to the community," Noah answered.

Teresa began to pace up and down the screened-in porch. "That's a small price to pay for not coming back to see her, and it's something we'd both enjoy, so we wouldn't get any stars in our crowns for doing it."

"We all have to shoulder that load about not coming around often enough. I didn't do my duty there, either, but we're here now, and she needs us more right now than she ever did before," Noah said. He sure couldn't throw stones—not with his past. "Give it some thought," he continued. "According to her will, this house is mine, but it's never to be sold because she wants you girls to always have a home to come back to. You've got time to talk about your idea and figure things out—at least I hope you do." He picked up another cookie and went back inside the house. He opened Miss Janie's door just a crack and found her wide awake, sitting up in the bed and staring out the window. He pulled the rocking chair over closer to her and sat down.

"Did you have a good nap?" he asked.

"No. I only slept a few minutes, and I dreamed that y'all were at my funeral. I feel like I'm dying a little more every day. I stay in a state of confusion. Noah, I don't have much time left," she sighed. "Pretty soon my mind is going to be gone completely, and I'll always live somewhere in the past."

"Something you want me to do?" he asked.

"No. Everything has been signed over to you, and I've told you how I want things done. You can make the decisions. While I'm clear, though, I want to say thank you again," she said. "I know this isn't easy for any of you, but I want to die at home."

"And you will," he said.

"I think that dream was an omen for me to talk to you about my funeral. I want it to be graveside only, with only close friends and family. Did I already tell you that?"

He took her frail hand in his. "No, ma'am, but if that's what you want, I'll take care of it."

"I don't want a preacher to go on and on. I want each of you kids to have a little word. No church songs, but you can play that song 'Angel.' It tells my story in music. I wasn't in a dark hotel room, but I was in a stark maternity ward, and when it was time for me to give birth, no one was there with me. The song talks of glorious sadness. That's the way I felt when they took my precious babies away from me, and the way I feel now about leaving y'all."

Noah had cried several times since the morning that he'd hit rock bottom and staggered into his first AA meeting, but the hot tears that rolled down his unshaven cheeks that morning had come straight from his soul. "I'll write it all down so I don't forget anything. You want to talk to the girls while you're . . . ?" He paused. "Well, you know."

She began to hum the tune to the song she'd mentioned. "I spent years and years waiting for a second chance, like the song says, and God gave it to me with Kayla and Teresa. I should've insisted that they stay with me, but what was there for them in an old ghost town with a few scattered houses? Lord, I missed them. Now, get on out of here. I want to be alone and think about how lucky I am while I've got my right mind. Please know that I love you, Kayla, and Teresa like you were my own."

"I love you, too," Noah whispered as he left her side.

He went straight to his office, found the song on his phone, and cried through all three times he listened to it. He'd thought *he'd* had a rough path to walk, but it was nothing compared to what she'd endured.

He wondered how things would have been different if Miss Janie had been born twenty or thirty years later. Would she have kept her twins, or would she have realized that at sixteen, she'd have a tough time raising them as a single mother?

"Whatever, it would have been her choice," he said out loud.

Give back to the community to honor her kept running through his mind.

His phone rang and startled him. "Hi, Daniel," he answered. "What's going on?"

"I was checkin' in to see if you changed your mind," Daniel said. "We've got a case in your neighborhood that we could use some help with. It's not a tough one. Client says his wife is cheating on him. If you could do one last case for us, I'd appreciate it so much. I'll send you her picture and the file."

"Promise you won't ask me again?" he said.

"Cross my heart," Daniel said.

"Okay, then, shoot me the stuff," Noah said. "I'll probably have it wrapped up in a week."

"Comin' your way as we speak," Daniel said. "And thank you. Send me the bill when you're done."

"You know I will," he said, glad for work that would take his mind off Miss Janie's mind getting worse and worse.

The picture of a pretty blonde-haired woman came up on his computer almost instantly, and then an attached file with all the information

Daniel had on her. Priscilla Wilson Carlton was probably at the top of Santa's naughty list from what he read even in the preliminary report. His brow wrinkled as he tried to remember where he'd heard that name.

"No!" he gasped when he finally remembered. Prissy Wilson was the girl who'd given Teresa and Kayla fits in high school. It had to be the same woman. Born in Sulphur Springs in 1992. Married five years ago, and from the copy of the newspaper article, it had been the wedding of the county that year.

He was bound by confidentiality not to say a word about this to Teresa, but that didn't mean he wouldn't enjoy the case more than any other one he'd ever had. He rubbed his hands together and began to make phone calls.

Chapter Twelve

One day blended into another, and Teresa could hardly believe that she'd been in Birthright almost three weeks. She stopped ironing Miss Janie's little floral dusters long enough to snap her fingers. "Just like that, time has flown by. I'm not ready for Miss Janie to be gone," she muttered.

"Hey, would you mind if I bring my shirt in here and iron it?" Noah interrupted her thoughts.

She whipped around, iron in hand like a weapon, to find him standing in the open doorway. "What did you say?"

"I wondered if it would be all right for me to iron my shirt in here," he answered. "It would save me having to tote that board and the iron into my room. I've got to do some research this afternoon, but I'll be back home by bedtime. That looks like a lethal weapon there with steam coming out of it."

"Sorry." She set the iron back in the holder. "I'll take care of your shirt. Bring it on in."

"For real? That's so sweet." He disappeared and returned a few minutes later with a long-sleeved, pale-blue shirt that matched his eyes perfectly. "I usually have my things done at the laundry, but . . ." He raised a shoulder in a shrug.

"But there's no dry cleaners in Birthright, and Arlene Patterson passed away at least ten years ago." Teresa stretched the shirt out on the ironing board.

"Everyone in the community misses Arlene?" Noah sat down in the rocking chair at the foot of the bed.

"Miss Janie loved to cook and clean, but she hated to iron, so she sent her things over there until she brought me home with her and found out I liked to do that job."

"My mama hated anything to do with housework. She always, *always* had a job somewhere on base, usually in a civilian secretarial position. So she had a housekeeper who did everything from cooking and cleaning to the laundry and ironing, and served as my nanny at the same time."

"What's your very favorite memory of your family?" Teresa asked.

He rocked back and forth for several minutes before he answered. "Sunday afternoons. That was what Mama called family day. We'd go to chapel and hear Daddy deliver the sermon and—"

She butted in before he could finish the sentence. "Your dad was an alcoholic and a preacher? How did that happen?"

"My dad, General Adam Jackson, always said he was a social drinker," Noah answered. "He got the best of both worlds—his love of liquor from my granddad Luther and his love of preaching from *his* granddad, Arnold. The General served as base chaplain when he was needed, but that didn't keep him from having his Jameson every evening."

"Sounds like one of those oxymorons they talked about when we were in school," she said.

"Kind of does, doesn't it? Or maybe a little bit hypocritical," he chuckled. "After chapel, we'd go out to eat, and afterward we would go exploring. That meant driving around whatever country or state we were stationed in for a couple of hours. Then we'd go home, have pizza and popcorn, and watch a movie on television together. Sometimes that was the only time I'd see my folks. They left for work before I got up and some days didn't get home until I was in bed. How about you? Got any good memories?"

She finished the last of the shirt and hung it on the doorknob. Then she crawled up in the middle of her bed and crossed her legs. "Mama took me to school when I started kindergarten and enrolled me. She got all dressed up and looked like the other mothers, and she'd gotten me a cute little dress with flowers on it." She remembered the pink ribbon in her memory box and almost smiled.

"Didn't she do that every year?" he asked.

"Yes, she did, but the rest of the years after that first one were not good. I found out later that she was trying to impress the elementary principal. He'd spent a few nights at the trailer, and she thought maybe he would marry her. She even told me to call him Daddy, but none of the other kids did, so I was afraid to," she answered.

"How did you ever turn out to be the person you are today? You had more reason to be an alcoholic than I did," he whispered.

"Your grandfather was a preacher, at least some of the time," she answered.

"What's that got to do with anything?" Noah asked.

"He was respected even if he drank," she replied. "My mama was trailer trash. They both drank too much. He was respectable and loved you enough to provide for you. My mama's liquor wasn't as expensive as his, but it was more important than me or what I needed."

"Think you'll ever forgive her?" Noah asked.

"Already did," Teresa said. "I wish she would have signed the papers so Miss Janie could have adopted me. The Social Services folks tracked her down, but she wouldn't sign unless she got money for doing it. When they told her there wouldn't be any payment for letting Miss Janie adopt me, she told them to go to hell and take me with them."

"They told you that?" Noah asked.

"No, they told me that she didn't feel right about it, but I eavesdropped when they talked to Miss Janie. They told Mama that it was illegal to sell a child, and her reply was 'No money, no kid. You can go to hell and take that brat I birthed with you.' I wasn't alone, though. When they found Kayla's mother, she pretty much said the same thing."

Noah got up from the chair and picked up his shirt. "I was raised in a fairly good environment and became an alcoholic, and you were raised in a horrible situation and don't drink."

"Don't matter if you're brought up in a rich, comfortable world or a poor one, whatever your home life is like, it definitely will affect who you become," she said.

"You got that right." He started toward the door. "Thanks a lot for ironing my shirt. This looks like it came right from the professional cleaners." He nodded and stepped out into the hallway.

"Hey, where are you off to?" Kayla asked him as they crossed paths right outside her door.

"My friend talked me into taking care of one last PI case, but this is absolutely the very end. I took it because it's right around here," he said.

"Who does it involve?" Teresa called out. "Do we know them?"

"I'd tell you, but then I'd have to kill you and Kayla, because you'd talk about it to each other." He laughed and kept walking.

Kayla giggled at his comment and went on into the bedroom. Her hands shook and her pulse raced. Had she been out of her mind to let Teresa and Miss Janie talk her into going to that damned reunion? It was still two weeks away, but she couldn't sleep for thinking about it. What if she hated that dress Teresa offered to let her borrow? She would be obligated to wear it or hurt her foster sister's feelings.

Well, you sure never minded hurting her feelings before, the niggling voice in her head reminded her.

She never did anything nice for me like this before, Kayla argued right back as she took a deep breath, crossed the hallway, and knocked on the edge of Teresa's open door.

"What do you need?" Teresa hung the last duster on a hanger.

"I was wonderin' if . . . ," Kayla stammered. Dammit! She hadn't thought it would be so hard to ask to simply try on a dress. "I don't want to wait to the last minute to try on that dress you said I could borrow." Asking for help did not come easy for her.

"Sure thing," Teresa said. "But sit down and let me press it first. Cotton wrinkles real easy, and it needs a good ironin' before you try it on. Just remember, it's not a hanger outfit."

"What are you talking about?" Kayla asked.

"Some things look fantastic on the hanger, and when you put them on, they look like crap," Teresa explained as she brought the dress out of the closet and began to iron it. "Never judge the way an outfit will look on you by the way it looks on the rack."

"Where did you learn that?" Kayla asked.

"I bought my scrubs for work at a secondhand shop, and I over-heard the lady who owned the place telling a customer that very thing. I got to paying attention and found out she was right." She sprayed each section with a light layer of starch. "Even older things take on a new life if you get the wrinkles out."

"Kind of like our lives, right?" Kayla asked.

"How's that?" Teresa moved on to the next section of the full-skirted dress.

"Our regrets and sins are the wrinkles. If we can get all that smoothed out, then our lives are better," Kayla said.

"Never knew you to be a deep thinker." Teresa would have never believed that she and Kayla would be having such a serious conversation.

"Didn't think I was until I came back here, but it seems like every day I turn loose some of my anger. Sometimes it scares me, though. That was what I've always had to fall back on when things got rough. It's been my salvation even if it did take me a long time to get mad enough to leave Denver," Kayla admitted.

"Me too." Teresa finished the last of the ironing. "There you go. All ready to try on. I'll get the wide belt out that goes with it."

"Are you crazy?" Kayla raised her voice. "I do not wear wide belts or any kind of belts for that matter."

"You've got a tiny waist, so you should accentuate it," Teresa told her. "Trust me. I'm thinking that we should get you some wedge heels to go with this."

"Are these shoes going to float out of heaven?" Kayla asked. "I'm not spending any part of my paycheck on shoes I won't wear but one time."

"And new underwear." Teresa acted like she didn't even hear her. "Who says you won't wear any of that again? Someone at the reunion may ask you out on a date, and you'll be glad you've got good under-britches and nice shoes to go with this dress." Teresa pulled a bright-red belt from her dresser drawer. "Maybe we should find you some red high heels instead of wedges, and red earrings. Those big ones that will almost touch your shoulders. Remember watching that old movie *Dirty Dancing* with Miss Janie?"

"Nobody puts baby in the corner," Kayla recited her favorite line.

"That's right. You walk into that reunion like you own the place. Now, take off your jeans and shirt, and let's try this on you," Teresa said.

Kayla peeled off her clothing. "I'll be surprised if they don't assign one of the cheerleaders to watch me the whole time I'm there to make sure I don't steal the plastic forks. I guess I could use part of my money for shoes and a new bra. How much do you think is in that trust fund? Wouldn't it be something if we could save up enough in a year to open our business?" Kayla asked as Teresa helped her into the dress.

"We'll figure it all out in good time," Teresa said.

Kayla smoothed the dress over her hips. "I've never had anything fit me like this, and the material has some stretch."

"Now this." Teresa held out the belt.

Kayla tucked her head down to her chest and raised both eyebrows. "I'm not so sure about that thing. I usually wear baggy things to cover up my butt and boobs."

"Would you put it on? It came with the dress and matches the trim around the top. I would have never thought that red and army green would go together, but it does."

"Kind of like two foster kids who can't stand each other." Kayla smiled as she roped in her waist with the shiny red belt. "Oh. My. Goodness! Would you look at that? I could run Dolly Parton a race for a tiny waist in this."

"Yes, you could," Teresa agreed. "Now, sit down in the rocking chair, and let me pull your hair up into a messy bun. You need to own your curls, not fight them."

Kayla didn't argue but did what Teresa asked. Who'd have ever thought they'd bond over a silly red belt?

Teresa combed Kayla's hair with her fingers and tied the bun with a piece of leftover ivory lace. "Stand up, close your eyes, and walk backward to the door."

Kayla wasn't ready to look in the mirror, so she had no trouble following Teresa's orders. She'd never been good at hiding her emotions. Her mother had told her time and time again that anyone could look at her face and see exactly what she was thinking.

Teresa slowly turned her around and then said, "Open your eyes."

Kayla couldn't believe what she was seeing. Was the mirror lying? Her hands went to her cheeks as she stood in awe. "Is that really me?"

"It is." Teresa smiled. "Those girls who made fun of you are going to be so jealous, and the guys are going to need bibs for their drool."

"This is better than all the money in the world," Kayla whispered as she turned around slowly to catch all the angles. "And it's even comfortable. I love it." She whipped around and wrapped her arms around Teresa. "You are a genius. Did I tell you that I talked to Will Barton and he said he might go to the reunion if I was going? He manages the grocery store where we shop in Sulphur Springs. Do you think he might ask me to dance with him?" Kayla gushed.

"Will Barton was the biggest nerd in your class. I can't imagine him even showing up unless he brings his mama with him," Teresa said.

"Believe me, he's changed. I've talked to him when it's been my turn to go to town for groceries. He's pretty dang sexy these days, and he's so nice," Kayla told her.

"Why didn't you mention him before now?" Teresa asked.

Kayla ducked her head. "I didn't want you to tease me about him."

"Well, honey, if you want to dance with him and he's too shy to ask you, then you ask him," Teresa said seriously.

"I might do that," Kayla said.

Locating Prissy Carlton wasn't difficult. Noah put the address into his GPS, and a nasal voice directed him right to her house. He wasn't even surprised to find that she lived right in the swankiest part of town in the biggest house on a cul-de-sac, or that two huge Dobermans roamed loose inside the ornate wrought-iron fence that surrounded the place.

He was surprised, though, when tall, blonde Prissy herself came out of the house in jogging clothes and took off down the street. He'd figured that she would've had a gym in that fancy place, with all kinds of equipment to keep her fit. He kept her in sight but followed at a discreet distance, driving slowly a block behind her. She ran about a quarter of a mile and then went into a house in a much more modest neighborhood. He parked across the road and got out one of the maps from his back seat, unfolded it, and spread the thing out across the steering wheel. If anyone stopped and asked, he was a guy in a truck who might need directions.

He thought it strange that three identical cars were parked in the driveway and against the curb. He took down all the license plate numbers and sent them to Daniel, and then he waited. Thirty minutes later, a tall red-haired woman wearing a business suit came out of the house Prissy had gone into. The skirt stopped at midthigh, and the top of a black lacy bra showed at the top of the snug-cut jacket. She got into a gray car that was parked in the driveway and drove away, never knowing that Noah had taken a dozen pictures of her.

Two more women—a blonde and a brunette—left the house in the next hour. Each drove away in one of the gray cars. Whatever Prissy was doing, she must have a thing for economy cars that were basically nondescript. Noah took pictures of each woman and fired all of those off to Daniel, too. Then he pretended to study his map some more.

He'd almost dozed off when his phone rang, causing him to jump and drop the map. He saw that it was Daniel and answered on the second ring. "Hey, did any of that help?"

"Not much," Daniel replied. "The women must be local. The cars are all rentals for the day and will be returned by midnight tonight. Looks like they're all pretty, rich girls, so it seems strange that they've rented cars. What kind of news have you got?"

Noah told him what he'd done and gave him the address of the place where Prissy was holed up. "Whoa! Wait a minute. Got some action going on. Don't hang up."

Prissy came out wearing a bright-red suit, cut pretty much like the others had been, with the short skirt, only her bra was ivory and matched her high-heeled shoes. She drove away in a little low-slung sports car. That seemed strange to Noah. Why would the other three use rental vehicles and Prissy drive something different?

"I'll get back to you in a little while," Noah told Daniel and ended the call. He flipped the map over into the back seat without folding it and drove off behind the sleek black Corvette.

He followed her all the way to Paris, Texas, where she got off the highway and nosed the fancy little car into a parking spot in front of a hotel, right beside the three gray vehicles that had driven away from the house in the first place. She took time to check her makeup in the rearview mirror before she got out, flipped all her luxurious blonde hair over her shoulder, and went inside.

"Probably some kind of woman thing, like a makeup party," he grumbled as he nosed his truck into a spot at the back of the lot and walked up to the lobby.

"Can I help you?" the cheerful little lady behind the counter asked.

"My friend will be checking in pretty soon. I came from a distance and got here early. All right if I wait in the lobby?" he asked.

"No problem," she answered. "There's coffee and cookies."

"Thank you." He sat down in what looked like a comfortable chair, but it turned out to have a hard seat and a back so straight that he couldn't find a good position no matter how he wiggled. He situated his phone on his lap so he could take pictures with a touch, picked up a magazine from the coffee table, and pretended to look at it.

After two hours the shift changed, and a guy took the girl's place. Evidently, he thought that Noah was a guest because he simply nodded at him and started reading a book between phone calls.

At six o'clock on the button, the redhead got off the elevator and took a seat beside him. Within five minutes, the blonde and brunette joined her. Then Prissy came through the lobby, and they all three followed her outside. Each of them handed Prissy something that looked like an external hard drive, and they drove off in their cars.

Noah waited another five minutes, and then a man stepped out of the elevator, turned in his room key, and left. Over the next several minutes, three more did the same thing, and not a single surreptitious photo showed a smile. After what evidently had gone on upstairs, he'd have thought they'd be a lot happier. Once the last one had gone, Noah went straight to his truck and fired all the pictures off to Daniel.

"Looks like the client was right. His wife is having an affair, but not like he thought. Those are credit card machines that the women gave her. Priscilla has been very naughty. She's running a little escort service on the side."

"My! My!" Daniel chuckled.

"Are you going to turn all this over to her husband?" Noah asked.

"He's my client and he's paid for the information, so the answer is yes, I will. What he does with it is his business. He can cause a dustup with the guys or the girls, involve the police or whatever, but he gets all this. It's not on us to judge or make decisions," Daniel said. "That's the dirty little side to this business. I did some digging while I waited on you to send more pictures. That house they left from used to belong to her grandmother and was left to her when the old gal died last year."

"Then my job is done?" Noah asked.

"Not really, because we didn't actually catch her in the act," Daniel said. "She could make up all kinds of excuses about what she and those girls were doing in that hotel. Follow her back to the house and see if they have any more business tonight."

Noah rolled his blue eyes, but he'd said he'd do the job, and he understood the need for undeniable proof. He drove back to the house, got out his map, and spread it out over his steering wheel, again.

The little sports car pulled into the driveway not long after he'd parked, and all four women got out. Evidently, the rentals had been taken back. The women all went into the house, and three of them emerged a few minutes later in jogging clothing and took off in different directions. Noah was about to leave when a ratty old pickup that reminded him of the one Teresa drove parked out on the curb. The guy who got out of the vehicle unzipped his coveralls and let the top hang to his waist. When Prissy met him at the door, she was wearing a filmy little teddy. With a little hop, she wrapped her legs around his waist and her arms around his neck, and they were locked together in a kiss when the man kicked the door shut with a heel.

Noah got out his camera and put a long lens on it. Right through the bedroom window, when the wind blew the lacy curtains off to the side, he shot several pictures that were proof positive Prissy was not a faithful wife.

"You should have pulled the blinds, lady," he muttered as he sent the pictures to Daniel.

"Now your job is done," Daniel said when he called a few minutes later. "You can't trust women. They'll nail your heart to the outhouse door every time."

"If you're ever up this way, come see me," Noah said.

"Will do, and thanks again," Daniel told him. "Same goes for you. Anytime you're in my area, we'll go out to dinner and talk shop."

They ended the call with goodbyes, and Noah sat there for several minutes with the words *You can't trust women* running through his head. That went for trusting men, too. He wanted Teresa to believe that he would continue to be a recovering alcoholic and that he would never go back to that lifestyle. She deserved someone to love her enough to stay sober and treat her right.

Chapter Thirteen

I can't believe that Miss Janie is giving us this much. Do you realize we might put in our business before long if we can find a decent place to rent?" Teresa hugged the copies of the papers the bank had given her close to her chest. She'd be getting twice as much every month as she'd made working at the nursing home, and she'd have room and board for as long as she wanted to live in Birthright.

"Don't pinch me," Kayla said as she got into the back seat of Noah's truck. "If I'm dreaming, I don't want to wake up."

"You aren't dreaming, and if there are a few more moments when Miss Janie is lucid, you should tell her what your plans are." Noah got behind the wheel and started the engine.

Teresa adjusted the air-conditioning and fastened her seat belt. "Does what Miss Janie left you have any bearing on what you intend to do with your life?"

"Yep," Noah answered. "For a long time, I thought that after she was gone, I'd rent out the property—if y'all didn't want to live in the house—and move to either San Antonio or Houston and keep doing PI work, but I've changed my mind."

"For sure, or are you toying with an idea?" Kayla asked.

"Pretty positive right now about changing my profession." He put the truck in reverse and backed out of the bank parking lot. "I'm going to hang out my shingle and do pro bono work. I don't really need the money, so I can choose the cases I'm passionate about, whether the client can pay or not. The words *giving back to the community* keep running through my mind. That's what y'all are doing, you know."

"That's pretty generous of you," Kayla said. "I can't believe I don't have to work anymore, or for some rich lady who acts like I'm something she tracked in on her shoes. To get to be help to people who will appreciate it just blows my mind."

"Me too." Teresa's voice was barely above a whisper.

Noah turned into the parking lot of the Dairy Queen. "Either of y'all up for ice cream? My treat. My truck automatically turns in when I see a DQ sign. I love their dip cones."

"Yes!" Kayla tossed her paperwork over on the back seat and was already undoing her seat belt when Noah braked and found a parking spot.

Not wanting to leave the paperwork was childish for sure, but Teresa had a hard time walking away from it. In all her wildest dreams, some of which included winning the lottery, she never thought she'd be able to even think about being her own boss. She gave the paper one last look and hurried along so Noah wouldn't have to hold the door open any longer.

Noah went straight to the counter but lingered back just a little to let her and Kayla order first. Luis had never done such gentlemanly things. He always told the lady what he wanted, and then she had to figure out what she could afford with the money she'd saved for them to have a burger or tacos.

"I want a strawberry sundae," Kayla said.

"Whipped cream and a cherry on top?" the lady behind the counter asked.

"All of it, and can you make that strawberry ice cream instead of vanilla?" Kayla asked.

"I sure can." The lady looked past Kayla at Teresa. "And for you?"

"Hot fudge sundae," she answered, almost tasting it as she said the words. When she celebrated something big, like a fifty-cent raise on her paycheck, she always treated herself to a hot fudge sundae on the way to work the next day, and she never told Luis about it.

"And you want a dip cone, don't you?" She waved at Noah.

Noah flashed a smile at her. "You know me too well, Miz Martha."

Even though the lady was at least twenty years older than they were, Teresa fought with a little streak of jealousy. Noah had not done one thing to suggest that he wanted to be anything other than friends, so she had no right to the feeling, but there it was in all its bullfrog-green glory.

"I'll bring your order to the table. Want a free cup of coffee to go with it?" Martha asked. "We make fresh every hour, but there's still half a pot and I hate to throw it out."

"We'd love that and thank you." Noah gave her another one of his sexy grins.

Kayla found an empty booth and slid into one side. "Hand me your purse, and I'll put it over here with mine."

Teresa handed over her purse and sat down on the other side of the table. The booth wasn't very big, so when Noah sat down beside her, their hips, shoulders, and knees were touching. She hoped that he couldn't hear the thumping beat of her heart, feel the heat that she did, or see the sparks dancing around the room.

"This is what I did to celebrate when I had a good-tip day," Kayla said. "I'd treat myself to a double strawberry sundae and eat it very slowly. Sometimes I'd get a cup of coffee afterward, but not always."

Teresa found it hard to believe that she and Kayla both celebrated victories, however small, the same way. She'd always thought that they were as different as night and day.

"Did you tell Denver?" Teresa asked.

"Hell no! I did not! He would've said something hateful about it." Kayla spit out the words in a rush. "What'd you do when you felt special?"

"Exactly what we're doing today. The Dairy Queen wasn't far from the nursing home. I'd go there on my way to work and eat a hot fudge sundae. And I didn't tell Luis, either," she answered, amazed that her voice sounded almost normal. "How about you, Noah? What'd you do to celebrate something big?"

"Until six years ago, I'd open a bottle of expensive whiskey," he answered.

Martha brought their ice cream and coffee, winked at Noah, and said, "Y'all enjoy, now."

"I'm sure we will." Noah grabbed a fistful of napkins from the dispenser and laid them all on the table. "I'm not being wasteful. I just know that when this thing starts drippin', I'll need most of those."

"Well, if I drop a single drop on the table or on my shirt, you can bet your sweet little butt I will lick it off. I don't waste DQ ice cream." Kayla dug down deep in the sundae and brought a spoonful to her mouth.

Like always, Teresa ate the cherry off the top first, chewing slowly and enjoying every bit of the flavor. With that taste still in her mouth, she took the first bite of the warm chocolate and soft vanilla ice cream. All those textures and flavors combined reminded her of the few good times she'd had since she had left Birthright. In among all the disappointments and regrets, she had her hot fudge sundaes.

Noah nudged her with his shoulder. "What are you thinking about?"

"I was thinking that the little things in life are pretty precious," she answered.

"You learn that real quick when you hit rock bottom," Kayla agreed.

"Oh, yeah," Noah said. "You sure do."

Miss Janie and Sam were on the back porch when they got home that afternoon. She'd been up more than three hours, but she didn't want to go to bed. She seemed agitated and kept leaning over in her wheelchair so she could see the dark clouds approaching from the southwest.

"We're going to have a storm," she declared.

The smell of rain was heavy in the air, and the sun had gone behind a layer of clouds so thick that the sky looked like a rolling bank of dark fog coming right at them.

Sam sucked in a lungful of air. "I love the smell of fresh summer rain, but I sure don't like a storm."

"Is it March?" Miss Janie asked.

Normally, after the first of June, folks in Birthright usually couldn't beg, buy, or borrow a drop of moisture—not until fall, and then it was iffy until after Christmas.

Kayla understood how difficult it would be for someone who could hardly keep a time frame in her head to keep the months straight. "No, it's the twenty-fourth day of August," she gently reminded Miss Janie.

Miss Janie pointed toward the sky. "The only thing in the whole world that scared Aunt Ruthie was storms. She wasn't afraid of the devil himself, and I always figured she could put out the flames of hell with a cup of water and maybe back old Lucifer down with a few well-placed cusswords. But a cloud like that would send her gathering up a picnic basket full of food for us to take to the cellar."

Kayla giggled at the image that popped in her head. She'd never met Aunt Ruthie, but she'd seen pictures of the lady. She was a short woman, and Kayla imagined her looking like an elf dashing around the house getting food ready to take to a storm shelter. Kayla remembered being afraid of the pictures of the old lady when she first came to live here because Ruthie's eyes looked like they could see right into her very soul. That scared her far worse than a storm or even a tornado.

"Were you afraid of anything, Miss Janie?" she asked.

The older woman toyed with the arms of her wheelchair for a while before she answered. Kayla thought maybe she'd jumped time frames again, but then she said, "I was afraid of my mama when I was a little girl, and I was afraid that no one would ever love me. I wasn't pretty like some of my classmates. Mama dressed me funny. Wearing bright colors or pants was considered a sin in our family, and makeup was a no-no. I was plain in every way. Then, when I was fifteen, Jesus came to work for my grandpa on his little farm. He told me I was pretty, and he flirted with me. He even came to church just so he could see me. For the first time in my life, I felt special. If he'd asked me to run away with him to Mexico, I wouldn't have even looked back as I left."

"Did you have a sad goodbye when he left?" Kayla asked.

"We both cried until our eyes were swollen, and we promised that we wouldn't love anyone else, and when we got old enough, we'd get married and be together forever." Miss Janie wiped a tear away with the back of her hand.

"Do you ever wish that you hadn't gotten pregnant?" Kayla asked.

"No sense in wishin' for what can't be undone. Aunt Ruthie said that he and his father didn't come back to work for my grandpa again. She never lied to me about anything, so I believed her," Miss Janie answered.

"I'm going to go home right now so I don't get caught in the rain." Sam got up and headed out the back door. "See y'all later."

Kayla had dropped her bank papers on the bottom step of the staircase, but Teresa kept the papers in her lap when she sat down in one of the chairs around the small table on the screened porch. She could understand how her foster sister felt about such a windfall, but she didn't have to hold the folder to prove that she'd never have to worry about her next meal again.

"How are you feeling this afternoon, Miss Janie? Did you and Sam have a good visit?" Kayla took a seat beside Miss Janie.

Miss Janie frowned and shook her finger at Kayla. "I told you to call me Mama. We don't have to pretend anymore. Did Noah get the banking done like I told him?"

"Yes, I did." Noah sat beside Teresa at the table. "Rain might cool things down a little bit."

Miss Janie began to wring her hands, and her eyes darted back and forth from the sky to the front door. "We should go inside and pack a basket to take to the cellar."

The first lightning streak zigzagged in a ragged pattern across the sky. A loud clap of thunder followed in a few seconds, and then the wind started blowing hard enough to knock a few tree limbs onto the roof.

"That's our cue to get Miss Janie into the house. We might be in for a bad one," Noah said.

Noah pushed Miss Janie into the house minutes before a fierce wind slammed the first drops of the rain against the screened wire around the back porch. Teresa brushed away a few sprinkles from her black hair as she closed the door behind them. She quickly checked her bank papers to be sure they hadn't gotten spotted by the rain. Then she laid them on the bottom step beside Kayla's. They were safe and dry right there. She patted them and then hurried into the living room, where Noah had taken Miss Janie.

"Someone needs to get the basket ready so we can go to the cellar," Miss Janie said. "We'll need to stay down there until the storm passes."

"Why do we need a basket?" Kayla asked.

Miss Janie raised her voice above the howling wind and rain. "Because we might have to stay in the cellar for a while, and we'll need food if we get hungry. Bread, peanut butter, jelly, cookies, and milk. We can't go to the cellar without the basket."

"I don't think we can get your wheelchair down the narrow steps to the cellar," Noah told her.

"Then pack a basket, get some blankets and pillows, and we'll stay in the hallway. It's in the center of the house, and there are no windows in the doors to blow out and hurt us." Miss Janie barked orders. "Right now, go! Aunt Ruthie's spirit is afraid."

"I'll get the food." Kayla took off for the kitchen.

"Blankets and pillows coming right up." Teresa headed upstairs. This was a new twist for her. Back when she was in high school and a storm came up, the only thing Miss Janie had said was that she hoped the wind wouldn't knock the power out.

"We'll be waiting right here in the hallway." Noah turned the wheelchair around and pushed it out of the living room.

Teresa took the stairs two at a time, threw open the linen closet between her bedroom and Noah's, and grabbed three blankets and as many pillows. Common sense told her that the storm would probably pass in half an hour, but logic didn't play a part in Miss Janie's world anymore. If it meant washing bedding because it had been on the floor, then that would be a small price to pay to keep her happy.

The load in Teresa's arms was stacked up above her eyes, so she eased down the stairs, one at a time. When she reached the last couple of steps, Noah rushed over and took the pillows from the top. His arms brushed against hers, and as usual, sparks that were brighter than the lightning and twice as hot lit up the whole area.

"Aunt Ruthie made sandwiches," Miss Janie said.

"Then that's what we'll have." Kayla got a loaf of bread and peanut butter from the basket.

Teresa laid the blankets on the bottom step and sat down in one of the three ladder-back chairs that Noah had brought in from the kitchen. "Do we spread the blankets on the floor, or would Aunt Ruthie mind if we use the chairs?"

Miss Janie shot a mean look her way. "Aunt Ruthie has been dead for years, but she was smart. She always said that you stay away from windows and glass during storms, and to go to the center of the house. If you can get to a cellar, there's cots to sit on and blankets. They're to wrap around you in case the power goes out in the storm and it turns freezing cold."

Anything other than stifling heat and humidity in Texas in August would break all kinds of weather records, Teresa thought as she took a seat in one of the chairs. "Why did you want me to bring pillows?"

"To put over your pretty face if glass starts flying." Miss Janie shook her head in disbelief. "I thought I taught you girls all this when you lived here with me."

"Yes, ma'am, you did, but we forgot," Kayla said.

"Oh, no!" Miss Janie's hands flew to her cheeks.

Teresa was instantly on her feet. "Did we forget something?"

Miss Janie shook her head. "No. We've got what we need, but I'm so sorry that you forget things." She removed her hands and wiped a tear. "The doctor didn't tell me this disease I have was hereditary."

Teresa bent and hugged Miss Janie. "It's not, Mama. Kayla meant that it's been a little while since we were here, and we might have let a few of your good teachings slip away from us."

"Well, thank God for that," Miss Janie said.

When Teresa sat back down, Kayla leaned over and whispered, "Guess we better be careful about using that word—*forget*."

Teresa nodded.

Noah had cracked the front door to peek at the storm, but he came back to sit down beside Teresa. Their chairs were close enough together that his knee brushed against hers every time he crossed or uncrossed his legs.

"You're fidgeting," Teresa whispered. "Are you afraid of storms?"

"No, but I don't like spaces with no windows," he admitted. "I feel like I'm in jail."

"How would you know what that feels like?" Teresa asked.

"Maybe someday I'll tell you," he said.

Before Teresa could say another word, Kayla said, "Miss Janie, why didn't you take other kids into your home after we left? I figured that you'd have a couple more when I got here."

"I didn't want just any girls. I wanted you two," she answered.

Teresa was afraid to blink for fear she would lose Miss Janie altogether. "What about Kayla?"

"I thought I'd hit the jackpot when they told me they needed a foster mother for her. That made my family complete." Miss Janie smiled. "I'm waiting on a sandwich. If we don't eat the food in the basket, the storm won't ever pass. That's part of the ritual."

"Yes, ma'am." Kayla handed her the first sandwich she'd made and went on to make another one. "You had retired when you brought me home. Did you ever regret having two arguing teenagers in the house?"

"Lord, no! I loved every minute of it." Miss Janie bit into the sandwich. "You girls kept me from going crazy, at least for a little while. I hate this worm in my head that lets me get all confused. I'm glad that you girls aren't going to inherit it from me. What were we talking about, and why are we in the hallway with the doors closed? I like to feel the breeze. Open the doors," she demanded.

"The storm," Noah said. "We have to keep the doors closed until the storm passes."

"We go to the cellar if the radio says there's a tornado," she said. "Not when there's only wind and rain. This is a very good sandwich, but I'd rather eat it at the table. Where is Sam? He doesn't need to be outside in this weather."

Noah stood up and pushed the wheelchair toward the kitchen. "He's gone home, and I'm sure he's inside his house, where he's dry and safe."

Again, Miss Janie drew her brows down. "After we have our afternoon snack, I think I'll be ready for a nap. Rain always makes me sleepy."

The storm pounded the house hard for an hour before the rain slacked up. Noah peeked out the door and checked the progress several times during that sixty minutes. At one time he started upstairs to his office, but Miss Janie became so agitated that he sat back down in a chair. They ate peanut butter sandwiches and drank milk from plastic cups until finally the thunder and lightning subsided. Noah opened the doors at both ends of the long hallway, and then pushed the wheelchair out of the kitchen.

"I'd like a nap now," she said. "We've survived, and that's a good thing."

"Yes, ma'am." Kayla stood up and pushed the wheelchair toward the bedroom.

Noah went ahead of her and opened the door. "Look at that, Miss Janie"—he pointed toward her bedroom window—"the squirrels are happy that the storm has passed. They're playing chase through the tree limbs."

"I'm glad it's over, too, but don't expect me to climb trees." She held up her arms for him to pick her up.

He scooped her up like a baby and gently laid her on the bed. "Please don't try to shimmy up a tree. It would make us feel bad that we couldn't go with you."

Teresa covered her with a throw, and Kayla removed her slippers.

"Honey, where I'm going, you all three can go, if your hearts are right with the Lord." She closed her eyes and was instantly asleep.

Teresa had tears in her eyes as she left the room. Kayla headed toward the kitchen, and Noah got busy returning the kitchen chairs to where they belonged. Teresa picked up all the blankets and carried them back up to the linen closet. When she turned around to go get the pillows, Noah was bringing them to her.

"Seeing her in her right mind, even for a little while, was sure nice." He stepped around her and laid the pillows on a shelf. "We might not get many of those moments."

"I don't want to think about that right now." Teresa wiped the tears away with the back of her hand.

Noah turned around and pulled a white hanky from his hip pocket. He gently took her hand from her face and dried her wet cheeks. Then he bent slightly and brushed a kiss across each eyelid. "Then we won't think about it. We'll just treasure what time we have with her."

Teresa laid her head on his broad chest, and he wrapped his arms around her. The steady beat of his heart assured her that Noah Jackson was a good man, one she could always depend on.

Chapter Fourteen

*T*eresa could hardly believe her eyes that Friday when she looked at the calendar on the kitchen wall. Surely the month of August couldn't be only two days away from gone. How on earth had the month gotten away from her so fast?

"Good morning." Kayla stared at the coffeepot. "Why haven't you got the coffee started?"

"Just got here. Do you realize I've been here only a few days shy of a month?" Teresa asked.

With a few deft movements, Kayla had coffee going. "And I've been here about three weeks. I was thinking of that last night when I went to sleep. Noah told us that the doctor said Miss Janie might make it six weeks, and if he's right, then we don't have a lot of time left. When I first got here, I figured the days would drag by, but just like that"—she snapped her fingers—"they're gone. What are you going to do when she's . . . ?" Kayla teared up. "I can't say the word, but you know what I mean? Do you think she'll even know us at the end?"

"When is the big class reunion? I saw a poster in town, but I forgot when it is." Noah entered the room and headed straight to the coffeepot. "I bet you can't wait to see how much all those kids you graduated with have changed."

"This year it's on Saturday after the homecoming football game, which is always on the first Friday in September. It used to be at the end of August, but there was a conflict in the school schedule," Teresa said as she reached for one of the cups and carried it to the table.

"I'm still pretty nervous about going by myself. One of y'all could be nice and go as my plus-one. I'd hate to give Prissy Wilson a black eye and not have anyone witness why I did it," Kayla said.

"Would that be Priscilla Wilson?" Noah asked.

"Yep." Teresa answered for Kayla. "She was *the* prettiest, most popular girl in high school, and she never let anyone forget it."

"I guess you haven't read the paper from a couple of days ago, have you?" Noah carried his coffee with him and left the room.

"Did she die?" Teresa called out.

"Nope." Noah returned with a newspaper in his hand and laid it on the table between them. "Third page, halfway down. She must have a lot of pull over in Sulphur Springs not to be on the front page. This is a pretty big story. I'm surprised y'all didn't see it. I read it to Miss Janie, and she got a chuckle out of it. She was having a lucid moment and said that she wasn't a bit surprised."

Teresa picked up the paper and read the headline out loud. "Local Women Busted in Prostitution Ring."

Kayla leaned over to read the article with Teresa. "You've got to be shittin' me."

"If you look on the fourth page, you'll see that her husband has filed for divorce and custody of their three-year-old son, too. From what I read, I guess he found out that she wasn't teaching a Bible class on the days she hired a sitter for their little boy, and he was the one who turned her in to the police," Noah said.

Teresa immediately wondered if that was the job Noah had done in Sulphur Springs. Had he been the very private investigator who'd discovered all this? She looked up to see a smug little smile on his face and knew, without a doubt, that her question had been answered even though a word hadn't been spoken.

"How the mighty have fallen." Teresa went back and read the article again, this time slower so she could get all the details. "Miss Janie used to say that when some hoity-toity person got their just due. I can't imagine why she and those other three would be doing something like that. They were all cheerleaders in high school, and Prissy was even the student senate president."

"They sure didn't need the money," Kayla said.

Teresa laid the paper aside. "Must have been for the thrill."

"And we thought it was a thrill to get ice cream from DQ." Kayla giggled. "Guess we're wired different than they are."

Teresa immediately thought of the differences in hers and Noah's wiring. Noah had been raised with plenty, and she'd had a horrible upbringing. Did that mean that they'd never be compatible?

"Miss Janie didn't have a hand in raising them," Teresa said.

"Amen." Noah smiled. "If Prissy is out on bail, and I imagine that she is, then I wonder if she'll even show her face at the reunion."

"She'll probably be there and brag about how much money she made before she got caught," Teresa said.

"Now I can't wait until next week." Kayla went to the refrigerator and took out a pound of sausage. "Miss Janie loves biscuits and gravy, so that's what we're having this morning."

Teresa hardly heard the last words she spoke for the buzz in her ears caused when Noah sat down and his knee touched hers. *Dammit!* she thought. *I've got to get ahead of this schoolgirl attraction or else come right out and ask him if he feels the same way I do.*

❖   ❖   ❖

The week went by in a blur, and when the evening of the reunion arrived, Kayla understood that old saying about being as nervous as a long-tailed cat in a roomful of rocking chairs.

Kayla turned to one side, then the other, and even looked over her shoulder at her reflection in the mirror after she'd gotten dressed.

"You look amazing," Teresa said from the doorway.

"Don't sneak up on me like that." Kayla's cheeks turned scarlet. Could her foster sister read her mind, too? Did she know that Kayla had been thinking about the biggest nerd in school?

"I didn't sneak up on you," Teresa argued. "I was on my way to my room, and your door was open. I mean it. There's no way anyone is going to outshine you at the reunion."

"I doubt that, but thank you, and I can't tell you how much I appreciate you loaning me this dress." Kayla took one more look at the woman in the mirror. The people who'd lived under the bridge with her would never believe that she was the same person.

Kayla picked up a small clutch bag that matched the shoes she'd bought on sale and started downstairs with Teresa right behind her. "Are you gloating?" she asked.

"About what?" Teresa shot right back.

"That you could take an ugly duckling and turn it into a swan?" Kayla turned around when she reached the hallway.

"You were only an ugly duckling in your mind. Shake it off and enjoy the evening," Teresa told her. "Your eyes look gorgeous in that dress."

Kayla appreciated how close they had gotten. She had no doubts that even though they might disagree regularly, they really could run a business like the senior place together.

Noah peeked out from Miss Janie's room and said, "You look like you belong on the cover of a magazine." He tossed her the keys to Miss Janie's car. "Have a good time."

"Thank you." Kayla smiled.

Ten years ago, she'd gotten into a car with Denver in the middle of the night, and the two of them had driven south. They'd thought they were doing something really wild until they had to use all their savings to rent a travel trailer in a park outside San Antonio. Reality hit strong a few weeks later, when Kayla was the only one holding down a steady job. She realized then what a mistake she'd made in leaving Miss Janie's house and packed her bags to go back, but Denver scared her into staying. He said that if she left him, he'd hunt her down, and no one would ever find her body. She believed him because the Bailey boys, Denver and Bowie, had a reputation for being downright mean. Thank God he hadn't come looking for her when she finally decided that being dead would be better than living with him.

She turned on the radio, more to ease her own jitters than to listen to the music, but the words of every song seemed to be aimed right at her. She needed to let go of all the pent-up anger, but it had been with her so long that she'd feel empty without it.

"And now," the disk jockey said, "we have news in brief. The Senior Citizens on Broadway in Sulphur Springs will have a domino tournament tomorrow from one o'clock until five. A reminder that the church on Seventh Street has a food bank for anyone who is in need . . ."

He went on, but Kayla's mind stayed on what he'd said about the senior citizens. If she and Teresa did start a little place for the senior citizens in Birthright and the surrounding area, the old folks would have a place to come and play dominoes. They could serve them a healthy lunch each day, and they could catch up on all the gossip and news about the town.

She was so excited about the idea that suddenly she was parking Miss Janie's car at the school, and she didn't even remember driving there.

Go on inside and knock 'em dead, the voice in her head whispered.

"Knockin' 'em dead is for the popular girls, not me," Kayla told her reflection in the rearview mirror.

A six-foot-long table was set up inside the lobby, with two high school students sitting behind it. "Good evening, and who are you?" a cute little brunette with a name tag that read *Emily* asked.

"Kayla Green," Kayla answered. "Starting off like I figured," she said under her breath. "They don't even know me."

"Hey, you came," Will Barton yelled from twenty feet down the hallway.

"You know my uncle Will?" Emily asked.

"Yes, I do," Kayla answered, but her eyes were on Will. He wore khaki pants, a light-blue shirt the color of his eyes, and a smile that was so bright it lit up the long hallway.

"He's my favorite." Emily laughed. "He's so funny and sweet. Mama says he was a nerd in high school, but I don't believe her."

In a few long strides, Will was right beside her. "Come with me, and I'll show you where the party is." He grabbed Kayla's hand and led her down the hallway. "I'm so glad you decided to show up—you look amazing. Did you read that story about Prissy in the paper?"

Kayla felt a little—no, it was a helluva lot of—heat rush through her body as they walked toward the cafeteria. "I couldn't believe it. She's always had the whole world falling down in front of her just to get to kiss her feet."

"She'll pay a fine and won't do a day's worth of jail time, but she's lost her husband and child because of it," Will said.

Kayla raised a shoulder slightly. "Makes a person wonder if she ever loved him."

Will's head bobbed in agreement. "She probably married him for his money." He opened the door to the cafeteria and stood back to let her enter first.

"Well, hello, Will. Who is your plus-one?" Amanda, one of Prissy's good friends and a member of her posse in high school, turned around and spoke to them.

"It's Kayla Green, darlin'." Kayla put on her best Texas drawl and pointed to her name tag. "And whose plus-one are you?"

"I'm Amanda Carson. I was voted prom queen our senior year." Her face registered pure shock that Kayla didn't know her. "I drove a cute little red sports car. I still have it, and I drove it here tonight."

"Sorry." Kayla shrugged.

"We only graduated eighty kids that year." Amanda seemed determined to force Kayla to remember her.

Kayla squinted a little and turned her head to one side and then the other. "Nope, sorry. Will, I thought we knew everyone, didn't we?"

"I thought we did, but maybe she's mistaken about the year she graduated." Will played along with a smile on his face.

"Didn't you graduate with my sister, Teresa, or was it a few years before that?" She leaned in a bit as if she was checking Amanda's wrinkles. "You're quite a bit older than us, aren't you?"

"No. I was in y'all's class," she protested. "Amanda Carson. Everyone remembers me. I'm a lawyer now."

"Guess not everyone. If you were in our class, you should have known *us*, dearie." Kayla turned her attention to Will. "You promised me a dance. They're playing 'The House That Built Me.' I love this song—it reminds me of Miss Janie's house."

Will wrapped an arm around Kayla's shoulders and led her away from Amanda and her friends. When they were in the middle of the dance floor, he took her by the hand and spun her around, then brought her to his chest and started a country waltz with her in his arms.

"That was brilliant," Will whispered for her ears only.

"Thank you." Kayla smiled up at him.

"And funny at the same time."

Will's surprising dancing skill made her feel like Cinderella. "I bet she didn't find a bit of humor in it," Kayla said.

"Probably not, but let's talk about you, not her."

"What do you want to know about me?" she asked.

"Everything."

One minute she was lost in Will's blue eyes. The next her back stiffened and she was frozen in the middle of the floor. Fight-or-flight adrenaline rushed through her veins, and she couldn't run because her feet wouldn't work. Denver and a tall, thin woman who looked like she'd just walked off a model's runway were standing not ten feet away, talking to Amanda and her cohorts.

"Ignore him and them, too." Will tipped up her chin and looked deeply into her eyes. "They don't matter. Pretend like we're the only two people at this reunion."

She did what he said, but she could see her ex in her peripheral vision. He wore expensive slacks, a button-down shirt, and loafers that most likely cost more than she had made in a month as a waitress.

She knew the minute he spotted her because his eyes went into what she called *the evil mode*, and he started across the floor toward her, dragging his poor woman away from Amanda and her crowd. Kayla stepped back from Will but kept her hand in his. "Hello, Denver. I wondered if you might be here this evening."

"Well, I never expected to see you here." His eyes started at her toes and traveled to her hair and then back again to stare into her eyes. "This is my wife, Dotty. Dotty, these are two of my classmates, Kayla and Will."

Dotty stuck out a veined hand and shook hands with Kayla. "It's so nice to meet you. This is a quaint little place, not at all like Atlanta, where we're making our home."

"My pleasure." Kayla held her cold hand a moment longer than necessary. Up close, Kayla could see that the woman was at least twenty years older than Denver, and that was being generous. She could be sixty with veins like that, but if all those diamonds that sparkled under the lights were an indication of her wealth, then Kayla knew exactly why Denver had married her.

"There's Bowie," Denver said. "It was nice seeing you again, but I haven't seen my brother since we flew into the little airport here in town. It's sure nice to have a private plane and not have to rely on commercial flights."

Dotty kissed him on the cheek. "He's such a sweetheart. The little things make him happy."

Oh, yeah, he's a real darlin', Kayla thought as the two of them walked away.

"That woman is old enough to be his mother," Will whispered.

"Love must know no age limits," she said.

"You really are funny, but would you look who Amanda flat-out kissed on the mouth?" Will glanced that way.

"Good God!" Kayla gasped. She hadn't thought that anything could get weirder than Denver showing up with a woman twice his age, but Amanda and Bowie? A hotshot lawyer lady with Denver's renegade brother—now, that would be something else to tell Miss Janie the next time she was lucid. "I wondered why he mentioned Bowie being here. He wasn't even in our grade."

"I heard they were sneaking around in high school, but I didn't really believe it. He's two years younger than us, and he's always going from one job to another. The latest news is that he got fired again last week," Will said. "I guess the Bailey boys like rich women, and the rich women like bad boys."

"Looks like it." Kayla couldn't take her eyes off Denver and his wife.

Wife! The word finally sank into her brain. He wouldn't marry Kayla, but he'd let an old gal come along with diamonds dripping off her ears and every finger and threw away all that ranting and raving about a marriage license being nothing but a piece of paper.

"You all right?" Will threw an arm around her shoulders. "You look like you could chew up railroad spikes and spit out thumbtacks."

"Now who's the funny one?" She smiled. "Thanks for being here for me, Will, and for the dance."

"Us misfits best stick together," he said. "Tell the truth, I'm a little lost in this crowd. I'm sure glad you showed up, so I don't feel like a fish out of water."

"Yes, we do, and I'm glad to have someone with me tonight. I'm shocked speechless, but I'm glad to see Denver tonight and to know that he's married and out of my life."

"That's called closure, my friend," Will said.

"That's a beautiful word and an even more amazing feeling," she said. "Let's find a table and visit awhile. You can catch me up on the past ten years and tell me the names of the people I don't recognize."

As luck would have it, they'd barely gotten seated when Denver and Dotty claimed the table next to them. Dotty constantly patted Denver on the shoulder or gave him cute little kisses on the cheek.

"Guess we chose the wrong table," Will said.

"Nope, the exact right one. I don't want to talk about him, though. I want to enjoy your company, and I refuse to let them spoil my evening," Kayla said.

"Spoken like a very wise woman. Thinking of wise women, how's Miss Janie doing this week?" Will asked. "I loved that woman when we were in high school. She let me cry on her shoulder more than once. My freshman year was pure hell. I was bullied every day."

"She is still an amazing person even when she does her time travel."

"What's that?" Will asked.

"One day she's sixteen, and the next she's seventy," she explained. "No, that's not right. She skips around several times in a ten-minute time frame."

"Are you going to be around for a while even after she's gone?" Will asked.

"Maybe," Kayla said. "Teresa and I have this idea, but . . ." She wanted to tell him, but she was afraid she'd jinx it.

"This is like Las Vegas," Will said. "What's said here stays here, but I understand if you don't want to talk about it yet. Just remember when you do, I'm a good listener."

Maybe it was the eagerness in his eyes, or the way he leaned forward to hang on her words, or perhaps it was just that she wanted to talk about her idea, but whatever it was, she couldn't hold it in.

"We're talking about starting a senior citizens place in Birthright," she said. "We'd like to serve lunch and take food to the shut-ins that couldn't come out that day. And the old folks could have a place to gather and play dominoes." She stopped for a breath. "It's a crazy idea, isn't it? Birthright is such a small place."

"Crazy, hell!" Will said. "It's a great idea. You know Sam Franks, don't you? He's Miss Janie's neighbor."

Kayla was amazed that he hadn't laughed at her. "Yes. Sam is in and out of our place almost daily."

"Talk to him. He's got a couple of empty houses for sale right there in town. He might rent one of them to you. I've been thinkin' about buyin' the one on the outskirts of town, to get away from the city," Will said.

"You don't think I'm totally insane?" she asked.

"I think it's downright sweet and kind to think about doing that for the elderly in that community. A lot of them can't get out. If there's anything I can do to help out, please let me know," he said.

The way that Will was staring at her, she felt like she'd won the lottery.

Teresa pushed the rocking chair close to Miss Janie's bed that evening. She had her sketch pad in her hands, but nothing came to her mind, so she hadn't picked up her pencil yet. Noah was in the living room with a book in his hands, and reruns of *The Golden Girls* played back-to-back on the television in Miss Janie's bedroom. Miss Janie was busy picking at the edges of her blanket when suddenly she looked up and clamped a hand over her mouth. "That woman looks and sounds like Aunt Ruthie did before I lost her."

The stringy-chicken character, Sophia, did look a lot like the pictures Teresa had seen. "She kind of does. Do you miss her a lot?"

"I did when she first died, but the last couple of days, she's come back to see me," Miss Janie said.

"Oh, really?" Teresa asked.

"Don't you doubt my word," Miss Janie scolded. "She's come and sat on the bed with me in the night hours. She says that it's time for me to go home with her, but I keep telling her that I want more time with you girls."

"Have I ever told you how much I love you?" Teresa had heard the old folks in the nursing home where she worked talk about seeing loved ones who had already passed away, and then a few days later they would die in their sleep or have a heart attack. Her heart clenched at the idea of Miss Janie's time drawing to an end.

"Not in so many words, but I know it in my heart." Miss Janie reached through the bars in her bed.

Teresa took the frail hand in hers. "I do love you. I love you for taking me in when my own mother didn't want me and then for giving me so much. I'm so sorry I didn't come and see you after I left. I was ashamed of the decisions I'd made, and I sure didn't want you to know what a mess I'd made of my own life. I'd had two mothers. You were amazing and kind and good to me. The other one was the opposite, and there I was acting more like her, rather than using your example."

"Were you drinking? Were you ignoring your daughter? Were you bringing men into a dirty house and sleeping with them with your daughter right there?" Miss Janie asked.

"No, but I let a man use me, cheat on me, and treat me like trash because I thought I didn't deserve any better," Teresa answered.

"Don't ever let it happen like that again." Miss Janie yawned. "And, darlin', I love you, too. You girls brought so much sunshine into my life. Those were the best years I ever had." Her eyes fluttered shut, and she began to snore.

Teresa tiptoed out of the room and crossed the hallway to the living room. Noah looked up from the sofa and laid the book to the side. "Wonder how things are going for Kayla?"

"So far, so good. The police department hasn't called yet." She sat down on the other end of the sofa. "Miss Janie was lucid for a few minutes, so I got to tell her how much I love her. It felt good to get to say the words even if tomorrow morning she's probably going to be sixteen again."

"I had a talk with her a couple of days ago," he said. "I don't think she remembers much of anything, but it does us good to bare our souls."

"Amen," Teresa agreed. "When are you hanging out your shingle?"

"Soon," he said. "Six years ago, when I hit bottom, I'd been thinking I wanted to be a big-shot criminal lawyer. I was going to set the world on fire, and by the time I was thirty, I'd be a household name. People would come from far and near to get the great Noah Jackson to represent them."

"You weren't even through law school at that time," Teresa said. "We all dream big at some time in our lives. You did become a lawyer, so what makes you think you hit bottom?"

"I already told you that I'm a recovering alcoholic," he answered. "I was twenty-two, had my bachelor's degree, and had been accepted into Texas A&M University School of Law. They have only a twenty percent acceptance rate, so I was feeling pretty damn good about myself. I stayed about half-lit most days, and I still had the smarts to get into the best law school in Texas. Two years later, everything changed."

"How's that?" Teresa asked.

"I was one notch away from being kicked out of school for bad grades. My girlfriend told me that she was in love with my best friend, and they'd been having an affair behind my back for six months. I went out and got so drunk that I woke up in jail the next morning," he said. "I was sweating bullets by the time my mother bailed me out. I didn't know if I'd killed someone in my drunken stupor, or raped a woman, or had gotten in a fight and put someone in the hospital. The entire previous two or three weeks were a blur."

"And?" she asked.

"Mother bailed me out of jail, took me back to school, and told me that the next time she was sending the General. I suppose she thought that would scare me into not getting drunk again," he said.

"Did it?" Teresa asked.

"I went out that very night, intending to go to the liquor store, but I saw a light in the window of a church, and something drew me over to peek in the window. The folks were having an AA meeting in one of the basement rooms. Maybe a dozen people were sitting in a circle, and this guy looked up and saw me. He motioned for me to join them, and I shook my head. I wanted to go buy a bottle of whiskey, but my feet were frozen to the cold ground. The man who had invited me in with a flick of his hand came outside and sat down beside me. I wound up attending my first meeting right then, and Jeff became my sponsor. I might add that he was one of my law professors. I haven't touched a drop of liquor since then, but I have had issues with trusting women."

Teresa scooted closer to him and laid a hand on top of his. "And, I've told you before, I'm afraid to drink because I'm afraid I'll turn out like my mother if I ever start. And, honey, trust is hard for me, too. Even though you're educated and I'm only a glorified nurse's aide, we're a lot alike."

"I guess we are." He tipped her chin up with his fist and brushed a sweet kiss across her lips.

"What was that for?" Her voice sounded breathy.

"For listening and not judging me," he said. "You are a good person, Teresa Mendoza."

"I should probably go back to Gonzales now that I have the time to do the paperwork."

"I know a good lawyer who's about to start up in town," he said as he brought her lips to his for a long, lingering kiss.

Teresa wrapped her arms around his neck with a smile and tangled her fingers in his hair. Every nerve in her body tingled as she pressed closer to him, wanting more. Each kiss got deeper and hotter. The temperature jacked up at least twenty degrees, and not even the cool night breezes helped cool her down.

Finally, he drew back, traced her lips with his fingertip, and whispered, "Ever since you arrived in Birthright, I've wanted to see if that first kiss we had as teenagers was as good as I remembered."

"Was it?" She smiled.

"No, darlin', this was ten times better, but if we don't stop now . . ." He paused.

She put her fingers to his lips. "You are right."

She laid her head on his shoulder and was satisfied just knowing that maybe in the future there would be a time and a place to go beyond making out.

Chapter Fifteen

Teresa and Noah wandered hand in hand through a field of wild-flowers. She liked the way her small hand fit right into his and the sizzle between them when he caught her staring at him and smiled. Someone whispered her name, but she didn't want to share the time she could spend with him, so she didn't turn around to see who was calling out to her. Then he let go of her hand and disappeared into a gray fog. She awoke from the dream in a horrible mood and got out of bed. On her way across the floor, she stopped long enough to see that Miss Janie was still breathing and then cracked open the door to see Kayla out in the hallway.

"Did I wake you? Can we talk?" Kayla whispered.

"Yes, and yes." Teresa left the door cracked. "Kitchen or living room?"

"Kitchen," Kayla answered and led the way. "I made a pot of hot jasmine tea, and there's cookies. I couldn't wait until morning to tell you everything that happened tonight. I had a wonderful evening with Will, and I put Amanda Carson in her place. I'm so glad y'all talked me into going. And then Will and I sat out in his truck and talked for hours and hours."

Teresa sat down in a chair and poured herself a cup of tea. Kayla told her all about what she'd said to Amanda, ending with, "And she was hugged up to Denver's brother, Bowie. I sure didn't see that coming."

Teresa laughed so hard that she had to grab a tissue to wipe her eyes when Kayla was finished with her story. She was still giggling when Noah came in from the back porch and got the milk from the refrigerator.

"I thought I heard voices, but I'd been dreaming, so I wasn't sure." He smiled. "I fell asleep in the chaise lounge on the back porch. What's so funny in here?" He poured himself a glass and carried it to the table. There were two empty chairs, but he chose the one right beside Teresa. She caught a whiff of something woodsy and musky that reminded her of the make-out session they'd had just hours before, and it sent her senses reeling.

Kayla repeated the story. Noah chuckled all the way through the tale, but Teresa laughed as hard the second time as she had the first.

"And why was Denver at the reunion, and who is Amanda?" Noah asked.

"Amanda is one of Prissy's posse, and she wasn't there, by the way. And Denver actually graduated with me—by the skin of his teeth, but he did graduate," Kayla explained. "I'm surprised that Amanda wasn't one of the call girl ring that Prissy had going, but I don't want to talk about her or those people. I'd rather talk about Will. Guess what he told me?"

"That he's always been in love with you?" Teresa teased.

"No." Kayla blushed. "He said that we should talk to Sam about our senior citizens idea. Sam has a couple of houses here in Birthright for sale, but he might rent one to us."

"Well, ain't it a small world." Teresa wanted to hear more, but Kayla veered off in a different direction.

"I'm so glad Denver came because now I know he's not going to show up and kill me, like he threatened to do if I ever left him. He's married to a woman who is probably twice his age and a thousand times as rich, so I don't have to worry about him coming looking for me ever again. He was acting like a big shot—same as if he'd been chosen king of the prom back in high school."

Teresa spewed tea across the table. "Are you lyin' to me?" She hopped up and grabbed a fistful of paper towels from the dispenser by the stove.

"Honey, I might have done some bad things in my life, but I'm not a liar," Kayla protested. "I wish you could have seen her. I'm not sure, but her hands are as veined as Miss Janie's, and the hands never lie. She might not be seventy-five, but she's old enough to be his mother. Her name is Dorothy, but she very proudly said that Denver nicknamed her Dotty, and she got all moony-eyed when she said it."

Teresa cleaned up her mess, sat back down, and poured herself another cup of tea. "I'm so glad you went to that reunion."

"Me too, and guess what else?" Kayla asked.

"There's more?" Noah picked up a cookie and dipped it in his milk. "That must've been some reunion."

Kayla's eyes glistened with excitement. "Will asked me out on a date next Saturday night. We're going to have dinner and go to a movie, and he danced with me and told me the news about each of our classmates, and he's so nice." She stopped for a breath.

"Out with the old, in with the new, all in one night," Noah joked.

"Those were Miss Janie's words when we did spring cleaning, except with the one-night stuff." Teresa reached for a cookie at the same time Noah did, and their hands touched again. There it was—proof positive that time, situation, or place had no bearing on the sparks that danced between them. She could get that warm, fuzzy feeling in the pit of her stomach anytime, even at three o'clock in the morning.

"I had to share all that," Kayla said. "I was too wound up to sleep."

"I can see why." Teresa nodded. "I can't believe that Denver is a gigolo."

"Well, you should have seen all the diamonds Dotty was dripping with. I bet she had twenty carats or more in her ears, around her neck, and on her fingers. If Denver is a good boy, he'll have all he's ever wanted." Kayla yawned.

"We could send him a large supply of paper bags," Teresa said.

"What for?" Noah asked.

"Because if he uses plastic bags to put over his gift horse's head when he goes to bed with her, he might smother her." Teresa giggled.

"You!" Kayla's finger shot up so fast it was a blur. "Are a bad foster sister, but that was funny. On that note, I'm going to bed. Good night to y'all. Turn out the lights when the party is over. How about we have breakfast at eight instead of seven? Miss Janie hasn't been waking up until about then anyway." She left the room without even taking her cup to the sink.

Teresa cleaned off the table, put away the milk, and glanced over at Noah, who was staring at her. "What? Do I have cookie crumbs on my mouth?"

"No." He covered a yawn with his hand. "I was thinking about how cute you look in those Betty Boop pajamas. The night I kissed you for the first time, you were wearing a pair that had Minnie Mouse on them."

"You remembered something like that?" She certainly couldn't remember what he'd been wearing that night, but she'd never forget the way that kiss affected her, or the ones they had shared more recently— like about four hours ago.

"I'll get the lights," he said. "See you in the morning."

She touched her lips to see if they were still bee stung or as hot as they felt, but to her surprise they were cool to her fingertips.

She stood up and crossed the hallway and was about to go into Miss Janie's bedroom when he tapped her on the shoulder. When she turned around, he wrapped her in his arms and hugged her tightly. "I love having you and Kayla in the house. Please don't move out when it's over."

"I don't plan on it," she whispered. "If Sam will rent us a house, Kayla and I can get started on making our dream a reality."

"This old house would get lonely without you." He released her and kissed her on the forehead. "We'll need each other to get through the tough times." He took a step back and then disappeared down the hallway and up the stairs.

"As friends or maybe friends with benefits?" she muttered as she went back to Miss Janie's room and crawled back into the bed beside the hospital bed. She closed her eyes, but sleep wouldn't come, so she opened them and stared out the window at the stars. She wanted to be more than friends with Noah, but they didn't have to label whatever it was between them right now—just so long as there was a future somewhere up ahead that she could see, like the light at the end of a tunnel.

Kayla groaned when the alarm went off at seven o'clock on Sunday morning. She could have slept until noon with no problem, but it was her day to do the cooking since Teresa had spent the night in Miss Janie's room. Miss Janie might only eat a few bites or nothing, but Kayla would be sure that there was a good hot breakfast ready for her when she awoke.

She wasn't surprised when she found herself alone in the kitchen. She rather liked some me time, a few minutes alone when she could think about the night before. Knowing that Denver was out of her life was closure, but what was uppermost on her mind was the idea of starting a business, hopefully with Teresa, and those delicious kisses she had shared with Will. She hadn't told her foster sister about that part of the night because she selfishly wanted to savor the kisses for herself for a while.

She closed her eyes and relived the feeling of Will's arms around her, and the fire he'd created in her body. No one, not even Denver, in those rebellious teenage years, had caused such heat inside her.

"Good mornin'," Noah said right behind her. "I'll get the coffee going."

His deep voice scared her so badly that she got an adrenaline rush. "Sorry about not having it ready," she stammered. "I was off in la-la land."

"Hey, before y'all got here, I had to do everything but clean the house. I'm sure not complaining about making coffee," Noah said.

While the coffee brewed, he set the table for four and then sat down at one end. "Want to talk about your la-la land?"

"I was thinking about this idea that we've got for the senior place." She wasn't lying—she had thought about it for a split second before she'd begun to relive the experience she'd had with Will.

Teresa usually set an alarm on her phone, but after getting up at three a.m. to listen to Kayla's reunion stories, she'd turned it off. She awoke with a start, ending a dream about trying to get to the other side of a muddy river. With a shiver, she sat straight up in bed and glanced over at Miss Janie, still sleeping soundly. She couldn't shake the vision of that raging chocolate-brown water in her dream. Miss Janie had told her many times that dreaming about muddy water of any kind meant there would be a death in the family.

Teresa kicked off the sheet and slung her legs over the side of the bed. Miss Janie was still sleeping, so she made a quick trip through the bathroom and then pulled on a pair of shorts. She tiptoed across the room and made the bed she'd slept in the night before—wrinkle-free and tight enough to bounce a quarter on. That's what Miss Janie taught her about making up a bed.

As she rounded the end of the bed, she stopped in her tracks when she noticed Miss Janie's lips were a pale shade of blue. Teresa sucked in air and gently laid her hand on her foster mother's chest. She wasn't breathing and her body was stone cold, even through her nightgown and the sheet.

"No!" Teresa's whisper came out in a ragged gasp as she dropped to her knees beside the bed. "Wake me up, God," she sobbed. "Let this be a dream and not real. Kayla!" She moaned in a guttural voice so full of pain that she didn't even recognize it as being her own.

Kayla eased the door open and peeked inside. "Do you need me to bring the babies? Holy crap! Did you fall? Are you hurt?" She rushed to her side.

"She's gone." Teresa put her head in her hands. "Miss Janie is . . ." She couldn't force another word from her aching chest.

"No!" Kayla screeched and fell on the floor beside Teresa. "I'm not ready . . ." She grabbed Teresa around the shoulders and rocked back and forth with her as their tears mingled.

Noah poked his head in the door. "I heard weeping. Does Miss Janie want the babies? Are y'all all right?"

"No, we're not," Kayla said between sobs.

"What's wrong?" His voice sounded concerned.

Teresa looked up at him and tried to speak, but the words wouldn't come out of her mouth for several seconds. She felt as if they were all three frozen in a macabre scenario that would never end. Finally, she whispered, "She's gone, Noah. She died in her sleep."

His eyes had been locked on hers, but now they shifted to the hospital bed, and tears flooded his unshaven cheeks. He sat down with a thud, wrapped his arms around both women, and cried with them. "I thought we had more time," he whispered. "I wanted her to be lucid a few more times. I wanted . . ." He buried his head in Teresa's shoulder and wept so hard that her heart broke for him even more than for herself.

Chapter Sixteen

*N*oah thought he had prepared himself for this day. All the legal work was in order. Miss Janie had told him what she wanted done concerning her funeral. Somehow, during taking care of her, he'd forgotten to think about the hole in his heart that would appear when she was gone. He wanted to scream at God for creating diseases like cancer and Alzheimer's, but down deep he knew that her last breath had nothing to do with God or the doctors.

"Shhh . . . We'll get through this together." Teresa patted him on the back.

His dad had been right all along. Noah's heart was too soft. He should be comforting the two women, not blubbering like a baby.

"She was fine when I went back to bed at three," Teresa said, "but when I got up and checked her a few minutes ago"—she covered her face with her hands—"she was cold and she wasn't breathing. Maybe if I'd gotten up earlier, I could have—"

"Don't blame yourself." Kayla reached around Noah to pat Teresa on the shoulder. "If I hadn't gone to the reunion, it would have been my turn to sleep in the room with her. This isn't your fault."

Noah slipped his phone from his hip pocket. "I should call the coroner and the funeral people, but I can't bear to see them take her away."

Kayla reached up for the box of tissues on the nightstand, took out a fistful, and passed them around. "Miss Janie is the spirit that makes this house a home. How will we survive without her?"

Teresa dried Noah's wet cheeks before she took care of her own tears. "She looks so peaceful, like she's sleeping, but that's only the body that housed her sweet spirit. We have to remember that when they take her out of the house. Her spirit will stay in our hearts to help us when we need it."

"Promise?" Noah needed something to hang on to as much as the two girls did.

"Hey, where is everyone?" Sam's voice floated down the hallway from the front door.

"We're in here," Noah called out.

Sam eased down into the rocking chair and sighed. "When did she leave us?"

"Sometime after three this morning," Noah answered.

"She went peacefully," Sam said. "I hope that when it's my time, I go like that."

"How do you know?" Noah asked.

"She was having a wonderful dream when she stepped out of this world and into eternity. She's got a smile on her face," Sam answered. "My Delia fought death so hard that she had a horrible expression on her face when she went. Miss Janie accepted things, and she knew she was leaving her little family right here where you all belong."

"Thank you, Sam." Noah managed a weak smile.

"Losin' her will be hard on all of us here in Birthright, but even tougher on you kids. Folks didn't come around much this past summer because a lot of the time she didn't know them, but they'll be here for y'all." Sam reached for the tissues and pulled out a couple. "We've lost a pillar of our community." He wiped his eyes and laid a hand on Noah's shoulder. "I'm here to help. Want me to call the funeral home?"

"Yes, please," Noah whispered.

Sam pulled his phone from the bib pocket of his overalls and made the call. Then they all sat in silence for a few minutes. Noah felt like he should have said something, but there were no words—just a gaping black abyss.

"She'd hate this," Kayla finally said. "She didn't like people staring at her."

"You're right, but . . . ," Noah agreed. "I can't leave her alone. If y'all want to go, it's fine, but I have to stay until they take her away."

"Her last words to me were that the best years of her life were when we lived here with her." Teresa sniffled.

"She told me that pretty often," Sam said as he put his phone back in his pocket. "The funeral home will be here in twenty minutes. I'm glad for the times when her mind was lucid and we could talk about old times."

"I'm glad for all the times she talked about when she was younger because we got to know her better. She would never have opened up to us if she hadn't been able to flip back and forth from past to present." Kayla tossed her tissues into the trash can and pulled more from the box.

"Thank you, Noah, for finding me and Kayla and making it possible for us to come back to spend some time with her." Teresa wiped her face with the back of her hand.

"Past and present, she's been a counselor to all of us, and you don't have to thank me, Teresa. I would have done anything for her. She'd want us to get past this grief and get on with our lives, though."

"You are so right about that. She even said those same words to me when I lost Delia." Sam's voice cracked. "Y'all are going to make her proud by paying forward the love and kindness that she's shown you. That's the way to honor her memory."

"Amen," Teresa, Kayla, and Noah said in unison.

❖ ❖ ❖

Teresa appreciated the two men who came to take Miss Janie away for respecting her modesty as they lifted her onto the gurney with the sheet still covering her body. Miss Janie would have been mortified if her nightgown had slid up and shown her underpants. She and Noah walked on one side of the gurney, with Sam and Kayla on the other, as they carried her out to the hearse. Then they stood together until the vehicle was out of sight and the dust it left behind had completely settled.

"This is a small community, but we take care of our own," Sam said. "The food will start pouring in here as soon as the community knows she's gone. Folks used to bring in food for her before y'all showed up. I kind of took it upon myself to tell everyone to let her have the time with her family since we knew the end was in sight. I'll stick around and help y'all since I know everyone."

"Thank you," Teresa said. "I've never been involved with anything like this before. What do we do about the services, Noah?"

"First of all," Sam said, jumping in, "we go into the house and have something to eat. Then we can talk about what comes next. Y'all need to keep your physical strength up, or you'll get all depressed, and I'm talking from experience. Miss Janie saw to it that I ate three times a day when Delia passed. She fussed at me when I didn't think I could swallow a bite. It's my turn to be that person for y'all."

"I'm not hungry," Teresa whispered. "If I eat, I'll gag."

"Sam is so right," Noah said. "And after we have breakfast, I need you girls to help me pick out a dress to take to the funeral home for her burial. The florists are closed today, so we'll have to be ready first thing in the morning to go choose flowers for the casket piece."

"My mind is numb," Teresa whispered. "I don't know that I can do either of those things."

"You will take each step one at a time," Sam said. "The funeral home won't need her dress until tomorrow morning, so you've got time to think about that and the flowers."

Noah started back toward the house, but when he realized Teresa wasn't moving, he came back. "She wanted to be buried as quickly as possible, and she wants graveside services only. She told me what song to play, and she said that the preacher could say a few words, and each of us is supposed to speak, but nothing lengthy. I was thinking Tuesday morning."

"That's too soon." Teresa shook her head slowly. "I can't . . . We should . . . Oh, Noah." She buried her head against his shoulder. "How are we going to let them put her in the cold ground and cover her up with dirt?"

He wrapped his arms around her and mingled his tears with hers. He didn't care if the General did think he was too soft for a man. "Like you said earlier, that's only her body, darlin'. Miss Janie doesn't occupy that space anymore. She's with Aunt Ruthie now. She's not in pain, and she's got her right mind back."

Teresa took a step back. "I thought I was ready for when her time came, but I was so wrong."

"We are never ready." Noah laced her fingers in his and gently pulled her toward the house. "We all knew my grandfather wouldn't last long, and yet when he was gone, we weren't ready to lose him. My dad went suddenly, so we sure weren't ready. I remember thinking at the time that it didn't matter if we had weeks to prepare for a loved one's death or no time at all. We could never be ready no matter how hard we try or even think we are."

"I should have come to visit her more often, but I was so ashamed of what I'd made of my life that I couldn't face her. She did so much for me, and I wasted everything." Teresa wanted to stop crying, but the tears kept coming like there would be no end to them.

Noah opened the door for her. "You came when she asked for you, and you had time with her—and more importantly, she had time with you—so stop beating yourself up."

When they reached the kitchen, Sam had put a yellow legal pad and a pencil on the table. "That's to write down what each person brings in the way of food. Did she leave any directions about what she wants done?"

"She wants a blue casket like Aunt Ruthie's, and she said not to spend too much money on it," Noah answered. "We discussed all that when I first got here last June, and then again a few days ago."

"She likes red roses and yellow daisies," Kayla said. "She told me that when I was a senior in high school."

"She told *me* that her favorite color was lilac," Teresa added. "On Easter Sunday, before Kayla came to stay with us that summer, she said she loved pastel colors. Why don't we have the florist make a casket piece of *all* colors? When I think of her as a color, she's every color in the rainbow."

"We should bury her in one of her Sunday dresses," Kayla said. "Teresa and I can pick one out."

"See?" Sam smiled. "That wasn't so hard. You just think of her and what she liked, and it makes it easier. The sun is supposed to shine through Tuesday, but according to the weatherman, storms are coming through the area on Wednesday. Miss Janie liked to sit on the screened porch even on hot days, and she hated storms."

Thank God for Sam, Teresa thought.

"That's the day after tomorrow," Kayla moaned. "I'm not sure I can tell her goodbye that quick."

"Yes, you can, and the sooner the better. Once the funeral is over, we'll all begin to heal," Sam told them. "And yes, I'm speaking from experience. None of us will ever forget her, but we have to get through the grief in order to start living again."

"Are you over Delia yet?" Teresa asked.

"Nope, but I'm workin' on it. Grief ain't an overnight thing, but time and good friends help. Let's have some chocolate doughnuts and milk in Miss Janie's honor. Folks will have already seen the hearse and will be coming by soon. Y'all will need to be dressed and ready to talk to them."

Teresa looked down at her Betty Boop pajamas and started to laugh—big guffaws burst out of her.

"Have you lost your mind, Teresa?" Kayla scolded. "There's nothing funny going on here."

"Look at us." She waved an arm.

"Good God almighty!" Kayla gasped. "It's a wonder Miss Janie didn't crawl right off that gurney and fuss at us for going outside in our pajamas. And yours even have pictures of Betty Boop dressed in what looks like a teddy."

That turned into an infectious belly laugh that had all of them roaring in a matter of minutes when each of them realized how they'd been dressed when the coroner and the funeral folks had arrived. Noah in his white tank top and Aggies pajamas. Kayla in her baggy neon-green shorts and a nightshirt that looked like it had come from a rag bag.

"I needed that." Teresa wiped her eyes on her shirtsleeve.

"I think we all did," Noah agreed.

"Y'all go on and get dressed," Sam said. "I ain't much of a cook, but I know how to open a package of chocolate doughnuts and pour four glasses of milk."

"Thank you," Noah said, and then left the room with Teresa and Kayla right behind him.

"I didn't mean any disrespect, laughing like that," Teresa said.

"Of course you didn't, and if Miss Janie was here, she'd have got a big kick out of the way we all look." After giving Teresa a quick peck on the lips, Noah closed the door to his bedroom and fell back on his bed. "I'm going to miss you so much, Miss Janie," he whispered. "I can never thank you enough for what you did for me in the past or how much you've helped me understand myself during these weeks I've had with you."

He took a deep breath before he went on. "Or for the future. I would have never gotten to know Teresa as an adult if you hadn't brought us all together here in Birthright or have figured out what to do with my life."

Chapter Seventeen

On Monday afternoon Teresa looked around the kitchen and groaned. "What are we going to do with all this food? Do folks realize that there's only three of us in the house?"

Sam patted her on the back. "Country folks show their respect and love with food at a time like this. I knew this would happen. That's why I brought aluminum foil and different-sized containers. Miss Janie taught me how to do this when Delia passed away. We're going to divide the casseroles into portions for three to four people and put them in the freezer. We can do the same with most of the cakes, pies, and cookies, but we'll have to eat the jelled fruit salads and the puddings pretty soon. That kind of stuff don't freeze too well."

"I remember Miss Janie taking food to funeral dinners and to homes when new babies were born," Kayla said.

"Me too, and I even went with her sometimes." Teresa began to wash the containers.

"Military wives are pretty good at this kind of thing, too." Noah had barely gotten the words out of his mouth when his phone rang. He answered it, listened for a few seconds, thanked the caller, and shoved the phone back in his hip pocket. "That was the funeral home. Miss Janie is ready for the family to view."

Teresa's heart turned into a stone in her chest. Sure, she'd seen Miss Janie lying cold in her hospital bed the day before, and in her mind, she knew that her foster mother was dead. Her heart had refused to believe it, so she'd pretended that Miss Janie was just sleeping. Now she'd have to look at her in a casket, and that would make everything very real.

"Right now?" Kayla asked.

"Any time before five," Noah answered.

"Go now," Sam said. "Puttin' it off makes it harder to deal with."

"You're coming with us, aren't you?" Kayla asked.

"Nope," he answered. "Needs to only be you three together for that. I'll take care of this food while y'all are gone. I'm glad to be included in the family, but—"

"You are part of this family," Noah butted in.

"Thank you, son." Sam smiled. "But this is y'all's time."

Family.

That afternoon Teresa thought that was the most beautiful word in the whole world, and to think she'd wasted more than a decade trying to create something that had been waiting for her right here in Birthright.

The temperature flashing on the bank thermometer said that it was ninety-nine degrees, but when Kayla and the others walked into the funeral home, she felt like she'd gone from a hot oven right into the freezer. Chill bumps popped up on her arms as the lady greeted them.

"Hello, I'm Nadine. I'll show you to Miss Janie's room. She was a great lady. I remember her from my high school days when she was the school secretary. We always knew if we had a problem, we could take it to her and she'd help us if she could. You'd be her girls, right?" The woman talked as she led the way to a room off to the side.

To Kayla, it was a fancy place, with four pale-blue velvet chairs set in a semicircle in front of the casket. Miss Janie would have liked all the flowers and plants that surrounded her. She had liked puttering about with her roses, and always loved the wildflowers that sprang up in the springtime. Sunrays flowed through the window blinds, giving the room a warm feeling despite the chill from the air-conditioning vents above them. Several well-placed lights in the ceiling lit up the casket. Miss Janie wouldn't like that. She'd rather be the person in the background, not the one under the spotlight. She had always preferred to be the one who stayed behind during a funeral and got the dinner ready to serve.

Noah slipped his arm around Teresa's shoulders, and together they went to the end of the room, where the casket was located. That chemistry between them had gotten stronger. But Teresa would tell her all about it when she was ready.

Teresa stared down into the casket for a few minutes and then buried her face in Noah's shoulder. He patted her on the back and led her to one of the chairs. Then he started across the room toward Kayla. "We need to tell her goodbye," he whispered.

"I don't know if I can," she said.

Noah slipped an arm around her, and together they walked up to the casket. She took a deep breath, closed her eyes for a moment, and then looked at Miss Janie. All the strength she thought she had left drained from her when she realized the finality of death. In that split second she realized that her chance to tell Miss Janie everything she'd needed to say was gone. Everything would go unsaid forever now. Kayla's knees went weak. The room began to spin, and everything went dark.

When she came to, her head was in Teresa's lap, and Noah was fanning her with a brochure. "I'm all right," she muttered as she tried to sit up, but their faces seemed to fade into a thick gray fog. She lay back down with a groan.

"Do we need to call the ambulance?" Teresa asked.

"No!" Kayla protested. "I've done this before when I haven't eaten in a day or two. I'll be fine when we get home and I can eat something."

"With all that food at the house," Teresa scolded, "why didn't you?"

Kayla held up a hand. "I couldn't force anything down. If I could have a glass of milk or orange juice, I'll be okay."

"There's a convenience store down the street." Noah got to his feet. "Don't try to sit up until—"

"What's happened?" Nadine seemed to appear out of nowhere.

"She fainted," Noah explained.

"We have that happen from time to time," Nadine said. "Can I get you some crackers and juice, or milk and a candy bar? We keep a small supply of snacks in the kitchen."

"Yes, please," Teresa answered.

Nadine hurried out of the room and came back with a basket of snacks. "I brought several things in case the rest of you would like something. There's also bottles of juice and water if you need a little pick-me-up. This kind of event can drain your supply of emotions for sure, and some food helps the body keep going. Y'all stay as long as you want. I'll be here until five, but I don't mind sticking around longer since it's Miss Janie."

"Thank you so much," Noah said.

"You're very welcome. I really loved that woman," Nadine said as she left the room and eased the door shut.

Teresa opened a package of peanut butter crackers and put one in Kayla's mouth. Noah twisted the cap off a small bottle of milk for her and then removed the wrapper from a candy bar.

Kayla chewed and swallowed the cracker and then tried to sit up again. She still felt weak, but at least nothing around her was spinning. Teresa handed her the milk, and she drank all eight ounces of it at once. "You eat that candy bar," she told Noah. "I'd rather finish the crackers and have another milk."

"Don't mind if I do." Noah passed the basket over to Teresa, who took a bottle of water, then set the basket on a chair next to the one where Noah had sat down.

"I thought I was strong," Kayla said. "That I could march right up here and look at her, maybe cry at the idea of never seeing her again, and then comfort y'all. She's not even the first dead person I've seen, but . . ." Her voice faltered as the tears began to flow.

"But it's Miss Janie," Noah said.

Teresa grabbed the box of tissues from a nearby chair, pulled out a couple, and dried Kayla's tears. Then she started to cry with her, and soon Noah was wiping all their faces.

"She'd scold us for sure." Noah's voice sounded hoarse. "We're not supposed to grieve, but to rejoice that she's not in pain and that she has finished her race."

"Tell that to my aching heart," Kayla whispered. "I should've come back to see her."

"We all have regrets about that," Noah said. "But we also know that she didn't hold us guilty."

Teresa pulled a ponytail holder from the pocket of her jeans and whipped her black hair away from her face. "I know there's bushels of food at the house, but why don't we all go to the Dairy Queen, have a burger, and settle our emotions."

"Is that against the rules?" Kayla asked. "If someone sees us there, will they think we don't appreciate what everyone has already brought us?"

"We will be glad for all the food for weeks to come," Teresa said. "But right now I could use a big, greasy burger and some french fries."

"Me too." Kayla got to her feet and went back to the casket for a final look. "Goodbye, Miss Janie. I love you."

Noah dreaded the actual funeral service. The only people he really knew were Teresa, Kayla, and Sam, but several of the folks who brought food said they would see him at the graveside. Evidently, Miss Janie's close friends went beyond the four people that she considered family.

Having her service on a bright, sunny day seemed fitting. Storms might come tomorrow, but today was gorgeous, with a few white, fluffy clouds in the blue summer sky. Noah started out of his bedroom and found Teresa sitting on the top step of the staircase. She'd dressed in a simple little black dress, with her dark hair twisted up and held in place with a wide gold clip.

"I can almost hear Miss Janie whispering words of comfort in my ears. She's telling me not to grieve, but to get on with life," Teresa said when he sat down beside her.

"I was thinking the same thing," Noah agreed.

Kayla came up behind them. "We should all dive into getting our senior place ready if Sam is willing to rent us one of those houses."

"I agree," Teresa said. "But what about you, Noah?"

"I'll work from this house. I'll do pro bono when folks can't pay me, and charge those that can a reasonable fee for legal work. Y'all are giving back to Miss Janie's community, and so am I." Noah draped his arm around Teresa's shoulders and pulled her closer. He liked the way she fit so perfectly against him, the way her hair smelled, and everything else about her. When things settled down, he intended to tell her exactly how he felt about her. Sometimes, like right then, he wanted to spit out the words, but the timing simply was not right.

"That's wonderful," Teresa said. "Miss Janie would be so proud of you."

"And the two of you as well," Noah whispered.

Kayla gave them both a nudge with her knee. "It's time for us to go. Sam says we should arrive at the graveside and sit in the family chairs about ten minutes before the service begins. It's already hot outside. Do you think it will be a long, drawn-out thing?"

Noah stood up and extended a hand to Teresa. "She wanted one song, and the preacher and each of us to say a few words, and that's all." He wished that he didn't have to let go of Teresa's hand, but the staircase wasn't wide enough for two people to go side by side.

Noah helped Teresa into the front passenger seat and then opened the back door of his truck for Kayla. Driving from Birthright to Sulphur Springs took only ten minutes, even if he drove the speed limit. That morning, it seemed like they'd barely cleared the driveway of Miss Janie's house, and then *poof*, the time had passed and he was parking beside the tent that had been set up in the cemetery.

"I'm not ready for this," Teresa whispered.

"None of us are, but it has to be done," Noah assured her with a hand on her knee.

"Good Lord!" Kayla opened the truck door. "There must be a hundred people here."

"Or more," Teresa whispered. "Who's that man hurrying over this way?"

"Will Barton," Kayla answered. "Bless his heart."

"He did change a lot," Teresa said.

"I'm so sorry about Miss Janie," Will said as soon as he reached Kayla. "Here. Let me help you. If there's anything at all that I can do, please tell me. We can talk more at the church dinner." He offered her his arm and led her to the chairs set up in a row under the tent in front of the casket.

"And what church dinner?" Noah asked as he and Teresa made their way across the lawn not far behind Sam, Will, and Kayla.

"I didn't know there was going to be a dinner," she whispered.

Noah waited until the three ladies were seated; then he and Sam took the last two chairs on either end of the row. That still put him beside Teresa, so he reached over and laced his fingers in hers. He hoped that she felt the same support from having someone to hold her hand as he did.

For the trip to the cemetery to have gone by so fast, the next few minutes seemed to take forever. The preacher finally came out of the crowd and removed a piece of paper from his pocket. He unfolded it, laid it on the lectern by the head of the casket, and leaned in close to the microphone. "Thank all y'all for coming today. I'm Vernon Davidson, the pastor of the church that Miss Janie attended. She wasn't one to be the center of attention, but what she got done behind the scenes in her community and the church did not go unnoticed. She was a great lady who started to work in the Sulphur Springs High School cafeteria when she graduated from high school. In a few years she moved up to be the high school secretary and saw more than forty classes graduate before she retired. She even saw third-generation kids come through the school during those years. She wouldn't like for me to be telling much, but I want y'all to understand what an impact she had on so many lives. She left me this paper to read and told me explicitly that this was all I was to say, so don't tattle on me."

He cleared his throat and went on. "To my family and friends, don't weep for me. I'm going to a better place. To my girls, I love you, and I want you to be happy. To Sam, I couldn't have ever asked for better neighbors. To Noah, you've been like a son to me, and I love you more than you'll ever know. That is all. Now go home, enjoy life, and when you think of me, I hope it will be a happy memory that puts a smile on your face." The preacher removed a white handkerchief from his pocket and wiped his eyes. "It's signed Sarah Jane Jackson, but we all knew her as Miss Janie. I understand that she asked each of you kids to have a few words." He stepped away from the microphone.

Teresa had dealt with death in her job more than the other two, so they'd planned on her going first. Noah missed her touch when she let go of his hand as she stood. She took a few steps and leaned into the microphone. "Miss Janie had her struggles and faced a lot of demons in her life, like all of us have done. Today, as we put her to rest, I can hear her sweet voice singing with the angels. I want to live the rest of my life so that someday I can sing with her. Thank you all for attending the service today. Seeing so many folks would have made her happy."

Her hand was shaking as she sat down and slipped her hand back into Noah's. They hadn't discussed the order beyond who would go first, but Kayla stood up next. She reached out her hand for Will, and he joined her, standing firm beside her with his hand in hers as she spoke into the microphone. "I'm Kayla Green, but in my heart I'm Kayla Jackson and Miss Janie is my real mama. I can never thank her enough, but I intend to do my best to make her proud of the decision she made to give me a home and teach me how to love unconditionally."

When Kayla sat down, Noah let go of Teresa's hand and made his way to the lectern. "There is sadness in our hearts today, but happiness right along with it. We're all three very glad for the time we've had with Miss Janie, but most of all we appreciate the impact that she's had on our lives. We wouldn't be who we are or where we are without her, and we love her for giving so much of herself to make us the grown-ups that we are."

He sat back down and draped his arm over Teresa's shoulders. "That was tough," he whispered.

"Yes, it was," Kayla said from Teresa's other side. "Thank goodness for you and Will, or we'd have never made it. My hands are still trembling."

"Mine, too," Teresa admitted.

The preacher nodded toward someone behind the casket, and the first notes of piano music floated out across the cemetery. Sarah McLachlan's clear voice sang "Angel." Many of the people wouldn't understand why on earth the family had chosen that song rather than something more religious, but it's what Miss Janie had asked for, and Noah was honoring her last wishes.

Tears streamed down Teresa's face, and then Kayla followed suit. Noah was glad that the funeral home folks had thought to set a box of tissues beside his chair. "This was her choice of songs," he whispered.

"I don't know if she chose it for herself or for us girls. She knew all the reasons why we never felt good enough, like the song says," Teresa whispered.

"Even when she was dying, she left this for us. We were in the arms of an angel these few weeks for sure," Kayla whispered as the song was coming to an end. "In all the madness and the sadness, she was our angel."

"Not *was*," Noah said. "She *is* our angel."

"And she'll be watching over all of us forever," Teresa agreed.

When the song ended, the preacher focused on the family instead of the crowd behind them. "Miss Janie wouldn't want a fuss, but she's not here to argue with us. There's a dinner prepared in the fellowship hall of the church for any who want to join us and visit about Miss Janie and what she meant to us."

The funeral director came forward, moved the floral piece to the side, and then opened the casket. Sarah McLachlan's song played again as the folks walked past. Some just glanced at Miss Janie. Others said an audible goodbye to their old friend.

The last person walked past the casket as the final words of the song ended.

"You take all the time you need." The preacher came around and shook hands, starting with Sam. When he reached Noah, he said, "If you kids are going to make a permanent residence in Birthright, we'd love to have you in our church."

"Thank you," Noah said. "You might see us there next Sunday, but right now, I guess we'd better have some direction on how to get there for the dinner."

"I know how to get there," Teresa said.

"We went there with her every Sunday when we lived with her," Kayla offered. "It's only a few blocks from here."

"Good." Vernon mopped sweat from his brow with his handkerchief and then combed his thick gray hair back with his fingertips.

"We'll see you there in a few minutes, then. I'm going to go on and get out of this heat, but don't y'all hurry a bit."

The preacher left, and the five of them walked to the casket together. With their arms around each other's shoulders, they stood there staring down at the remains of their loved one. Noah couldn't wish her back, not with her health and mind in such a mess, but he wondered how or if he would ever be able to fill the empty feeling in his heart. Her death left him as the last living Jackson and with the responsibility of carrying on the family name.

Teresa was glad that Noah kept her hand in his on the way back to the truck. His touch filled part of the emptiness in her very soul.

Will had asked Kayla if she would ride back to the church with him, and she had said yes, so Teresa and Noah were alone in the truck. She fastened her seat belt and looked over at Noah. Their eyes locked, and they didn't even need words to say what they felt in that moment, but it passed quickly.

He started the engine and drove slowly out of the cemetery. "Like I said earlier, I'm going to run my practice right out of the house, so I'll either be there or in court. I'll be meeting with clients, sometimes unsavory ones, right there. Is that going to be a problem for you and Kayla?"

Teresa knew that he had to have something to occupy his mind to keep from thinking about Miss Janie, because hers was doing the same thing. She gave his questions some thought and then said, "You should know by now that Kayla and I have seen lots of what you call unsavory characters. Maybe they'd like some cookies and coffee while you visit with them. You never know what a small act of kindness will do for a person who's down and out. Miss Janie did that for me, so maybe I can pay it forward a little bit at home."

"Thank you. That makes me happy." Noah parked his vehicle behind Sam's.

"The thanks go to you for finding me and Kayla," Teresa told him.

"I'd say that they go to Miss Janie." He got out of the truck, rounded the front end, and opened the door for her. "I didn't know about this dinner. I would have told y'all if I had."

"But you knew about her wishes," she said as he tucked her arm into his.

The one thing Teresa had always liked about the small church Miss Janie attended was that the girls who had been so popular in high school, Prissy Wilson included, went elsewhere on Sunday morning. That day, however, the first face she saw when she walked into the fellowship hall was Prissy, standing against the wall with what everyone in high school had called her posse. Suddenly Teresa felt downright dowdy and underdressed.

They came in a group straight toward her. Noah squeezed her hand and whispered, "I'm right here."

"Teresa, we want to tell you how sorry we are for your loss. Miss Janie was loved by us all. Every one of us four can remember a time when her advice helped us. We went in together and brought a ham to the dinner," Prissy said.

Miss Janie's words about Prissy being such a brat came back to Teresa. She was almost tempted to come up with a smart-ass remark, but she just smiled sweetly and said, "Thank you for that. We appreciate your kindness."

"You're welcome," Prissy muttered. "And I'm sorry for the way we treated you and Kayla when we were in high school."

Teresa looped her arm into Noah's. "Thank you for your apology, Prissy, but we shouldn't hold up the line."

"I can't believe you accepted her apology," Kayla whispered.

"That's what Miss Janie would have wanted me to do," Teresa said out of the corner of her mouth.

"Well, I'm not to that place yet," Kayla said.

"If I could have everyone's attention." Pastor Vernon tapped a glass with a spoon. "We'll have grace now that the family has arrived, and we'd like to invite them to go down the buffet line first." He bowed his head and said a short, heartfelt prayer giving thanks for Miss Janie, for the food, and for the hands that had prepared it.

"And who is this man with y'all?" Prissy asked the minute the preacher was finished.

"He's Miss Janie's nephew," Teresa answered. "Good to see you, Prissy. Sorry about your troubles."

Prissy's face turned red, and she whipped around and headed out the door with her posse right behind her. Evidently, they didn't eat tuna casserole or homemade brownies. By the time the family had gotten through the line and sat down at one of the long tables, Teresa had forgotten all about Prissy Wilson. Some people simply didn't matter anymore, she decided, and Prissy was one of them.

Kayla liked that Will made sure he was in line behind the family and then sat beside her. "Noah, this is Will Barton," Kayla said.

"Pleased to meet you officially, Will." Noah nodded across the table at him. "How did you know Miss Janie?"

"I graduated with Kayla, and Teresa was a year ahead of us. Miss Janie was tough but fair, and it didn't matter to her if a kid was poor or rich—she treated us all the same," Will answered, and then chuckled. "She could tell if we were really sick or fakin' it, and believe me, she knew if we skipped school and tried to get by on a forged note that wasn't written by our parents."

"You should have lived in the same house with her." Kayla raised both dark eyebrows. "There was no skipping classes or fakin' sickness with me and Teresa. We toed the line worse than the teachers' kids did."

"I don't doubt it, but was she really your mother?" Will asked.

"In every way but blood," Teresa answered. "She fostered us and wanted to adopt us, but it wasn't possible."

"Where have y'all been all these years?" Will asked. "I asked Miss Janie about you when she came to the store, but all she'd say was that y'all were out finding your way. I had no idea what that meant."

"That's a story for another day," Kayla told him.

"Sorry." Will blushed. "I didn't mean to pry."

"No problem," Noah told him. "None of us took the time to visit like we should, and we all feel guilty for the choices we made."

"Don't we all, for one thing or another," Will replied, then turned his attention to Kayla. "If you aren't up for our date on Friday, we can reschedule."

"Thank you." Kayla smiled. "I'll let you know how things are going later."

"Fair enough." Will nodded. "You've got my number. Did you ask Sam about his houses?"

"What about my houses?" Sam suddenly appeared and took a seat beside Noah.

Will shook his head slowly. "I think I just put my big foot in my mouth."

"No time like the present to lay it out there," Kayla said. "Sam, you and Miss Janie were talking on the porch a couple of times about how nice it would be to have a senior citizens place in Birthright. That kind of got me and Teresa to thinking about putting one in. We kind of like working with elderly folks and . . ."

"We can't do that in Miss Janie's house. Noah is already starting up his law business there," Teresa said.

"I've got two houses settin' empty, and the real estate agent hasn't had a bite on either in a year. One would be perfect for a senior citizens place. It's that place next to the old post office. Big old living room, but it's only got two bedrooms. I'll let you have it rent-free for as long as you want," Sam offered. "I don't know what kind of legal stuff you'll need to do, but I reckon Noah can take care of that. The place has two bathrooms, one off each bedroom, so you'd have a ladies' room and one for the menfolks built right in. It's in bad need of paint, but other than that, I believe it would work. Want to go see it when we leave here?"

"Are you serious?" Teresa asked.

"You bet I am." Sam nodded. "I've wanted a place like that for years, and we all need somethin' to do to move forward. It'll give us old guys who hate to cook a place to have lunch, and one of the bedrooms can be for playin' dominoes. I'll even donate a few boxes. In the summertime, I'll bring garden vegetables, and I'm sure old Lucien Williams would be willin' to donate a hog in the winter. Will, are you up for a paint party this weekend?"

"I'm in," Will agreed. "I get off work about five on Friday, and I'll bring the pizza."

"That quick?" Noah asked. "Friday is only three days away. That won't give me much time to investigate the legalities."

"Might as well have it ready when we get the green light to open up." Sam grinned.

Kayla was stunned speechless, but she could feel Miss Janie's approval down deep in her soul.

"Which reminds me, Sam," Will said. "Do you think maybe I could also look at that other property you've got for sale? The big old two story on the other end of town? It keeps calling out to me every time I'm in that area. I realize it's too big for one person, but I'm tired of living in a tiny apartment, and I've been thinkin' about getting a dog."

"You bet we can." Sam grinned. "It needs paintin', too. You help us, and we'll all pitch in and help you if you decide to buy it."

"Sounds like a fantastic deal to me." Will grinned back.

Kayla had thought he was handsome before, but when he smiled, the whole room lit up for her like fireworks on the Fourth of July. That might be a strange way to feel at a funeral dinner, she thought, but Miss Janie would like that a lot. Now the week ahead of her didn't look so bleak and empty.

Chapter Eighteen

*T*eresa pulled the covers up over her head on Wednesday morning when the alarm went off. She'd awakened every hour through the night and sat straight up in bed, thinking that she should check on Miss Janie. Then she'd realize that she was in her own room, not Miss Janie's, and that her foster mother was gone.

"I don't want to face her room without her in it," she muttered as she finally threw off the covers and headed downstairs.

"Well, don't you look chipper this morning," Kayla said in a flat voice. She pointed toward the cabinet. "Now that you're finally awake, I heated up a breakfast casserole, and there's blueberry muffins in the cake plate."

"And you sound downright grumpy," Teresa said.

"I am," Kayla told her. "I'm mad at Miss Janie for dying before I could tell her how much I really loved her."

"I've moved past that one," Noah said as he joined them. "I was in denial when I first got here in June. Then I got mad at myself for not coming sooner and at her for not seeking out a doctor before the cancer got so bad that she couldn't be treated. After that I tried bargaining with God. If He would let her live to see another Christmas, I'd go to church every Sunday. If He would let her be able to walk again, or not be in so much pain, I'd be a better person. It's the stages we all have to go through to find peace."

"Where are you this morning?" Teresa asked.

"Somewhere between depression and acceptance," he admitted. "We really lost Miss Janie a while back and were lucky to get a few glimpses of her before she left us. I peeked into her room when I walked past it and found it depressing."

Sam stuck his head in the back door and said, "I've come to help y'all with the next step."

"What step is that?" Teresa asked.

"You can tell me no if you want to, but we need to clean out Miss Janie's bedroom. The clothing can go to the church clothes closet for folks in need. Prissy Wilson's great-uncle needs a hospital bed and can't afford one. If y'all don't want to donate it to him, we can take it to the veterans center, along with the shower chair and the bedside potty." Sam helped himself to a cup of coffee and sat down at the table with them.

"Why would we need to do that now?" Kayla asked.

"I waited three months to take care of Delia's things. Every time I went into her room, I cried. Miss Janie came over one day and told me that it was time to take care of her things. It was one of those days when Miss Janie was in her right mind, and she wouldn't take no for an answer. Crazy thing was, afterward, I dreamed about Delia for the first time, and she told me she was at peace," Sam answered.

"I have no problem giving the bed and other things to someone who needs them, and I don't think Miss Janie would mind if Prissy's great-uncle got them," Noah said. "I was thinking about turning that room into my office eventually. That way my clients wouldn't have to climb stairs or be peeking into bedrooms, and the smaller downstairs bedroom could become y'all's office for the senior business stuff, if you need extra space."

Teresa was still emotional from the funeral the day before, so that offer brought more tears to her eyes. "That's a sweet idea." She nodded.

"We might get them both cleaned out today. What have you got in mind for the regular furniture?"

"I'm not ready to get rid of that yet," Noah said, "so I guess I could rent a storage unit."

"I've got a barn I don't use since me and Delia quit runnin' cattle several years ago. You could put it in there for free, and it would be close by if you decide you want to bring some of it back at any time," Sam offered.

Teresa got up and rounded the end of the table to give Sam a hug. "You are a godsend."

"Thank you, but what I really am is a friend who's been through something like this and wants y'all to finally have peace." He smiled.

"This isn't going to be easy," Kayla said.

"I'm here to support y'all through it all." Sam stood up, went to the stove, and uncovered the casserole. "I haven't eaten breakfast. I'm inviting myself to eat with y'all, and when we finish, we can get busy."

Teresa locked gazes with Noah and whispered, "You ready for this, or do you want to wait a while?"

"Miss Janie would want us to move on," he answered. "I'll never be ready, but by putting it off, we'd only be hanging on to the past."

There were parts of the past that Teresa desperately wanted to let go of, but her memories of Miss Janie she wanted to wrap a warm blanket around and store deep in her heart.

"Thank you, again, Sam, for helping us get through all this," Kayla said.

Teresa and Noah both blinked after staring at each other for a minute. Kayla and Sam had both already filled their plates and were on their way back to the table. Noah pushed back his chair and stood up at the same time Teresa did.

"After you." He made a sweeping motion toward the stove.

"Thanks." She smiled.

There it is again, Kayla thought. *That chemistry between them, and if I can see it, they must feel it. Do people see that kind of thing when I'm around Will Barton?*

Sam touched her on the arm, and she came close to jumping out of her skin.

"Where were you?" Sam's old eyes twinkled. "Were you thinkin' about Will Barton? He's a good, hard-workin' man, and he's talked to my real estate lady. He's made an offer for my house."

Kayla lowered her voice to barely a whisper. "Can you see the sparks between them?" She glanced over her shoulder at Teresa and Noah.

"Of course." Sam grinned. "They've been skirtin' around their feelings all month, but they'll figure it out."

"What are y'all whispering about?" Teresa put her plate on the table and then sat down.

"I was asking if I might donate some card tables to the senior citizens. Me and Delia used to have the elderly folks' Sunday school class at our place for the Christmas party. We got about eight of them tables so we could all have places to sit and play games," he answered with a broad wink at Kayla.

"You've already done so much," Noah answered.

"I'm tryin' to show you kids how important this is to me and the rest of the community. I mentioned it to several folks, and they're as excited as I am," Sam said. "Soon as we get the place painted, I'll clean up them tables and bring the folding chairs with them."

"Thank you." Noah finished off his muffin and went back for a helping of casserole. "Anyone need a refill on coffee?"

Kayla shook her head. "I'm good."

"I'll take one." Teresa held up her cup.

Noah refilled Teresa's cup and then topped off his own mug.

Teresa swallowed the food in her mouth and then took a sip of coffee. "I can't believe how well everything is falling into place. I feel like it's Christmas one minute, and then I feel like the other shoe is going to fall if I blink."

"Me too," Kayla said.

"When the other shoe does fall and y'all have a big argument, are you going to throw up your hands and leave Birthright?" Sam asked.

Kayla shook her head. "I don't intend to skate on thin ice. If I've got something to say, I'll spit it out, and I fully well expect you to do the same"—she raised a dark eyebrow—"and to do it in English, not Spanish like you used to do when you cussed me out for something."

"No pidas lo que no estás dispuesto a aceptar." Teresa spouted off a string in her parents' tongue.

"And that means?" Noah chuckled.

"It means not to ask for something unless you want it," Teresa answered. "As you know, sister, I don't hold back when I've got anything to say."

"I guess that answers my question." Sam laughed out loud. "They may attempt to scratch each other's eyes out, but I've got a feeling if anyone messes with either of them, they'll stand together to take care of the matter."

"That pretty much sums it up," Kayla said out loud, but her thoughts were going to the idea of giving Miss Janie's things away and storing her furniture. Would she think they were forgetting her too easily?

Miss Janie's voice popped into her head. *Get on with your life. This is all just stuff I left behind. Use it, give it away, or burn it. I don't need it anymore. I only need you girls to be happy.*

Kayla had her answer, so she pulled a ponytail holder from the pocket of her jeans and whipped her curly hair up off her neck. "I'll start in the closet. Do we leave the clothing on the hangers, Teresa?"

"That's the best way." Teresa followed her into the bedroom and set a box of garbage bags on the dresser. "It turned out to be a pretty day in spite of the weatherman's forecast, so we can line the bed of Sam's truck with a sheet and lay them back there."

"I'll drive slow to the church so they don't blow out," Sam said. "Folks there will be glad to help me unload them. While y'all do that, me and Noah will take down this hospital bed and deliver it, then come back and take the other furniture to my barn."

"I'd like to keep the last dress I remember her wearing when I was still here," Kayla said. "I saw it in her closet when I was hanging up her dusters last week. It's the bright-pink one with white polka dots."

"I want to keep one, too. The navy-blue one that she always wore to funeral dinners at the church," Teresa said.

Teresa removed a garbage bag from the box and pulled open a dresser drawer. She had filled one with nightgowns and slips when she heard Kayla gasp.

"What?" Teresa asked. "You find a dead mouse? I remember you being terrified of mice. Never could figure it out, since we both lived in places that had critters and bugs."

"If I'd seen one, I would have left footprints on you as I left this room," Kayla said. "You've got to come help me get these two boxes down. I can't reach them."

Kayla watched Teresa looking up from her place on the floor. The boxes were on the top shelf. Getting them down would require a ladder or a kitchen chair.

"Too bad Noah's left with Sam," Teresa muttered as she got up. "I'll get a chair."

Kayla couldn't take her eyes off the two boxes. One had her name printed in big block letters on the end, and the other one was marked with Teresa's name.

Eternity plus three days passed before Teresa came back with a chair, climbed up on it, and gasped when she saw her name.

"This is kind of spooky," she said as she pulled the first one down and handed it to Kayla. "I've gotten clothes out of this closet and hung them up in here for weeks, and I never noticed these."

"Me, either." Kayla sat down on the floor and removed the top of a box that once held reams of paper. An envelope with her name on it lay on the top of everything else. She recognized Miss Janie's perfect penmanship and held what she hoped was a letter to her chest.

Teresa plopped down beside her and set her box on the floor. "What is that?"

"Don't know. Open it up and see. I think I've got a letter," Kayla answered.

Teresa flipped the lid off her box and set it on the floor in front of her. She grabbed the envelope and opened it carefully, exactly like Kayla had seen her opening her Christmas presents. Kayla ripped into hers like she had when she'd unwrapped the gifts Miss Janie had put under the tree for her. When she started to read, the first line brought on a fresh batch of tears:

> My dear child, Kayla,
> Everyone needs good memories from their past to overcome the bad ones. When you came to live with me, I started this little box of memories for you—pictures, recipes I cut out of magazines that I thought you might like someday, your report cards from school, and even your high school transcript, just in case you ever needed it. There's a copy of your birth certificate and your shot records. I had so much fun putting together the album of pictures for both you girls. Christmas had a whole new meaning to me when you came to live with me. Oh, how I enjoyed buying presents for you two. The privilege of walking into church with two daughters all dressed up on Easter was such a blessing. You'll find the Mother's Day cards you made for me in this box, along with that last note you left on the table. I'm sorry I didn't come to find you and

drag you back home, but in those days, I was both sad and angry. I hope you will forgive me for that. I've been diagnosed with Alzheimer's, so I'm writing now and hoping and praying that the time will never come when I don't know you girls if you should decide to come home. Remember that you are loved and enjoy the memories. I hope they make you happy.

Love,

Miss Janie

With tears leaving wet spots on her T-shirt, she looked over at Teresa, who was now holding her own letter close to her heart. "I expect," Kayla sobbed, "that yours pretty much says the same as mine. She thought of everything. Even after we didn't treat her right, she's given us a past."

"My biological mother didn't keep anything for me. When I came here, it was with the clothes on my back and one picture of Angel in my purse." Teresa scooted over and hugged Kayla. "Angel just flat-out didn't have the ability to love me, but Miss Janie loved me enough to do this. I'm going to add everything in here to what I've kept through the years."

"I know." Kayla wept with her. "I can't go through the rest of this stuff right now. My feelings are too raw. I'll do it another day. Right now we've got to get her room cleaned out. I was worrying about doin' this, and I heard her voice this morning. She told me that it was all just stuff and to move on."

"You hear her voice, too?" Teresa asked.

"I did this morning." Kayla moved away, laid the letter in her box, and put the lid back on it. "I take it that you do, too?"

"Not often, but sometimes." Teresa returned her letter to her box and stood up. She extended a hand toward Kayla. "We should get back to our jobs. We don't want to disappoint her after what she's done for us."

"Amen!" Kayla replied, and took the offered hand.

Chapter Nineteen

So many paint swatches in one place downright bewildered Teresa. Even when she narrowed it down to only the minty-green colors, the selection was huge. She had thought that they would walk into the store, choose between two or three hues, and leave with gallons of paint.

"This is way too much," Kayla sighed. "How will we ever choose?"

"Each of you will pick out three colors and then compare notes without even looking at the rest of the swatches," Sam suggested.

"That sounds like a solid plan." Kayla pulled two swatches out and couldn't decide between three others, so she took them all.

Teresa only liked two, so that at least narrowed the selection down to seven. When they laid them on the counter, they discovered that two of Kayla's were the same as Teresa's. They tossed the other five to the side and asked Sam for his opinion.

"You'll be happier with the lighter one," Sam suggested.

"Why?" Teresa questioned.

"Because you want the place to have a light, airy feel to it. Think about the smell of sugar cookies and homemade banana bread baking in the oven. That's the kind of feel you want. That dark one will make people feel like they're going into a cave, and us old people need lots of light. Our eyesight isn't what it used to be," he answered.

"Then we should consider white, and make sure we raise the blinds up every morning," Kayla said.

"I believe you're right," Teresa agreed. "Keep everything as simple as possible."

"With that in mind, me and Noah and Will were thinkin' maybe we'd put a ramp on the end of the porch so folks in wheelchairs would be able to join us. What do you girls think of that?" Sam asked.

"I love it," Teresa told him. "It would make it easier for those with canes, too."

They left with plastic drop cloths, paint pans, rollers, brushes, and tape. Sam drove on to the feedstore to buy fertilizer for his fruit trees, and Teresa and Kayla headed to the house where they planned to put in the center. Teresa had parked Miss Janie's car and had opened the trunk when Will's shiny black SUV pulled in behind them.

"Hello. I was out this way delivering groceries to one of the ladies in our church. She's not able to get out anymore, so she calls in her list. Saw y'all drive up. Need some help unloading that stuff?"

"We never turn down help." Kayla waved Will over.

"Methinks you've got a boyfriend," Teresa teased.

"That would be the pot calling the kettle black," Kayla said out of the side of her mouth.

"What do you mean by that?" Teresa picked up the bag with the drop cloths in it.

"Exactly what I said. You can't deny the electricity between you and Noah," Kayla answered.

"Y'all leave that heavy paint for me to take," Will said. "Guess what? Sam took my offer for the house on the other end of town. I'll start getting it ready to move into in a couple of weeks, so I'm holdin' y'all to that promise to help me paint. And, Kayla, do you reckon once I'm moved in that you'd be interested in helping me choose a rescue dog for a pet?"

"I'd love to," Kayla told him. "I love dogs and cats both, but never was able to have a pet."

Will flashed a big smile toward Kayla. "Then it's a date."

Teresa used the key Sam had given them on the day of the funeral and opened the door. A musty, unused smell greeted her. She made a mental note to bring some scented candles to the house once they'd finished painting.

"Good thing there's wood floors and not carpet," Will said. "That'll make it easier for old folks to get around on."

"I guess you see lots of elderly people in your grocery stores," Kayla said.

"Yes, but . . ." He set the paint down. "My mama was past forty when she adopted me, and Daddy was fifty. I've lived with older folks my whole life." He shrugged. "I kind of know them better than most people our age. My folks live in an assisted living place up in Paris these days. I drive up there, bring them down to our church in Sulphur Springs, and take them out to eat, and we go see a movie every Sunday afternoon. And everyone thought it was nerdy when I was a kid, but I always got a home-cooked meal." He chuckled.

"If I'd known your mama cooked for you every day, I'd have begged you to take me home with you," Kayla said.

"I'd have done it." His grin got even bigger.

"I'll see you Friday evening soon as I get off work." He waved and closed the door behind him when he left.

Teresa nudged Kayla on the shoulder. "He likes you."

"How do you know?" Kayla asked.

"You know those sparks you said you saw between me and Noah? Well, I see them with you and Will. Quite the pair, aren't we? Two good men have been flirting with us, but we're hangin' back because we don't trust men," Teresa said.

"Amen, sister." Kayla nodded.

On Thursday morning, Kayla went to the grocery store, leaving Teresa and Noah alone in the house. Her foster sister wasn't fooling Teresa one little bit. Her trip was twofold—she wanted to see Will, and she was playing matchmaker between Teresa and Noah.

As Teresa helped Noah move his desk and file cabinet downstairs into Miss Janie's old bedroom, she thought about the first days when Kayla had come to live in Birthright. Lord, she'd hated that girl, and there was no doubt Kayla had felt the same. Looking back now, Teresa knew she'd only had those feelings because she'd seen herself in Kayla and didn't like what she saw.

"What do you think?" Noah asked, breaking into her thoughts.

"About what?" she shot back.

"How does it feel?"

"Empty." Teresa glanced around the room. "You need a couple of chairs and maybe some bookshelves."

Noah hiked a hip on the edge of the desk. "I mean about us three being here together without Miss Janie."

"If I take a deep breath, I can still catch a whiff of her rose-scented perfume and dusting powder. I feel like her spirit is still among us and always will be. I can't speak for Kayla, but living here feels right. You are helping people who can't pay high-dollar lawyer fees, and that is a good thing. This idea of making a place for senior citizens to go brings peace to my soul," Teresa answered.

"I've been looking into that, and I need to know what services you are going to offer. We need to figure out if you're going to offer house-cleaning services, medical help of any kind, or taxi service," he said.

She hopped up on the desk beside him. "No, no, and maybe."

"Basically, what you and Kayla plan on doing here at the beginning is offer a hot meal at noon and a place for folks to gather and play games or do craft things. Is that right?" He turned to face her.

She didn't want to talk about chicken and dumplings and domi-noes. She would far rather lean in, moisten her lips, and kiss him.

"Right," she said.

"Is this going to be a business or nonprofit?" he asked.

"Nonprofit," Teresa answered. "If the folks around town want to bring in a sackful of green beans from their gardens in the spring, or if Sam wants to donate a pot roast every now and then, that's fine, but we won't be in it to make money."

"Then we don't need to do anything. You are just making free food for a crowd and opening up a property for the elderly to meet and visit. You will need to have each of them sign a form relieving you of liability in case of an accident." Noah didn't blink as he seemed to search her very soul.

"Can you draw one of those up?" She glanced down at his lips and then brought her eyes back up to his.

"Of course I can." He lowered his voice to just above a whisper.

Then his lips barely touched hers, and that old familiar fire was kindled between them. He cupped her face in his hands and kissed her eyelids, the tip of her nose, and then kissed her with so much passion that the smoldering embers turned into a hot blaze.

"Whew!" She wiped at her brow in a dramatic gesture when the kiss ended.

"Want to drive up to Sulphur Springs and get some ice cream?" He grinned.

"That's a weird question right now." She tried to keep from panting, but it was impossible after a kiss like that.

"Evidently that didn't make you as hot as me. We either need to cool off with a ride and some ice cream or take this up to one of our rooms and set the bed on fire," he teased.

"Are you asking me on a date?" Teresa fired back at him.

"I believe I am," Noah drawled. "And maybe we can go on the sec-ond date after church. I could take you to Sunday dinner at this sweet little place I like in Paris."

"Are you telling me that you have a private jet?"

"No, ma'am," he chuckled. "Not Paris as in the Eiffel Tower, but Paris, Texas, as in Aunt Mamie's Diner. Turkey and dressing is their specialty on Sunday."

"Yes, to both, but you should know I don't kiss on the first date," she teased.

"Does that mean the third date might be the lucky one?" he asked.

"Oh, honey, that kind of thing doesn't fly until the fifth or sixth date," she told him.

"Look at us flirting," he chuckled. "I like it."

"Me too." She wiggled out of his embrace. "But if we're going to go on our first date, I should get cleaned up."

"You look beautiful just like you are. Grab your purse and let's go," he said.

Never—not once—had Luis ever said something that nice to her. Looking back, she couldn't remember him paying her compliments before they got married. After that day, everything seemed to go downhill. There were *no* compliments and very little communication, and mostly, when they talked at all, it was to argue about him spending more time with his friends than with her. Maybe it was cultural, but after the first year, she'd asked him why he'd wanted to marry her if he couldn't even stay home with her a night or two a week. He'd told her it was because he didn't like to cook or clean house. In his opinion that was the only reason a man needed a wife anyway. She had judged all men by Luis after that.

She shook off the memory, took the hand Noah offered, and hoped that she had been dead wrong.

Noah slowed his truck down as he passed the house where the new business would be going in. "Looks like Kayla stopped by here on her way to the grocery store. Want to go in and look at the place, maybe invite her to go with us?"

"Are you having second thoughts about our first date?" she joked.

He drove on past the place. "Not a bit, other than that we should have had our first date right after that first kiss when we were teenagers. Our lives might have been different if we had."

"We are who we are today because of what we've been through," she said. "If we'd had a first date then, we wouldn't be who we are. Does that make a bit of sense?"

"More than you'll ever know," he replied. "Let's play pretend. We're teenagers. We've had our first kiss, and even though neither of us can drive, we take a picnic lunch out to the backyard and call it a date. We write notes to each other, call on our cell phones when we are apart, and eventually we wind up married. You go to college with me, and I'm drinking every day like my dad did."

"I don't like you passing out on the sofa every night, and you don't like listening to me nag about it. Neither one of us is happy," she added.

"Point proven. We weren't right for each other then, like you said. We needed to go through what we have so we could be who we are and fall in love now, right?" he asked.

"L-love?" she stammered.

"If everything goes right, isn't that the logical end to this first date?" he asked as he turned south toward Sulphur Springs. "It may not be in two weeks, or even in two months or a year, but that's where we'd like for this to wind up, right?"

"Are you summarizing, like you do in court?" She smiled.

"I haven't spent time in court in a couple of years," he answered. "I'm not sure if I could even present ending arguments, but I'll give it my best shot." He cleared his throat, took her hand in his, and held it on the console between them. "Ladies and gentlemen of the jury, today's question for you to ask yourselves is whether or not two people begin to date so that they will eventually find something in each other that makes them fall in love. I believe that any other reason is simply tagged *booty call* or *friendship*. What you must decide is whether Teresa Mendoza and Noah Jackson should or should not go on a second date. The decision is in your hands."

Teresa's laughter bounced around the inside of the truck. "You convinced me, but I'll have to persuade the rest of the jury. I believe that Will won't be difficult. I admit I'm a little worried about Kayla. She seems a little smitten with Will right now, but I'm afraid she's still got a bad taste left over from living with Denver."

"As the elected spokesperson for the jury, you will have to use your powers to convince any of the diehards."

"They'll be tough," she sighed, but he could tell by her expression that she was enjoying this as much as he was. "They'll throw up all kinds of obstacles, like us living in the same house. What if this doesn't work out and then things get weird between us? What if one of us falls head over heels in love with the other one, and that one is kind of ho-hum after a couple or three dates? Would it be painful for the one in love to see the other one bringing someone home and sleeping with him or her?"

"Sounds like logical questions that might come up." He nosed the truck into a parking space at the Dairy Queen. "What kind of arguments are you going to give them?"

"That love isn't logical. It's trust," she said.

"Good answer." He got out of the vehicle, rounded the front end, and opened the door for her. "Without trust, all relationships die. Do you trust me, Teresa?"

"With my life." She squeezed his hand. "Maybe after a while I'll even trust you with my heart."

"I hope so," he said. "You'll let me know when the jury is ready to pass a verdict, won't you?" Her hand in his felt small, but he had no doubts about Teresa's strength. She'd endured a horrible childhood, and that had to have made her strong as steel.

"I can't believe you never found someone to settle down with before now," she said as they walked inside.

"Had to get my life in order first." He looked up at the menu board and told the guy waiting for their order, "I want a hot fudge sundae."

"Me too," she said.

"Have them right out," the fellow said when he'd taken payment from Noah and made change.

"This must be a special day, if you're having a hot fudge sundae." Noah ushered her to a booth with his hand on her back.

"It isn't only a celebration day." Once they were sitting, she reached across the table and took his hands in hers. "This is the most special day I've had since I left home eleven years ago. I feel like my life is finally beginning to fall into the place it was meant to be."

"Let's make a pact to always come here when we get to celebrate something," he said. "Whether it's getting past our first fight or if we're happy about me winning my first case."

"I love that idea." She squeezed his hands. "No matter what happens, this can be our place."

"We'll even claim this booth." He brought one of her hands to his lips and kissed the knuckles.

"Shall we carve our initials in the tabletop?" she asked.

"I left my pocketknife at home," he answered. "Next time we come here, I'll bring it." He nodded.

Yes sir, life with her was going to be a fun trip.

Chapter Twenty

When they were all gathered at the new house, Kayla took one look at the walls and said, "Teresa is a perfectionist, so she can tape off the woodwork, so paint don't get on it. I will do the trim work that the rollers can't reach. Since Noah is tall, he can paint the upper half of the rooms, and Sam can work on the lower parts. How's that sound? When Will gets here, he can relieve Sam and Noah."

"You're not my boss, and why do you think I'm a perfectionist?" Teresa asked.

"Hey, I've seen you cook. You count the grains of sugar that go into making a batch of peanut butter cookies," Kayla said with a laugh.

"I do not," Teresa argued. "And in my defense, you have to be precise if you want a good outcome."

"Miss Janie and Delia both measured things like that, and I got to admit, whatever they were making was always perfect," Sam said.

Teresa picked up a roll of blue painter's tape and sat cross-legged on the floor. "I've seen you cook, and you're as careful as I am when it comes to baking."

"Exactly like Miss Janie taught me." Kayla poured paint into a cup and started working right behind her.

"I've never done this before," Noah admitted, "so I'm going to watch Sam for a couple of minutes before I start."

The smell that filled the room brought memories back to Teresa's mind that she thought she'd forgotten years ago. She was four years old when Angel decided to paint her bedroom bright red.

"Can I help, Mama?" Teresa had asked.

"You don't call me that again, or I won't even let you watch. I told you time and time again to call me Angel." She had swept back her dark hair with a flick of her wrist and gotten a bit of paint on the ends, but Teresa didn't say a word about it.

At that age, Teresa couldn't understand why she would call her mother Angel when her name was Angelina. Angel and Angelina didn't even sound the same. When she went to first grade and discovered that the two words were spelled alike, she understood a little better. In the second grade, she figured out that other kids did not call their mothers by their nicknames. She was in the third grade when she invited a little girl over to her house to play and found out that all little girls didn't have mothers who brought men home.

The second time she invited her friend over, the little girl said, "My mama says that your mama is a whore and I can't go home with you."

Teresa had gone home that evening and asked her mother if she was a whore. Angel had slapped her across the face, told her to never say that word again, and made her sit on the porch until dark. Whatever that word meant, it had to be worse than the swear words that Angel spewed when she was drunk or angry. Teresa was careful not to say it again, or to invite kids to come to her house.

Not long after that, she realized that leaving kids alone in trailers until the wee hours of the morning wasn't what other mothers did. Some little girls had mothers who combed their hair and made them breakfast every morning before they went to school. The whole concept had seemed strange to Teresa back then, but when she had come to live with Miss Janie, things had changed. Miss Janie took her to the beauty shop and had her hair thinned and layered to make it more manageable, and Teresa learned what it was like to have a hot breakfast every single morning.

Noah startled her when he touched her on the shoulder. "Earth to Teresa."

She looked up from the floor where she was sitting. "Sorry about that. I was living in the past for a moment."

"Want to talk about it?" he asked.

She watched him load a roller and expertly cover a section of the yellow wall. "Good job. You're a fast learner."

"Sam's a good teacher, but I don't think you were woolgathering about paint. The expression on your face was pure sadness. Were you grieving for Miss Janie?" Noah asked.

Teresa finished taping off that section of baseboard and scooted down a few feet. "No, not this time. I was thinking about my mother. I should probably just say Angel. I was not allowed to call her Mama, or Mother, or Angelina, for that matter. She was Angel, and she got really mad if I called her Mama."

Sam added, "When Angelina was a toddler, her mother went to prison for a drunk-driving accident that killed an elderly man and left her in the care of her grandmother. Her grandmother died not long after Angelina moved out. The poor girl didn't have much of an upbringing, but that doesn't excuse the way she treated you."

"How did you know that?" Teresa asked.

"Miss Janie told me y'all's stories when she first took you girls into her home," Sam answered.

"Is her mother still in prison?" Teresa had never heard anything about a grandmother or great-grandmother, other than when Angel told her now and then that she hated churches because Mama Lita made her go every time the doors were open.

"Miss Janie kept tabs on all that and said she was leaving you girls as much information as she could. Did y'all find those boxes she put together for you? I bet you'll find most of that in there," he answered.

"We found those boxes, and I'll look into mine later," Teresa said. "Life sure does have some twists and turns, don't it? But me and Kayla will still be here for a long time, and Will is moving here, so maybe we'll start a trend and the town will come back."

"Miss Janie used to say, 'It is what it is.'" Kayla had moved to the other side of the room with her can of paint and small brush. "I never understood what she was talking about until lately. Life is what it is. We either repeat what we know, or we learn from it and go forward in a better direction. Wouldn't it be something if folks started moving back here, and we even became a little bedroom community for folks working in Sulphur Springs and Paris?"

"It sure would," Sam replied. "What time did you say Will is going to show up?"

"He is supposed to head here as soon as he gets off work, no later than five, and he is bringing pizza with him," Kayla answered. "Don't worry. There'll be plenty for him to do. We've still got bedrooms and the bathroom to paint." She nodded. "I'm glad we changed our mind and didn't use the yellow that we thought about."

"What color would you choose if we repainted Miss Janie's place?" Noah asked Teresa.

"This isn't my favorite work in the whole world," Teresa answered, "so it'll be a while before I want to do it again after we help Will get his house redone and ready to move into. What about you?"

"The only thing I really like about what we're doing is the fellowship," Noah said. "I'm already feeling like I'll need a good massage tomorrow morning. You up for that?" He raised an eyebrow at Teresa.

"Only if it's a mutual thing and I get one first," she told him.

Kayla sat in the middle of the kitchen floor and admired the new walls. In one of the dozen or so places she and Denver had lived, she'd painted the walls a pale blue. He had come home about half-lit that night and told her that he'd quit his job. There was no way, he had said, that someone was going to boss him around like his supervisor had been doing, so he had told the guy to take the job and shove it. That meant they had to move from the apartment back into the travel trailer where they had been living between times when they could afford a real apartment. After that happened too many times to count, she'd finally given up on making a home. She had kept whatever place they lived in clean—whether it was a month or a year—and had paid the bills, but none of the apartments and certainly not the old stand-by travel trailer in a ratty park was ever what anyone could call cozy or homey.

She closed her eyes and felt at peace with the universe and with herself, so this must have been the right decision. When she opened them, Teresa was sitting beside her.

"Holy crap! You scared the hell out of me." She shivered.

"Then I guess you're an angel now, since there's no more hell in you," Teresa teased.

"I don't want to be an angel if that's what our mamas were," Kayla said.

"Me, neither." Teresa nudged her with a shoulder and then waved a hand to take in the whole kitchen. "White was the right color. Sam did good by suggesting it. I can't wait to start cooking and for the old folks to come in every day. Noah was asking me about what services we plan to offer, and that got me to thinkin' about something. Why don't we put a bulletin board on the living room wall and let folks that clean houses or do home health care know that they can advertise there?"

"I love that idea. We're going to be happy here," Kayla said. "Think we could have our grand opening by October first?"

"I don't see why not. Basically, we need to buy some big pots and some dishes," Teresa said.

"Not real dishes," Noah said as he joined them. "If you do that, you'll have to install a dishwasher to keep things up to code. As it is, you'll have inspections a couple of times a year, but if you use disposable stuff, it'll make things a lot simpler."

"What about our pots and pans and silverware?" Kayla asked.

"You have to be sure everything is sparkling clean and show them you are using throwaway stuff," Noah said. "I thought we could get away without any paperwork, but there is an upside to what we do have to take care of—since Sam is donating the space, it becomes a tax write-off for him, and all the food y'all buy will be a tax write-off for your company. I'll have all the permits and papers taken care of in a couple of weeks."

"Thank you." Teresa smiled up at him.

"No problem." Noah sat down on the floor beside Teresa. "It feels good to be giving back to the community. Have y'all decided what you're going to call this place?"

"I've been trying to come up with something. Birthright Senior Citizens sounds so generic. Either of you got any ideas?" Kayla asked.

Sam came around the corner. "I heard that last sentence, and I do have an idea. How about Miss Janie's Senior Citizens Place?"

Kayla clapped her hands. "Yes! Yes! Yes! That way she'll be remembered. Folks will say, 'We're going down to Miss Janie's for lunch, or for a game of Monopoly or dominoes.'"

"I wish we had food cooking on the stove right now," Teresa sighed. "I'm hungry. I hope Will brings lots of pizza. I could eat a whole one all by myself."

As if on cue, someone knocked on the front door, and then Will's deep voice floated into the kitchen. "Pizza delivery."

"We're back here." Kayla didn't even have time to stand up before Will was in the kitchen.

"I wasn't sure what kind everyone liked, so I got four different ones." Will set them on the counter. "I'll be right back with the ice, cups, and a gallon of sweet tea."

"Need some help?" Noah asked.

"Nope. It's all in one bag." He disappeared out the back door and returned in a couple of minutes carrying a tote bag printed with Disney characters on it. "Don't judge me." He grinned. "My Sunday school class gave me this for Christmas last year. I think maybe the little girls won the fight on which one to buy. And if I had to guess, the little redhead named Zoe led the pack. Y'all remember Tammy Revas, who graduated with Teresa? That's her mother." He set a bag of ice in the sink and took out half a dozen red plastic cups.

Kayla got up with a groan and said, "Let me help with that."

Noah followed her lead, picked up all the pizzas, and set them on the floor. "With no table, we'll have a picnic."

Will and Kayla brought cups filled with ice and tea and joined Sam, Teresa, and Noah on the floor. Kayla opened the boxes and said, "Dinner is served."

"I forgot!" Will jumped up and pulled a roll of paper towels from the tote bag. "I even brought napkins. This white paint sure does make the place look lighter and brighter. I think I'll go with white, too, when we start painting my new place. I'm pretty pumped about having a house." He tore off a couple of napkins for each one of them. "I've lived in an apartment since my folks sold their place and went to the assisted living place. I'm pretty excited to think about putting some roots down."

"I'm gettin' too old for this." Sam chuckled. "I'll let you kids do that job and finish up here as well. Soon as I get done eating, I'm going home to stretch out in my recliner and moan about my sore muscles, but when y'all paint Will's place, I'll smoke a brisket and y'all can come over to my place to eat, but I'm not painting any more houses." He finished off his pizza and got to his feet with a loud groan.

"I'd paint the White House for good brisket," Noah said with a laugh. "But I thought you didn't like to cook."

"I don't, but smoking or barbecuing ain't cookin'." Sam grinned as he waved goodbye to all of them and left by the back door.

Kayla couldn't keep her eyes off Will or her mind off the kisses they'd shared after the reunion.

You never felt this way with Denver, the voice in her head reminded her.

No, I did not, but then Denver never looked at me the way Will does. I always felt like I was only a step up from him being my pimp. He never asked me to go out on the street, but he always took whatever money was left after the bills were paid, she thought.

As if he'd read her mind, Will said, "I was surprised to see Denver at the reunion with a new wife. How long have y'all been divorced? Don't answer that. I have a habit of saying things before I think, and that was rude."

"Not rude at all," she said. "We never got married. We had lived together for nearly nine years when I finally left him. For several months, I was off the grid, as they say on the cop shows. Cash-only jobs, and for a while I was sleeping on park benches or in a bus station, anyplace where it was warm in the winter or cool in the summer. I was living with a homeless group under a bridge before I landed a job working as a housekeeper for a cranky old lady. Denver was a mistake, and I'm glad that he's in the past."

"I imagine all of us have made our fair share of mistakes," Will said, not a flicker of judgment in his eyes at her revelation.

"I'm done." Noah downed the last of his tea. "It's time to start on the bedrooms and bathrooms. We sure appreciate the pizza, Will, but most of all we're glad for your help. We're getting pretty tired, and we've still got the bedrooms and the bathroom to go. I'm especially glad that you are a tall guy, so I don't have to reach all the way to the ceiling anymore."

"I'm glad to help, but y'all are helping me more than I am you. My house is at least twice this big, and I expect it'll take a couple or three Friday evenings and/or Saturdays to paint it." Will stood up and gathered up the empty boxes. "I'll toss these in the back of my SUV when I leave."

"Thanks again." Kayla nodded.

"Where are you workin', Kayla?" Will asked.

"In the bathroom. Teresa's already got it taped off, so I'm in there doing the work that a roller can't do," she answered. "Sam left his paint pan and roller right outside the door for one of you guys."

"Are y'all tellin' secrets over there?" Teresa asked.

"Nope. We were talkin' about going down the hall and startin' on the bathroom. If we get this job done tonight, then we can get Sam's tables and chairs moved in. These walls look pretty bare right now. We talked about a bulletin board, but some pictures might be nice," Kayla answered.

"How about some old movie posters?" Will asked. "I've got a *Gone with the Wind* one and one of John Wayne when he played in *True Grit.* You can have them if you want. One could go in the ladies' room and one in the men's room."

Kayla must have had a strange look on her face, because Will chuckled and said, "I don't have them hung up in my house. Through the past ten years, I've gotten all kinds of strange but cute gifts from my Sunday school kids. You mentioned a bulletin board? I've got one of those in my office at the store that I was about to toss in the trash. The company sent a new one last week. It's yours if you want it."

"That's fantastic," Kayla said. "We'll take all three, and as payment, anytime you're in this area at noon, stop in and eat with us."

He offered her a hand. "That sounds great. I'll bring the stuff to y'all Sunday after church if that's okay."

Kayla put her hand in his and let him pull her to her feet. He let go as soon as she was standing up, but not before she had a vision of taking him down the hall, closing the door on any of the rooms, and having a nice, long make-out session.

Teresa and Noah sat there for a few minutes after Will and Kayla had left. She had been this tired after working double shifts, but that had been weeks ago. Since coming back to Birthright, she'd gone to bed at a decent hour most nights.

"You sure you're up for a commitment like this?" Noah asked. "I'd hate for you to get bored or tired with it and let all the old folks around here down."

"I'm excited about it," she answered. "I thought you had faith in me, and you thought this was a good idea for me and Kayla to work together."

"Don't get your dander up," he chuckled. "I do have faith in you, but let's play hypothetical like we did with the jury that evening. Let's say that Will and Kayla fall in love and get married. After a year or so, she gets pregnant and has a baby and wants to stay home and raise it. What do you do?"

"I talk her into bringing the baby to work, where we have dozens of grannies and grandpas who'll be happy to rock a baby and watch it grow up," Teresa said without a moment's hesitation. "When the baby or babies get ready to go to school, our old folks will help them with their homework and tell them fantastic stories, and they'll love their extended family of grandparents, because they won't have day-to-day love and care like that."

"Will's folks are still alive," Noah reminded her.

"Yes, but the babies raised in this house will have everyday love, not only on Sunday afternoon," Teresa argued.

"I see you've given this a lot more thought than I have." He stood to his feet and held out his hand. "Guess we'd best get back to work."

She put her hand in his, and he pulled her to his chest. She didn't even have time to moisten her lips before he kissed her.

"I might be too tired to even pucker up when we get home, so that could be your good-night kiss," he told her when it ended.

"I don't believe that for a minute." She picked up a roll of blue painter's tape from the cabinet and grabbed his hand. "If we ever expect to go home, we'd better get busy."

"Bossy, ain't you?" He let her lead him into the bedroom.

"Yes, I am." She grinned.

There was no way Kayla couldn't notice Will's muscular thighs, not in the cramped bathroom space—not when all she had to do was turn her head slightly and they were right there. He was wearing a pair of jean shorts that already had paint stains on them and a T-shirt that was printed with a sign saying that Will was a 1989 model that was aged to perfection and still had all the original parts. A slow heat started up the back of her neck when she let her mind wander to all of his parts—especially those covered by his shirt and shorts.

She shook her head to get rid of the vision of his body without that T-shirt or shorts. Lord have mercy! She'd vowed not to trust a man again, and now Will Barton had stirred up emotions in her that she'd thought had died.

"So you've been teaching Sunday school since we graduated?" She did her best to keep her eyes on the taping job instead of sneaking peeks at his body.

"Yep," he answered. "My mama and daddy both taught a class, and when I graduated, I wanted to help out like they did. I took online college courses so I could stay home and help them while I got a business degree, and I taught my class of second and third graders on Sundays."

Kayla could tell by the tone of his voice that he dearly loved his family and his class of little kids. "Ever think of having kids of your own someday?"

"Have you?" He looked down at her.

"I've always been afraid I'd be a terrible mother," she blurted out.

"Why would you feel like that? Miss Janie mothered all of us at school and you at home, too. She was tough, but there wasn't a one of us, rich or poor, that doubted her love for us."

"I never knew my biological father. He got my mother pregnant, then got killed. Mama married my stepdad before I was born, and they had a couple of kids, but . . ." She stopped. "This isn't important at all."

Will sat down beside her. "If it has to do with you, then it's important, because you are."

"Okay, then." She smiled. "My stepdad and my mother constantly reminded me that I should be grateful that someone was willing to adopt an ugly mixed-race kid like me."

"Was the man blind?" Will raised his voice a notch. "You are beautiful, Kayla Green."

"No. His vision was fine until he got drunk," Kayla answered. "His brother or uncle or someone in his family got him a job in California, and at the end of summer they moved. They said there wasn't room for me in the car and they'd send money for me to come on the bus in a couple of weeks. The food ran out, and the landlord kicked me out when I couldn't pay the rent. Social Services stepped in, and Miss Janie said she'd foster me. I was almost fifteen at the time."

"Holy hell!" Will gasped. "If my mama had known that, she would have brought you home with us."

"I'm glad she didn't." Kayla grinned.

"Why's that?" Will stood up and began to roll paint again.

"Because we'd be kind of like brother and sister right now if she had," Kayla answered.

"You got a point there."

He finished painting the bathroom and then added, "Think that maybe I could talk you into dinner on Sunday after church? I'd like you to meet my folks. You'll love them."

"Will Barton, are you totally insane?" she asked.

"Nope, and I know because Mama had me tested when I was a little boy," he joked. "But why would you ask?"

"Think about what I told you about my folks. I would imagine that your mama lived in Sulphur Springs her whole life. She would remember my mother and all the scandal. I'm not like my mother, and I'm comfortable in my skin these days, but are you sure about this?" She sighed.

"That's funny as hell," Will said. "Did you ever meet my mama or my daddy?"

Kayla's brow wrinkled as she tried to remember if she'd seen them at church, but then she remembered that they'd probably attended services in Sulphur Springs.

"I don't think I ever did meet them," she answered.

"They are both black. I'm the little white boy that Mama's neighbor's daughter died giving birth to, and the neighbor let them adopt me," he said. "Mama was a registered nurse. Daddy was a lab technician. Both of them worked at the hospital in Sulphur Springs. I don't think they'll mind you being half-black."

"You're kiddin' me," she whispered.

"Nope, not one bit," he declared.

He set his roller down, stepped over to where she was still sitting on the floor, and sat down beside her again. He removed his wallet from his back pocket and flipped it open. "Here's me when Mama and Daddy brought me home, and here's me with them on high school graduation night. Surely you noticed them then?"

She shook her head. "I'm so sorry. Denver and I were planning to run away, and we didn't stick around after graduation very long. You were still wearing thick glasses then." She touched his face in the picture.

"Yep, my biological mother smoked and drank, and God only knows what else, so I was born with poor eyesight. The doctors weren't sure that I wouldn't have mental issues or impaired motor skills. That's why my biological grandmother didn't want to try to raise me," he said.

Kayla was struck speechless. The love in his mother's eyes was undeniable in the picture. Will had wrapped his tiny fingers around his adopted father's hand, and Mr. Barton was looking down at the baby as if he had been sent straight from heaven.

"So now," Will said, "one more time, will you spend the day with me on Sunday? Meeting the parents is usually after many, many dates, and I'm sure Mama wouldn't mind if I skipped going to see her for a few weeks, but—"

"I'd love to go with you and see these two folks." She looked up at him.

"Great!" His head bobbed once. "I'll pick you up at nine o'clock. That'll give us plenty of time to drive to Paris, pick them up, and get to church on time."

"Hey, y'all done in there?" Teresa called out from the other side of the hallway.

"Yes, we are," Kayla answered. "We'll meet you on the porch for a glass of iced tea."

"Sounds good to me," Teresa said. "Noah and I will pour the tea."

"Thanks for sharing your story with me." Kayla handed back his wallet. "I guess we have a little bit in common, don't we?"

"Looks like it, and thank you for sharing with me." Will stood up again and opened the door for her. "I guess I got in on the tail end of this painting job. I feel a little guilty about y'all doin' so much for me when I've done so little."

"That's what friends do," Kayla told him. "They help when and however much they can."

Chapter Twenty-One

*W*ill left pretty quickly after he'd drunk his tea, leaving the three of them sitting on the porch together. The sun had sunk below the far horizon in a bright array of colors that reminded Teresa of Miss Janie's casket flowers and of the idea that the woman's spirit really did represent all the shades of yellow, pink, purple, and light blue in the beautiful Texas sunset. Yellow represented her sunny disposition; pink and purple, her fantastic ability to love; and light blue was her understanding heart.

"I've got a few things I need to do at home." Noah got up from the porch step where he and Teresa were sitting. He still had her hand in his when he looked down at her and asked, "Are you ready?"

"Not just yet," she said. "Kayla can bring me home after a while."

"See you there, then." Noah let go of her hand. "I'm really not looking forward to painting a two-story house after doing this one."

"But we get smoked brisket afterward," Teresa reminded him.

"We've had so much fun with this one, I'm kind of looking forward to starting on Will's place," Kayla said. "I asked Sam about it when we were working in the living room, and he said that it's got three bedrooms and a bathroom upstairs. There's a living room, dining room, and kitchen on the first floor and a completely finished basement that's paneled, so it won't need any paint."

"That's good news." Noah waved and disappeared.

Both women waited until the dust had settled behind Noah's truck, and then they started to talk at once, realized what they were doing, and stopped.

"Guess we better slow down and go one at a time," Teresa said. "Maybe you better go first."

"His folks are up in Paris at an assisted living center, and we're going up there to take them to church and then dinner and a movie afterward. If you'd told me six weeks ago that I'd be double-dating with his parents, I'd have told you to go have your head examined," Kayla spit out. She took a deep breath and went on. "Did you know that he was adopted, or that his parents are black?"

"Are you serious? We were out of the gossip loop, I guess," Teresa said.

"Serious as a heart attack. He carries pictures of them in his wallet. I thought I was agreeing to dinner after church and maybe a movie, but then he said he'd pick me up for church. Going to a black church, meeting the parents, eating with them? Lord, I'm getting hives thinking about all that." Kayla sighed. "What if I don't use the right fork, or they remember my mama, and . . . ?"

Teresa threw an arm around Kayla and gave her a side hug right there on the porch steps. "You'll do fine. Miss Janie taught us all we need to know."

"If Noah's parents were still alive, would you feel like you were ready to meet them?" Kayla asked.

"Hell, no!" Teresa's voice went all high and squeaky in her own ears.

Kayla giggled. "Just as I thought. Maybe I won't think of this as a date, but as two new friends getting together for church and dinner."

"If it sounds like a date, waddles like a date—even if it's going to church—and looks like a date, then it's probably a date," Teresa teased.

"I'm not strong like you. I'm ninety percent bluff and only ten percent mean," Kayla admitted. "The thought of bringing a man into my life terrifies me."

"Honey, I'm not nearly as tough as you think I am, but we are both survivors, and that comes from the way we were raised. We had to be or we'd both be dead by now," Teresa told her.

"He has always been a churchgoing man. If we got into a serious relationship, I'd feel like I should tell him more than I have about life back then. I was more than just abandoned and homeless, Teresa. I had a horrible example for a mother, and I don't know if I can even talk about it," Kayla admitted.

"You might want to be up front and honest before the third date, though." Teresa moved over a few feet. "It's too hot to sit close together."

"Why the third?" Kayla asked.

"The first one is Sunday, when you meet the parents and his mama gets to know you. Believe me, the second one will be with only the two of you, and you'll kind of know at the end of that one if you want a third date. If so, you should tell him what's on your mind so you don't get your heart broken down the line," Teresa answered. "That's my honest opinion."

Kayla threw up her palms. "Have you had a lot of dates since you and Luis separated? I was so glad to be free of Denver that I didn't want to even look at another man until I ran into Will in the grocery store a few weeks ago."

"What changed your mind, even then?" Teresa asked.

"I don't know, but some of the chains that I imagined were wrapped around my heart to protect it fell away when he looked at me," Kayla said.

"That's strange." Teresa smiled.

"Why is that strange?" Kayla asked.

"Because that's the way I felt when I saw Noah again. Did I ever tell you that he was the first boy I ever kissed?" Teresa asked.

"No!" Kayla clamped a hand on her mouth. "When did that happen?"

"Before you came to live with me and Miss Janie. We were barely in our teens, and we had a little moment on the back porch," Teresa told her. "I kissed other boys after that and even had a short-lived relationship in college before I met Luis, but nothing ever compared to that first kiss I had with Noah."

"I've never kissed or been with another man other than Denver, and he's the only man I've had sex with. With my wild reputation, I bet that's hard for you to believe."

"Not one bit," Teresa said. "Like you said, ninety percent of you is bluff."

"Do you ever worry that if we were to have kids, we'd be like our mothers?"

Teresa shook her head. "I refuse to be like that, and I give you permission to yell at me if I ever am."

"You've got the same permission," Kayla said. "When Denver told me that I was pretty and he loved me, I was willing to do anything he asked because somebody finally loved me. Will has wonderful parents and comes from a really good background. I can see this developing into something really good, but after he thinks about what I told him about being afraid to be a mother, he may not ever want to see me again."

"If he likes you, then he'll help you get past your demons," Teresa told her, but she wondered if she was talking to her foster sister or to herself. "Now it's your turn. Noah is so far above me, smart-wise, background-wise, and every other way in the books, that I wonder if we got into something very serious"—she paused—"if he would ever be ashamed to introduce me to his lawyer friends."

A few long sighs pierced the silence, but nothing else, not even the sound of a cricket or a bird, could be heard. Then Kayla said, "The same right back at you. I can't imagine him ever being ashamed of you, but if it happens, kick him to the curb. We've come too far to let anyone make us feel ugly and unappreciated just as we are."

"Take me as I am or shut the door," Teresa said.

"Something like that," Kayla told her.

"We are tough," Teresa declared. "If these guys don't like what we have to say, the world won't end. The sun will come up in the east the next morning and go down in the west that night."

"Amen," Kayla said.

"And on that note, let's lock this beautiful place up and go home." Teresa got up and headed inside. "I'll turn out the lights and bring out our purses. You can go on and get the car started." Who would have thought that she and Kayla would ever be close enough to share their deepest fears? She only wished that they could have trusted each other enough when they were teenagers and had talked to each other back then. Maybe if they'd been friends, neither of them would have made so many mistakes in their lives.

Cooking was what Kayla did when she was nervous, and she sure enough had a case of jitters that Saturday morning. Will had sent her a text message and asked her to go to supper and take in a movie with him when he got off work. By Saturday evening she'd made six dozen peanut butter cookies, as many chocolate chip cookies, and four loaves of banana-nut bread. She had also made a pan of hot yeast rolls to go with the potato soup for dinner, since they were all tired of leftover casseroles.

Still the day seemed to drag by—probably because she wanted to talk to Will some more about this thing lying heavy on her heart.

"You're sure a bag of nerves today," Teresa told her as they cleaned up the kitchen after dinner. "Are you that nervous about going to supper with Will tonight? You don't have to talk to him about motherhood, you know. Matter of fact, that might scare him off."

"I've worried about this all night and all day. I have to get it off my chest." Kayla washed the last bowl. "He's so kind and sweet. He doesn't deserve to be led on, so I'm telling him tonight. I got to admit, though, I'm afraid of what I'll see in his eyes when I tell him."

Teresa threw an arm around Kayla's shoulders and hugged her. "You'll feel better once you get it off your chest."

Kayla laid her head on Teresa's shoulder. "My mother didn't want me, but she kept me anyway, and I might be just like her. Is that what I say?"

"Miss Janie was our real mother, and she not only wanted us but loved us," Teresa said. "Want me to wait up for you? I can always put in the time looking at pots and pans on Noah's computer. I've got two sets picked out for us to consider already."

Kayla took a step back. "Knowing you'll be here to talk to when I get home would make me feel better." She finally smiled for the first time that day.

Teresa laid a hand on Kayla's shoulder. "That's what sisters do. I'm glad we have each other."

"Amen to that." Kayla felt much better, but she still made a batch of raisin-filled cookies to keep herself busy until it was time to get ready for her first real date. What she and Denver had done couldn't even be considered dating. They'd sneak around during their noon hour at school and have sex in the back seat of his car. If there was a pep assembly at school the last hour of the day, they'd sneak into the auditorium and have sex behind the stage curtains. Denver always loved the thrill of doing something he shouldn't.

Strangely enough, Kayla's nerves had begun to settle down when it came time for her to start getting ready that evening. What Teresa had said about what sisters do had run through her mind all afternoon.

Kayla realized that she hadn't been a very good sister, either, in the time she'd lived with Miss Janie, so she couldn't fault Teresa for anything.

I loved being here, she thought, *but I had so much anger in me those years; my attitude stunk. I was a lousy daughter to Miss Janie and a worse sister to Teresa.*

Half the battle of getting through a tough situation is admitting that maybe part of it was your own stupid fault. Miss Janie's voice was strong in Kayla's head.

"Yes, ma'am," she said aloud.

"Who are you talking to?" Teresa popped into her room as if on cue.

"Miss Janie and I were having a visit," Kayla answered. "Would you twist my hair up, please? You do it so much better than I do."

"Sure. Be glad to." Teresa pointed toward the chair in front of the dresser. "And by the way, you sure look pretty in that dress. Aren't you glad that you bought a couple of outfits with your paycheck?"

"Yep, but if it hadn't been on sale for half-of-half, I wouldn't have bought it."

"There you go, and three, two . . ." Teresa giggled.

"Why are you counting down?" Kayla asked.

"One!" Teresa finished a few seconds before the knock came to the door, and they could hear Noah telling Will to come on into the house.

Kayla's eyes widened. "How did you know?"

"I heard the gravel crunching when he drove up and his car door slam. You're so worried about everything that your heart was probably pounding too hard for you to hear. You'll be fine. I have faith in you," Teresa said.

"I'm damn sure glad someone does," Kayla muttered. "If you've got any points with Him"—she pointed toward the ceiling—"you might put in a prayer for me."

"I will, but you don't need it." Teresa gave her a reassuring hug and headed back across the hallway.

Kayla was halfway down the stairs when she realized that Will was standing at the bottom of them, staring up at her.

"Oh. My. Goodness." He held out his arm for her when she reached the bottom step. "You are even more gorgeous than you were in paint-stained jeans last night."

"Y'all have a good time," Noah said, and disappeared into his office.

Kayla looked up at Will. "Thank you. You clean up pretty good yourself."

"Aww, shucks." He ducked his head like a little boy might. "I ain't used to pretty women sayin' things like that to plain old Will Barton."

"Don't you talk about my friend like that." Kayla looped her arm into his. "He's one handsome fellow, and I like him a lot, so don't be putting him down."

"Is that so?" Will laid a hand over hers, and together they went out to his SUV. "I thought I'd let you choose where we eat tonight." He opened the door for her.

That was a new twist from what she was used to with Denver. When they had the money to go out for something other than hamburgers, he made the choices, and usually it was a steak house.

Do not compare men. Miss Janie's voice was back in her head. *Will is rock solid and kindhearted, but he won't ever be as dangerous and thrilling as Denver was to you in the beginning, so it's not fair to him.*

Kayla had closed her eyes and was nodding when Will got into the vehicle.

"Are you listening to music in your head?" he asked.

"No, I was listening to Miss Janie," she said truthfully.

"Shh . . ." He put his finger on her lips. "Don't tell anyone, but I hear voices, too. They usually give me really good advice."

His gentle touch sent a jolt through her heart, releasing even more of those icy chains. She knew that she could so easily fall for this guy, and she had to tell him about her past even before they had supper together.

"I'm choosing Sonic," she said.

That was a safe place, she thought—a place where folks ordered from their vehicle. A carhop brought out the food, took their money, and went on to the next customer. It was probably the cheapest place in Sulphur Springs and wasn't where guys took women on a date to impress them. No point in making him spend a lot of money if this was going to end up being their first and last date.

"I believe I can afford to take you somewhere nicer than that," he protested as he started the engine and drove away from Birthright.

"I want to talk before we go out. I have things to say, and if I don't get them out, I won't enjoy the food," she explained.

"I have a better idea then. Let's go to the park. You can say what you want to, and then we'll go have some Italian at Roma's Restaurant," he told her.

He drove to Cooper Lake State Park and nosed the SUV into a spot that overlooked the lake right beside a concrete picnic table. The setting sun made a path of orange across the still waters of the lake.

"Shall we get out and sit at the table?" he asked.

"I'd like that," she answered.

He was the perfect gentleman again, opening the car door for her and then ushering her to the table with his hand on her lower back. She had no doubt that the heat from his handprint would still be there the next day. A soft breeze blew the hem of her dress up, and she held it down with one hand, tucking it under her thigh when she sat down on the table, her feet on the bench. The pungent smell of wet grass where the lake water splashed, keeping it moist, filled the air. A few tree toads joined their voices with dozens of crickets to provide music for her ears. Somewhere off in the distance, she could hear the putting of a motorboat, probably folks out at night, doing some fishing.

Will sat down beside her and took her hand in his. "Look at me, Kayla."

She looked up into his eyes, and the words tumbled out so fast that she had to take several deep breaths before she got finished. "I told you what kind of mother I had and how afraid I've always been to have children. I've probably scared the hell out of you by saying that. We are barely in the dating stage, but I'm afraid you'll rethink going out with me after what I told you." She held her hands tightly in her lap.

He brought her hand to his lips and kissed each knuckle. "I wish we had been better friends when we were in school and I hadn't been so afraid to ask you out, and then we'd be way past this point in our relationship. I know how much you love old folks, and I'm guessing that you like little kids, so I'm not worried about your fear of motherhood, darlin'. I've been just as scared about fatherhood. I have had wonderful examples, but I have no idea who my biological father is or what kind of genes he might throw into the already-muddy pool. We'll simply have to trust each other and leave the rest up to God."

She was astounded. Of all the scenarios that had played out in her head throughout the day, that certainly wasn't even on the list. "Are you serious?" she whispered.

"Oh, yes, I'm serious, but I'm also starving. If that's all you have to tell me, can we, please, go have some Italian? I said you could pick, but I want to go someplace where we don't eat in the car," he teased.

"Yes," she said, and smiled at him. "And thank you."

"You, my sweet darlin', are welcome, but the thanks go to you for going out with me tonight. I'm lucky to get a second chance with you. I was and still am a pretty big nerd." He pulled her up to her feet and kissed her on the forehead.

Every one of those chains around Kayla's heart fell away, and she felt ten times—no, a hundred times—more blessed than Will could ever know.

Teresa got tired of waiting for her sister to come home and went out to sit on the porch at midnight. She heard a car out on the road and thought Kayla was finally back, but then a car door slammed and the sound of the engine faded.

"Probably someone who's been out partying too much and lost their supper," she muttered. In a few minutes she heard faint crying sounds coming from the backyard and went to investigate. The whimpering got louder with each step she took, and all she hoped was that, surely to goodness, no one had left a baby on their back doorstep.

When she rounded the corner, she saw Noah sitting on the porch step with a puppy in his arms. He caught her gaze and pointed at the dog. "Look what found us this evening. I imagine someone dumped it out on the road, and the little thing went to the first light it saw. Think we should take her to the pound up in Sulphur Springs or keep her?"

Teresa sat down beside him, and the puppy licked her hand. "I don't think we have a choice. She found us. We didn't find her. She wants to live here. Man, she's got some big feet."

"If we keep her, she will have to be an outside dog," Noah said, "because she'll grow up to be half the size of a Shetland pony. She looks like a cross between a yellow Lab and one of those big old white sheepdogs to me, with maybe a little plain old mutt thrown in for good measure."

"Why would anyone throw something like her away?" Teresa asked, then wondered the same thing about herself and Kayla.

"Who knows." Noah shrugged. "But their loss will be our gain. I've always wanted a pet, but I want one we can keep inside. Will talked about a dog. Think he'll adopt her?" He hugged the puppy and let it lick him in the face. "I'll go into town tomorrow and get her some good dog food and some bowls, but she'll have to make do with leftovers tonight. She looks pretty well fed, and she's got teeth, but I imagine she was nursing her mama this morning. We might keep her here until Will can get moved in, if he'll take her."

Teresa had often thought of getting a pet, too, but she hadn't wanted to leave even a cat alone, as many hours as she worked. This puppy would be one more thing she'd have to leave behind if things didn't pan out for her and Noah. She decided right then that she wouldn't get attached to the animal. Then it looked up at her with big, sorrowful brown eyes, and she lost a piece of her heart.

"Can I hold her?" she asked.

Noah passed her right over, and the puppy licked her face until she giggled and put it down on the grass. Then it chased fireflies and stalked crickets for the next hour while Noah and Teresa laughed at its antics.

She couldn't help but envision their children playing on a summer evening—little dark-haired children with Noah's blue eyes and maybe her high cheekbones. She had never wanted children with Luis, but now the thought of having babies with Noah put a smile on her face.

Whoa! Slow this wagon down! The pesky voice in her head shouted so loudly that it hurt her ears. She shook her head to get the visual out and laughed when the dog came running over to plop down in front of her and then promptly fell asleep. Noah scooted over next to her and draped an arm around her shoulders. When she looked up at him, he lowered his lips to hers in a fiery kiss that raised the temperature of the already-hot night by at least ten degrees. When that one ended, he deepened the next one and picked her up to settle her on his lap.

They were so lost in one another that if the dog hadn't jumped up and barked, neither of them would have heard someone walking across the kitchen floor.

Teresa jumped out of Noah's lap and was standing three feet from him out in the yard when Kayla came through the back door.

"You said you'd wait up and you did, but Noah didn't have to stay up, too," she said.

"I couldn't sleep," Noah said. "Look what showed up. We've got a puppy."

"It's cute." Kayla yawned. "I'll get excited about the new baby tomorrow. Right now I'm going to bed while I'm still in a state of euto-pia . . . No, that's not right . . . It's *euphoria*, like when you're walkin' on clouds, right?"

"That's right," Teresa answered. "What happened tonight?"

"I'm going to church with him and his parents in the morning. Thanks for waiting up for me, but right now I'm going to bed so I can have sweet dreams of Will. We'll talk more in the morning, and you were right about talking to him. Everything is right with the universe." Kayla grinned and then disappeared.

Chapter Twenty-Two

Kayla tried on all three of her nice outfits on Sunday morning, but she wasn't satisfied with any of them. They were all lying on the bed when Teresa knocked on the bedroom door and poked her head inside.

"Need help with your hair?" she asked.

Kayla rolled her eyes toward the ceiling. "I need help period. I wore that dress to the reunion, and you loaned me that one"—she pointed to the slim dark-green skirt and cute sleeveless blouse—"for the funeral. That leaves the third one, and it's really too tight."

Teresa crooked her finger at Kayla. "Follow me."

"In my underwear?" Kayla frowned.

"Noah has already gone downstairs. The smell of coffee woke me up." Teresa disappeared.

Kayla looked both ways and then darted across the hallway.

Teresa opened her closet doors and brought out a flowing, multi-colored, gauze skirt that skimmed her ankles, an olive-green shirt with a lighter green undershirt, and a pair of sandals that matched the shirt. "Here, wear these," she said.

"Where did all that stuff come from?" Kayla asked. "When you loaned me a dress for the reunion, you only had a few things in your closet."

"The other day, when I drove up to Sulphur Springs to the grocery store, I noticed a little thrift store with a 'Going out of business' sign on the window, so I took a few minutes to go inside. Sit down and I'll twist your hair up."

She motioned toward the rocking chair, laid the clothing on the bed, and kept talking as she started in on Kayla's hair. "That was the last day the place was going to be open. They handed me a brown paper bag at the door and said I could fill it up and only pay five dollars, so I did. Stuff was pretty well picked over, but Noah mentioned that Sam wanted us to go to church with him, and I knew you would be going out with Will, so I crammed it full."

"I'm not taking what you planned to wear, am I?" Kayla asked.

"Nope. There now, see if you like that," Teresa told her.

Kayla went over to the mirror and gasped. "I love it. How did you learn to do hair like mine?"

"I had a couple of black patients in the nursing home, and I used to get them all fancied up when we had a party," she said.

"Well, bless their hearts, and I mean that in a good way," Kayla said as she got dressed and took another peek in the mirror. "Oh, Teresa, I'm so sad that we weren't sisters before now."

"Me too," Teresa said. "But we weren't the people that we are today. Back then we were just two discarded girls. Now go get a muffin and some milk so that your stomach won't growl in church."

"Miss Janie used to tell us that." Kayla turned away from the mirror. "For years I thought it was a sin if my stomach grumbled in church."

"So did I." Teresa led the way out of the room.

When they reached the kitchen, Noah was coming in from the back porch. "Well, you sure look nice this morning." He smiled at Kayla.

"Thanks to Teresa." She picked up a muffin from under the cake dome and poured herself a glass of milk.

"I can't believe what I just heard, and it was said with heart," Noah teased.

"Shhh . . ." Teresa laid her forefinger over his lips. "Don't jinx it."

Kayla giggled. "And don't expect it every day."

She finished eating, poured herself a cup of coffee, and had taken the first sip when the doorbell rang. She set the cup down, put on her best smile, and started down the hall.

"Got breakfast ready?" Sam yelled.

"No, but it will be in a few minutes," Teresa hollered back. "We're in the kitchen."

"I'm bringin' company with me," Sam said.

Kayla had almost never seen Sam in anything but bibbed overalls, so her focus was on him wearing khaki slacks and a plaid shirt. She didn't even see Will until he said, "Good mornin'. You sure look beautiful."

His deep drawl sent sweet shivers up her backbone. "Thank you. That shirt sure brings out the color in your eyes."

"I do the best I can with what I've got to work with." He grinned. "Are you ready?"

"Want a cup of coffee before we go?" she asked.

"I've got two Starbucks lattes in the car," he said. "Hope you like caramel with extra foam."

Kayla had never bought Starbucks in her life. Lord have mercy! Those things cost as much as four cups of coffee at a convenience store.

"I love caramel, so I'm sure I'll like it." She picked up her purse.

He ushered her out to his SUV with his hand on her lower back. "I told Mama you were coming with me today. I'm glad you didn't stand me up. That would have disappointed me and her both."

She slid into the seat and fastened the seat belt with shaking hands. In less than an hour, she would meet his parents, sit with them at a church she'd never attended, and then have dinner with them. That was as scary as the day she'd walked away from Denver, and yet she was more excited than she'd ever been in her life.

"Will you teach Sunday school this morning?" she asked.

"Not today," he answered. "The preacher's wife is stepping in for me. We're just attending church this morning. I usually try to get the folks back to the center by four so they can get a little nap before their supper is served. I was wondering if you would walk through my new house with me after we get back to Birthright. I could use some help before I buy paint. I like the idea of white, but I'm not sure."

"I would love to see the inside. Are you going to take that dog that wandered up to our place?" she asked.

He shook his head. "I want something smaller when I adopt a dog, and I'm thinking about an older animal instead of a puppy. Not many people want the old dogs, but they need love, too. Besides, Noah's already named the critter, and when a man names a pet, it's hard to give it up."

A wide smile spread over Kayla's face. "I think that Teresa is already attached to her, too."

"Then all's well that ends well," Will said.

See his house. Pick out a pet with him. This all sounded too serious to Kayla, and she felt herself taking two steps back.

Will Barton is a good man. Miss Janie popped into her head and scolded her. *He's not rushing you. He's grateful for new friends and happy that he's moving to Birthright. Don't be afraid to enjoy the move with him.*

That settled the angst in her heart. Miss Janie knew everything, maybe even the future, from where she was sitting these days. Listening to her had never proven wrong in the past.

Kayla had almost calmed herself down when Will parked right in front of a lovely stone place. "Be right back," he said as he opened the door and slid out of his seat. "Guess they're eager to get away today." He grinned and pointed to two smartly dressed people coming toward the SUV.

"Good mornin', Mama and Daddy." He waved and then went to give them both a hug.

Mr. Barton was as tall as Will, and his wife was only slightly shorter. His hair was totally gray, and her close-cut natural hair had a good amount of salt sprinkled through it. Other than his height, Will looked nothing like either of them.

"Of course he doesn't," Kayla whispered.

"Hello, I'm Dulcie," Mrs. Barton said as she got into the back seat. When she was settled, she reached up and laid a hand on Kayla's shoulder. "You are a very lovely woman, Kayla."

"Thank you." Kayla wondered if she'd died and this was heaven. "I'm very glad to meet y'all."

"I understand you graduated with our boy." Mr. Barton got into the seat behind Will. "I'm Thomas. I hear you're puttin' in a senior citizens place in Birthright. That will be good for the old folks down there. Mama and I were regular visitors at the one in Sulphur Springs until we moved here to Colonial Lodge."

"We hated to leave our friends, but it was time for us to downsize our house," Dulcie said. "What we hated most was leaving our church family, but Will said he'd come and get us every Sunday for church so we could see everyone."

"We knew Miss Janie through the school when Will went to high school, and we are very sorry for your loss," Thomas said.

"Thank you." Kayla wasn't prepared for conversation. When she'd worried about this day, she'd thought the only time they would visit would be over dinner.

"I was hoping that after we have our usual pizza Sunday, we might drive through Birthright on the way back to Paris and take a look at the house you've bought," Dulcie said.

Oh, great, now she would be seeing the house for the first time with his parents.

But at least you don't have to worry about using the right fork. Miss Janie's giggles bounced around in her head. *You can eat pizza with your fingers, and there will only be one fork.*

262

"Oh, hush!" Kayla said under her breath.

"What was that?" Will was absolutely beaming.

"I was arguing with myself," Kayla answered.

"I do that all the time," Dulcie chuckled. "Most of the time when I want my way and the Good Lord is telling me that's not the way to go."

"She gets cranky on those days." Thomas laughed with her.

The forty-five-minute drive back to Sulphur Springs seemed to speed by, and when Will parked beside a small church, several folks were making their way inside. Dulcie was the first one out of the vehicle and opened Kayla's door for her. "Come on, darlin'. I'll introduce you to some of our friends before services start. We're always glad to have new folks, especially young ones, join us."

"Mama, you're steppin' on my gentleman's toes," Will said.

"Oh, be quiet. You get to spend time with her all week," Thomas scolded him. "Let Mama have her day. This is the first time you've ever brought a girl to church."

Kayla met dozens of folks that morning, and even more at the pizza place. Names and faces were a blur in her head by the time they'd started back north toward Birthright and Paris. She could remember a few things about church—the beautiful singing, that Will shared a hymn book with her like his folks were doing, and that he held her hand all through the preaching. Everything was entirely too perfect, and she'd learned from experience that life was not like that. There had to be a hidden bomb somewhere, and when it went off, everything, including her heart, would be shattered.

She was still deep in her thoughts when Will parked in front of the house on the east end of Birthright. The house was set back on a lane a good eighth of a mile and wasn't even visible from the road. Big oak trees lined the lane leading up to it, and there was a circular drive—gravel but still in good shape—in front of the place.

"Needs some paint on the outside, but you got time to have that done before winter sets in," Thomas told him as he got out of the vehicle. "Did you have the plumbing and wiring checked out?"

"Is the kitchen in good repair?" Dulcie added before he could reply. She went straight to the porch and then turned around. "Come on, Kayla. Us girls would rather see the inside."

Kayla couldn't imagine ever living in such a quaint little home. She felt at peace when she walked inside and could easily picture a sofa in front of the stone fireplace and bookcases on either side. "This is amazing," she whispered.

"It's a lot of house for one man," Dulcie said, "but he sure is taken with it and this area. It is closer to where we live now, and you are here in Birthright."

For the first time Kayla felt uneasy. "We are just starting to date, ma'am. I hope he's not buying a place here because of me."

"Honey, I didn't mean to spook you." Dulcie patted her on the shoulder. "But we're glad he's finally got to date you and that you're part of both our worlds."

"Thank you," Kayla said, and meant every word.

Chapter Twenty-Three

*B*irthright didn't see fall many years. Usually the weather went from scorching-hot summer one day to icy-cold winter the next. But the year when Kayla and Teresa came back to town, the hot weather gradually got pushed into the history books by lovely, cool sweater weather. The morning of October 17 was an absolutely perfect day for Miss Janie's Senior Citizens Place to have its grand opening. The leaves had begun to turn colors and fall from the trees. A crisp breeze blew them around in circles, but it wasn't so cold that the old folks couldn't get out that day. Sam had spread the news, and he and about twenty other folks were waiting in their vehicles, or on the porch, at eleven o'clock, when it was time to open the doors for the first day.

When news got out about what they were doing, folks began to call to ask what they needed. One lady donated two bookcases—one for each of the gaming rooms. Others sent over boxes of dominoes, Monopoly, Chinese checkers, and other games. Then someone brought about forty jigsaw puzzles.

Eight tables for four had been set up in what was now the dining room, and the first day's meal of tossed salad, hot rolls, and pot roast cooked with potatoes, carrots, and onions was ready to serve. Dessert was chocolate sheet cake, and there were cookies and some sugar-free treats, too, for those who wanted to snack that afternoon while they played games. Carafes of lemonade, sweet tea, and water were already on each table, along with four red plastic cups of ice. "The countdown begins." Kayla pointed at the clock.

"Ten, nine, eight . . ." Teresa counted off the seconds.

Kayla crossed the floor, and when Teresa said "one," Kayla opened the door. "Come right on in here. We're so glad to see you," she said with a smile.

Sam was the first one through the door, and he stopped right inside to take a deep breath. "Is that hot rolls? Sweet Lord, I'll be here every day if y'all are making fresh bread."

Car doors began to slam, and soon the room was filled with elderly folks, all seeming to talk at once about how much they'd looked forward to this day.

Sam ate dinner, made six deliveries to folks who were shut in, and then came back to play dominoes for a spell.

"Anyone need a ride home?" he called out in the middle of the afternoon. "I'm taking my golden chariot to the house, but I'll be glad to give anyone a lift."

He wound up with three elderly women who'd had their kids drop them off, and it was a few minutes after four when the last elderly person left. Teresa locked the door and sat down at one of the tables. "It went well." She beamed.

Kayla poured two glasses of lemonade and sat down on the other side of the small card table. "How do you feel about today? Not just that we managed to serve lunch and visit with everyone, but how did it make you feel?"

"Oh, honey! I feel so good about today that I'd dance a jig in a pig trough if I wasn't too damned tired to move. I'm so glad you got this idea."

"Me too." Kayla nodded. "I could feel Miss Janie patting me on the back all day."

"I could, too," Teresa agreed. "I felt like she was right there beside me when we were rolling out the pie dough for tomorrow's cobblers, and Sam was fairly well strutting when he showed the folks the other rooms."

"Yep." Kayla took a long drink of her lemonade. "We should get on home now, though. Will is picking me up right after five. We're going to Sulphur Springs to look in his storage place at the furniture his folks stored there when they moved to the assisted living center. He wants me to help pick out the furniture for his new house."

"Would you have ever thought things would fall into place like they have?" Teresa asked.

"Not in a million years." Kayla pushed up out of her chair. "We've only reconnected for two months, but I think I'm in love."

"You just now figuring that out?" Teresa teased. "I knew it weeks ago. You'll be moving into that house with him before long."

"Nope. I'm not living with any man again until I have a marriage license in my hand," Kayla declared. "Besides, I have a nice warm nest in Miss Janie's house that I'm in no hurry to leave."

"Perfect weather. Perfect day," Teresa said when they stepped outside. She turned when they reached the car and pointed to the sign that Noah had paid to have painted on the picture window. *Welcome to Miss Janie's Senior Citizens Place* was in the middle of a wreath of multicolored flowers.

"Doesn't that sign give you all the good feels in the whole world?" she asked.

"I agree." Kayla got behind the wheel. "Did you say that about me moving in with Will so I'd get out of the house to give you and Noah more privacy?"

Teresa air slapped Kayla on the arm. "I figured you'd be of the same mind I am. I do not ever intend to marry anyone again until I've lived with them at least a year. That way if it doesn't work out, I might have a broken heart, but I won't have to go through a divorce."

"I'm right the opposite." Kayla started the car. "Like I said, I'll never *just live* with another man. If he can't commit to the whole nine yards, including a ring, a marriage license, and a wedding cake, then"—Kayla shrugged—"he's out of luck with this girl."

"I had a cheap ring and a marriage license. Didn't have the wedding cake—maybe that's why it didn't work out," Teresa said with a laugh. "I want to be certain the two of us are compatible before we make it permanent, and I've already told Noah that."

Kayla could well understand her sister's reluctance. "Do you really think if you and Luis had lived together, it would have made a difference? I think he would have been nice to you no matter where you lived, right up until you were legally married."

"Maybe so, but I'm not taking chances," Teresa said. "You better get on inside and grab a quick shower. You smell like onions."

"So do you," Kayla shot back. "I'll save you some hot water. It might not be easy to seduce Noah with that smell all over you."

"Maybe he likes onions," Teresa teased.

Kayla parked the car, got out, and jogged across the lawn to the house, leaving Teresa alone in the vehicle. She sat there for a long time thinking about the past few months and what a life-changing experience it had all been. Will and Kayla were getting more serious with each passing day. Teresa and Noah were learning to live in the house with Queenie, the big blondish-white pup that Noah declared grew a foot a day. The first time it rained, the puppy had shivered, and the idea of her being an outside dog came to an end. Except in bad weather, her place was on the back porch at night, but other than that, she could go where she wanted in the house.

A good man. A spoiled dog. A home. A business—everything that Teresa had ever dreamed about. She shivered at the thought of losing it all now that she'd found it, and then she felt Miss Janie's presence right behind her. She glanced over her shoulder to be sure the old girl wasn't really there.

"What?" she asked.

Be happy. Miss Janie's voice was loud and clear in her head.

"What if happiness is jerked out from under me? I know you had it taken away from you when me and Kayla left home and didn't come back to see you, and when you had to give up your babies," Teresa argued.

But I died a happy woman. Make each day happier than the one before and you'll die the same way.

"I hope so," Teresa said as she got out of the car.

Noah had finished working on his first pro bono case. He'd poured himself a glass of sweet tea and was settled down on the sofa when Teresa and Kayla came home that evening. Teresa kicked off her shoes and snuggled down beside him.

"How did the first day go?" he asked. "I really wanted to come down there and have lunch with Sam and meet all his buddies, but I was tied up with this case all day."

"I understand, and, honey, it went well enough that my feet hurt," she told him. "I didn't have time to sit down for even a minute all day. We had an amazing day, and Sam and the old folks thanked us for everything and even tried to pay us for the dinner, but we told them it was taken care of already." She stopped to catch a breath and went on. "And I feel like I'm floating on clouds and nothing can ever go wrong."

"That's great." He tipped up her chin and kissed her. "You taste like lemonade, but you smell like onions."

"Kayla and I both do. We chopped about five for tomorrow's lasagna. You can come eat with us anytime you want, too. Today was just the beginning," she said.

"Are you telling me that I'm old?" He put his arm around her and drew her closer to his side.

"I'm not saying you're old, but you can come eat with us anytime you want. You might even get some business while you're there. I heard Sam telling one old guy that he should come talk to you about his will," she said.

"Lay down and put your feet in my lap," he told her.

"Why? I'd rather be snuggled up right next to you," she argued.

"I give a wonderful foot massage." He grinned.

She had heard of such things but had never had one, so she did what he asked. He removed her socks and began to rub her left foot.

"Sweet Jesus and all the angels in heaven!" she groaned. "I've sure enough been missing out on something amazing. You have six hours to stop that."

"I'm leaving," Kayla called out. "Will is pulling up in the driveway right now. See y'all later."

"Be safe, and don't do anything I wouldn't do," Teresa yelled.

"That gives me lots of freedom right there," Kayla giggled, and then the door closed.

Freedom.

The word stuck in Noah's mind. At one time, he wouldn't have given up his freedom for a million dollars, but that day he gladly would've handed it to Teresa on a silver platter, along with a wedding band.

She'd told him that she'd never really commit to a man until she'd lived with him at least a year, and he didn't want to rush her. If it were up to him, he'd propose to her on the spot and ask the preacher to marry them the very next day, but Noah was a patient man.

When he'd finished with both feet, Teresa shifted her position to sit in his lap. "I love moments like this, when it's so quiet I can listen to your heartbeat," she said softly. "It's like hearing drums beckoning to me."

"What do you think my heart is telling you right now?" Noah ran his hand down her bare arm.

"It's sayin', 'Take me to bed or lose me forever, Noah Jackson,'" she said.

Noah could hardly believe what he'd heard. "Say that again." He pushed her back a little so he could look into her eyes.

"I want more than kisses. I want to go to sleep in your arms and wake up with you beside me every morning, to have a relationship with you that goes all through this life and into eternity. That's what I want for the long term, but tonight I want to know that when I go to sleep, you will be right there beside me and that we will open our eyes together when the alarm goes off tomorrow morning," she said. "What do you want?"

"Everything that you just said." He stood and scooped her up into his arms, carried her up the stairs, and stopped in the hallway. "Your room or mine?"

"It doesn't matter to me," she whispered.

He was still thinking he might be dreaming, but if he was, he hoped no one would wake him up for a long time. If he wasn't walking in his sleep, then his patience had finally paid off. He stepped into his bedroom with Teresa in his arms and kicked the door shut with his heel.

Chapter Twenty-Four

Noah and Teresa had planned to go to the haunted house in Sulphur Springs on Halloween, but a storm came up that evening, both outside and inside the house. The wind blew like crazy, bringing sheets of cold rain with it. Terrified of the thunder and lightning, Queenie refused to go outside and made a nasty mess on the living room floor. Noah was furious with her for making a mess and banished her to her doghouse on the screened porch. Then he said he was doing the dog a favor by letting her stay on *his* porch (as he said) and this was how she repaid him.

Teresa cleaned up after the dog, but she damn sure didn't like the way Noah had acted with Queenie. If they ever did have children, would he raise his voice to them when they had an accident?

"A pet is like a child. You train them. You don't yell at them like that," she said.

"It didn't hurt me to get yelled at," he argued.

"It did me." She looked him right in the eye and didn't blink. "Queenie is afraid of storms. They scared me when I was a little girl, too. If things got tough in the house, I could always hide out under the trailer porch, but if it was storming, even that was taken away from me."

"Oh, grow up, Teresa, and stop living in the past," he'd said before storming out of the room.

His tone sounded so much like something Luis might have said that she followed him into the hallway. "What's wrong with you? This is a brand-new side I'm seeing, and I don't like it. I knew things were too good to last. I'm not that lucky."

"I lost a case in court yesterday," he admitted as he put on his coat and pulled the hood up. "A good man went to jail for something he didn't do."

"And you're taking it out on me and Queenie?" She could almost feel fire shooting from her eyes.

"No, but I'm leaving before I say or do something else wrong," he said.

Teresa saw red when Noah walked out of the house, got into his truck, and drove away. She had put up with Luis leaving her alone and running off to a bar to get drunk, and by damn, she wasn't going through that again. She still had a vehicle of her own, even if she hadn't started the old rusted-out truck in a while. She'd put four new tires on it, and it had gas in the tank.

She got into it, slapped the steering wheel a couple of times, fired it up, and started driving south toward Sulphur Springs, hoping that maybe he'd gone to the Dairy Queen for ice cream to cool his temper. When she arrived, she drove around the lot twice but didn't see his truck, so she went to the park, pulled to the side of the road, and sat listening to country music for half an hour in the pouring-down rain. Every blasted song seemed to speak right to her, as if the words had been written with her and Noah in mind.

She should've known that the only place "happily ever after" happened was in romance books and movies. She thought she had learned that from Luis, but she'd let her guard down and found out that all men were alike, after all.

The rain stopped as suddenly as it had begun that afternoon, and when she drove through town, she passed an area where trick-or-treaters were out in full force. Little ghosts, goblins, and princesses ran up and down the streets with sacks and plastic pumpkins in their greedy little hands, expecting candy and treats. She remembered going out on Halloween night when she was a little girl, and what happened afterward. Angel let her have a few pieces of candy and took the rest. Teresa never saw any of it again. Her mother got the munchies pretty often and had a terrible sweet tooth.

She went back to the park, got out of the truck, and kicked at the wet leaves that had fallen on the ground, but even that didn't help ease her anger. Halfway to the swings, she realized she needed to talk to someone, so she sat down on a picnic table with her feet on the bench and called Kayla.

"Hello, what's going on?" Kayla whispered.

"Are you with Will?" Now, in addition to being angry, Teresa felt guilty.

"We're at a movie. I'll step out into the lobby so we can talk," Kayla said.

"No, don't do that," Teresa whispered, even though there wasn't another person in the entire park to overhear.

"Already on my way," Kayla said. "Talk to me. Are you all right?"

"No, I'm not," Teresa answered. "Noah and I had our first fight, and he left, and he's not at the Dairy Queen, and I'm afraid he might have gone to a bar, and I'll feel terrible if I drove him to drinking again." She sucked in a lungful of air. "What did *you* do when you and Will had your first argument?"

"First of all, we agreed to step back and let our tempers cool down, and then we sat down and talked it through." She giggled. "After that we had makeup sex. What did you fight about?"

"Our dog, Queenie," Teresa sighed. "She's afraid of storms, and she made a mess on the living room floor. Noah yelled at her and put her on the back porch. He bought her one of those igloo doghouses for out there, but I know she's scared to death. We argued, and he said he was doing her a favor letting her stay on the porch at *his* house."

Kayla laughed out loud. "That's a stupid thing to fight about."

"I can see that now, but I got really mad when he set his jaw and said *his* house. And his tone reminded me of Luis when he was angry, so we had an argument," Teresa said. "What do I do?"

"Cool down and talk it out like adults. I bet this is the tip of the iceberg about what's really wrong, isn't it? You needed something to argue about, and the dog got the job, right? You're afraid of commitment, and if something is his fault, then you feel justified in not being in love with him, right?" Kayla asked.

"Probably," Teresa had to admit.

"You don't have to tell me what the big problem is, but face it, talk it out, and if you don't want to live with him anymore, you can move out and get your own place. I'll go with you. We don't have to live in the house with Noah forever, you know. We could even sleep in the senior citizens place if we needed to for a few nights. There's always room for you at our place whenever Will and I decide to get married," Kayla told her.

"Thanks, and I'm sorry I ruined the movie for you," Teresa apologized.

"No problem," Kayla said. "We can talk more tomorrow, right?"

"Sure we can," Teresa agreed.

A stool in an old country bar wasn't a new thing to Noah, but the one he sat on on Halloween night was. As a matter of fact, he felt downright out of place in a bar now that he'd been sober for so long. Located south of Sulphur Springs, it was a tin building with a rough wood facade and swinging doors that made its patrons feel like they were walking into a honky-tonk out of a Western movie. Noah had been there more than an hour, and the ice was melting in the double shot of Jameson that sat right in front of him. An old man with a scruffy gray beard and a mop of hair the same color, drawn back in a ponytail, slid onto the barstool right beside him. He ordered a shot of Jack Black and tossed it back like an old bowlegged cowboy.

"I'm Orville Jones." The old guy motioned for the bartender, who was dressed up like Minnie Mouse, to bring him another one. "Who are you? Can't say as I remember seeing you here before, and I'm here most every Saturday night."

"Noah Jackson," he answered.

"Well, Noah Jackson, are you going to drink that whiskey or let it sit there and mold?" Orville grinned, showing off a mouthful of crooked teeth.

"I haven't decided. I've been sober for six years," Noah said.

"Then what the hell are you doin' in here, son?" Orville frowned. "I'll bet dollars to cow chips that it's money or a woman. Am I right?"

"Yep," Noah answered.

"Want to talk about it?"

"We had our first fight after a bad workday." He toyed with his glass, swirling what was left of the ice around in circles. He started to bring it to his lips, but then set it back down.

Orville got up and went to the jukebox, plugged a few coins into it, and then came back. "You need to listen to Miss Miranda sing this here song before you drink that watered-down stuff."

The country beat of Miranda Lambert singing "Storms Never Last" filled the whole place. A few folks got up and two-stepped to the music. Noah wished he had Teresa in his arms rather than the whiskey tempting him right there at his fingertips.

"You hearin' the words to that song?" Orville asked.

"Yes, sir, I get the meaning, and you're right," Noah answered.

"Well, son, the clouds that's brewing now won't last, like the pretty lady is singing, so leave that drink alone and go home to your woman. If you're lucky, she'll still be there." Orville picked up Noah's drink and downed it one gulp. "Wouldn't want you to lose your six-year chip."

"Thanks." Noah threw a bill on the bar. "This is for your next drink, sir."

"Appreciate it." Orville gave him another big grin.

Teresa was still sitting on the swings when her phone rang. "Go watch your movie," she answered.

"I'm not at the movies. Where are you?" Noah's deep voice sounded worried. "I came home, and you were gone. We need to talk."

"I'm at the park," she said.

"Will you meet me at the Dairy Queen in ten minutes?" he asked, and then added, "Please. And you can bring Queenie, since we can eat at the outside tables."

"I can be there, but I'm not bringing Queenie," she said.

Different scenarios played through her head as she thought about going back to the house to get Queenie, but eventually she decided against it. No way was she taking her dog with her to experience a sad moment. As she drove to the ice cream store from the park, her thoughts kept circling back to the fact that Miss Janie had left him the house, so it was legally his. He could do what he wanted with it, and that included telling her to go somewhere else.

The drive to the Dairy Queen took less than three minutes. She went inside and headed to the booth that she and Noah had chosen as their favorite. The next few minutes went by so slow that she wondered if the big Coca-Cola clock on the wall had stopped.

Finally, the door opened and Noah walked in. He looked every bit as miserable as she felt, and it broke her heart to see him like that.

He went straight to the counter and ordered something. How could he be hungry? Her stomach was tied up in knots with worry about what they were about to say or do. He paid with a bill, stuffed the change into the pocket of his jeans, and took his own good easy time getting back to the booth.

"We need to talk," he said. "Why didn't you bring Queenie? I said we could eat outside."

"She's sensitive," Teresa said. "She doesn't need to hear you yell or see me cry."

"All right." He nodded. "Now let's talk."

"You already said that," she told him. "You go first."

"I don't care if that silly dog sleeps in the house," he said.

She looked him right in the eye and didn't blink. "I don't care if you put her in the screened porch."

"Then what are we fighting about?" he asked.

"Where have you been?" she threw back without answering his question.

"I went to a bar and ordered a double shot of Jameson on the rocks. I stared at it for an hour, but I didn't drink it. An old guy sat down beside me and made me listen to a song on the jukebox, and then he threw my whiskey back and I left," Noah answered. "After I listened to the words of the song, I didn't want a drink. I just wanted to come home to you."

"Play it for me," she said.

He glanced around the room. "There's no jukebox in here."

"You've got a phone," she reminded him.

He found what he was looking for, adjusted the volume, and laid the phone on the table between them. The song came up, and Teresa recognized Miranda's voice right away. Storms never last, the lyrics said, and bad times could pass right along with the wind. Teresa looked out the window and watched the wind blowing the leaves from the trees. Could this storm she and Noah had faced be blown away like that? Would they be all right when they got to the root of their problem?

"We had our first fight. What we do now is what will define our relationship. The dog isn't what's wrong with us right now, is it?" he said.

"What do you think our problem is?" she asked.

"Trust," he answered with one word. "You don't trust me. You're measuring me by Luis, and I'm not like him at all. I'm not going to cheat on you, and I think I proved tonight that I won't be going back to my old drinking ways. I love you, Teresa, but I can't live with you if Luis is still in your life. I want more than us just living together. I want us to be together forever. I want children and to grow old with you."

"Luis has been out of my life for more than a year," she declared.

"I know that, and I don't think you still love him, but until you can trust me with all your heart, he's still right there between us," Noah said. "You told me you want to live with me for a year. I feel like we're wasting time that we could spend being totally committed to each other. I don't want to rush you, but darlin', I want the world to know that you are my wife, not my girlfriend."

The lady brought a banana split with two spoons stuck in the top and set it between them. "Y'all enjoy. I'll bring your coffee when you finish. That way it won't get cold," she said, then went back to wait on a group who were pushing their way inside.

"Thank you," Noah called after her. He picked up one of the spoons and laid it to the side, then picked up the other one. "This is our life here between us, darlin'. One spoon. One banana split." He dipped into the ice cream and the caramel and held the spoon toward her mouth.

She wrapped her hand around his, ate the ice cream, and then took the spoon from him. She filled it with hot fudge and vanilla ice cream and offered it to him. He ate it and smiled for the first time.

"I'm sorry," she said. "You're right. I've been measuring you by Luis, and that's not fair. I thought we had to live together a year before I really made a commitment. I wanted to be sure that we would last, but I really believe in you and trust you."

"I apologize for not speaking my mind, but, honey, I am serious," he said as he slid out of the booth. He dropped down on one knee right there in the Dairy Queen, took her hand in his, and said, "Teresa Mendoza, will you marry me? I don't have a ring yet, and it doesn't have to be next week, but I want to know that we are committed wholly to each other, that the past is totally gone from our lives."

"Yes!" She leaned in to kiss him. "And, Noah, you have my whole heart, every bit of it. I think you always have."

He kept her hand in his as he stood up, and then he slid right next to her. A verse from the Bible came to her mind. "And they two shall become one." She had no idea why it popped into her mind, but it sure made sense right then. Her heart and Noah's were one, and there would never be room for anyone else ever again.

"I love you," she whispered, "and we don't have to wait a year."

Epilogue

One Year Later

*T*eresa picked up the two pink gift bags on her way out the door that Sunday evening. The sun was just setting, and a cool breeze let her know that summer was gone and fall had arrived. Queenie was sprawled out on the porch that fine fall morning. Noah had been right when he said she'd be half the size of a Shetland pony. "You protect the place," she told the dog. "Don't let any mice or two-legged critters on the property until we get home."

"Are you ready for this?" Noah slipped an arm around her waist, and together they crossed the yard to the truck.

"Yes, and I'm ready to start our family," she said. "If we have a baby nine months from now, we might have four or five by the time we're forty."

Noah's bright smile lit up the truck. "We'll see what we can do about that when we get home from church." He started the vehicle, and loud music filled the cab. "Guess I know who was driving this last." He turned it down far enough that they could talk above it.

"Yep, I like my music loud when I'm alone." She wasn't afraid to have children anymore. She no longer believed that she would be a terrible mother. Miss Janie had taught her better than that. She and

Noah had been married six months now, and there had been a few arguments, but they'd worked their way through them. Every day they were together, their love for one another seemed to grow even more.

"Remember this song?" he asked when Miranda began to sing "Storms Never Last."

"It's kind of been our theme song for the past year, hasn't it?" she said. "Did I ever tell you about my drive up here last year? About fifty miles out, I thought for sure I'd run out of gas or that one of my tires would blow out. That song came on the radio, and I remember wishing that it was true, that storms didn't last, but I sure didn't believe it. Now I do."

"I believe it has been our song, and I'm glad that you changed your mind about it." He laid a hand on her shoulder. "The wind really has taken any bad times with it, just like the words say."

She covered his hand with hers. "I've heard that the first year of marriage is the hardest. If that's the case, we should make it all the way to that eternity you talked about the night you proposed to me."

"Maybe after the party this afternoon, we should go to the Dairy Queen and share an ice cream sundae just for good luck on starting our family," he suggested.

"Couldn't hurt a thing." She smiled as he found a parking spot at the church.

Kayla forgot to pick up the hostess gifts and didn't remember them until she and Will were in the SUV and halfway to church. When she brought it to his attention, Will turned the vehicle around right there in the middle of the road and went back to the house.

"You stay in the car, darlin'," he told her. "With that big old belly, you can't hurry."

Kayla laid her hand on her stomach. "You're probably right. I don't rush too well anymore. When the babies get here next month, you won't have to do so much."

"Honey, I don't mind doin' anything at all. I still can't believe I'm going to be a daddy and that I'm married to my high school crush." Will left the vehicle running and jogged into the house. When he returned, he set a box containing small gift bags onto the back seat. "Do you think they'll have your curly hair?" he asked as he got behind the steering wheel.

"God, I hope not." Kayla groaned. "They can have eyes like mine and your good hair."

"I hope they look just like you, right down to every cute little freckle on your face."

"You are a sweetheart," Kayla said.

In a few minutes, they turned into the church parking lot.

"Good grief!" Kayla gasped. "Look at that parking lot. The church is going to be packed this morning."

"Don't worry," he laughed. "Mama will throw anyone out of our pew if they try to move in on her territory. I hope our girls have half her spunk."

"I wish Miss Janie would have lived to see her granddaughters." Kayla sighed.

After they'd found a spot and parked, Will opened the door for her and helped her get out of the vehicle. They spotted Dulcie and Thomas waiting for them outside the church and made their way over to meet them. Will then leaned over and laid his hand on her stomach and said, "Miss Sarah and Miss Marie, I can't wait to carry you into church."

"You could do that today," Kayla sighed, "but the weight would break your back."

"I couldn't be happier than I am today," Dulcie said. "And to know that y'all are naming the babies after me and Miss Janie is an honor that brings tears to my eyes. I always wished my mama would have called me by my middle name, Marie, rather than Dulcie, and now I get a granddaughter named that."

"We do get to babysit for you once a week, don't we?" Thomas asked. "I've already told all the folks at the center to expect to see babies pretty soon."

"Of course." Kayla nodded. "And thank you for the offer. I'm sure we'll look forward to a little time each week."

"Oh, honey," Dulcie laughed. "You really do need time for the two of you. When we got Will, we made ourselves a promise that we'd always have date night, and even if we were tired, we hired a sitter on Saturday nights and went to dinner."

Kayla still had trouble believing that Will's folks had taken her into their family, that they'd insisted on paying for a wedding six months ago, and that they'd been delighted when they'd told them that she was pregnant.

A few minutes later, Noah parked his truck right beside Will's SUV. As Noah opened the door and jogged around to help his wife out, Will hollered over to him, "You didn't have any trouble finding the place, did you?"

"Not a bit," Noah said. "We brought Sam with us, and he's been here before."

After Teresa, Noah, and Sam had joined the others, Teresa said to Kayla with a laugh, "Are you sure that's just two babies in there? Looks like a litter to me. I just saw you yesterday, and you look bigger than you did then."

"Oh, hush up." Kayla shook a finger at her. "Your time is coming, and I fully well intend to make fun of you when you look like an elephant."

"But you're such a beautiful elephant." Will slipped an arm around his wife's shoulders. "And we get a double blessing. Noah and Teresa might not get two at once."

"I hope not," Teresa said.

The preacher stepped up behind the lectern, cleared his throat, and said, "I don't know that we've ever had a Sunday-evening crowd this big." He chuckled before getting serious. "We are fortunate when we bring a new baby—or, as the case is with Will and Kayla, two new babies—into our church family. Our children are our future, and we need to remember that. Jesus said, and it's written in red in our Bibles, 'The kingdom of heaven belongs to these,' and He's talking about the little children. Our father in heaven sent His only son to earth to live and die for us. He didn't send Him as a grown man but as a baby, so we need to remember just how precious our children are to our spiritual kingdom."

Teresa pondered those words and didn't hear a word of the rest of the sermon. If she hadn't been ready for motherhood before, she was after hearing the preacher say those words. She and Noah would be good parents in spite of their pasts. They would use their pasts as an example of how not to be, rather than let them define their methods of parenting.

She was jerked back to the present when the preacher said, "And now, if our guest, Sam Franks, will deliver the benediction, we will all go to the fellowship hall for our potluck and baby shower."

After Sam delivered a short prayer, Will helped Kayla up from the pew. "Twins! We're so lucky."

"What would you do if we had twins?" Noah whispered in Teresa's ear.

"I'll be grateful for whatever we get," she said, "and I want to name our first daughter Jane. Kayla done already got the name Sarah."

"We can always lay claim to Ruth, since that's not only Aunt Ruthie's name but also my mother's middle name," Noah said.

"I like that, but we got to get pregnant before we start thinking about names," she said.

"What are y'all whispering about?" Kayla asked.

"We've decided it's time for us to start our family. I figure if we get pregnant soon, we might have time for four kids by the time we're forty," Teresa told her.

"Now, that's the best news I've heard all day," Kayla said. "Mine and Will's daughters will have some little cousins to grow up with."

As everyone filed into the fellowship hall, an elderly lady came up to them and touched Kayla on the arm. "You and that one right there"—she pointed at Teresa with her other hand—"I recognize you now. I used to work in the cafeteria back when Miss Janie was secretary at the school here in Sulphur Springs. Aren't y'all Miss Janie's girls?"

"Yes, we are," Teresa and Kayla said in unison.

Dear Readers,

There really is a Birthright, Texas. There really is a church there, but the people I met and fell in love with are fictional. I'm having trouble as I finish the book convincing myself of that, though. Miss Janie and her girls, Sam, Noah, and Will have become very close friends of mine as I've gotten to know and love them through all their struggles. I hope that you fall in love with the folks as much as I have and that when you read the last page, you'll wish for one more chapter. I've said before that it takes a whole team to take a book from a simple dream to the finished product that you hold in your hands today. My Montlake team is totally amazing for all they do—from edits to covers. A simple thank-you seems so small, but I want them to know that it comes right from the center of my heart. I'm sending love and appreciation to my Montlake editor, Alison Dasho; to Krista Stroever, who always manages to help me take a chunk of coal and turn it into a diamond; to the whole team who has put together this amazing book; to my awesome agent, Erin Niumata, and to Folio Literary Management;

and once again, big hugs to my husband, Mr. B, who continues to support me even when he has to eat take-out five days in a row so I can write "just one more chapter" or finish another round of edits.

And thank you to all my readers who buy my books, read them, talk about them, share them, write reviews, and send notes to me. I'm grateful for each and every one of you.

Until next time,

Carolyn Brown

About the Author

Photo © 2015 Charles Brown

Carolyn Brown is a *New York Times*, *USA Today*, *Publishers Weekly*, and *Wall Street Journal* bestselling author and a RITA finalist with more than one hundred published books to her name. Her books include romantic women's fiction and historical, contemporary, cowboy, and country music mass-market paperbacks. She and her husband live in the small town of Davis, Oklahoma, where everyone knows everyone else, including what they are doing and when—and they read the local newspaper on Wednesdays to see who got caught. They have three grown children and enough grandchildren and great-grandchildren to keep them young. For more information, visit www.carolynbrownbooks.com.